BLOOD OF KINGS
THE SHADOW MAGE

Paul Freeman

LIR PRESS

Blood of Kings: The Shadow Mage

Paul Freeman

Copyright © 2016 Paul Freeman

Published by Lir Press
First Edition, 2016

All rights reserved. No part of this book may be reproduced or transmitted in any form or by any means, electronic or mechanical, including photocopying, recording or by any information storage and retrieval system, without written permission from the author, except for the inclusion of brief quotations in a review.

This is a work of fiction. Names, characters, businesses, organizations, places, events and incidents either are the product of the author's imagination or are used fictitiously. Any resemblance to actual persons, living or dead, events, locales is entirely coincidental.

ISBN – 13: 978-1537185361

ISBN – 10: 1537185365

Table of Contents

Jarl Crawulf: Wind Isle, Nortland ... 1

Lorian: Alcraz, capital city of Sunsai Empire ... 5

Duke Normand: Besieging the walls of Eorotia ... 11

Tomas: Woodvale Village ... 18

Princess Rosinnio: Wind Isle ... 24

Duke Normand: Eorotia – The Thieves Citadel ... 32

Tomas: Woodvale Village ... 38

Lady Rosinnio: Wind Isle ... 44

Tomas: Woodvale Village ... 49

Lorian: The house of Lorian, Alcraz, Sunsai Empire ... 55

Duke Normand: Duchy of Lenstir ... 62

Lady Rosinnio – Jarl Crawulf: Wind Isle ... 67

Tomas: Woodvale Village ... 75

Djangra Roe: Flagston ... 83

Jarl Crawulf – Lady Rosinnio: Wind Isle ... 88

Tomas: Woodvale Monastery ... 98

Duke Normand: Duchy of Lenstir ... 106

Lady Rosinnio – Jarl Crawulf: Wind Isle ... 112

Tomas: The Great Wood ... 120

Djangra Roe: Woodvale Monastery ... 126

Jarl Crawulf: Wind Isle ... 132

Tomas: The Great Wood ... 140

PART II ... **149**

Jarl Crawulf: Seafort, the Duchies ... 150

Duke Normand: Mountains of Eor 156
Tomas: Alka-Roha 164
Jarl Crawulf: Northern Duchies 172
Duke Normand: Mountains of Eor 181
Tomas: Alka-Roha 190
Jarl Crawulf: Northern Duchies 198
Lady Rosinnio: Wind Isle 206
Duke Normand: Eorotia 215
Tomas: The wild lands beyond Alka-Roha 222
Lady Rosinnio: Wind Isle 229
Duke Normand: Rothberry Castle 238
Tomas: Temple ruins, wild lands of Alka-Roha 245
Aknell: The house of Lorian 255
Lady Rosinnio: Wind Isle 261
Duke Normand: Duchy of Lenstir 268
Tomas: Temple of Eor, wild lands of Alka-Roha 273
Jarl Crawulf: Wind Isle 278
Duke Normand: Eorotia 290
Tomas: Temple of Eor 298
Jarl Crawulf – Lady Rosinnio: The Duchies ... 305
Duke Normand – Tomas: Hidden valley 312
Lady Rosinnio – Tomas: Hidden valley 319
Hidden valley, Mountains of Eor 325
Jarl Crawulf – Tomas: Hidden valley 335

Dedication

For my family

Acknowledgements

Many thanks to Ivan Amberlake and Sharon Van Orman.

Cover design: EJR Digital Art

Also by Paul Freeman

Tribesman

Warrior

Taxi

Season Of The Dead

After The Fall: Children Of The Nephilim

www.paulfreemanbooks.com

Jarl Crawulf: Wind Isle, Nortland

Crawulf gazed over the battlements at the vast expanse of turbulent water, its iron grey reflecting the angry sky. He could taste the salt borne on the bitterly cold wind washing over the dark walls of the keep. Far below, waves battered the bottom of the cliff in an endless assault on the jagged shore, as froth from the boiling sea spiralled upwards. He pulled the bearskin cloak he wore tight around his shoulders, a vain effort to ward off the cold. His long dark hair, not yet speckled with as much grey as his beard, whipped behind him.

"They come."

Crawulf spun around to face the source of the words, as his hand slid to the hilt of his sword. "Have a care, Brandlor. It is unwise to creep up on a man so," he said, relaxing when he saw the thin frame of his advisor.

"These old bones know no other way to walk, my jarl." The wizened face cracked into a smile that stopped short of dark sunken eyes.

A growl rattled in the throat of Crawulf before he returned his attention to the sea. "You are right! I see them," he said, craning his neck as he spied a dark speck in the distance. "How is it you see these things before I, old man?" he asked as he watched a small ship being tossed from one swelling wave to another. "He will do well to make the channel in that soft bottomed, southern boat."

"He will make it. He has no choice with the cargo he carries. He will make it or he will lose more than just his life."

Crawulf glanced at the old man, as always finding his intense gaze unsettling. "The fat bellies of the southern ships are ill suited to these waters," he insisted, thinking of his own smaller, sleeker ships – dragon-prowed sharks compared to the bloated whales of the southerners.

"Aye, but he will make it."

Crawulf watched the ponderous craft draw closer to the rocks far below that had claimed the lives of countless vessels and crews down through the years. "How many of the king's jarls would sabotage that ship if they knew what she held in her belly?"

"All of them," Brandlor answered. "Long years of planning will soon bear fruit. When your uncle dies, you will be king."

Overhead the sky grew darker as clouds whipped by a growing wind tumbled past. Sheets of rain, from a sudden burst, lashed the faces of the two men. Still they held their ground. "If he comes aground on yonder rocks all will be lost." Crawulf returned his attention to the ship.

"He will make the channel, my jarl. And you will be king."

"They will fight. Every one of them." He scratched at coarse bristles once black, now flecked with grey. His hand reached for the leather grip of his sword as if even the mention of his rivals would summon them closer.

"Yours is the stronger claim."

Crawulf turned two grey eyes on his counsellor. "Strongest but one," he said.

"Your brother is dead, my jarl. Died these past three years," the white-bearded counsellor answered.

"I will believe him dead when I see his body," Crawulf snarled.

"You worry overmuch. Your uncle will be dead before winter, and you *will* be king. You are his closest kin." The two men turned once again to the distant vessel as it bobbed into view before disappearing again beneath another, white-capped, wave.

"I'll warrant the captain longs for sunnier climes and calmer seas," Crawulf said.

"He will make the channel, my lord."

Crawulf dwarfed his advisor, where one embodied the spirit of the bear whose hide he wore, on his broad shoulders, to stave off the bitter northerly wind, the other was frail, with thin white hair and wispy beard. He gripped the battlements with two, large, calloused hands. He could feel the raw coldness of the rough stone. The castle, like the cliff, was weather-beaten and constantly assaulted by the power of the sea, yet unbowed and defiant. "He drifts closer to the rocks. Does he even realise the peril he is in? Gods protect us, does he know how to do anything about it?" He leaned over the battlements, as if stretching a few short inches over the wall would give him a better view."

"He will make the channel, my lord," the counsellor said. Unseen to his jarl, he raised his eyes skywards and offered a silent prayer to Alweise, father of the gods, beseeching him to allow the foreign captain to reach the bay, and safety. The king of gods sent his answer with a loud rumble and an electric flash across the sky.

"Baltagor, Lord of the Sea is angry this day. If that ship goes down all will be lost," Crawulf was shouting now to make himself heard over the breaking storm. The wind howled around the watchtower looming over them, casting a dark shadow across the rampart they stood on.

"He will make the channel," Brandlor insisted. His words were swept away even as they were uttered.

Dark hair, unusual amongst the mainly blond and red-haired Nortmen, clung to Crawulf's face, soaked within minutes of the downpour. "Look!" He pointed. "He's changing course. He's turning her!" Brandlor nodded sagely. The fat-hulled ship bobbed and tossed in the raging sea. "I should have sent one of my own ships. With a captain who knows how to sail these waters," he said.

"You know that was not possible, my jarl."

"Aye," he answered softly. Slowly, as both men held their breaths, the fat ship rounded the headland and disappeared from sight. "She's in the channel!" Crawulf beamed.

"Gods be praised," the advisor muttered.

"I'm going down to the harbour to greet her." Crawulf suddenly leapt into action.

"Wait," the counsellor called after him. "Let them come to you." Too late, he was gone.

The hollow clatter of shod hooves echoed around the keep as Crawulf and his housecarls filed out of the gate and made the short journey to the harbour. All the while the wind and rain grew in intensity. By the time they marched along the wooden pier they were soaked through, their moods as dark as the sky. Most of the fleet of sleek, single-mast longboats were tied up, leaving few berths for visiting ships. The jarl of Wind Isle, the southerly most island of the Nortland Isles, waited impatiently with his entourage as the pot-bellied ship sailed ponderously into the harbour, battered but unbowed.

A nervous, swarthy-skinned captain walked down the gangplank, followed by several of his officers. "My lord." He bowed extravagantly from the waist.

"Well met, Captain. I witnessed a fine piece of seamanship today," Crawulf said, inclining his head.

"You have wild seas, my lord. I did not think we would make it."

"I was never in doubt, Captain. But praise the gods. And your cargo, is it safe?"

"A little shaken, my lord, but yes, quite safe."

Crawulf beamed a smile at the news.

"So where…" he began but stopped short when he saw a dark-haired girl, dressed in an unseasonal, and impractical, emerald green gown, so thin and delicate he thought she might be swept away by the wind. She glided down the gangplank with a stiff back, her hair tied on top of her head with ribbons and pearls. Crawulf's jaw dropped. Never before had he seen such exotic beauty. "Princess Rosinnio," he whispered her name.

The princess approached him, curtsied, and promptly threw up all over his leather boots.

Lorian: Alcraz, capital city of Sunsai Empire

"Gods curse this heat," the fat noble grumbled as he fanned his face with a silk cloth. Even the overhead canopy failed to keep him cool. He snatched a goblet from a tray held by a tall servant standing, stiff-backed, in the full blaze of the midday sun.

"Oh, drink your wine and stop grumbling, Lorian," a second man, seated beside him in the second tier of the arena said. Below them on a dusty playing field thirty men stripped to the waist and armed with sticks fought over an inflated pig's bladder. Half of the players wore a red ribbon tied around their arm, the other half a blue one. A cheer reverberated around the arena as a melee broke out between the opposing teams. Neither of the two men reacted to the excitement.

"What else is one to do in such heat?" Lorian complained. He leaned in closer to his companion, glanced about conspiratorially and lowered his voice. "Have you heard the latest rumour coming from the palace?"

"No," the second man answered, leaning closer.

"Word is... the emperor has sent Rosinnio north." He smiled as he sat back in is chair. He rolled a date between his forefinger and thumb before popping it into his mouth. Each finger, on a fleshy hand, bore a heavy gold ring.

"Well stop looking so pleased with yourself, Lorian, and do continue."

Lorian mopped his glistening brow with a square of bright silk, shifted his huge bulk and smiled. "He has sent her to become bride to some king of the Pirate Isles."

"No! His favourite? Surely he would not subject his youngest daughter to such a life," he said, looking thoughtfully over the fat noble's shoulder.

"Remember Brioni, his eldest? He sent her to the nomads of the Uncha Mort. She roams that desolate desert with all she owns packed on the back of a horse now. When it comes to politics he has no favourites. Poor Brioni, she was such a fun girl too. And now Rosinnio. The poor little bird will never see the sunshine again. They say the Pirate Isles are forever shrouded in mist, and the rain only ceases for the snow."

"How is it you come by such information, always ahead of time?" the second man asked as he stroked his trimmed beard, still staring into the distance.

The fat man smiled. "I have my ways, my friend, I have my ways."

"Incidentally, I would not use the name, 'Pirate Isles,' in front of a Nortman or you will likely lose your head," the man said, a smile spreading across his face.

"Ha! I think it unlikely I will ever visit Nortland. The very thought sends a chill into my bones. Is this wretched game nearly over yet?" Lorian then grumbled as he turned his attention back to the thirty players almost made invisible by a swirling dust cloud. Barely had the fat man finished when a horn sounded. "Praise the gods," he said, raising his eyes towards the clear blue sky.

"Don't you have a taste for clubs?" his companion asked. "Surely the sight of athletes in their prime is enough to stir the blood. Do they not at least whet your appetite for the main event?"

"No, they do not. Watching two groups of men chasing a bladder and trying to hit it and each other with sticks does not appeal to me," he replied, before turning around to his servant. "More wine. This jug is empty." The servant bowed and silently took the empty vessel from his outstretched hand.

"Do not think of it as sport, think of it as war. The two teams are opposing armies, the field of play a battlefield. From the sideline the generals give their commands and their troops act upon those instructions."

"You have not convinced me," Lorian said.

"You know it is not so long since they used the heads of captives instead of a bladder."

Three blasts of a horn sounded, sending an excited ripple through the crowd. "Ah, at last! Now we will see real battle." The fat man grinned.

"Who are the fighters?" the other man asked.

"The Summalian, Bordron, and Rolfgot." Lorian grinned. "A Nortman." The grin turned to laughter.

"Oh. How ironic."

"Yes," Lorian agreed. "I do enjoy the little jests the fates throw at us from time to time." A cheer rose and washed over the crowd as a fanfare sounded announcing the arrival of the combatants. They entered the arena from either side, to be greeted with a wall of thunderous noise. Lorian and his companion rose to their feet and joined in the applause.

"Is it to the death?"

"Yes!" Lorian beamed. "Yes, it is."

The crowd settled as an announcer walked into the centre of the arena. He first introduced, to muted applause, the Nortman, Rolfgot. A massive blond warrior strode confidently from a dark tunnel at one end. He was stripped to the waist; his hair fell loosely down his back. Muscles bunched and rippled across his back and down his forearms. In his hand he carried a huge, two-handed great-sword. He came to a halt yards before the announcer, spat once and glared disdainfully into the crowd. A rumble of boos echoed around the arena.

"Huror, Huror! Where is that wretched man?" Lorian turned agitatedly in his seat.

"You sent him for wine."

"Curse his eyes, how long does it take to fetch a jug of wine?"

"Oh, calm down, Lorian. What is the matter?"

"I wish to place a wager on the bout. They will not take it once the fight has begun. Huror!" the fat man bellowed.

"Yes, Master." The servant hurried over, placing a jug in front of Lorian.

"What took so long?" he snarled.

"The crowd, Master. It is not so easy to pass through it."

"Never mind. Here, take this, and place five gold crowns on the Summalian. And see that you get favourable odds." He fished the coins from a purse on his belt and dropped them into the servant's open palm.

"Yes, Master." The tall servant bowed deeply before closing his fist around the coins and turning away.

"Five crowns?" the other man whistled. "What about a side wager? What odds on the Nortman?"

Lorian looked at his companion with narrowed eyes. "Are you holding information back from me?" he asked suspiciously.

"No, of course not. The other man laughed. "I pride myself on being a good judge of men, and I like how he moves."

"So you would wager your intuition against the three times arena champion?"

"Yes."

"Very well." Lorian grinned. "Ten gold crowns will get you twenty."

"Twenty? An unknown against the undefeated arena champion? Make it fifty."

"Fifty?" Lorian spluttered a mouthful of wine. "Do you take me for a fool? Anything could happen out there."

"Forty then."

"Thirty, no more."

"Done!" The other man grinned.

A thunderous noise rolled around the arena. The two men could feel it reverberating up from the platform where they stood. All around them people were stamping their feet and clapping their hands together, chanting a chorus of, Bordron! Bordron! An ebony-skinned giant strode towards the centre of the arena. He wore a leopard skin loincloth, the head still attached and hanging over his shoulder. Strapped to his left arm was a round wooden shield, in the other he carried a long spear.

"Lords, ladies, and all others assembled here today!" the announcer bellowed, his resonant voice silenced the crowd as his words carried to every part of the circular arena. "Salute the men who will die for you this day!" The arena shook with the noise. With a sharp nod of his head towards the combatants he scuttled away and disappeared from sight.

The two warriors circled each other warily, tension and excitement rippled through the crowd. The Nortman was tall and broad, his upper body heavily muscled, the Summalian taller again, but lighter. Rolfgot struck first, hefting the great-sword with both hands. He spun on his heel, the blade swinging through the air in an arc. The dark-skinned fighter snarled, a flash of white teeth contrasting against his complexion, he deftly blocked the sword with his shield and stabbed out with the spear, catching the paler-skinned man in the side. The crowd erupted at the first sight of blood. Both men stepped back from each other.

"First blood to me." Lorian grinned at his companion, who did not answer.

The Nortman lunged again, leading with the point of his blade this time. Again the taller warrior sidestepped and smashed his shield into his opponent's face. Rolfgot staggered back and spat out a mouthful of blood. The Summalian lunged with his spear, catching the swordsman in the shoulder, another wound opened. Bordron openly grinned now.

"Oh, he's toying with him, this will be over soon and I will be considerably richer." Lorian beamed and gulped back his wine, the red liquid dribbling down his chin, drops pooled on the wooden floor at his feet.

Both spear wounds bled visibly on the white skin of the Nortman. His face too had a crimson smear across his mouth. The crowd urged the tall Summalian to finish him off. Those few who had backed the Nortman with their gold turned away in disgust, as once again the spear point found soft yielding flesh. The Nortman dropped to one knee, and the crowd erupted in a wall of noise. Spurred on by the adulation of the crowd, the dark-skinned Summalian advanced, drawing back his spear. Rolfgot leapt up, apparently not so injured as he at first appeared, driving his sword under the ribs of his opponent and wrenching it up with a grunt. Bordron's eyes opened wide. The big Nortman pulled his sword free and spat a mouthful of blood at the falling body of his opponent. The crowd was stunned into silence, their favourite, the three times arena champion, the undefeated Summalian, Bordron crashed to the dust, dead.

Lorian scowled at his grinning companion as Rolfgot spun around raising his sword as he did so and brought the blade down on the neck of Bordron, severing his head. The gods themselves could not but have heard the thunderous noise coming from the arena moments later.

Duke Normand: Besieging the walls of Eorotia

Duke Erik Normand glanced up from the parchment stretched out on the table in front of him. Fanned out before him were his chosen men, a collection of knights and advisors. Rain drummed a steady beat on the canvas tent which had been his home and central command for the past weeks. "Are the engines in place?" he asked.

"Yes, my lord," a young warrior answered. Duke Normand regarded him coldly before turning away in silence. He traced out, with a finger, the dark lines scratched onto the parchment, a map of the Duchies, and the lands beyond its borders. Spidery script marked his own small segment of the kingdom, the duchy of Lenstir, a tract of boggy and mountainous territory gifted to his ancestor by the then king for his loyalty and bravery in battle. He had grand aspirations to increase its size and with it his standing at court.

He dismissed his momentary lack in concentration and snarled at his knights, "Well get to it then!" A chorus of, 'Yes, my lord,' followed, as the men filed from the tent in a rattle of swords and armour. He poured a rich amber liquid into a silver goblet. He grimaced as the strong brandy burnt all the way down, before turning his attention to the only remaining occupant of the tent. A man with shoulder length grey hair and thick, wiry beard sat in a chair in the corner. He wore a simple, hooded woollen robe. If there had once been any colour to the free flowing garment, the dye had long since washed out, leaving it a dull brownie grey. Duke Normand rubbed his eyes with the palm of his hand and refilled the goblet.

"You should sleep, my lord. I can see the weariness in you," the grey-beard said, as he stood up.

"Sleep? Are you jesting with me? Here of all places, under the walls of the Thieves Citadel?"

"You need to trust me, my lord. The priestesses will not enter your dreams while I protect you."

"So you say, Mage. Did you see the fear on the faces of my men? They all know the legends, they have grown up with the stories..." He half drained the goblet again without finishing the sentence. Worry lines creased his forehead. He could hear the sounds of a mobilising army just beyond the entrance to his command tent – barked orders from officers and sergeants, the rattle of bridles and snorts of horses. Beyond his lines lay the fortified city of Eorotia or, as it was more commonly known, the Thieves Citadel. A thorn in the side of every Duke of Lenstir since his family had been granted the duchy. The city was a den of brigands, assassins and pirates, yet successive generations of dukes had allowed it to flourish on their doorstep. Until now. The reason: the city was sanctuary to the Priestesses of Eor, some called them the Shadow Sisters, others the Dream Cult, for they possessed the power to enter a man's dreams and kill him while he slept. There was no defence against them, no wall could stop them, no barred gate or armoured sentries would deter them.

"You have nothing to fear from the Shadow Sisters. They will not penetrate my wards," the mage answered.

"For centuries Eorotia has been an embarrassment, a festering wound to the honour of my family. Our rivals have mocked us, called us impotent and worse. Yet, not even the king would move against the citadel while the Priestesses of Eor claimed sanctuary there and ownership of the surrounding mountains. They are all that stands in the way of its destruction. The collection of rogues and pirates behind those walls are not an army, most of them have probably fled already." He drained the goblet again and refilled it one more time.

"Getting drunk will help no one," the older man said.

"It will help me," the duke growled. "I have put my faith in you, Mage. See that I am not disappointed. Six of my men failed to wake this morning. There isn't a man among them who doesn't fear to fall asleep."

"You have over a thousand men, if you take an entire city with your losses in single figures, I would call that a good day's work," the mage answered. Normand glared at him coldly, before ducking his head and walking from the tent.

Rain fell in a hazy mist over an open plain in front of the citadel. Beyond the walled city a dark mountain rose steeply towards a grey sky, its peaks shrouded in cloud. Huge, wooden war engines stood in silent rows arrayed before the crenellated walls. A dark, iron studded door stood firmly closed before them. *It is not too late to turn around and march your army off the mountain,* a stray thought crept into his mind like a thief in the night. He dismissed it with a nod towards one of his sergeants, who in turn raised an arm. Barked orders echoed in the air. Huge wooden arms crept ponderously upwards in unison, before releasing a barrage of heavy rock towards the walls and beyond. *So it begins.*

Duke Normand had been present at many sieges, but none where such a poorly defended city would cause such terror in the men assaulting it. Eorotia had no standing army, other than bands of brigands who used it as a base to plunder the local countryside. His countryside. He felt secure moving his siege engines almost up to the wall without fear of them coming under any sort of organised attack. He stifled a yawn, reminding him of the sting the city of thieves was armed with.

"What are your orders regarding the aftermath of the assault, my lord?" one of his warriors asked. The man stood stiff-backed in a shiny breast-plate and open-faced, peeked helm. His red cloak rippled in the breeze, signifying him as a member of Lenstir's elite Dragon Knights.

"It is a city of thieves and cutthroats, the women are either whores or assassins. Once those walls are down and the gate breached, unleash the men. Allow them to plunder as they will, this is my gift to them. If there is not a man or woman left alive, or one brick left stacked upon another by the day's end, it will make no matter to me."

"My lord." The knight bowed stiffly and turned to go.

"One thing," the duke's words immediately halted the man. "Bring me the high priestess. There are thirty-three priestesses in all, see that they are all accounted for. Let none escape." The man swallowed, failing to conceal the flash of fear in his eyes.

"A wise move, my lord. It would be most unfortunate if any of the Shadow Sisters were to escape," the mage said.

"Gods curse them," Normand grumbled.

A roar went up from the besiegers as the first missiles hit home. Huge rocks struck the walls with mighty crashes, while flaming barrels filled with tar rained fire down on top of the defenders. Normand imagined the panic the barrage would cause inside the citadel.

"For how long will you assault the city thus?" the mage asked.

"For as long as it takes," the duke answered as he turned back towards his tent.

"Where are you going now, my lord?"

"To do as you suggested," Normand answered before ducking low inside the tent. "To get some sleep. Wake me when the walls have been breached."

"Sleep well, my lord." The mage bowed low.

***

The boatman stood anxiously on the quayside. He licked his lips as he scanned the empty dock. A thick mist had risen suddenly, obscuring the light of the silver moon. It was an unusual assignment to be called out so late at night. The river was a treacherous stretch of water in the middle of the day, he was not happy having to navigate it in the inky black of night. His heart beat rapidly as he heard boots clicking off the cobblestones. His breath caught in his throat when a hooded figure emerged from the mist. His natural inclination was to tip his head in deference. He swallowed hard as the stranger brushed past him. He caught the scent of jasmine in the air.

Afraid to make eye contact or even look in the direction of the black-cloaked passenger, the boatman dipped his oars into the slow-moving water and began to row. His instructions were to collect one passenger and return to the castle. That was it, see nothing, say nothing. The sound of the oars gently pushing the water brought some sense of peace to his anxious mind.

Normand paced the empty hall, his steps echoing from the flagstones. In the hearth a fire blazed. Above it, pinned to the stone wall, his banner rippled in the heat, a red dragon on a green background. It never ceased to invigorate him, to remind him of the glory he had earned leading his Dragon Knights into battle. He allowed himself a self-satisfied smirk.

A serving girl approached, her eyes to the floor. He arched an eyebrow. *A pretty wench,* he thought. "Come here girl!" he barked.

Nervously she approached. He smiled at the sight of her heaving chest. He could feel his blood rising at the power he held over this girl.

"Yes, s-s-sir," she said. He dragged the back of his hand across his mouth, feeling the prickle of his whiskers on his skin.

"You are a pretty little thing." He leered. He was the king of the castle, he could do whatever he liked. He reached out and took a blonde curl in his hand, wrapped it around his finger as he pulled her towards him. She whimpered, but did not struggle. She knew her place. He reached down and grabbed a fistful of skirt as he pushed her against a wall.

Looking her in the eye, he could see tears glisten.

"My lord, the barge has arrived," a male voice said from behind him.

Normand snapped his attention around and released the serving girl. "Excellent." He beamed, before marching into his bedchamber. It was a fitting place for a duke to slumber. Weapons and banners adorned the walls, animal furs were sprawled about the floor, a fire blazed, casting an orange glow about the room. Normand waited impatiently.

"My lord, your... guest," a servant announced. The duke's lip curled into a sneer, as the man led a figure concealed by a dark hooded-cloak into his bedchamber. "The High Priestess Elandrial."

He could hardly contain himself. Elandrial herself was here, his prize, his spoils of war. He took a step towards her and pushed back her hood.

The Thieves Citadel had fallen, their small army vanquished, their treasuries plundered. Only one thing saved them from utter destruction. They had only one thing left to offer to save themselves from annihilation.

Her green eyes shone in the firelight. He could not help but gasp at her beauty, her skin, so pale and soft, her hair jet black, her lips so full. She was the most exquisite thing he had ever seen. He was almost afraid to touch her lest she would be revealed as an apparition and would disappear… almost.

Lust raged like a wildfire through him. He yanked the cloak down from her shoulders. His eyes opened wide in surprise, she was naked. He drank in the sight of her body, her heavy, round breasts and pink nipples, the curve of her hip and neatly trimmed triangle of dark hair. Her eyes met his. His blazed with lust and passion, hers were blank and unreadable. Without a word or even a sign she dropped to her knees. He closed his eyes and gasped.

No, stop, he thought, *this is too quick*. He wanted to savour the moment, to savour her. With an enormous strength of will he pulled back and lifted her to her feet. Then he guided her onto the bed. She complied without objection. *You're enjoying this,* he thought to himself, genuinely surprised at her reaction. His eyes travelled up the length of her, along her flat belly lingering on her breasts and hard nipples, to her face, creased in rapture. Her body tensed, and a gasp escaped her lips when he ran his hand up her bare leg. He could control himself no longer. She started to groan, pushing her hands against the back wall and wrapping her legs around his hips as his passion grew in intensity.

At first he didn't notice her eyes glow, so busy was he wrapped in her warm embrace. He felt a sharp pain in his back, saw her face transform into a hideous mask of terror, all the while he drove into her. She rolled him over and straddled him as her teeth became fangs, her fingers ending in claws. Yet he could not stop, as he built to a crescendo. The mouth that had given him so much pleasure moments before was now a grotesque ruin of needle sharp teeth reaching for his throat. The priestess growled and hissed as she tore at his soft flesh, her face awash in his blood.

Suddenly she stiffened, and then wailed an ear-piercing shriek of pain. Standing over them both was the mage. In two hands he held a glowing spear which he drove into the priestess's back. His mouth was moving, but Normand could not hear or understand the words at first.

"Wake up, my lord. Wake up!"

***

With a gasp and a shudder the duke was awake. He gulped down ragged breaths as he sat up straight. He swallowed hard, as he took in his surroundings, the small cot he used as a bed while campaigning, the canvas tent all around him. The mage. "What happened?"

"You were dreaming, my lord," the older man answered.

"The Shadow Sisters?"

"Yes," the mage confirmed.

Normand swung from the cot and stood up, looming over the mage. "I trusted you to protect me from those witches!" he bellowed. "You were to be my protector."

"You yet live, my lord," the unbowed mage answered, before turning his back on the duke and walking away.

Tomas: Woodvale Village

Moonlight poured through the open window, bathing the entwined couple in its silvery glow. A cool breeze caressed the glistening skin of the lovers, as two bodies and minds became one. Tomas gazed at his wife's face, marvelling at her beauty. Her eyes were closed, her bottom lip caught between her teeth, as he gently pinned her beneath him, clasping both of her slender wrists in his, much larger, hands; rough, calloused hands of a worker. She stretched her neck back, as she slid her legs over his hips. Blonde curls fanned out behind her, like waves on a sea of gold. She opened her eyes then; liquid sapphires looked into his own. He clamped his mouth to hers as an urgency built inside him, an unconquerable desire to possess, totally, the woman he loved, to give her his soul, even as she opened herself up to him. But, as their lovemaking built to a crescendo, a loud bang on the front door shook them from the moment. Whoever it was rapped again, urgently.

"The All Father curse whatever whoreson is banging on that door," Tomas grumbled in a deep, cracking voice.

Aliss inhaled deep breaths as he rolled off her making the wooden-framed cot creak. The floorboards groaned beneath his weight when he stood on them. As he dragged a linen shirt over his head, he caught sight of her watching him, appraising his hard, muscular body.

"See who it is and come back to me, my love," she said in a breathy voice, a smile twitched at the corner of full lips. *A mouth to savour*, a wicked thought slid into his head.

"Don't move," he said, pulling on coarse woollen breeches.

Blood Of Kings: The Shadow Mage

"I'll be right here." She grinned back.

The banging continued, the stout wooden door shaking under the onslaught. "Alright, alright, I'm coming," he shouted back, becoming increasingly annoyed at the incessant knocking. Not to mention, concerned, at what could be so urgent at such an hour. He was the village blacksmith, who would need a batch of nails made, or a horse shod, in the depths of night? He paused and pulled down a crossbow hanging above the door and loaded a short arrow. Then he opened the door a crack. "Who is it?"

"Tomas, come quick!" He heard a familiar voice, although out of breath, and with an edge of panic to it.

"What is it, Comal?" he asked, recognising one of the young men of the village. The baker's son if he remembered rightly.

"You need to come. Marjeri's baby has been taken."

"Taken?"

"Yes, snatched from its crib as it slept. The mother is distraught, all of the men are gathering in the village square. They say it must be wolves come from the Great Wood. They are going after them. We need your help."

"Wolves?" Tomas tried to process the information coming at him in waves of hysteria from Comal Bakersonn. "Has the magistrate been sent for?"

"Yes, yes, but there is no time. We need to go after them if the child is to have any hope."

"Okay. Give me a minute. I'll follow you down to the square." Tomas collected his thoughts as he closed the door on Comal.

He sighed with regret, as he thought of his wife waiting for him in the bedroom. Instead of returning to her, he removed the bar from the back door and walked out into the cold night air, and out to his workshop. He put the crossbow down on a workbench and then heaved the bench away from the wall.

"What is going on?" Aliss came out covered in a woollen blanket.

"A child has been snatched from its bed by wolves. A hunting party is going after them," he answered. He wiped away a thin covering of dust on the stone floor, to reveal a square wooden door, barely visible in the flickering torchlight. Sliding his fingers into the creases at the edge he lifted the hatch, and sat back on his heels as he regarded a wooden chest concealed there.

"Why do you need that?" she asked, as he hauled the chest out. "You made a promise to me."

"Because wolves do not come into villages and take children from their beds," he answered.

"Please," she pleaded. Tears glistened in her eyes.

"This is different," he said.

"Not if you open that box. Once it's open you will never close it again." Beads of moisture leaked from her eyes. "You swore to me…" She trailed off as he stood and pulled her into his broad chest.

"Okay," he said, running his fingers through her cascading, golden curls. He let her go, and slid the chest back into the slot in the floor, covered it again, then pulled the workbench back over it.

"When will you be back?" she asked, as they stood in the front doorway of their small stone cottage. The earthy perfume of the overhead thatch filled the air, along with the other night smells – the peaty aroma of the nearby forest, the icy touch of an early morning frost.

He slung a pack onto his back and the crossbow over his shoulder. "I'm not sure. It shouldn't take long."

"Be careful," she said. He could see concern written on her face in worry lines across her eyes.

"Don't worry. I should be back before supper." He smiled reassuringly. "We have some unfinished business to attend to." His smile turned into a wicked grin. Aliss blushed and returned a shy smile. It was enough to send renewed fire washing over him. "Go back inside out of the cold and bar the door until my return." He kissed her hard before turning away and walking the short distance from his cottage and workshop at the edge of town to the village square.

"Tomas!" a man called to him as he approached the gathered group. He could hear the hoarse sobs of a woman drifting on the night breeze. Dark shapes congregated around the well at the centre of town, elongated shadows made from orange torchlight stretching out from each of them.

"Daved," Tomas greeted the man, as he approached the group. The moment the blacksmith arrived he became the focal point of the gathering. Men spoke in hurried tones, talking over one another to give him the news. He stood a head taller than the tallest man there. His broad chest and powerful arms giving a hint to the power contained in his wide frame. Dark brown hair tumbled down to his shoulders, a beard of the same colour covered his face.

"My baby! My baby!" a woman wailed in the background. "Who will save my baby?"

"A bad business," Daved said, offering his hand to the big blacksmith.

"I'm told wolves snatched the child from its bed," Tomas said.

"Aye," Daved answered. "Morten here has spoken of a large pack taking several of his sheep in the last few days. They must have come from the Great Wood."

"We'll see," Tomas answered, unable to keep the doubt from his words.

A group of twelve men filed from the village, with a round yellow moon and the torches they bore to light their way. They were armed with an array of weapons, from axes normally used to fell trees, to clubs and hoes. And the crossbow Tomas slung over his shoulder. Morten led the way. He would take them to where he had caught a glimpse of the pack, two days previously, at the edge of his land, where it bordered the Great Wood.

When they arrived they found more evidence of the wolves' presence. Half-eaten remains of sheep lay scattered about, barely visible in the silver glow of the moon. In the background the Great Wood loomed, a wall of darkness bordering the valley. A wolf howled, sending a shiver down Tomas's spine.

"Curse their flea-bitten hides. They have feasted royally on my livestock," Morten grumbled.

"So it would seem," Tomas agreed, as he toe-pocked a woolly carcass. "So why risk coming into the village to take a child?"

"Because they are savage beasts who do not think like men," Morten spat. "They should all be hunted down and skinned. We must rid the valley of their scourge once and for all."

"All beasts understand fear, and all are wary of man," the big blacksmith said.

A second wolf answered the call of the first followed by many more until the dark forest seemed to ring with the sound of their cries. The men shuffled nervously.

"They are close. Now is our chance to rid the valley of their curse," Morten said.

"Do we enter the forest in the dark? The Great Wood is not such a good place to become lost in at night. The stories..." one of the villagers began.

"Pah! Stories? Are you afraid of tall tales told by your grandma, while you bounced on her knee? I have lived on the forest's edge all my life. There are no spirits and sprites of the forest, only beasts who kill sheep, and snatch babes from their beds," Morten raged.

"Enough!" Tomas interjected. "Let's get this done and return to our homes."

They marched, in single file, into the gloom of the Great Wood, all eyeing their dark surroundings nervously, each of them with a feeling of being watched. The wolves were not happy with the beasts who walked on two legs encroaching on their territory. They put up a display of defiance, and a show of strength, unsettling the men at first. But when Tomas fired two crossbow bolts in quick succession, taking down the big alpha male and one other, the men calmed, and the beasts learned to be warier of man.

They hunted and they killed more wolves, as the sun crept higher into the sky. They heaped the carcasses in a big pile to be skinned later, but found no sign of a babe. Although none voiced it, they all thought the same thought, *the child was surely dead by now*. Silence prevailed now that man had found his quarry, and all other beasts remained hidden and out of sight.

"If the babe was taken by wolves, it was not by this pack," Tomas finally said. Tired men bowed their heads, none disagreed.

Although it had not been their reason for journeying into the forest, they collected a fine haul of wolf skins. Three of the men were left to the dirty work of skinning and butchering the beasts, while the rest set out for home, to replenish supplies and head out in another direction in search of the missing infant. They were tired and hungry when they finally emerged from the forest. Already the sun was beginning to slip below the tree line. One of the men suddenly stopped and sniffed loudly. Tomas got it too, a faint smell of smoke, drifting on the breeze.

"There! Look!" Daved suddenly said. Tomas followed the direction he was pointing, towards the village. A thin line of dark smoke drifted into the air.

Princess Rosinnio: Wind Isle

Princess Rosinnio could feel tears well in her eyes. She squeezed them shut lest the man grinding on top of her should see them and mark it as a sign of weakness. She may have lost many things in the past weeks, but her pride she would keep. The beast of a man finished with a loud grunt and a shudder. It was not the pain that had her wanting to cry, although that was enough reason in itself. She had been warned the first time would be painful, and she would bleed. Had she known at the time that her first experience of love making would be with a bear of a man, a Nortman, she would probably have run away and hid herself. No, she thought, she would not, she was her father's daughter and she knew her duty, even if she did not understand it.

Her new husband, Jarl Crawulf rolled off her and lay on his back gulping down breaths. Soon his chest rose and dipped rhythmically as a deep rumbling sound rattled in his throat. Now the tears came. She pulled the silk sheet up to her neck, a wedding gift she had carried across the sea with her. She was surprised the man had even been capable, he had drunk so much at the wedding feast. Rosinnio had sat, stiff-backed by his side, barely touching her food. She doubted she would have had the stomach for the great hunks of half-cooked meat put in front of her, even if she were not fretting over the activities to come. Or contemplating the rest of her life marooned in Nortland, as the wife of a jarl. *How could you, father?* The words tumbled through her mind. She remembered when she voiced them to the emperor, 'you will be a queen, my sweet,' he had said, and that was that, she was dismissed. When it came to affairs of state, and the running of the empire, there was no room for sentimentality. She, as a princess, was a commodity to be traded. What did her father receive in return? A powerful ally in the north, potentially the king of Nortland. *All those pirate ships and sea wolves at his beck and call.* He had done the same to her older sister, Brioni, who he had married off to a desert nomad to ensure peace on his southern border. She had not been heard from since. *At least she will feel the heat of the sun on her face,* Rosinnio thought, as wind howled beyond her window, rattling the wooden shutters.

   Crawulf snored loudly before turning over and flopping a huge muscular arm onto her thin frame. In time sleep finally came to her, it was not a restful one. She tossed and woke on several occasions, as dark shapes chased her through her dreams. Giant wolves with flesh-ripping teeth and jaws hunted her. She dreamt she could feel the hotness of their breath on the back of her neck. In the distance the wind howled as it bore other terrors towards her, huge winged creatures swooping at her from above. Each time she woke she could hear the wind outside rattling the wooden shutters. She could hear the sea crashing against the rocks below the castle. Each time she woke she could feel the wetness of her cheeks. The dreams were not new to Rosinnio. Ever since she'd been a child she'd suffered night terrors and premonitions. She had hoped they would not follow her to the ends of the world. It seemed they had.

   In the morning, Crawulf leered at her like a wolf from her dream, and without so much as a word he flipped her over and lifted her nightgown. He stank of grease and stale beer. She endured in silence, thankful she, at least, did not have to look upon his face. She felt him spill his seed inside her, and could not help but wonder how long it would be before she was with child.

   How much worse can life become?

   "Gods, girl, the very sight of you stirs my loins every time I look at you. No man has ever had to withstand such torture as I, while I waited to do that."

   "You are too kind, my lord. I am happy I please you," she answered as she pulled the hem of her nightgown back over olive-skinned thighs. *The oaf has forgotten last night already*, she thought.

"I am a jarl not a lord. It is time you saw some of your new country. My people are anxious to greet you. You have been hidden away behind these walls for too long now. It is many weeks since your arrival. Later I will take you on a tour." His voice sounded harsh and coarse to her ear, as he stumbled over the words of the common trading tongue. The language of Nortland sounded more like guttural barks, harsh to her ears and utterly incomprehensible.

"And I am anxious to meet them, my lord... my jarl. It is taking me time to adjust to the climate, the weather is not so damp or cold in Sunsai," she replied, dropping her gaze as his eyes bored into her.

"Aye, the winds are likely a little brisker than you are used to. You may call me Jarl, or simply Crawulf. Have no fear, my princess, a few days aboard my ship and you will feel at home here as if you were born and raised on one of the isles." He grinned.

To Rosinnio his smile was more of a feral snarl. She had to bite back a protest at the thought of going to sea again. Her stomach lurched at the memory of her last voyage, three weeks of sickness on raging seas, and that in one of her father's great warships, where she was provided with her own living quarters, a large, triple mast vessel designed for long ocean voyages. Her heart sunk into a cold pit in her stomach at the thought of setting out to sea on the much smaller longboats the Nortmen used for pirating and raiding the coastal towns of their near neighbours. "My lord... jarl... Jarl Crawulf," words caught in her throat.

"Get some sea air into those lungs." He grinned. "For now though, come. My men are still below in the feasting hall. They have celebrated our wedding throughout the night. The feast will continue for the next three days."

"My lord!" Rosinnio exclaimed. "I cannot possibly just go out in public. A lady must prepare first. My handmaiden will need to dress me, style my hair..."

Crawulf shook his head. "Women and their secret rituals. I will have your girl sent to you. Do not keep me waiting too long."

Rosinnio nodded and forced a smile for the benefit of her new lord and husband… *jarl*. Once Crawulf had closed the heavy wooden door behind him, she finally gave free rein to her tears. She ran to the window and threw open the shutters. Far below the tower the grey sea boiled, crashing against the cliff. *If only it would wash the cursed castle and all of Nortland away with it*, she thought. She imagined climbing out and up onto the uppermost battlements. Giving herself to the wind, arms outstretched, a sacrifice to the harsh northern gods. Would they embrace her and wrap her in a blanket of snow and ice, or would they spit her back onto the shore? What would her father think if she were to truly give her life to the Nortmen? She pictured his kindly face, and saw it quickly clouding with anger. Just as she had seen it transform from beauty to ugliness a thousand, thousand times before. She dismissed the image and gently closed the shutters. *Did you really believe this was in my own interest, father?*

"Highness." A young woman bowed before her. Rosinnio smiled and raised her handmaiden to her full height. A familiar face in a land of strangers, a land of monsters and demons.

"Marta," she squeaked her servant's name, resisting the urge to fall into her arms and cry on her shoulder.

"Your husband, highness, he bade me come to you with haste…"

Rosinnio suddenly straightened her own back, and her lip, as she gazed upon the girl who was strikingly similar in appearance to herself. Both had long dark hair and olive skin. Both had dark brown eyes and full lips. They were of an age, Rosinnio was fifteen, and Marta had served the princess since she was a young girl. If not for the difference in bearing, and the silver chain worn around the maidservant's neck, a mark of bondage, they could easily pass as sisters. "Do not call me highness. You will address me as, my lady. I am no longer a princess of Sunsai, no longer a daughter of the emperor. Henceforth I am the wife of a jarl, a lady of Nortland." Her stare was cold and hard making the servant dip her head to avoid the determined gaze of her mistress.

"As you wish, high… my lady."

"My husband requires us to return to the wedding feast. I wish to be dressed in the pale blue silk gown, with the lace trim, and decorate my hair with the pearls my father gifted me on my fifteenth birthday." Rosinnio sat in a hard wooden chair, and waited, stiff-backed, while her servant readied her gown and accessories.

"They were very noisy. They drank all night, and I'm sure I heard the sounds of fighting," Marta said, as she dragged a comb through Rosinnio's hair. "They scare me. When they talk they sound like dogs barking, and when they look at me it makes me feel like they want me to be their next meal."

Rosinnio took her servant's hand in her own, stopping the languid strokes with the comb. "They scare me too, Marta, but this is our home now. We must be brave, both of us."

"Yes, my lady," the servant girl answered and then continued. "Did you see the statue of the hideous creature at the entrance to the castle?"

"The one sculpted from wood, taller than a man, at the main gate?"

"Yes, my lady, the very one. I asked one of the kitchen slaves about it. It is supposed to depict the goddess Boda, Mistress of their Underworld. They call it the Nacht Realm or Shadow World. One side of her face is fair and beautiful, the other a horror of dead and rotting flesh. She was once queen of the gods, wife of Alweise, The All Wise. She was famed for her beauty and gentle nature, but she was seduced by the warrior Ronawn the Swift who used his great speed to flee the wrath of the gods and the vengeance of Alweise. Boda was not so lucky. He cursed her, leaving one side of her face and body hideous to behold, but he left the other side untainted to forever remind her of what she had lost when she betrayed him. Then he banished her to a desolate place filled with the lost souls of the diseased and the cowardly."

Blood Of Kings: The Shadow Mage

"Why would they worship such a god and place an image of her for all to see when they enter the castle gates?" Rosinnio asked.

"Out of fear, my lady. They worry that if they do not worship her and give her due respect she will inflict a great pestilence on them."

"They are a strange people," Rosinnio answered and then said, "I have a task for you. Find an apothecary somewhere in the town, but be discreet. If anyone asks, what you purchase is meant for you and you alone. Do you understand?"

"Yes, my lady." Marta began the fluid motion of combing her mistress's hair once again.

"In time I will bear my husband the sons he no doubt craves, but I am not ready for that at this moment."

"I understand, my lady." Marta tied up the princess's hair in ribbons and curls before threading a string of pearls through the creation.

"There are eight main isles that make up Nortland, as well as a smattering of other, smaller islands. This is Wind Isle. There is also Sea Isle, Sun Isle, Land Isle, Dark Isle, Rock Isle, Green Isle and Black Isle. We are the southernmost isle." Rosinnio barely heard a word said by Crawulf, as she sat, biting her lip, beside him at the head table in the great hall. Dozens of other wooden benches filled the hall, each one, beneath a burden of half-eaten food and slumbering men. Rosinnio's eyes could not be torn from the dark red patches staining the stone floor. They were not there when she retired with her new husband the night before. "The sunny southern isle, they call us." Crawulf laughed.

"There was bloodshed here last night?" Rosinnio interrupted her husband.

"Hmmm?" The big Nortman followed her gaze to patches of blood. "Oh, yes, more than likely. The men can become excited and argumentative when they've taken ale." He shrugged. "Black Isle is where my uncle, the king, rules from Castle Ice," he continued, barely drawing breath.

"But, my lord, so much blood," she interrupted again.

"Do not trouble yourself, my love. I doubt there were more than a handful of fatalities."

"A handful! You mean men died here? Were murdered in my name?" Rosinnio failed to keep the horror from her voice.

"It is nothing..." Crawulf's words were suddenly interrupted by a loud roar. A huge man, with long braided hair and a bushy red beard was bellowing so fast and loudly Rosinnio could not understand the words. She was reminded of her servant's remarks earlier when she likened their speech to that of barking hounds. "Sit down, Rothgar!" Crawulf leapt to his feet. The big Nortman, who only moments before, had been in a drunken slumber continued to shout. "You are disrespecting my bride, Rothgar. Sit down!"

Rosinnio could taste bile in her throat, she wanted to be sick. She was a daughter of the Emperor of Sunsai, and as such was unused to such explosive displays of violence, at least not at such close quarters. She had attended the arena games many times, where men often fought to the death, but they were far more distant in mind and body. Rothgar jabbed a finger in her direction, making her pale with fear. She had no idea what she should do. Sit where she was and say nothing? Run for her life? No one would dare address a member of royalty so, in the court of the emperor. She felt rooted to her chair. Even if she were capable of standing she was sure her legs would give way beneath her. Her new husband was roaring and exchanging insults with the man. Other Nortmen now joined in. Rosinnio searched with her eyes for her maidservant. She saw Marta standing in the shadows, her face as pale as Rosinnio's own.

Crawulf leapt over the table, an axe appeared in his hand. She had no idea where it had even come from. Rothgar was not expecting it either and received the flat of the blade in the face. One blow sent him crashing to the floor in a heap. "Get him out of here! Let him sleep it off with the hounds in the courtyard," the big jarl fumed. When he turned back to his young bride, she could see a smile play at the corner of his mouth. *He's enjoying this*, she thought. She had thrown up all over his boots the first time they met. A repeat performance was not far off.

"W-what was he saying?" she stammered.

"Do not concern yourself. He was drunk. In a few hours he won't even remember anything happened." Crawulf picked up a tankard of ale and finished it without taking breath, half of it spilled down his front.

"What did he say?"

"He called you a witch." Crawulf shrugged.

"I? A witch?" The words floated between them, she could not understand why anyone, least of all, one of her husband's housecarls would label her so. She had spent the weeks, and especially the previous night contemplating her new life, and how she could possibly tolerate becoming the wife of a Nortman. Now she was beginning to wonder how long her life was likely to be with such animosity and suspicion towards her.

"What is to be his punishment?" In her father's court, such disrespect would result in the forfeit of a life.

"Ack, the sore head he will have will be punishment enough." Crawulf dismissed her strangled protest with a wave of his hand.

"But, my lord, he called me a witch. He disrespected me, you said so yourself. He threatened me. I am your wife!"

"Enough," he barked. "I will make him apologise and that will be the end of the matter." Crawulf suddenly rose again, pulling her to her feet as he did so. "Come, wife, all this fighting has stirred my blood. I have other sport in mind." He laughed as he dragged her from the hall. Princess Rosinnio, daughter to the Emperor of Sunsai, blessed of the gods, bit back a protest and did as she was bade by her new husband.

Duke Normand: Eorotia – The Thieves Citadel

"Wowza! Kaboom!" The mage chuckled as rocks, fired from the swinging arms of trebuchets, arced through the air and crashed against the solid stone walls of Eorotia.

"I am glad you find sport to amuse you," Duke Normand spat as he watched, grim-faced, the assault on the Thieves Citadel. Behind him, his knights, resplendent in their red cloaks, calmed restless mounts as they waited impatiently for a breach in the walls, and for the real slaughter to begin.

"Is it not often one witnesses such beauty in destruction, such grace. Not to mention the ingenuity in the design of the machines. They are like giant wooden swans."

"Have you been struck on the head?" the duke asked, irritably.

"No, my lord." The mage chuckled. "You and I just see the world differently."

"Well stop your jabbering, man." Normand threw back a goblet of red wine, spilling much of it on his chin.

"They say dragons once nested in these mountains." The mage indicated the jagged peaks behind the city, with a sweep of his arm.

"Dragons? Pah! Now I know your mind is addled," Normand said, his words laced with scorn. "Are you to tell me you are a believer in dragons now?"

The mage turned towards the duke, his eyes full of determination. "Oh yes, my lord. Oh yes indeed. I have seen, with my own eyes, the bones of huge creatures that could have come from nothing other than a dragon. Ancient bones dug from the ground while mining for precious stones deep in the Sunsai Empire. Dragons are real, my lord. Oh so very real."

Duke Normand held the mage's eye-contact momentarily before turning away, with a dismissive wave of his hand. "Nonsense, nonsense and more nonsense."

A wave of excitement rippled through the spearmen lined up before him, as masonry dust clouded the air and chunks of the outer wall crumbled away.

"Your men are anxious to partake in the coming jovialities," the mage said, turning away from the duke again.

"What of it?"

"Your order to unleash, and unmuzzle them and allow free rein on the unfortunate citizens of the town, may have been…. hasty, in my, ever so, humble opinion."

"Oh just speak your mind, Mage. I have not the patience for your riddles and games. The 'citizens' of that city are nothing but brigands, whores and thieves. It has been a blemish staining the honour of my family for far too long. I would see it dismantled brick by filthy brick, and the inhabitants with it."

"Just so, my lord, and who would blame you? Perhaps, though, you are not seeing the wood for the trees in this matter. These mountains are a gateway to the south, and Eorotia is its key. Think of the huge trade caravans snaking their way around the mountain to avoid the very brigands you are about to put to the sword. Think of what they would pay to save a journey of hundreds of miles, especially if there were a warm welcome, and safe passage. They would be more than happy to pay a small levy, and pass a night or two in a hospitable town to break their journey, and spend some of their coin. Handled right, it could become a trading hub itself. Where would be the sense, for southern traders in travelling for weeks north, when they could unload their goods and make their profit here?"

"I am a soldier, not a trader nor an innkeeper," Normand responded.

"Soldiers need gold too, my lord."

A cheer rang out from the men, echoing through the valley. "The wall is breached, my lord." A man-at-arms hurried up to the duke.

"Ready the men to advance, Malachi," Normand said, turning towards his most senior and trusted knight.

"Yes, my lord."

"Oh, and Malachi," the duke called back the grizzled warrior. "See to it that the destruction of the town is kept to a minimum. And I want all of the priestesses accounted for."

"My lord." Malachi bowed, before running off to carry out his orders.

Normand drew his sword. "Shall we, Mage?"

"You are going in with the vanguard?"

"Oh yes." Normand smiled, a cold, humourless smile.

"Well, I shall wait here, my lord, and leave you to your fun."

Normand pulled his helmet over his head, leaving the visor raised. He ordered his one hundred knights to dismount and join the front ranks on foot. They were his heavy horse, his battering ram, but there was no place for cavalry when storming a castle, and he would have his Dragon Knights—an order of fighting men formed by his great grandfather in the dim and distant past—around him when he entered the Thieves Citadel.

He was hot and uncomfortable inside his armour. His legs and arms ached from the weight. His throat was parched, as dust and smoke from countless fires choked the air. Yet he was exuberant as he led his men over the crumbled masonry and into the town. Everywhere he looked, people milled about in panic, struck dumb by the chaos of war. A woman stood screaming in a street, blood staining the skin of her cheek and neck where she had been hit by flying shrapnel. A spearman drove the point of his weapon into her as he leapt bits of broken wall, silencing her screams for good. More devastation was wrought on the citizens of Eorotia, as Duke Normand's warriors piled into the city.

A thin line of defenders rushed to meet them. The duke's knights led the charge against them with his spearmen following close behind. The ragged band of brigands was quickly broken and those not left lying silently in pools of their own blood, or screaming for their mothers, wives, or whores, fled from the savage assault. Normand passed a man on his knees, whimpering as he held a string of his own pink guts in his hand. The duke ignored him and pressed deeper into the city. Soon the pain-filled cries of dying men were replaced with the screams of women as the sack of the city began in earnest. There would be no mercy for the citizens of the Thieves Citadel.

Normand led his knights through the mayhem; all were under strict instructions to round up the Shadow Sisters, priestesses of the Dream Cult. It was imperative that none of the white-robed women were allowed to escape. As well as their distinctive garments, his men would recognise the priestesses by a tattoo of an eye burnt into their foreheads.

They swiftly put down any resistance and pressed deeper into the city. Normand and his knights ignored the fleeing citizenry, even as his foot soldiers put the town to the sword and began the rape and slaughter in earnest. The duke led his men onwards towards the town square, and there he found what he was looking for. Dominating the surrounding buildings and open spaces of the square stood an imposing structure. Two huge wooden doors were flanked by massive circular pillars. Above the entrance, carved into the stone was an eye. Painted in blue and black it stood out from the white façade of the building, as if it watched all who approached. The temple of Eor.

"Bring up a ram, get those doors down!" Normand barked. "And fetch the mage here, now!" Knights scrambled to do his bidding, issuing orders and threats of their own to the common warriors.

"My lord," the mage greeted Normand, just as a loud crack echoed around the square. The double-doors guarding the entrance to the temple smashed inwards in a cloud of dust and splintered wood. The duke glanced at the mage, his jaw set in steely determination as he drew his sword. The air hung heavy with smoke and dust as all around him his men sacked the Thieves Citadel. Rape, slaughter and looting abounded. Normand ignored it all, as he stepped over rubble and entered, sword in hand, inside the Dream Cult's temple.

Inside the temple was dark. There were no windows or any other doors to give access to sunlight and all of the torches and lanterns lining the walls of the entrance hallway had been extinguished. The air was thick with the heady scent of burning incense. Normand pushed forward as men lit his way, rushing ahead with flaming torches. The duke glanced in the direction of the mage several times, making sure the practitioner of magic, and his only defence against the dark arts of the priestesses of Eor, was still at his shoulder.

The long corridor opened into a wide, circular chamber, the high roof supported by towering columns. Men quickly filed into the chamber, putting flame to the sconces on the wall; their shadows danced across the marble floor. Their echoing boots broke the eerie silence. Normand stopped suddenly, letting his sword drop by his side as the flickering torches bathed the chamber in orange light. Lying, in a circle, with their eyes closed and their arms by their sides, as if in peaceful slumber, were the priestesses of Eor.

"Are they?" he began, but a knight answered for him.

"Dead, my lord." He moved to each one, putting his cheek to their faces before touching his hand to their cold skin. "All of them."

"How many?" he asked irritably, even as he heard the mage's mumbled counting behind him. Cautiously he stepped towards the bodies, the lifelike eye tattoo on each of their foreheads made him shiver involuntarily.

"Thirty-two, my lord," the mage answered.

"One missing," Normand answered, unable to shake the feeling of being watched by thirty-two false eyes branded onto thirty-two foreheads. "Make sure they are all really dead," he said to the knight moving among the bodies. He drew his sword and plunged it into the heart of the first, before moving to the next. The duke then swung back towards the mage. "There is one missing!" he growled.

"Aye, the high priestess herself," the mage answered.

"Find her!" he growled at the mage, before turning to his knights. "Tear this place apart brick by brick, until you have found her. Pull the city down if you have to, just find her!" He stormed from the chamber then, with the mage hurrying behind him.

"Calm yourself, my lord. She will be found, and in the meantime you have my protection. She will not harm you," the mage panted.

Normand stopped and whirled around. "And is your magic powerful enough to protect us all? Can you guard the dreams of my men too?"

"No, my lord, I cannot," the mage answered, dropping his head.

"She must be found! Tell me, why did they take their own lives?"

"There is power in death, my lord. Especially if a life is freely given."

"She sacrificed them all to make good her own escape? Be on your guard, Mage," Normand said and then barked an order to one of his knights. "Should I fail to wake from sleep, at any time before the high priestess is caught, slit his throat." He pointed at the mage before turning to face the smaller man. "On your guard, Mage, the stakes are high!"

The mage swallowed hard and nodded. "Of course, my lord."

"A purse of gold to the man who brings me her head, attached or not to the rest of her," Normand bellowed to all within earshot.

All around him was devastation and mayhem as his army put the Thieves Citadel to the sword. The blemish, for so long, staining the honour of his family would finally be eradicated, and the brigands and whores, thieves and assassins who populated the city would suffer badly at the hands of his soldiers. But the High Priestess of Eor had escaped. His greatest fear, literally his nightmare was loose, and likely thirsting for vengeance.

"Find her!" he barked again and strode from the devastated city.

Tomas: Woodvale Village

The sun sank below the distant mountains, draining all light from the sky. Any sign of the trailing smoke had disappeared with the inky backdrop of the night sky. Tomas led the small group of men to the edge of town where they were met by Rorbert, a village elder, whom Tomas knew had once served in the King's Lancers. The loss of an eye and a severe limp that made him grumble in cold weather was proof that he had seen action.

"Tomas," the grey-beard began, unable to meet the blacksmith's eye. "I'm sorry, Tomas."

"What has happened, Rorbert?"

"The magistrate came. He..." Rorbert dropped his head. "Aliss..."

Tomas heard no more. He was off and running as words drifted on the wind. He was unaware of the doors and windows being barred as he ran past, of husbands pulling wives, and wives pulling their children from the street.

At the far end of the village the blackened carcass of his house stood stark in the moonlight. Behind his ruined home, his blacksmith's workshop bore the scorch marks of the flames, but at least still stood relatively untouched.

"Aliss!" he cried out, twisting this way and that, looking for his wife. "Aliss!" he yelled until his throat was raw and his voice hoarse.

"She's gone, Tomas. They took her," Rorbert said softly, coming up behind him, panting.

"Why?" Tomas asked, the anguish he felt in his heart clearly evident in his voice. In truth he was still in shock as he tried to fathom what had happened while he was gone. As he stood amidst the destruction of his home tears glistened at the edge of his eyes. "What happened here?" His eyes bored into those of the shorter man, searching for answers, searching for truth.

"The magistrate was sent for, to report the missing babe. He and his soldiers were only a short distance away dealing with a matter in Dortia. He came straight away." The grey-beard paused, rubbing greasy hands into his tunic.

"Go on," Tomas encouraged as he became irritated with Rorbert's nervousness.

"The story of the missing babe was related to him and he asked to speak with Marjeri. She... she," Rorbert stumbled over his words.

"Tell me."

"She denounced Aliss as a witch. She said, it was your wife who had stolen her baby to use his blood to make potions, and feed the demons she summoned."

"What nonsense is this?" Tomas could not believe his ears. It was true, Aliss had often made potions and elixirs, but from plants and herbs she collected in the forest, and only to help folk. People came from miles to visit her with their ailments. She was certainly not a witch, at least not one who would cause mischief. "Marjeri called her witch? Why would she even think such a thing, let alone voice it? Who was it she called when her other boy took ill last winter and almost coughed up a lung? Aliss cured the lad," he spat out the last part.

"Her mind is addled with the loss of her child. She doesn't know what she is saying." Rorbert shrugged, half-heartedly defending the accuser.

"I spent the day searching for her child! Aliss aided in the birth of the babe!" Tomas could feel his anger building up. He picked up the crossbow he had left leaning against a blackened post.

"What are you going to do?" Rorbert asked, suddenly anxious.

"I'm going to get her back," he answered and headed towards his stable. He kept two horses there, a luxury he could ill afford, but Aliss loved to go riding whenever she could and he could never deny her anything.

"Tomas... they were not gentle with her," Rorbert called after him, dropping his head as he did so. "The magistrate's eyes were filled with lust when he saw her."

Tomas growled as hatred darkened his face. "Did not one among you try to help her?"

"I'm an old man, Tomas. The rest of the folk were scared. What could we do?"

Tomas spat his contempt into the scorched earth at his feet and strode to the stable. He led a dun-coloured gelding by the reins, and quickly tacked up his horse. "Which way did they go?" Tomas growled.

Rorbert pointed east away from the setting sun. "Have a care, Tomas. He has half a score of armed men with him. And he is the law in this part of the country. Do not throw your life away."

Tomas scowled at the older man as he hauled himself into the saddle. "He has not the right," he said before urging his mount forward.

"Aye, but he does," Rorbert said sadly, as the sound of hoofbeats disappeared into the darkness.

Tomas was wary of pushing the horse too hard in the darkness. One misplaced foot, or a divot on the well travelled road and it would be disaster. He needed to catch the magistrate before he made it back to his keep or it would make rescuing Aliss so much harder, but a horse with a broken leg or neck would be of no use to him.

As it happened, he was hailed on the road far sooner than he had imagined. In his mind, the magistrate and his entourage were hurrying to get to the safety of his walls, eager to put to trial and pronounce judgement on his prisoner. In his mind, the magistrate was fleeing. Not so, the king's official had taken a leisurely pace and had made camp by a small stream a short ride from the village.

"Halt and identify yourself!" Tomas was challenged as he approached the camp by two liveried guardsmen. Both wore shirts of chainmail and round helms with a long nose guard protecting the upper half of their face. Although both were armed with swords, neither had drawn their weapon.

"I wish to see the magistrate," Tomas declared impatiently. In the distance he could see a small campfire glowing in the darkness. Several dark shapes huddled around the fire, but he could not identify anyone. The stream gurgled over stones behind them, as the fire crackled sending sparks into the air.

"And who might you be then?" one guard answered.

"The magistrate is busy," the other said. His companion chuckled.

Just then a scream pierced the night. Instinctively, Tomas kicked his horse forward between the two guards, catching them unawares. He guided the mount towards the cry of distress as the two guards picked themselves up while shouting warnings to the camp. The shapes stirred from the around the campfire. The sound of steel being drawn from sheaths filled the air.

Tomas unslung the crossbow from his back and fumbled for a bolt from the quiver on his belt. Guards rushed forward from the darkness startling his horse. The beast reared up on its hind legs and threw Tomas from the saddle. He hit the dirt with a thud he felt travel up his spine to the base of his skull. The horse screeched and scrambled to safety as Tomas groaned on the ground. Rough hands hauled him to his feet.

"What is the meaning of this?" a voice bellowed. Tomas saw an older man approach. He wore a thunderous expression on his face, his expensive cloak fanned out behind him as he marched towards the blacksmith. "Who are you? And what in The Hag's Dark Pit do you want?"

"The magistrate asked you a question. Answer his lordship!" Tomas felt the sting of a gauntleted fist connect with the side of his head. He would have fallen again if he had not been held between the two guards. "Valley scum," the guard added pushing Tomas to the ground at the magistrate's feet.

When he looked up it was not the magistrate he saw. Staring straight at him, through tear-filled eyes and bruised face, was Aliss. She had been tethered to a tree, her dress was ripped exposing one breast. Her lips trembled and she was shaking her head, mouthing the word, 'no'. Tomas felt his rage burning inside him. He spat a stream of blood onto the ground and turned an icy glare towards the magistrate as he looked up at the king's official. The magistrate took an involuntary step backwards from the intensity of the stare. "What," he began levelly, "have you done to my wife?" Although the words were spoken softly, the threat lacing them was clear.

"The witch is your wife?" one of the guards chuckled. He wrenched Tomas back by the hair. "You'll not satisfy her again now that she's tasted a real man."

"Aye, and more than one," another guard added, laughing.

A smirk spread across the magistrate's face. "She will face the flames before the week is out. Find another." With the dismissive uttered, he turned his back on the stricken Tomas and walked away.

The blacksmith glanced over at his wife and saw the shame written plainly in her eyes and in every mark, every bruise on her face. She looked away unable to meet his eyes, knowing that he now knew. It broke his heart. Then the mist descended. Working as a blacksmith had developed his upper body muscles, giving him the strength of a horse, but Tomas had speed too, and surprise. The guard was still chuckling when Tomas leapt up and punched him so hard in the face that he fell to the ground and lay still. He grabbed the second by the throat, effortlessly throttling him and flinging him away where he heaved and gasped in an attempt to suck in air. Tomas followed through with a kick to the side of his head. It knocked the helmet of his head and sent him sprawling to the ground.

The magistrate whirled around at the commotion and fumbled for the sword at his belt. Tomas grabbed his wrist and squeezed until he heard a crack. The man who would judge his wife and brand her witch, screamed at the agony of his broken hand. The big blacksmith drew his head back before whipping it forward. His forehead connected with the magistrate's face with a spray of blood. His legs buckled and he collapsed to the ground beside his guards.

"Tomas!" Aliss screamed. Pain exploded in his shoulder driving him to his knees. The rest of the magistrate's compliment of guards were roused now. One was pointing a crossbow at Tomas. The blacksmith clawed at the bolt protruding from his back, but could not reach it.

"Run, Tomas! Please, just run!" Aliss screamed at him. The guards approached warily, swords drawn. Tomas pushed himself to his feet, grabbing the magistrate's fallen sword as he did so. "Run!"

Tomas hefted the blade. He would give his life for his woman, but if he died, who then would be left to help her? "I'll come for you," he said. All he saw were her tears.

He turned then and ran for his horse, ignoring the burning pain in his back. Time ceased to exist for him then, as he fled into the darkness. If pursuit came he did not know, nor how he had lost them. He kicked the horse and let it take him away, his mind clouded by the memory of his wife tied to a tree, surrounded by men who had abused her and named her witch. And he had left her with them. He had no idea when the darkness came and took him.

Lady Rosinnio: Wind Isle

Lady Rosinnio, wife of Jarl Crawulf, Lord of Wind Isle and all of the surrounding seas, stood stoically at the prow of the ship as it dipped and rose, seeming to smash into every wave while sending a jolt through the vessel. Beside her, her handmaiden knelt over the side, whimpering and retching into the grey and white swell beneath her. Rosinnio would not succumb. She who was of the Royal Sunsai household would not yield to anything so base as the Nort Sea. Even though her stomach was as turbulent as the waves beneath the hull of the wooden boat, she would not give in. Her heart leapt at every creak and groan of the thin planks beneath her feet, her mind raced as she envisaged a watery doom. Although land was still visible through mist and the spray of the sea, she knew it was too far to swim, even if she had the strength to fight the roiling water. She swallowed back a mouthful of burning bile, while her imagination made every motion of the sea a giant arm made of salty water reaching for her. *How was it possible to undertake vast sea voyages in such flimsy crafts?* she wondered, as behind her the crew busied themselves at oars or bailing water. *There is more water inside the cursed boat than in the ocean!* Even so, she would not give in to her fears and treacherous stomach. She did not notice her husband come up behind her, until his harsh, guttural voice sounded in her ear.

"How does it feel, my lady, to rule the waves?" he asked. She found it difficult to tell when he was jesting and when he was serious. It infuriated her, especially at a time when speaking a few simple words was a major chore.

"Am I queen of the sea?" she asked, her words impossibly lighter and more playful than she felt.

"Aye, girl, you will be queen of Nortland and all the seas around her, one day."

"Jarl Crawulf, perhaps it would be best if some sentiments and aspirations were kept secreted for the time being," the voice of her husband's advisor slithered across the wind, making her wonder had they been uttered at all, or were they conjured from her imagination. She did not like the man. She did not like the way he appeared as if from nowhere. No sound or sight and then suddenly he was standing behind her, staring at her. *Was it magic?* She found herself wondering every time her thoughts turned to him.

"Nonsense, Brandlor. She is my wife and will be my queen. I will be my uncle's successor. Have you not said so yourself?"

"Yes, my Jarl, but patience is…."

"…is for women and weak-willed men!" Crawulf cut him off.

"As you say, my Jarl." The older man bowed, the wind whipping the thin wisps of white hair. As he rose, his eyes met Rosinnio's. They were dark like the overhead sky, and hungry as the bottomless sea. They reminded her of a wolf stalking his prey. She looked away first, unable to shake the feeling of insects crawling all over her body. "A storm is coming." He changed the subject with a glance towards dark clouds on the horizon.

"Aye," Crawulf agreed, and turned away barking orders at the men as he walked between the rowing benches. A wide rectangular sail crept up the mast, the fabric had been dyed red, the colour of blood. It made Rosinnio shiver at the thought of the vessel creeping inland in some far-off place. Its dragon skull prow-head chasing away the spirits and gods of the poor folk the fearsome Nortmen would regularly raid. They were her people now.

With the wind filling their sail and the angry Baltagor, Lord of the Sea, leading their path, the ship easily reached port before the black rolling clouds and the oncoming storm. Lady Rosinnio had never felt such relief as the moment she took one delicate step onto the dock. Behind her, her handmaiden was all but carried ashore by a giant Nortman covered in furs and unkempt hair. She, however, would disembark without the aid of any man. She met the eyes of her husband as she did so, and the secret smile and wink he gave her filled her with pride. The depth of which took her by surprise. *Did it matter to her that the barbarian warlord she now called husband was proud of her?* It would seem so.

"My lady, we have a carriage waiting to return you to the castle," a member of Crawulf's household staff greeted her, an elderly man, with the leather bond of slavery wrapped around his neck. She nodded her thanks and took charge of her maidservant from the huge Nortman warrior, stifling a smile at the poor girl's suffering and green complexion.

She sat into the back of the wooden cart and pulled a woollen blanket over her and the other girl. Her husband's bondsman had called it a carriage, a far cry from the ornate transport made from polished wood and inlaid gold she was used to being ferried in as the daughter of an emperor.

The cart rocked and bounced over the uneven surface the Nortmen called a road, little more than a worn path through the countryside. Each jolt sent a wave of pain up Rosinnio's spine. "I do not know which is worse, the sea or this gods cursed road," she grumbled. Her maidservant was not listening. She leaned her head against the wall of the carriage, with her eyes squeezed tightly shut. Rosinnio put her head back and tried to ignore the discomfort of the ride. She pulled the woollen blanket up over her shoulders, ignoring the musty smell. The wind picked up blowing rain in through the uncovered windows, landing little icy kisses on her exposed face. Even so, she allowed herself the briefest smile of self-satisfaction. She had not given in to the sea, not this time.

Her mind wandered back to another time, what seemed like a lifetime ago. She was a child, playing in one of the many courtyards throughout the palace. The sun beat down, warming her skin and touching her soul with tendrils of light and warmth. The air was filled with the musky scent of jasmine as she glided across the paving slabs, ducking behind fountains and flat-leafed plants, as she played some game or other conjured from her imagination. Then she heard voices.

"No, father, please don't do this to me." She heard her older sister's voice. She could hear the tears in her words and knew she was crying.

"Enough! You are a daughter of the Sunsai Empire, Brioni. Your duty is to obey your emperor, and you will obey me!" It was rare for her to hear her father's voice raised. He was usually such a soft-spoken, kindly man… at least to her. She knew, however, that it was wise to avoid him, or at least do his bidding, when dark clouds fouled his mood.

"You would send me to die in the Uncha Mort? Your own daughter," Rosinnio's sister cried.

"I am not sending you to die. It is time you were wed, and I have chosen a husband for you," the emperor answered.

"It is a desert. They are savages. They live in tents and never stay in one place for more than a season. Do you expect me to live that way? I, a princess? Prince Egron of Tarnaia will…"

"Forget Prince Egron! And all of the others. You will marry Khan Bordon, and that is my final word!" From her hiding place, secreted behind a fountain depicting a boy playing a flute, Rosinnio flinched at the anger she heard coming from her father. Her own tears welled at her sister's sobs of despair. The Uncha Mort was a desert of sand and hard-baked earth dried out under a relentless, burning sun, stretching for hundreds of leagues. Several nomadic tribes roamed there, carrying all they owned on the backs of herds of camels and horses. The desert was a buffer between the southernmost border of the Sunsai Empire and the wild lands beyond. Even as young as she was, Rosinnio could see the need to secure that border, and aligning with the strongest of the nomads was certainly one way of doing it, although she did not envy her sister and the life her father was forcing upon her.

Her eyes snapped open as the cart found a particularly deep pothole, the entire frame shuddered as the team of horses, under the encouragement of a cracking whip, dragged the vehicle onwards. She had not seen her sister since that day. In a cruel turn of events, her next eldest sister was married to Egron the following year. The Prince of Tarnaia did not seem to mind which princess was to be his bride, despite the love Brioni swore he bore her.

To wither away beneath a scorching sun, or bear children with salt in their veins? If she had to choose which would it be? She pictured her father's face, the strong jaw carpeted with an oiled and sculpted beard, his shoulder length hair, once jet black, now flecked with grey, slicked back from his forehead. His dark, piercing eyes, capable of exposing your soul, your every thought, with one withering look, stared back at her.

"I have defied the great Nort Sea and not been found wanting. Neither ice nor rock, fire nor wind shall break me. I am my father's daughter," she said in a low, even voice. Beside her, her servant stirred and suddenly wretched, spewing black bile onto the floor of the carriage.

Tomas: Woodvale Village

Tomas was falling, tumbling head-over-heels into darkness. When he stopped, Aliss was waiting for him, an uncertain smile twitching at the edges of her full lips. Crimson tears leaked from her eyes dripping onto his chest. He could feel the wetness of the blood pooling there. He reached out to catch the red tears on his finger, but when he touched her cheek the image faded. He called out, aching to see her face, to hear her voice again.

Back into the abyss he fell, falling through the ages until he saw a figure he recognised as himself, but it was not he, not Tomas the blacksmith. It was a younger version of himself, with a harder edge to his eyes, his mouth curled into a snarl. Aliss was there again. This time there was fear in her expression. *Why was there fear in her eyes?* His mind worked around the question, trying to comprehend; yet no understanding came. He took a step towards her, to reassure her. She turned away and fled, throwing cautious glances over her shoulder. When he tried to follow he could not. He realised he was weighed down and anchored to the ground by the weight of heavy armour covering his body. When he lifted his arm slowly and with great effort, a struggle even for the strength of a blacksmith, he saw a sword in his hand, the blade smeared with blood. Aliss stopped and doubled over, agony plainly written on her face. Her dress was stained red.

"Noooo!!!!"

She fell to the ground, and all went dark.

"Shhh. For the love of the gods, quieten down, damn you." His eyes snapped open. Several moments passed as he, first, tried to figure out who he was, and then where he was. His mouth was parched, his whole body ached, especially the back of his shoulder, where he was sure a flame raged there, blistering his skin and boiling his blood.

"Where…?" His voice cracked, agony shooting through him in waves as he struggled to sit up.

"Hold still, Tomas, you are safe here for now, but if you continue to yell I'm not sure that will continue to be the case for much longer," Rorbert said.

Memories began to tumble together. A cold feeling of dread washed over him. "Aliss!" He sat up with a jolt, and pain erupted all down his back, bringing tears to his eyes.

"Lie still, you fool, or you will rip open the stitches." The old villager eased him back down onto the straw-filled bed.

Finally he recognised Rorbert and his cottage. "Water," he said. The older man quickly held a cup to his lips. Tomas pushed his hand away and gulped the liquid down greedily.

"Easy, too fast and it'll make you sick."

Tomas drained the cup and handed it back with a nod of thanks. "What has happened, Rorbert? How am I here?"

"First, let me warn you, keep your voice down. The magistrate's soldiers are in the village. They are looking for you. They've been here for two days, so I'm guessing they're not going anywhere until they find you. They're making such a nuisance of themselves that I suspect any one of the village-folk would turn you in just to be rid of them." Rorbert refilled the cup from a small jug and handed it to Tomas. "As to the second question, Brother Joshan brought you here three days ago. He found you by the river and came to me for help. We would have brought you to the monastery, but it was too far and you were close enough to death as it was. He patched you up and applied the poultice to your wound. If you were wondering what the stink is, it's the salve Brother Joshan applied." In truth, Tomas had yet to regain full control and awareness of all his senses, but now that Rorbert mentioned it, his nose wrinkled at the pungent odour. "What happened, Tomas? I was long enough in the King's Lancers to recognise an arrow wound."

"Aliss," he answered, "they took her to the keep. I have to get her back!" Tomas tried to sit up again. This time he took it slower, and with a little help from the village elder, he managed to attain a seated position. Pain still shot though him, forcing a grimace and several silent curses.

"You are in no condition to go anywhere." Rorbert shook his head.

"Where is Brother Joshan now?" Tomas asked through gritted teeth.

"He was here this morning. He said he would look in later."

"Find him," Tomas interrupted.

"You are in no position to…"

"Find him!" Tomas insisted, causing Rorbert to take a step back.

"Okay, but first eat something." Tomas nodded his assent and eased himself off the bed, while Rorbert piled some bread and smoked meat on a wooden plate, before placing it on the only table in the room. "I'll be back shortly. Don't leave this room," the village elder said before turning and leaving.

Easing himself into a rickety wooden chair, Tomas contemplated the meal. His stomach growled loudly reminding him he had not eaten in days.

A little while later, exactly how long he couldn't be sure, he was woken from a restless slumber by the sound of the door creaking.

"Come in, come in quickly," Rorbert instructed anxiously. Behind him a figure in a grey-hooded robe ducked through the narrow doorway. Once inside, the priest pushed back the cowl to reveal a worn unshaven face, with tufts of grey hair standing on top of an otherwise bald head. Cold, hard eyes, the colour of a winter sky regarded him.

"So he yet lives," a rasping voice came from the throat of the stooped priest.

"Aye. Tomas is a strong one."

"You speak as if I am not here before you," Tomas said.

"Whist, boy! Let me see the wound." The priest fumbled none too gently at the dressing, releasing the vapours from the poultice. Tomas flinched when he probed the wound grunting in satisfaction. "The gods will not claim you for a while yet. Now tell me, what has happened?"

"The magistrate has taken Aliss," Tomas snarled. The priest shook his head and turned to Rorbert for an explanation.

"Aye, what Tomas says is true. The magistrate was called here on another matter. A charge of witchcraft was levelled against Aliss by another woman. It was her baby the men searched for…"

"Hold," the old priest cut Rorbert off. "Another woman? A baby? How does this concern Aliss and the charge of witchcraft? Please, start from the beginning."

Rorbert began again. How the men of the village went in search of the missing baby, what happened while they were away in the Great Wood. Tomas too listened to the story intently, a pained expression crossing his face when the older man related how his wife had been taken.

"Hmmm." The robed priest sat back into a chair. "The babe may well have been taken to the Great Wood, but not by any wolves."

"What do you mean?" Rorbert asked.

"Enough on that for now." He turned towards Tomas then. "And you, like a big dumb ox went thundering after them, facing the magistrate's guards all alone."

"They are hypocrites. The king surrounds himself with mages and then orders the arrest of women who are just helping their community with simple healing gifts. And the church who have whole orders who practise magic…"

"Enough! Do not mock the church in my presence," the priest fumed.

"You know I speak the truth, Joshan."

"Brother Joshan." The priest regarded him levelly with his grey, cold eyes.

"Aye, Brother Joshan if you prefer." Tomas met the stare of the older cleric unflinching.

"So what will you do?" Brother Joshan asked as Rorbert handed him a steaming cup. He blew gently before sipping from the edge. His face relaxed as the hot liquid worked its magic.

"I will go to the keep, and I will get her back."

"And how do you propose to do this?" the priest asked between hurried sips. "You will simply throw your life away, and the girl will die anyway."

"We shall see."

"Yes, yes we shall," the robed cleric answered.

"I don't believe I'm hearing this," Rorbert cut in. "Are you going to allow him to go through with this foolishness?" He turned his eyes on the priest.

"How do you propose I stop him?"

"You are a priest," Rorbert said, as if that alone could halt the raging storm.

"Perhaps I could call on the All Father to freeze his legs and hold him here trapped until the girl perishes..." Joshan raised one bushy eyebrow as he spoke, his sarcasm not lost on the village elder.

"You still have your cavalry sabre?" Tomas' eyes bored into the older man.

"If you go out to that street you will die. They will cut you down."

"Bring me the sword," the blacksmith insisted.

"I will not be party to your death." Rorbert turned to the priest, opening his arms while his face pleaded for assistance.

"Bring me your sabre or by the All Father I'll tear this place apart until I find it."

"You are a strong man, Tomas, and a skilled hunter, but you are sorely wounded. They will gut you in a heartbeat."

"Bring me the sword!" Tomas fumed.

Rorbert turned to Brother Joshan again, but the cleric simply shrugged. Silence descended leaving the room thick with tension.

"Very well, throw your life away. Rorbert opened a chest at the back of the house and reverently took out his sheathed weapon and handed it to Tomas.

The big blacksmith drew a hand-span length of the blade from the leather sheath exposing the polished steel. Rorbert looked on in silence.

"It all changes from here," Tomas said looking up from the blade and towards Joshan. The priest regarded him with unreadable eyes.

"What does?" Rorbert asked.

"He knows, ask him," Tomas answered, his eyes still on the cleric. He looked away then and turned to Rorbert. "I was not always a blacksmith, old friend." He brushed past the confused older man and out onto the street.

At first nobody noticed him as he walked between the scattered dwellings, then after several double glances people stopped and stared as he calmly made his way towards the blackened shell at the edge of town. As he approached his burnt-out home he drew the sabre, flinging the leather sheath away. Two liveried guards peeled away from the house when they saw him approach. The first died with a smirk still on his face. The second was cut down while he fumbled for his sword. Overhead dark clouds suddenly burst spilling rain onto the heads of the village folk as they looked on in shock as their blacksmith cold-bloodedly slaughtered two of the magistrate's guards. A clap of thunder rumbled in the darkening sky. In the distance Rorbert watched with his jaw open, uncomprehending at what he'd just witnessed. Beside him the grey-robed priest shook his head sadly.

Lorian: The house of Lorian, Alcraz, Sunsai Empire

"Master, your guest has arrived." The tall servant bowed low, keeping his eyes from Lorian's. A grin spread across the fat noble's fleshy face as he plucked a small, cooked and peeled egg from a silver bowl on a table before his couch. Along with the eggs the table was packed with all manner of savoury treats, steaming bowls of fish stew, roasted ducks, legs of mutton, platters of bread and cheeses, and silver jugs full to the brim with ruby-red wine.

"Excellent. Show him in." Lorian popped the whole egg into his mouth and sat back into a sea of cushions.

"Lorian," the man greeted his host as he walked calmly into the room. "No, no, don't get up," he said to the fat man. Lorian raised an eyebrow and grinned not giving any indication of attempting to extract himself from the mass of cushions surrounding him.

"Sit, Aknell, I have had some refreshment prepared."

"Ha, your refreshments, my friend, would shame any of the emperor's feasts," Aknell answered, allowing his gaze to fall on the mountain of food before him. "Before I do, I have a small gift."

"A gift? For me?" Lorian beamed. He pushed himself up into a sitting position. His eyes brimmed with unconcealed eagerness.

"Oh, do not get too excited. It is merely a small token." Aknell clapped his hands and turned towards the door. A tall fair-haired man walked through the doorway, his arms and shoulders rippled with power beneath a sleeveless leather vest. He held his head high with an arrogant sneer playing across his face.

Lorian's breath caught in his throat. His eyes darted over to where his own servant stood impassively. He was suddenly acutely aware of how far away his two armed guards were, even if it was just out in the hallway. There was something familiar about the pale-skinned northerner, he thought, once his initial panic subsided.

"What have you brought me, my friend?" he asked, managing to recompose himself quickly.

The big Nortman approached, his blond hair tied back from his head at the nape of his neck. He held out a polished wooden box caught between two powerful hands. Lorian glanced again at his servant. Although the man was little more than a body-servant, Lorian knew he had once been a warrior before his captivity. It gave him little comfort when the giant before him dominated the room so. Their eyes met; the fat man bit back his outrage at such impudence and looked away, his confidence overwhelmed by the burning arrogance in the pale blue of the other's.

He turned his attention to the box and lifted the lid. A jewel of sublime clarity sparkled on a velvet cloth. "It is beautiful," he said as he gently fished it out by the chain of gold it was attached to. He reached out with a chubby finger, hesitant to touch such perfection... yet, he knew he must possess it.

"This stone was mined from beneath Mount Draknoir and cut by the dark elves a thousand years before men walked on the surface of the world." Aknell gently took the jewel from Lorian's hands and eased the chain around the fat noble's neck.

"Elves?" Lorian chuckled.

"I swear it is true." Aknell smiled.

"It is beautiful," Lorian beamed as he clasped his hand around the gift now hanging from his neck. "But why...?"

Aknell cut off the question with a raised hand. "A token of friendship, that is all."

"I have never seen its like."

"The dark elves are long gone but their treasures remain to amaze us yet."

"You do amuse me, Aknell but elves are nothing but tales for children. Elves, dragons and the magical knights who fought them should remain between the pages where they belong."

"As you say," Aknell said smiling, before helping himself to a goblet of wine.

"I recognise your new friend from the arena. I am thinking I may have been cheated out of a goodly sum of gold when last we met."

Aknell laughed then and patted Lorian on the shoulder. "Come, let us eat. I am famished. A jewel crafted with elf magic is worth far more than thirty gold crowns."

Lorian scowled but relented and helped himself to a whole roasted fowl. "So tell me," he said as he tore soft white flesh from the bones of the bird, "how is it you are in possession of such a prize as an arena fighter? Not just any but the most talked about fighter in years."

"Rolfgot is not a slave. I do not own him."

"But he fights in the arena!" Lorian's incredulous eyes opened wide. "How did you convince him to that insanity?"

"It was not I who convinced him, but the other way round." Aknell grinned.

"He volunteered?"

"Not volunteered, demanded."

"Why would he do such a thing?" Lorian's head shook in incomprehension.

"Because he likes to kill."

Lorian shivered involuntarily under the scrutiny of his friend. "Where did you find him?" he filled the nerve-wracking silence.

"He was literally washed up. He was found on the beach close to my villa by some of my field workers. When I first laid my eyes on him he was close to death. He had been in the water for some time, and had been stabbed several times in the chest and back. It was quite miraculous he still lived. I was curious to find out how he had landed there, so I bade my physician do what he could. He still has not told me what happened to him. I suspect he was part of a Nortman pirate crew and fell out with them for some reason and was tossed overboard. Who knows? A rumour has begun circulating among my workers that he is the son of Possodon, and that the sea god evicted him from his watery domain."

"Ha, the son of a god in your employ. I can see how that would appeal to you." Lorian chuckled. Aknell smiled in return.

"To be truthful I think he has no memory of the incident, or if he does, he is guarding it well. But, he has served me well, and I can't say I've been out of pocket with him in my employ." A smile crept across Aknell's face.

"Hmmm," Lorian grumbled. A single drop of red wine dribbled down his chin as he drank from a silver goblet. He wiped the trailing drip with a swipe, staining the sleeve of his white robe.

"So, my friend, tell me what news from the palace. I do so look forward to the titbits of gossip you are ever a font of."

"Are you buttering me up with flattery? Now that you have stolen my money and scared me half to death with your pet Nortman?"

"Oh come, Lorian," Aknell said. "The jewel I have gifted you is worth a hundred times our wager. If you are that sore I shall return the gold."

"No, it is a lesson well learned." Lorian grinned. His eyes narrowed then over the rim of his goblet. "The emperor has sent a ship laden with gold to his new son-in-law," he blurted out then, giddy with excitement.

"Really?" Aknell stood up and refilled Lorian's cup. Wine spilled over the rim and both men laughed. "A dowry to be spent on gowns and jewels for Rosinnio perhaps?"

Lorian leaned in, his voiced dropping to a whisper, "To buy a crown. The king of Nortland is dying. He has no direct heir, only a collection of nephews and lords who all claim to be next in line. The strongest claim is Crawulf's, Rosinnio's new husband. There is one other whose is stronger, Crawulf's elder brother, but he was lost at sea..." Lorian suddenly stopped and glanced over at the big Nortman standing like a statue against the far wall. Aknell followed his gaze.

Blood Of Kings: The Shadow Mage

"Do not trouble yourself." Aknell laughed. "Rolfgot is no heir to a throne. He is too young to be the elder brother of this Crawulf, for a start."

Lorian examined the lean, muscular figure of the tall Nortman. He nodded in satisfaction, before his eyes darted back to Aknell. "Yes. Perhaps though, it would be wise to learn a little more about your new pet." When he glanced back at the Nortman he was met by a pair of unnaturally black eyes boring into him, undisguised contempt written there. He did not let his stare linger.

Aknell saw the exchange and turned to Rolfgot. "Perhaps you should wait outside. My carriage is in need of a guard." The Nortman nodded and slowly departed the room. "Please, continue. So, this Crawulf is next in line for the throne. What need does he have of the emperor's gold?"

"His is the strongest claim, but that does not mean the Nortlanders will follow him. They will only bend the knee to a strong ruler. The gold is to give him that position of strength."

"And to eliminate his enemies?"

"Indeed." Lorian drank again before lying back into his cushions, his demeanour more relaxed now that the Nortman arena fighter was gone.

"So the hearts of the Nortlanders can be swayed so easily that a show of strength... or weakness can determine who they choose to rule them? Interesting, don't you think?"

"What more would you expect from a race of barbarians." Lorian glanced nervously at the door, seeking any sign of the giant Nortman; There was none.

"And Rosinnio is in the middle of all this. What is her role to be in this game of kings? The emperor has played his pieces well, but why? Why such an interest in the north? The Pirate Isles are so far removed from here that most of the empire's citizens either don't believe it exists, or that it is a mystical land shrouded in mist and populated with ogres and giants."

Lorian sighed. "The emperor had a dream, many, many moons ago. He told no one but his most trusted mages and advisors. He told them his dream was so strong and powerful that it could only be a message from the gods, and it was they who should interpret it."

"Dreams can be powerful," Aknell agreed, "and one would imagine, the emperor being so closely related to the gods themselves that they would communicate through him."

"Just so. He dreamt he was a small boy scampering up a rocky peak, on the scent of the great eagles and their nesting place. He wanted to steal their eggs and raise the chicks himself. Of course, the higher he got, the stronger the wind and the more nervous he became, especially when the powerful birds of prey, with their vicious talons and beaks saw him stealing into their nests and gathering the eggs. They attacked him until he was bloody and raw and chased him from the mountain.

"When he reached the ground his whole body was covered in deep wounds. His clothes were torn and hung from him in strips. On the way down, as he fended off the attacking birds, he had dropped all of the eggs, save for one. A dark, hard egg like none other he had ever seen. He could hear the eagles high overhead laughing at him. All that endeavour and all he had left was one malformed egg. His efforts wasted. He took the egg home, deciding it would at least make a decent supper, but when he hit it off the side of the pan he could not crack it open. So, he called out for a chisel and a hammer to go with it. As hard as he tried to smash the hammer off the chisel head, the egg would not break. He flung it against the wall in frustration. Still, it would not break. He bashed it directly with the hammer, over and over, but still he could not open the dark, ugly egg. He gave up and flung it with all his might into the fire." Lorian paused to take a drink. He grunted in satisfaction, smacking his lips as he sat back into his couch and nest of cushions.

"So what happened to the egg?" Aknell asked.

"Nothing."

"Nothing?"

"The emperor woke the next morning feeling ill-rested and frustrated. He spent the next day unable to accomplish anything as the dream played on his thoughts. That night he dreamt the same dream, with the same outcome. When morning came he resolved to climb the mountain, as he had recognised it as one he had often played on as a child, although never before had he tried to reach the summit to where the great eagles made their home. So he scaled the rocky peak, following the trail of the boy from his dream. The giant birds chased him from their lofty perch just as they had chased the boy in the dream.

"On the third night he dreamt the dream again, only this time the egg began to crack as the flames burned brightly around it. Bit by bit, lines appeared in the hard shell until a scaly head emerged from the top of the egg. With a squawk it breathed fire at the boy who jumped back in fear. A scaly body emerged slowly from the egg, unfurling a pair of leathery wings. When it hopped from the flames it began to grow, its scales turning golden as it did so. The boy remained trapped in shock and fear unable to move as the creature craned its neck towards the ceiling until it was so large the house could no longer contain it. The boy croaked in fear, drawing the attention of the monster. With one snap it devoured him whole.

"The boy did not die though. He grew inside the beast and recognised it for what it was – dragon! Their minds melded, becoming one, neither in control of the other, nor of themselves. The dragon leapt into the sky and returned to its nesting ground where all of the birds of prey gathered and bowed down before it.

"The emperor woke then with fire raging in his soul, with one thing certain in his mind; that blood and fire would come to the world of men."

Duke Normand: Duchy of Lenstir

Duke Normand stretched back on the sumptuous bed his eyes fixed to the blonde curls slowly bobbing below him. The walls of his chamber were adorned with weapons and tapestries of battle scenes long since played out. The polished wooden floor was covered in rugs and made from animal furs. He could feel the urge for release build inside him. His eyes lingered on the creamy-white shoulders of the girl, allowing himself a moment of indulgence where he did not have to think about war, or dream-witches. His hips arched as he got closer. The girl sensed it too and pulled back. Normand grabbed a handful of curls holding her in place. She gasped and gurgled but stuck to her task. He gripped her head firmly as he climaxed with a grunt and a shudder, only releasing her from his iron grip when he relaxed with a sigh. His eyes lingered on her full breasts when she sat up and wiped her chin with the back of her hand.

"Leave me," he growled and shoved her away. She quickly gathered up her dress and scampered from the room. Normand allowed himself a moment to admire the curve of her hips and fleshy buttocks as she hurried from his presence.

He dressed quickly and strapped his sword to his waist. A painting of a grey-haired man in chainmail armour and brandishing the same broadsword loomed over him. His great-grandfather, a famed warrior and king's champion, or so Normand had been taught by a succession of tutors. It was he who had formed the Dragon Knights of Lenstir, and he who had gained most fame and glory leading them. *We shall see who will be ranked the most famed Normand of them all,* he thought to himself before spinning on his heel and following the girl from his chamber.

His boots echoed off the flagstones as he marched towards a roaring fire at the end of his hall. "Bring me wine," he instructed a girl hovering nervously at the entrance. She curtsied and hurried to do his bidding.

"She's a pretty little thing." A hushed voice startled the duke. He swung around to confront whoever had spoken. A dark-cloaked figure emerged from the shadows. Normand's hand dropped to his sword. "Beg your pardon, my lord. Did I startle you?" A humourless smile twitched at the corner of his mouth.

The duke watched as a small man moved cat-like towards him. His eyes darted about the hall as if they could not focus on any one thing for more than a heartbeat. An angry red scar ran from his temple to his cheekbone. He pushed back his hood to reveal shoulder length, brown hair. Aside from his constant fidgeting and ugly scar he was a handsome enough man with powerful arms and shoulders.

"Mortaga. One day you will crawl out of the shadows onto the point of my sword."

"I earn my coin by being discreet, my lord. Have I yet to displease you?"

"No, you have not," Normand agreed. The girl arrived back carrying a clay jug. He took it from her and filled two cups he snatched from a long feasting table. He handed one to the smaller man and drained one himself, while his eyes followed the girl as she hurried from the hall. He scratched his chin and indicated for Mortaga to sit.

"I prefer to stand, my lord." His eyes continued to dart about the hall, searching, probing the unseen.

"I prefer you to sit." Normand's voice was level, his glare iron. The smaller man sat. "Have you found her?"

For the first time, the cool façade dropped, just for an instant before Mortaga replied. "I lost three men. All died in their sleep, all with looks of terror on their faces when they were found. This is no ordinary task you have set me, my lord. My men have no defence against this witch. Each time she kills one the trail goes cold once again."

"Are you not being paid sufficiently?" Normand raised an eyebrow.

"It is not the coin, my lord."

"Are you saying you are not up to the task?"

The smaller man frowned, pushing strands of greasy hair back from his face. "My men are spies, thieves and assassins. There are none to rival them in the Duchies or beyond, but this witch has powers we do not understand." His eyes dropped from the duke's heavy glare.

"You displease me, Mortaga. This is not news I wish to hear." Normand's hand trembled for an instant as he raised his cup to his lips.

"I am sorry, my lord. I have failed you in this."

"Yes, you have. It will not be forgotten, Mortaga. Now tell me, what other news has your unrivalled," he spat the last word, "spy network to report."

"*This* will interest you, my lord. The emperor is building an army, a large army."

"The emperor is always building an army. He is fighting wars on two of his borders already, not to mention countless insurrections. He cannot even trust his own family. His half-brother claims the crown is rightfully his. His sons are waiting on the day he dies, to fight their own war of succession, and all the while, the desert nomads to his south constantly raid and harass his border, despite him marrying his eldest daughter to the chief of the largest tribe. And you tell me he is building an army?" The duke's eyes narrowed. "My faith in you, Mortaga, Chief of Spies, is rapidly dwindling."

"He has also married his youngest daughter to a jarl of Nortland?"

"Why would he do that? I did not know he had a love of the Pirate Isles, anymore than we do here in the Duchies. Thieves and cutthroats every one of them. The All Father damn them to The Hag's Pits!"

"Aye it's a mystery. The Empire is a long way from here, farther again to the Pirate Isles. It's hard to understand why he would wish to have any influence there. Perhaps he wishes to keep his own ships free of their pirating, but a daughter seems a large price to pay for free passage for his trading vessels."

"No, that makes no sense. I will think on it. Leave me now."

The cloaked man skulked from the room, while Duke Normand rubbed his temples. The heat from a roaring log fire warmed the air around him as a blanket of tiredness weighed heavy upon him. His eyes drifted shut for an instant before he snapped them open again. "Curse you, witch!" he roared and flung his cup into the fire.

"You would be wise to listen to him."

The duke swung around at the sound of the new voice. "Stay out of my affairs, Mage. All but the one you are here for."

The grey-haired mage shrugged and took a seat. He poured a goblet of wine before sitting back into the heavy wooden chair. "Mortaga is an excellent spy-master. You are lucky to have access to his network."

"What do you know of the weasel?" Normand snarled.

"Enough to know the thin threads of his web spread far. Listen to what he says."

"And what would you have me do now?"

The mage selected a ripe peach from a wooden bowl on the table. Juice dribbled into his beard as he savoured the flavour. "Elandrial is no mere woman. Sending spies and assassins to kill the High Priestess of Eor is akin to setting a mouse to catch a cat."

"What gibberish are you speaking now? Speak plainly, man. I am far beyond tiredness for riddles."

"You need a witch."

"You talk nonsense! Do I not already have a mage in my employ? And where would I find a witch, let alone one who would agree to work for me. The king banned witchcraft. He is burning them the length and breadth of the kingdom. Witch? You are as big a fool as that spy."

"The King would ban all magic if he could. He does not trust those of us with the gift, but he is afraid to. Afraid of what would happen if every practitioner of magic were to turn against him. And with good cause. So, he has turned on the magic of the small folk, mainly women who heal the sick and concoct love drams that maybe work and maybe don't. They are out there. The good ones will avoid detection. They know the sound of every creature, animal or insect in the countryside. They can tell you the name of a tree just by the sound of a leaf falling to the earth. And they can track a magic trail as if they were following footprints through the mud. Find a powerful witch and have her lead your assassins to the Priestess."

"And in the meantime?" Normand asked, a gentler tone in his voice.

"In the meantime you are safe. Elandrial has fled far from your borders. She is being hunted and constantly on the move. What she does, entering the dreams of men, takes an enormous amount of energy and power. It is exceedingly dangerous for her to travel the dream-path. Although she can kill and manipulate the dreams of a man, it is when she is most vulnerable. The greater the distance the more the danger to her. She will not trouble you, my lord, unless she can get a lot closer."

"That gives me little comfort, Mage." Normand stood up and glared into the fire, hypnotised by the dancing flames. "So, how do I find a witch?"

"I will do that for you."

Lady Rosinnio – Jarl Crawulf: Wind Isle

Rosinnio could feel the heat of the sun on her upturned face as she looked into the clear azure sky. The warmth made her skin tingle pleasantly bringing a smile to her full lips. A faint taste of cherries lingered in her mouth while the scent of cinnamon hung in the air. The thought of such treats made her smile wider. Closing her eyes, she turned towards the sun, allowing its rays to absorb beyond her flesh and warm the spirit at her core. When she opened them again she could see the fertile plains of Sunsai stretched out before her, a myriad of colours in a patchwork of fields fed by the river named for the goddess Neline, queen of the gods. It meandered a course, nourishing the soil for thousands of leagues, bearing a fleet of water-borne traffic throughout the empire and out to the Fiery Sea. Although she had never seen it, she had heard many stories told, of how its waters burn red at sunrise and sunset as Possodon the lord of the sea bleeds his own life force that every sea creature may have life. Silently, she thanked the sea god for providing them with the bounty of his realm.

Her pleasant thoughts were dispelled by a dark shadow creeping over her. Suddenly she felt a wave of pain ripple through her. She cried out, falling to her knees as she clutched her stomach. The sun and blue sky were gone now, replaced by eternal darkness and cold. So cold. The pain grew in intensity, pulsing through her, making her wretch. Harsh, bitter voices grated on her ears adding to her discomfort. She tried to shut them out, but they were relentless. The pain spread up to her head, throbbing at her temples.

Memories came to her then of other, similar dreams in her past, a dark shadowy figure always hovering just beyond her vision.

"Make it stop," she whimpered. *Or had she just thought it?*
"Wake, girl!"
"My lady." Voices spoke over each other. She tried to focus, but the pain was unbearable.

A vision appeared before her. She wanted to scream as she stared into cold, cruel eyes. *The Lord of the Dark has come for me,* she thought.

"My lady, what is wrong?" a softer, more familiar voice.
"Move aside, girl." The pale eyes bored into her, chasing away the sun, snatching her from the ramparts of her father's palace.

The Lord of the Dark has abducted me to his own realm. She wretched again, choking back tears. *Bring back the sun, please.* She choked as her throat burned raw.

"Poison," someone spat the word.
"Aye, and there's sorcery at work here," another said.
Poison - sorcery, the thoughts reverberated around her mind. She coughed, expelling bile and dark viscous blood in equal quantities. Her head throbbed, her stomach burned like she'd been run through with a spear. Slowly the room came into focus. Her handmaiden was there, her face twisted in concern. The cruel eyes watched her too, and she recognised them. Those very same ones had watched her every night since she had been wed, filled with hunger and lust. How many times had she been unable to look into them as he rutted on top of her. The eyes that had taken her from her home, maybe not those of The Lord of the Dark, but not so far away as to make little difference to her. Crawulf, her husband, barked orders she did not understand, to men she did not recognise. She was confused. Had one dark figure controlling her life been chased back into the shadows by another?

Pain gripped her like a fist clenching and twisting in her gut. *Sorcery.* The word echoed in her mind.

"Seal the gates! No one leaves or enters the castle until I have the heart of whoever has done this in my hand!" She could hear Crawulf barking orders.

Rough hands pulled and prodded her. Her jaw was pulled open and a cool liquid slid down her throat, making her gag and cough. Yet, she still had not the strength to lift her head. *It burns.* She wanted to protest, but no words came out. Blackness beckoned her. *Oblivion calls to me.* She yearned to see her father's lands again, to feel the heat of the sun on her face. Her head throbbed, making her wonder if the darkness would be such a bad place after all. To feel no more pain. A release from the captivity of her marriage and life in a harsh, new world.

"Drink this, child." Words drifted over her, she could no longer place voices with faces.

I did all you ever bid me do, Father. I don't want to die. A chasm yawned before her, cold and dark.

A sharp pain stung her cheek. "Come back to me, girl." She felt another slap on her face. It was enough of a shock to snap her attention from the darkness. "The potion will soothe your pain."

I don't want to die.

***

Crawulf stood behind his counsellor, Brandlor, as the old man gently pulled down his new bride's jaw and poured a vial of creamy liquid down her throat. Rage ignited inside him as he watched the stricken princess gag and choke on the elixir. The depth of feeling he bore her took him by surprise. He had not realised how he had grown fond of his exotic new wife, with her odd southern ways and delicate sensibilities. The sight of her unblemished, olive-coloured skin sent a fire raging through his loins every time she disrobed. Yet, there was more to it. He enjoyed her company, felt a ridiculous thrill when she smiled. Seeing her face contorted in agony set anger boiling through him.

"Whoever has done this shall suffer like no man has ever suffered before!" he stormed. He clenched his fists until his knuckles turned white, gritted his teeth as his eyes bulged and his face flushed red. Rosinnio's handmaiden flinched when he glared at her, fear in her eyes. He ignored her.

A warrior rushed into the chamber. "Jarl Crawulf, riders have been spotted fleeing the castle beyond the west wall," he said, gulping down breath.

Crawulf slammed his fist against the hard stone wall. "Bring my sword and armour! Prepare my horse. We will ride them down before they reach Whalebone Beach."

"Aye, my lord," the warrior answered as men hurried to do their lord's bidding, grabbing weapons, barking instructions into the air. Crawulf stormed from the chamber and through the castle with thunder in his eyes.

He climbed into the saddle with the aid of a stable boy. A dozen riders, with armour and weapons jingling, pulled on reins to control restless horses as the beasts stomped excitedly in the courtyard. The breath of mounts and men misted in the cold morning air as the heavy wooden gates slowly creaked open.

"I want them alive!" Crawulf roared over the noise as he kicked his horse's flanks, urging the animal onward. The sound of clopping hooves reverberated around the courtyard and beyond. Men and women rushed out beyond the gate, to watch their jarl lead his small band of men west, until they were dark specks in the distance.

He was sure he knew where they were headed, a small cove to the west of the island often used by fishermen and others who were not inclined to announce their arrival on his shores by entering the main harbour. If he had to kill his horses to catch them before they reached the vessel which was surely waiting for them, then he would.

As it happened there was no need to destroy the mounts as Crawulf and his housecarls rode down their quarry before they reached the beach. They had stopped in clear view on the open grassland, which dominated the windswept island, close to a small copse of trees. Perhaps they had sought to seek shelter in the trees, or perhaps they had not expected to be followed, Crawulf thought. No matter, they had been caught and he would ensure their deaths would not be easy.

"Hold!" he barked at them when they came into sight. The three men made no attempt to escape. He kicked his horse towards them, anger coursing through his body, an image of the lady Rosinnio choking on her own bile fresh in his mind.

As the group of riders neared the three men, one of Crawulf's warriors let out a cry of warning, "The trees!" He turned to look where his man was pointing. Dark shapes melted from the copse. Shadows that became men. The three assassins kicked their mounts and galloped towards the line of warriors.

"What's this?" Crawulf growled.

"I count three score, my lord," a grizzled grey-beard, with a scar running from forehead to chin answered. Crawulf watched as they formed a battle line, three deep. The clatter of wooden shields locking together reverberated around the rock-strewn grassland. Wind bearing the smells and sounds of the sea made his eyes water as he stared at the strangers.

"We will easily outrun them, my lord, and return with a larger force."

Crawulf ignored his man's words as he tugged at the end of his beard. Something did not sit right here, he thought. He watched as the opposing force began moving slowly towards his small band of horse-men, beating their weapons off their shields. Crawulf was familiar with the rhythm – the symphony of battle.

"Aye," he finally agreed, "they are too many. We will return with more men and chase these whoresons to the bottom of Baltagor's realm. Even so, it left a bitter taste in his mouth to run from the challenge of battle as insults and the barking jeers of men filled the air. "I will have all of their heads placed on spikes and left for the sea air to rot the flesh from their skulls," he snarled. It hurt even more to know that the three would-be assassins had slipped from his grasp.

"Gods protect us," one of the men gasped. Crawulf swung around in his saddle just as a noise like thunder rolled over them. More shapes darkened the horizon as mounted men crested a hill behind them. "Trapped," the same man spat.

Trap, the word crept into his head. "This smells of trickery and deceit," he growled. "Ride!" he barked then, kicking his mount's flanks.

A black cloud suddenly launched into the air above the shield-wall and travelled at speed towards the fleeing horse-men. A hail of arrows rained down on them. Most clattered harmlessly off mail armour. Some though found a mark leaving three riderless horses running amongst Crawulf's group of housecarls. Warriors ran to intercept them, while behind the same number again of horsemen galloped towards them. A horse screeched and then its legs collapsed bringing down its rider. Crawulf kicked his own mount and vaulted the stricken beast and man, as more arrows studded the ground around him. He wheeled in the opposite direction to turn away from the warriors attempting to intercept him. *This is no way to die,* he thought and turned back again, pointing his horse directly at the line of warriors. He drew his sword, sensing his men around him do the same, even as they urged their mounts onwards.

"Kill the bastards!" he shouted over the din of battle.

"Crawulf!" his men roared back, and "Wind Isle!"

The small band of horsemen formed a line as they galloped towards the enemy. As one, they lowered the points of their swords, aiming them at the line of shields before them. Behind them mounted warriors whipped and shouted at their own horses, eager to join the battle.

For Crawulf, everything slowed down, even as he sped towards the wall of round wooden shields and bristling spear points. His mind empty of all thought as instinct and battle-sense took over. He heard a roaring sound like the ocean breaking over rocks as the familiar battle-rage overcame him. Then, it was chaos. The sound of iron beating on wood and mail, of men screaming and dying sang loudly in his ears as he smashed through the line, swinging his sword at all who stood in his way. His horse reared and trampled a warrior who tried to block him, while he swept the head off another with a single blow, the momentum of the charge adding the strength of a war-horse to his stroke.

The line was thin and the charging band broke through to the other side, leaving devastation in their wake. They had not emerged unscathed either, two more of Crawulf's men had fallen, leaving only six left alive. All were bloodied from both their own wounds and of the men they had killed. Another charge and the spearmen would break. They had advantage of numbers, but facing down the charge of mounted warriors on horses bred for battle is no easy thing. The large group of riders were now almost upon them. *Now this is a way to die*, he thought, as a bitter smile touched his lips. Sucking in deep breaths, he prepared for one more charge.

"Jarl Crawulf," the scarred grey-beard spoke up. He had fought alongside Crawulf, and his father before him, for a score and ten years, earned the scar in defence of his jarl while raiding in lands to the far south. His name was Jarnheim. "Ride, my lord, this is not a place for you to fall." Their eyes met, and Crawulf read the implacable strength there. The resolve to die. "Go, we will buy what time we can. Avenge us!" He roared the last part as the remaining men dug their heels into the flanks of their mounts and turned to face the enemy again.

Crawulf paused for only a heartbeat. It cut deeper than any blade to flee the battle, leaving his own men to die for his sake. Dying with them though would serve no purpose. "Ha!" He slapped his mount's rump with the flat of his blade, not looking back as the sounds of screaming men and horses washed over him, ending all too briefly.

Keeping low in the saddle, he raced towards the coast, if for no other reason than the way back to his castle was barred by mounted warriors. He knew they were following him, could hear them urging their own beasts to keep pace with him. When he glanced over his shoulder he could see them, all too close for his liking. As the wind grew in intensity carrying the salty smell of the sea and white puffs of foam, he knew his horse was tiring. He had ridden him hard in the pursuit of the assassins, rode him into battle and now he had reached the end of his endurance.

The great grey sea stretched out before him all the way to the horizon where it became one with a cloud-filled sky the colour of iron. If only he rode Greystorm, the mighty steed of Alweise, who could sprout wings and carry his master across the sky.

Man and beast slowed as his horse's heart could take no more. He slid from the saddle, leaving the sweating and panting animal and dragged his sword from its scabbard. The riders made a semi-circle in front of him. He glared at their triumphant faces. Behind him was a cliff and beyond that the ocean for as far as the eye could see. Four men dismounted. All hefted great double-bladed Nort-axes.

Crawulf spat and planted his feet firmly in the ground. More than one would die before he fell. The four circled him warily. All knew of the fearsome reputation of Crawulf and his prowess with a blade. He snarled and leapt towards the one closest, swinging his sword as he did so. He was rewarded with a cry of pain as one of his assailants dropped to his knees. Before he could deliver a killing blow, the other three rushed him. He parried one axe and kicked out at another attacker before pain erupted in his head. He staggered back, his sword slipping from his fingers. He heard a laugh as he tried to keep his balance. A blurred silhouette of a figure on horseback dominated his vision.

"Good-bye, Jarl Crawulf."

He had the briefest sensation that he was flying, he could taste the brine as water washed over him, just before all went black.

Tomas: Woodvale Village

Tomas stepped over the bodies of the two guards and walked into the burnt-out rubble that was once his home, now little more than a fire-blackened shell. His jaw was set hard in grim determination as he picked through the destroyed wreckage of his belongings. Nothing it seemed had survived the fire. Out back his workshop remained unscathed, although the door hung open and he could already see the carnage caused by the magistrate's guards. He eyed the mess with a cold detachment, no longer caring about his life as the town blacksmith. His eyes quickly scanned for the hidden hatch beneath a workbench. He heaved the bench away from the wall, grunting with the effort as pain flared in his shoulder.

"So, two men dead and in sight of the entire village." Tomas turned around to see the grey-robed priest standing in the doorway. He sagged against the bench, taking deep breaths as he grimaced in pain.

"I did not start this. This was brought to my door!" Tomas spat bitterly. "Do you think I want this? I was happy here… we were happy…" He trailed off as memories of his life with Aliss tumbled through his mind. "This valley was my home. They've taken that from me, they will not take Aliss too!"

"Tomas! Tomas!" Rorbert cried from outside before coming to a sharp halt in the doorway. "Tomas? What have you done?"

Tomas ignored the village elder and returned his attention to the hidden hatch. He knelt down and opened it before hauling out the wooden chest.

"Go," Brother Joshan said to the village elder, "saddle the soldiers' horses and pack supplies for a number of days in the saddlebags."

"I don't understand..."

"Just do it!" the priest snapped. Rorbert looked to Tomas who nodded slowly. Reluctantly the old man backed away from the workshop.

"You are not coming with me," Tomas said.

"Ha! Even if I wished to I'm getting far too old for such adventures," Brother Joshan answered. He walked slowly over and watched as the blacksmith swung open the lid of the chest.

"It all ends here," he said, looking at the contents.

"Yes," Tomas answered. He fished out a sheathed sword and placed it on the bench, before holding up a dull grey shirt of interlocked metal rings.

"Does it still fit?" the priest asked.

"Aye," Tomas nodded, "it still fits."

"Not many men get a second or even a third chance. There will be no turning back from this." The priest wrapped long, almost skeletal fingers around Tomas' arm; his grip was like iron. "You made a good life here. You could do the same somewhere else."

"A life with Aliss," the blacksmith replied. "It was she who gave me the second chance. I will not abandon her now."

Joshan released his hold on the younger man, nodding sadly. "Well, it's probably safe to tell you this now – you were a terrible blacksmith!"

Tomas laughed and then winced as he felt the wound in his shoulder stretch with every movement. Brother Joshan smiled.

"Will you tell Rorbert?"

"The truth? All of it?"

"Aye, he deserves that much," Tomas replied.

"He will take it hard," Joshan said. The blacksmith's head dropped, before he slowly nodded. "Let me take a look at that shoulder before you ruin all my work with that mail shirt." Tomas stripped off his shirt and sat still while the old priest probed his wound. At first, darts of pain shot through him as prodding fingers pulled and tightened stitches. Then a new sensation trickled into his upper body. He felt a warmth creep through him, easing the pain, giving him back strength.

"Did you not take a vow never to use magic again?" he asked enjoying the relief from pain.

"Aye, well, the king may frown upon the use of magic by his subjects, and the abbot may wonder why a simple monk has much success with fighting infections with poultices and a few wild herbs, but sometimes it is hard to just watch."

"The king is a hypocrite and a fool," Tomas declared.

"Such talk will see your head on the executioner's block," Brother Joshan tut-tutted. Tomas glanced over his shoulder and out of the open door, to where two of the magistrate's guards lay dead in the street.

"I think it's too late to worry about that now."

The priest chuckled then, as both of them turned at the sound of footsteps. "The All Father watch over and protect you," the old priest said and made a protective sign on the blacksmith's forehead.

Rorbert walked cautiously into the workshop. "The horses are ready for you," he said.

Tomas stood up testing his shoulder by rolling his arm back and forth. He nodded in satisfaction and dressed quickly. As well as the mail shirt in the chest there was a padded leather jerkin to be worn under the mail, a round helm with nose guard, and a dagger with a thick blade housed in a leather sheath. Once dressed, he attached the dagger to his belt and strapped it and the sword around his waist. All the while, Rorbert stood watching in silence, his eyes questioning.

He clasped the village elder on the shoulder as he walked past. "I am sorry, old friend. I think it unlikely we will meet again."

"I-I don't understand," the old soldier stammered.

"Brother Joshan will explain. When you hear the truth, try not to think too hard of me." Tomas climbed aboard a dapple grey gelding and took the reins of a chestnut mare in his hand—a mount for Aliss. He kicked his heel into the horses flank and left, without a backward glance; the valley and the life of a blacksmith.

He pushed the horses as fast as he dared without killing them, they would be little use to him if they came up lame on the journey, or collapsed from exhaustion, even so, he fought hard the feelings of frustration threatening to overwhelm him. He knew he was at least two days ride from Flagston. Tomas could picture the magistrate's keep at the heart of the busy market town, where he lived and dispensed justice for the region. Although he was answerable to his lord, and he to the king, in the Valley and surrounding lands, the magistrate was the ultimate power, he who could condemn a man, or woman to death, empowered to dispense the king's justice and collect taxes due to the duke.

There would be a trial, Tomas thought as he stared into his small campfire. Dry wood cracked as orange flames swayed in a hypnotic dance before him. There was still time. He reflected on his life in the Valley with Aliss—a town blacksmith—an honest trade, it had been his father's and his father's before him. Tomas, too, had been marked to carry on the line, but in his youth, he had not the patience for hard graft which offered little return. Although he learned how to beat metal into a new shape, to create and give it life, at his father's shoulder, his head was full of dreams of adventure and lofty ideas beyond his station. "Can we make a sword, Father?" he asked once.

"This is not the king's armoury, boy. Horseshoes and broken wheels is our trade. Nails and scythes put bread on our table, not idle dreams of young boys."

Funny how things work out, he thought as he closed his eyes. An image of Aliss appeared before him, as she always did before he slept. She was smiling at him, her golden curls framing a soft face. "Beautiful," he whispered in his sleep.

When he woke in the morning she was there again, only this time her face was creased in terror as she pleaded for his help. He relived her molestation, at the hands of the magistrate and his guards, powerless to intervene. His eyes snapped open as rage boiled inside him. He had not slaved at his father's forge, he had chosen a different path, learned a new set of skills, skills with which to better himself, to raise his station in life. Yet, he had returned to the forge and his own workshop. Where was he when he could have used those skills to defend his woman? To protect the life he shared with her? He was not there. He jumped up, cursed as he kicked earth over the smouldering fire.

Before the sun had risen and the air still held the cold bite of night, he was mounted and on his way.

A day and a half further in the saddle, through well-worn forest trails and over churned up, cultivated land, the grey walls of the town shimmered beneath a low lying sun. The bite of autumn was in the air, turning the forest into a dazzling display of orange and brown beneath a vibrant blue sky. Ahead of him a small convoy of wooden carts bounced along a crooked, uneven road, pulled by wretched looking, half-starved horses. Small children clung to the sides with grim determination to avoid being flung overboard, while their older siblings walked alongside with their parents and other relatives. Tomas pulled up alongside the first cart.

"Is it a market day today?" he asked.

The driver regarded him coldly, hawked and spat. "Every day is a market day in Flagston, but that's not why we're headed there, if that's your reason for asking."

"How so?" Tomas felt a cold feeling of dread pool in the pit of his stomach.

"Magistrate's burnin' a witch today. Whole town and folk from all over the countryside'll be there to witness that. Might be we've missed it already on account of us havin' wheel trouble along the road."

Tomas turned away from the gap-toothed grin and kicked his horse on.

The closer to the town he got the more the traffic increased. He ignored shouts of protest and waved fists as he bludgeoned his way through the crowds, using the weight of the horse if needed. The gates of the walled town hung open, allowing in a steady stream of would-be voyeurs as well as farmers and traders with goods to sell. A small group of guards slouched lazily against the wall, paying scant attention to the growing crowd filing into the town.

Once inside the gates, the stench and sounds of humanity, living tightly packed, washed over him. So many people in one place with buildings leaning one on top of another, and all around, the outer wall looming, made Tomas dizzy. It had been a long time since he lived among so many people. By now he was forced to dismount lest he attract the attention of curious guards. He led both horses in the direction of the swelling crowd, borne along a sea of grinning and excited townsfolk.

A great cheer went up as he approached the town square, followed by a high-pitched wail. The screech made both his mind and stomach lurch. "Aliss!" He barged his way through now, shoving any obstacle roughly aside. "Make way! Make way!" Ignoring any protestation, he kicked and prodded a path through the crowd.

More screams sent a ripple of laughter though the crowd drawing shouted insults and taunts. "Burn, witch!"

Tomas' sword was drawn now as he moved into the square. At the centre was a raised platform, on that platform, tied to a stake and surrounded by a wall of fire, was Aliss. Thick, cloying smoke filled the air. Her agonised screams reverberated around the square.

Tomas shoved his way through, sword in hand, not registering how it was now stained red as spectators failed to move out of his way quick enough. Panic was a trailing snake following where he went as he snarled at people to move and used his naked blade and blacksmith's strength to clear a path. Suddenly he was in open space. Three guards moved to intercept him. The first put up a hand to stop him. Tomas took his arm off at the elbow. The other two hesitated, expressions of shock creasing their features. Tomas stabbed one in the chest and viciously wrenched his blade free, before swinging it full force into the exposed neck of the third. The guard fell as a geyser of blood sprayed the panicking crowd.

As he mounted the wooden steps of the platform he could feel the ferocious heat pulsating from the fire. His heart wailed a silent scream of ache when he saw his woman at the centre of the inferno, her hair and clothes burnt away, her skin scorched and blistered. He ignored the burning agony of the flames as he beat away the fire with his own bare hands and lifted his woman free.

He carried her down, not knowing if she were alive or dead, barely able to look at her disfigured face, where the skin was black or red-raw. Charred meat sprang to mind, the thought sickening him. A line of guards waited. When he reached the bottom of the steps he gently placed Aliss down. He thought he heard her groan, but couldn't be sure. *Don't let her die like this*, he offered a silent prayer to any of the gods who bore witness to such injustice.

He turned to face the guards as one stepped out. "Drop your sword," he demanded. Cold, hard eyes regarded the blacksmith.

Tomas looked beyond the guards at the devastation he had caused. Small knots of people littered the square, tending to folk he had injured because they would not move out of his way fast enough. The bodies of two guardsmen lay where he had cut them down when the black rage overcame him. A third screamed in agony, calling for the All Father to aid him, as the bloody stump that was once his arm was wrapped in bandages.

"I fear it is too late for that now," Tomas answered. He met the glare of the guard captain without flinching. "Stand aside or you will all die," he added coldly.

"Who are you?" the captain asked. Tomas could hear a tremor creeping into the man's voice.

"I am the terror of the night, he who walks in the darkest places with death as a shadow. I am the force that will not bend nor stop. I feed on fear and pain, my thirst for blood is unquenchable." Tomas brought his sword up.

"I can't do that. You have murdered two soldiers, injured a dozen people here. And you are in league with a witch!" The captain's eyebrows shot up. "I know your face," he suddenly said.

"I am not the man you think I am," Tomas replied and then lunged.

The captain's head spun on his severed neck, before hitting the cobbled ground with a sickening squelch. Two more soldiers dropped, one clutching his belly, the other grabbing at a slash down the front of his chest that ripped open his chainmail armour before rending flesh and bone. The others fled from the whirlwind of death.

Tomas cradled his woman in his arms and rode though the deserted streets of Flagston, the smell of blood and burned flesh lingering in the air.

Djangra Roe: Flagston

Djangra Roe climbed the steps of the platform, his boots echoing off the wooden planks as he crossed the raised structure. He examined the fire-blackened pole at its centre before turning to look out over the town square. From his lofty perch he could see where the cobbled stones were still stained red in patches. He scratched the grey bristles covering his chin as his gaze wandered across the square, down a street flanked by two-storey dwellings, picturing in his mind the route used by the witch to escape.

Waiting for him at the foot of the steps was the magistrate along with a handful of his guards, and none too pleased to be made to wait on the pleasure of Duke Normand's mage. He reflected on his parting from his lord. The duke had not wanted him to leave, still living in fear of the dream-witch. Roe had assured him that she had flown far too far to have the power to manipulate his dreams. "I need to find a witch who can follow her trail, otherwise she will haunt you for the rest of your life," he had explained.

"Send someone else," the duke had responded in his usual gruff manner.

"No. This is a thing I must do." And that was that. Djangra had left a fretful duke behind while he searched the countryside for a witch, one powerful enough to follow the thin trail of magic left by the priestess of Eor, yet not so wilful that he could not bend her to his own. Now here he was, after travelling many days around Normand's small duchy, standing in the spot where a witch made good an escape from a raging mob. *Had she used magic?* he wondered, he could find no trace of a taint that surely would have lingered, a faint crackle in the air, a taste of... of what? What does magic taste of? He mused. Cloves, he decided, bitter like cloves.

He climbed back down and approached the magistrate. "She was aided in her escape, you say?" he said.

"Aye, by a blacksmith. I have men out searching for the pair of them now. They won't get far," the magistrate answered. "Now, I have business to attend to..."

"You may attend to your business when I say you can," Djangra answered, his voice low and even.

"And who in the name of the All Father do you think you are to be giving me orders?" the balding, official spluttered.

"We have established that already," the mage said. He could sense the tension building from his own men at his back and those of the magistrate's, fingers edged towards swords, feet shuffled on the cobbled street.

"Yes, you say you are Duke Normand's counsellor. As a courtesy I have given my time and answered your question, but this is my town. This is..." Djangra interrupted by stretching up to whisper in the ear of the taller man. All colour faded from the magistrate's complexion. Suddenly he clutched his chest as he sucked in deep breaths. He dropped to his knees, a strangled sound coming from the back of his throat. His men stared at him, confusion written on their faces.

"Well, help him up. The man has obviously taken a turn," the mage instructed the magistrate's guards. "Have a good day, sir." He bowed to the kneeling official who was still struggling for air as his men gently eased him to his feet.

Djangra Roe calmly walked from the town square, Three men-at-arms, bearing the red dragon of Lenstir on their white tunics, fell in behind him. "This is not the work of any ordinary blacksmith," he muttered to himself, as he mused over the tale he had been told of the witch's escape and the role of the blacksmith. He doubted there were more than a handful of men in the entire kingdom who could boldly interrupt an execution, literally pull a condemned witch from the flames while slaughtering a handful of trained guards in the process.

"Horace?" he addressed one of the men-at-arms.

"Aye?"

"Do you think it possible to decipher a trail from all the tracks leaving town? If the girl is a witch she has left no signs of magic for me to follow, so, we must assume the rescue was all the work of our blacksmith… or whatever he is."

"Aye, perhaps. A horse leaving at speed and carrying an armoured man and girl will leave deeper tracks than most, if they have not been trampled already."

The mage looked into the pockmarked face of the warrior, briefly wondering the reason for his scarred skin, a pox of some sort no doubt, he decided. "They tell me you are the best tracker in Lenstir. I have been told your skills are legendary. The word mystical was used." Horace's expression remained the same; if he was affected by the flattery he showed no sign. "Is what they say true?"

"Aye." The answer was simple and direct. Djangra smiled at the honesty of it. Surely there was no idle boast here.

"Do not fail me. I shall wait in yonder tavern. I have a strong urge to clear the dust from my throat."

Horace nodded before ambling off.

The tavern was quiet with very few patrons to approach. Djangra instructed his remaining two men-at-arms to wait outside, no point in intimidating the locals if he wanted to glean some information from them. The ceiling was low, the room filled with smoke from a turf fire blazing in the hearth. Three off-duty guardsmen huddled together in a corner supping tankards of frothy ale. An old man appeared to be sleeping at another table with his sleeves soaking up liquid from an upturned cup, with his head resting on his arms. A woman, displaying ample cleavage and looking bored slouched against the bar. Her eyes shot to the entrance when the mage walked in, lighting up at the prospect of custom.

"Good day, sir." A portly innkeeper with tufts of grey hair either side of a bald head, greeted the mage. "What's your pleasure?" He wiped his hands on a stained off-white tunic. The woman sidled over, managing to display even more flesh than before. Djangra stopped her with a raised hand. Her eyes dropped in disappointment as she slumped against the bar once again.

"Wine would be nice," he answered with a smile. "Tell me, friend," he said, handing over a couple of copper coins in payment and then adding a silver to the small pile, "there was a witch burning here a day ago. You've a pretty good view of the square from here. Did you see much of what happened?"

The innkeeper scooped the coins into his hand before sliding them into a pouch which disappeared as quickly as it appeared. "Nah, not a lot. Jalia here." He indicated the girl with a nod of his head, "she were right outside, saw the whole thing."

"Is that so?" Djangra smoothed down his whiskers as he turned his attention to the girl. "Share a jug of wine with an old man, would you?" He slid a silver coin under her hand.

"Thank you, sir. That would be right nice." She beamed. The mage took the jug from the innkeeper and poured a dark red liquid into two clay goblets. He handed one to Jalia with a smile and sipped from the other.

"So what did you see? Did she use magic to escape her bonds and the flames?"

"No, sir, it were that blacksmith... leastwise they say he's a blacksmith. Never seen him before meself, but I wouldn't mind gettin' to know him a bit better, if you know what I mean. A fine figure of a man he was." She grinned and quaffed the wine, spilling much of it down her chin. Djangra smiled a painted on smile and refilled her cup.

"They say he's the blacksmith from the village Woodvale, up aside o' the Great Wood. Nothin' good ever comes out o' that cursed forest," the innkeeper joined in.

"How so?" the mage asked. "Enlighten a humble stranger to your fair land."

"It's haunted, sir," the girl said. "Full o' dark creatures and spooks that'd steal yer soul."

"All them valley dwellers and other folk what live next to the forest are a bit queer in the head," the innkeeper added.

"Is that so? So how is it you are so sure it was this blacksmith who rescued the witch?"

"She was his woman. Some o' the magistrate's guards recognised him. He attacked them several nights past when they was bringing her in for trial. They've been huntin' him ever since," the girl explained before helping herself to more wine.

"One o' them guards is a regular o' Jalia's," the innkeeper clarified.

"Ah, I see. So, how would a stranger find this village?"

"Go west out of town and follow the road for two days," the portly innkeeper answered.

"Thank you, you've been of great assistance." He placed two more silver coins on the bar. The woman's hand snaked out to claim one for herself. Djangra smiled and turned to leave.

"Don't go wanderin' into that Great Wood. Folk who go in there often as not don't come back out," the innkeeper called after him.

His two men waited outside, leaning against the wall. "Horold, fetch the horses and bring them here. Ronwald, find Horace. Tell him we are leaving."

"What if he hasn't sniffed out the trail?" the man-at-arms answered with a question.

"Never mind that." Djangra looked into the distance, a smile flickering at the corner of his mouth. "We're riding west. West, in search of a hamlet and a haunted forest."

Jarl Crawulf – Lady Rosinnio: Wind Isle

He opened one eye, struggling to exert the effort needed for that simple function. Ice water flowed through his veins in place of blood. He was beyond cold, he felt as if his very bones had frozen into strips of glacial ice. The muscles of his jaw clenched tightly as his teeth chattered uncontrollably. Hair – wet and greasy clung to his face. Darkness enveloped him; the sound of the sea breaking on rocks filled him with petrifying fear, making him groan and stir. Like a great, sea-creature rousing from slumber, he pushed himself up onto one arm. The effort required was too great, his own weight too much to bear and he dropped back to the hard ground. The smell of the ocean clung to him, lay thick in the air all around. His thoughts were too groggy to bring clarity to his thinking, everything felt out of focus to him. The how and the why of where he was, were questions beyond him, the where, even more so. *Falling,* he remembered falling. Perhaps he had sunk all the way to the ocean floor and was now in the dark realm of Baltagor, or had the Lord of the Sea's trickster daughters lured him to his doom? As they had tricked countless sailors into the turbulent seas, since time began. *Surely death would not hurt so much.*

He heard voices then. In the dark he could not tell if they were carried on the wind, from some far off place, or if they were close by and about to stumble on him. Either way it made no difference; he could not move. If he was not already dead, he soon would be. Perhaps the voices were the Soul Reapers come to harvest his soul for Boda's Nacht Realm. Such thoughts filled him with dread. As a warrior, it was his reward to spend eternity feasting in the hall of Alweise and fighting his enemies on the vast plains and in the high, rocky reaches of Eiru, home of the gods. Could some trick of fate deprive him of his ultimate reward? Who knew the minds of gods?

Memories came back to him—he had fallen from the cliff—had he died with a sword in his hand? Or had the watery depths of Baltagor quenched his life? Would fate be so cruel as to judge him by the manner of his death? Pain wracked his body, shooting through him in icy, dagger-stabs. He dug his fingers into the ground beneath him, cutting his hands and tearing the skin from his fingers on loose stones and the hard rock beneath.

The orange glow of torches, flickering in the wind allowed him to see the cave he was lying in. Huge dark shadows danced around the wet and jagged walls. Was it the Soul Reapers or his enemies come to finish him off?

The voices were closer now. He tried to focus on the words, but they made no sense to him.

"Over here!"

He was found. He dug his fingers into the hardness of the rock beneath him, ignoring the pain of breaking nails and shredded fingertips as he tried to summon the strength to get away. Grunting with the effort, he shifted his body.

"Hold still." Words drifted over him as blackness found him once again.

If he dreamed dreams good or ill, he had forgotten them when he woke. Although not quite as dark as before, it still took a little time for his eyes to adjust to the gloom. He lay on a bed with a straw-filled mattress beneath him. Stone walls surrounded him and above he could make out the dark reed of a thatched roof. The air was thick with the smell of wood-smoke and the strong scent of smoked fish. He reached his hand up to his aching head and felt a cloth tightly binding his scalp.

"You got a right nasty bang on your head there. The gods alone know how it is you were not dead when we found you in the cave. We was searchin' for shellfish washed in by the tide when we found you instead. Come off a shipwreck did ya?"

Crawulf regarded the man with narrowed eyes, taking in the small dwelling as he did so. The stranger was stirring a pot hanging over the fire. The smell of a fish stew drifted over to Crawulf, making his stomach grumble. He realised he was starving.

"How…" he began, struggling to rise, before failing and slumping onto his back. His throat felt constricted, his mouth parched.

"How long have you been here? We found you three evenings past. You couldn't have been in the cave more'n half a day, elsewise the tide would o' come in and washed you back out to sea," the man answered. "Here." He handed Crawulf a cup filled with water. "Supper'll be ready soon. I dare say you'd fancy a bite."

The jarl of Wind Isle needed aid getting up before he could take the cup from the fisherman. Once in a seated position on the low cot he could see that his leg was bound in a wooden splint.

The fisherman followed his glance. "It's broke," he simply explained and returned to his stirring.

Unable to express the gratitude he felt, Crawulf simply nodded, then drank. He drained the cup in one gulp. Never before had he experienced such relief and delight as the purifying water slid down his throat.

"More?"

Crawulf nodded in answer. The fisherman refilled his cup and then ladled a watery broth full of thick pieces of fish into a bowl and handed it to the jarl. He savoured every bite, without a word, his entire focus on the simple meal, a better feast than any he had tasted in his own hall. After a second and third helping he mopped the remnants from the bowl with thick chunks of black bread.

The room was suddenly bathed in bright light as the wooden door scratched across the hard-packed earth and reeds of the floor. A small, plump woman entered the dwelling. She was dressed in the local garb of drab woollen dress under a thinner, sleeveless linen apron, a white scarf covered her head.

"He's awake then," she said. Her eyes narrowed in suspicion as she nodded in Crawulf's direction.

"Aye," the man simply answered. Two younger men followed her into the room, glancing at Crawulf before turning their attention to the steaming pot. "My woman, and two boys. Twas the lads who carried you from the cave. She patched you up." The fisherman nodded towards his wife.

"More used to mendin' nets and worn breeches, but I fancy you'll live," she answered.

The two boys took a bowl of broth from their father and took it to separate cots lined against the walls of the single-room dwelling.

"Was ya shipwrecked?" one of the boys asked between mouthfuls. Crawulf reckoned both to be not long into manhood. He nodded in reply, realising that none of them had recognised him. He thought it best to leave it that way.

"Who might Rosie be then?" the woman asked. "You called out to her, in your sleep, more than once."

Crawulf glared at her. *Rosie*, the name he had taken to calling Rosinnio, of late. She hated it. Hearing it now was like a stab to his heart, as memories suddenly tumbled through his mind. She had been poisoned, how could he have forgotten? It was how he came to be fighting for his life on the cliff's edge. The bang on his head had addled his wits, he thought. *Was she dead or alive?* Another thought struck him then, *Had the raiders gone on to the castle?* It was a large raiding party, but not so large to attack his stronghold… unless there were others. He pushed himself up in a sudden movement. Pain shot through his leg, daggers of agony making him cry out.

"Here now, stay still," the woman said, rushing to his bedside. "Stay calm or you'll have all me work undone."

"I… need… to… get… back," he panted through gritted teeth.

"Nay, you'll not be going anywhere in the state you're in." She put her arm on his shoulder.

Crawulf's blood boiled, a red mist brought on by frustration and pain. He grabbed the woman by the throat. "I need to get back to..." He never finished. In an instant both sons loomed over him. Out of the corner of his eye he saw something coming towards him fast. Pain flared in his head. He released his grip on the woman and swung at the son nearest to him. The blow likely hurt him more than the young fisherman, as his shoulder, back and ribs all erupted in agony from the way he twisted himself.

The woman staggered back, gasping for breath while her two sons grappled with Crawulf. The jarl was powerless against the two boys as one took a hold of him from behind and the other balled his fists drawing back an arm.

"Hold!" the fisherman boomed. "Enough!"

"Let him go," the woman wheezed. Both young men did as they were told and released Crawulf.

"Both of you, gather more wood for the fire," he instructed his sons.

"But he..." the eldest began.

"Go. He is no threat in the state he's in. He cannot summon the effort required to rise from that bed. Go, I will deal with this."

Crawulf drew in deep breaths, each bringing a new wave of fiery pain to his ribs. His eyes were drawn to the knife in the fisherman's hand.

"You have a strange way of showing gratitude to people who only seek to help you." The fisherman finally turned his attention to the jarl. "What is your name?"

"Brandin," Crawulf instantly lied, his voice hoarse and barely above a whisper.

"Well, Brandin, I've a mind to have the boys cart you off that bed and toss you back into the sea." Crawulf made no reply. The woman, red-faced and trembling, moved behind her husband. The two men eyed one another. "I'll have no more trouble. We'll mend you and send you on your way. I've not the stomach for killing a man under my own roof, and putting you out would likely amount to the same thing. So, no more. Agreed?"

Crawulf regarded both of them with cold, grey eyes. He nodded once in response before sinking back onto the straw mattress. Losing his temper had been a mistake. The fisherman would likely as not slit his throat in his sleep now. He could reveal his identity and demand to be taken to the castle or have his men brought here, but he knew not if his enemies still searched for him, or if his hosts would turn him in for a purse of silver if they knew who he was and who searched for him.

***

Rosinnio opened her eyes slowly, a faint light bathing the room in yellow. She heard a soft rustle, and then caught sight of something out of the corner of her eye. An irrational fear enveloped her like a dark, hooded mantle. Something felt… not right. Memories of waking in the night, as a child came back to her, of dark dreams of someone, or something watching her from the shadows. But she was no longer a child. Had the Shadow Man followed her to the frozen north?

She pushed herself up, fighting back a wave of nausea. As she swung her legs gingerly out of the bed she heard a sound that filled her with terror, a bestial growl, then a shadow shifted in the gloom before taking shape. She screamed.

The door to her chamber crashed open, but Rosinnio was unable to tear her gaze away from the terror looming over her. In the dim light of a single lamp it looked like a beast of the forest crossed with a man, with a head like a wolf and its body covered in thick fur. It stood on two legs dwarfing the princess.

"Back to the Nacht Realm, foul demon!" The big warrior Rothgar burst into the room, swinging an axe at the beast. The wolf-man howled and swatted the warrior back-handed, sending him crashing against a wall. The beast turned back to Rosinnio drawing back dark lips to reveal wickedly sharp fangs. It snarled and lunged.

Instinctively Rosinnio flung up her arms in defence and closed her eyes, expecting the pain to follow swiftly. No savage bite came. When she opened her eyes the monster was howling and staggering back in obvious pain. Rothgar had recovered and with a mighty swing removed its head with a single blow.

Rosinnio fell back onto the bed, her heart racing, tears clouding her vision. Rothgar stood over her, his axe in his hands, the blade thick with blood and gore. She looked up and their eyes met. "You saved me," she said, remembering it was not so long ago that she had called for the man's execution after he insulted her at her wedding feast.

"No, my lady," he said, a concerned expression on his face. "When the beast reared up a blue flame erupted from your fingertips enveloping the thing, it was only when it was weakened that I finished it off."

"A blue flame?" Rosinnio said. staring at her hands.

"You are a sorceress," the big warrior stated.

"No, I…"

Before she could finish, her husband's Counsellor rushed into the chamber. "Please, my lady, we have to hurry." The words drifted into Rosinnio's consciousness. Her head throbbed; her stomach ached as she was supported, on one side, by her handmaiden, whom she realised was sobbing, and on the other by the counsellor. She offered no resistance as they led her through a narrow corridor, lit by torches lining the stone walls. "I know you suffer, my lady, but we must get you to the safety of the ships. There is a hidden passageway leading to the harbour."

"Please, highness… my lady, we must hurry. Men are fighting all over the castle," her handmaiden added.

Fighting? She suddenly wretched, as she tried to make sense of what she was being told, and what had just happened in her bedchamber. Her stomach cramped at the strain of heaving and having nothing to expel.

"The potion will take affect soon, my lady," Brandlor said. "It will ease your suffering."

Rothgar, who was leading the way, suddenly stopped and listened. Yellow hair hung loose down his broad back, save for two thick plaits either side of his face; the mark of a warrior. "There is fighting ahead," he said, his deep voice echoing in the corridor.

"There is fighting behind us too. We must go on," Brandlor answered. Rothgar simply nodded and moved forward.

Blood Of Kings: The Shadow Mage

The gods have truly deserted me in this forsaken place if the only man protecting me is the one who hates me above them all, Rosinnio thought.

"Where... where is my husband?" she stumbled over her words.

"We know not, my lady," the counsellor answered. "He rode out yesterday morn in pursuit of your would-be assassins. Neither he nor any of his men have returned." Brandlor's eyes were hard as he held Rosinnio's gaze.

She felt a warm sensation spread through her body, bringing relief to her cramping stomach and aching head. Even her blurred vision began to clear. She stood up a little straighter.

"The potion is taking effect, nullifying the poison," Brandlor said as he noticed the sudden change in her.

They came to a set of stairs leading down, the sound of battle drifting up from the lower floors. Rosinnio peered out through an arrow-slit to the courtyard below. To her eyes it was chaos. With only the light from the moon and flickering torches below it was difficult for her to make out who was who. Large groups of Nortmen hammered at each other with swords and axes. Battle-cries and screams of agony filled the air. All around men lay dead and dying while those still standing fought individual battles of life and death.

"What is happening?" she gasped, feeling as if she had woken from a dream and entered a nightmare.

"There is no time to explain, my lady. We must flee," Brandlor answered.

"Back!" Rothgar yelled as he swung a huge Nort-axe free. Three armed men ran up the stairs, yelling curses Rosinnio did not understand.

The giant warrior went to meet them swinging the axe. He sliced through the neck of the first man to make the top of the stairs. A red fountain sprayed the walls and floor as well as the axe-man. He kicked the falling body back down the stairs and into the other two rushing warriors. With a scream he brought the axe blade down on the head of a second, cutting through the iron helmet and cleaving his skull. The third stabbed him with a sword. Rothgar snarled and, using the extra height of the stairs, kicked him in the face. The warrior staggered back and screamed when he lost an arm to the whirling axe.

Rosinnio's handmaiden gripped her arm. The whole body of the servant trembled uncontrollably. Both women stared at the pile of bloody meat at the feet of the giant warrior. Rosinnio met his blazing eyes. She was mesmerised, appalled by the savagery and somehow drawn to the unbridled joy she saw there. She felt a new emotion rising in her, one she could not explain but felt as if her own heart was swelling. Rothgar, the man who had insulted her and whose life she had wanted her new husband to take, had now killed for her, was ready to lay down that life in defence of her. She could see the fierce joy brimming inside him. It overflowed, infecting her, filling her with anger and pride. The bodies lying at his feet were no longer men, they were trophies. These Nortmen lived, fought and died without a thought. Their daily meat was passion, raw and wild, and yes, cruel and fierce. She could never hope to understand them, would likely never be accepted by most. Even so, this was her home now, and if men were willing to die for her, men who despised her and thought her weak—well then—she at least would fight to defend that home.

"Rothgar," she said slowly to the big warrior, her eyes never leaving his, "give me your sword." Confusion spread across his face as his eyes dropped to the blade at his waist. Slowly he drew it with his free hand. In the other he held the blood-drenched, double-bladed axe. Rosinnio took the weapon, needing two hands to grip it and hold it up. "My husband's men are dying. Let us give them something to fight for."

Rothgar's eyes opened wide, then a grin spread across his face. Warrior and princess descended the stairs towards the courtyard leaving behind a confused Counsellor and handmaiden.

Weaponry was not a skill Rosinnio had learned in the courts of her father. Sewing needles and dance steps were her weapons and battle moves. It mattered not at all to the men who rallied to her that she struck not a single blow with the sword she held aloft. They were drawn to her as she walked into the midst of battle. At her side Rothgar wielded his axe, smiting down any who came close to her, his power and raw brutality immense. Many heads rolled that night, shorn by the double-bladed axe of the giant warrior. In the tales that followed the battle it was the southern princess, who held her sword aloft, vanquishing the enemy and driving the invader from their lands.

Tomas: Woodvale Monastery

The moon rose from behind a dark hill, on top of which was the outline of a building; jagged walls with a view over the entire valley and beyond. As day became night the buzz of life fell silent in the forest, save for the occasional cooing of some nocturnal animal scuttling though the undergrowth, or the shrill screech of a night hunter swooping in for a kill. Crashing and bellowing through the foliage a horse and rider, with a precious cargo on board, sent even these night-time dwellers scurrying into hiding.

Tomas gave no thought to his own, or the horse's safety as he pushed it beyond its endurance. Beneath him the animal snorted and choked in exhaustion, its hide bathed in a lather of sweat, the air misted from its flaring nostrils. Finally its muscled sides shuddered and its legs buckled beneath its own and the weight of the burden it carried. With an agonised cry it fell headlong, tumbling head over hoof to the ground, throwing its rider and the bundle he carried in his arms to the ground. It raised its long neck once before lying still on the forest floor, only its heaving flanks giving any indication it yet lived.

With a groan Tomas rolled onto his side, before quickly scrambling over to where his badly wounded wife had fallen from his arms. The cloak he had wrapped her in had come undone, revealing the terrible injuries she had suffered from the flames. "Aliss," he cried, panic welling inside him. Behind him, the horse he had ridden to its death snorted before giving its last breath. The blacksmith had no time for sentimentality and cursed the beast for failing before they had reached the monastery. He cradled the woman in his arms, his heart aching at the sight of her horrific injuries, her once beautiful face scarred and burned beyond recognition. Yet, she still lived, even if she had not regained consciousness since he plucked her from the flames. That in itself was a marvel, something to at least be thankful for.

Wrapping her once again in his cloak, Tomas scooped her up and stood on unsteady legs. His own body had reached and passed the point of exhaustion, having fled day and night without stopping to rest or eat, or even take a drink of water. Even so, Aliss was a light weight in his strong arms, muscles built from hard grafting over a forge these past years. Without a backward glance he left the body of the dead horse where it fell and continued the rest of the journey on foot.

By the time he stood before the stout wooden doors of the monastery, he was barely capable of holding himself up. His back, shoulders and legs ached. The slight frame of Aliss had grown heavier as the night wore on, the burden becoming almost unbearable as he carried her through the forest and then up the hill. Three times his legs had buckled and he'd fallen to his knees. Three times he picked himself back up, with one thought in mind – to reach the monastery, and place Aliss into the embrace of the monks and the healing prowess of Brother Joshan. He was not a man of strong faith. Oh, he knew the All Father existed. His influences were all around. He just had little time for bending the knee to some unseen force, oft as not as cruel and terrible as benevolent and kind. All of the gods—as far as he could see—worshipped far and wide, had a streak of nastiness in them. Brother Joshan had a gift though, Tomas knew this well, had seen what the old priest's powers were capable of from... before.

Before, he mused. He thought he had blacked out the past, almost to the point where, it seemed, as if he had always been a village blacksmith. Now that life was almost certainly dead to him. He suddenly became aware of the sword slung over his back and the woman, near to death, in his arms. Life had come full circle. It was a dark thought for him.

Holding his woman close to him, he pounded on the solid doors of the monastery. The cold, hard walls of stone reached up above him, almost to the stars, it seemed, from where he stood. With no immediate response, he hammered once again. The monks would be sleeping at this hour, even so, he would wake all if needs be.

Finally he heard footsteps from the other side of the door. A wooden slot slid back with a thud, echoing loudly in the otherwise calm and tranquillity of the night. A pair of eyes appeared in the gap. "Who is it that calls at this late hour? And making enough racket to wake the dead," a none-to-impressed voice said.

"Open the door!" Tomas bellowed. "I have an injured woman in need of urgent aid."

"Come back tomorrow, there is none here who can help you at this hour." The doorkeeper slammed the slot closed.

Tomas gently placed Aliss down, propping her against the wall. "Open these gates! Or by all of the gods in the heavens I will rip it off myself." With that he drew his sword, the length of the polished blade gleamed in the moonlight. He drew back and slammed it against the door. There was a mighty thud, and the hatch opened again.

"I said…" the monk began but was cut off by Tomas stooping to eye level with him.

"Your hide will be the first I skin from its wretched bones and pin to these gates. Now fetch Brother Joshan," Tomas said levelly, the truth of the threat as plain in the tone of his voice as in the words.

The gatekeeper swallowed hard. "Brother Joshan is abed, he will…"

"Wake him. Now!"

"Aye, very well. Wait here." The monk licked his lips and scuttled off.

Tomas closed his eyes, breathing in deep breaths as he struggled to rein in his emotions. Beside him, Aliss groaned.

Quickly he bent down to her, cursing himself for flinching at the sight of her wounds. Her once beautiful face was now unrecognisable, raw red where the skin had melted away, all of

Blood Of Kings: The Shadow Mage

her hair gone, her head scarred and scorched. Despair threatened to swamp him, manifesting as a physical ache in his chest. *He had arrived too late, and now she would die.*

The heavy door creaked open a crack. Yellow, flickering light spilled out from within as several, torch and lantern-bearing monks huddled together. Tomas looked up from his knees, exhaustion robbing him of the ability to even stand. His vision blurred as tears welled in his eyes. "Joshan…" he croaked.

"I am here, Tomas."

He felt a touch on his shoulder, and a warm sensation flowing through him, easing a hundred and more aches, soothing over-tired muscles. Grey-robed monks surrounded them, gently taking Aliss from his arms. He was powerless to resist them as he longed to give into the soothing touch of Brother Joshan. It was all he could do to grit his teeth and push the old priest away.

"No! Save it for Aliss. Save her for me, Josh," he whispered the name once used in affection… *long ago*… The older man's eyes narrowed as the blacksmith's words were snatched away by the night breeze.

"What have you done, Tomas?" Brother Joshan asked as he noticed the dried blood on the younger man's clothing and arms and face.

"I have been down roads not travelled in a very long time. I fear there will be no turning aside this time."

"Oh Tomas." Joshan sighed.

He followed the herd of cowled monks through the gate and into the courtyard of the monastery. Surrounded by sturdy walls and a stout wooden door, the home of the monks had the look of a fort.

"Take her to my room," Joshan instructed the monks. They carried her into the largest building in the compound and carried her up a set of narrow, wooden steps.

Tomas took in the sparse room of the monk, as he followed the small entourage through, having to stoop beneath the low doorway. A small wooden-framed cot lay against one wall. On the wall opposite covered in scrolls, leather-bound books, and ink pots sat a desk and one straight-backed, uncomfortable-looking chair. Aliss was placed on the bed.

"Thank you, brothers. Please leave us." The monks filed out the door, leaving Tomas alone, other than the still form of his woman, with the old priest. Joshan turned to him then. "How many did you kill?"

Tomas bowed and shook his head. "My recollections are vague," he answered, unable to look up and meet the glare of the older man.

"You will have to leave this place. They will hunt you down," the old monk said.

"Such concerns matter little enough now."

"Aye," Brother Joshan said, turning his attention back to the stricken girl. "She is beyond my help, Tomas."

"You have not yet tried." The blacksmith glared at the priest, rising to his full height.

"Tomas, she is beyond the help of anyone. It would be a kindness to ease her pain and allow her to pass into the arms of the All Father."

"I have seen what you can do. Watched you bring men back to life from terrible wounds. Why will you not help her?" Tomas' voice trembled.

"Sit, Tomas," the smaller man instructed, the tone in his voice brooking no argument. "She is sleeping now. I have helped ease her torment a little." His eyes strayed to where the woman lay on the narrow cot. "Sit, please." He produced a jug and two clay goblets, and poured a dark crimson liquid into both. "We have travelled a long dark road, you and I. It seems a very long time ago since we left the bosom of the king's court. A very long time ago indeed." Joshan sighed and sipped from the cup.

"Aye, a lifetime... two lifetimes," Tomas agreed. "You were once a trusted advisor to the king. You had wealth, position, fame. You need not have given that up," he said as he glanced around the sparse room.

"And you," a smile creased the monk's weather-beaten face, "once a headstrong champion, the best of them all. Now look at us." The humour made his eyes glow for an instant.

"Royal Guard or not, a low-born soldier is easily discarded by the nobility. Tossed aside like an expensive cloak, no longer in fashion at court," he spat the words bitterly.

Joshan smiled sadly. "You challenged the king's nephew to a duel, Tomas. And worse, you won! Do you even remember the name of the girl you fought over? I'll wager not. For that you will ever be a hunted man."

Both men sat in contemplative silence, savouring the wine, until a knock on the door interrupted their thoughts. "Brother Joshan, the brother abbot would have words," a muffled voice came from outside the room.

"Tell him I will come shortly," the old priest answered.

"I have brought more trouble to your door," Tomas said. "It seems it is all I ever do."

Brother Joshan smiled. "Aye well, you make an old man's life interesting and a little more bearable. He is likely concerned at having an armed man and badly wounded woman bang on his door at such a late hour."

"Will he bid us leave?"

"No, but he will be most anxious to know when you intend to do so."

"Why, Josh, why did you flee with me all those years ago? There was no need. It is I who was condemned. You had power, influence, wealth. Why did you give it all up?"

"Nigh on a score of years ago, I held a dying man in my arms. A friend, he bade me watch over his child and treat him as my own. I dare say he would have just cause to chastise me for the ill job I have done, but I have endeavoured to keep my promise... I have never told you this before, your mother..."

Tomas flinched when Joshan brought up the subject of his mother. "Died giving birth to me, yes I know," he said softly.

"It is not what I was going to say. Your mother was a most beautiful woman. When we were younger your father and I competed for her affections. I was young and fearless with a growing reputation at Court. Your father was an apprentice blacksmith. I promised her wealth and a life of adventure. She chose the dependable man that was your father over the uncertain future she would have with me. She chose right."

"You are one of a kind, Josh; a king's mage taking in a blacksmith's orphan." Tomas shook his head. "I was not so young that I could not have fended for myself."

"Aye, I don't doubt it. You were ever resourceful. It would not have sat well with me, though, seeing the child of an old friend, living on the streets. Mayhap, though, in the light of what has happened to us these past years, things may have turned out better.

"We have travelled down some dark roads, you and I, dark roads indeed. We've done things I'm not proud of. Perhaps this is why I chose to see out my years in this place. The All Father gave me two gifts, one, the ability to kill men with these hands, and the other, the power to heal with them. He opened two roads for me and left me to decide which to choose. I like to think the choice I made in latter life was the right path. It is not so bad here. We worship the All Father in quiet contemplation and in turn he answers ours prayers in his own way. It is not such a bad life. I thought you settled. It made my heart swell with pride when you took up your father's trade." Joshan wiped away a stray tear.

"Aye, I was happy for a while. I have no regrets over killing the king's nephew. It was a fair duel. Had I not been low-born and he royalty, no more would have been said about the matter, but…"

"Ah, it is always the 'but'," Joshan said.

"Aye. Afterwards though, I did some bad things. I was so angry…" he trailed off.

"Now the cycle continues," the old monk said, his mouth set in a grim line. "The All Father is the creator of all. He created the world and everything in it. Even the gods worshipped in other lands were created by Him. He also created The Pit, and The Hag and all of the demons who live in the dark depths with her. Why did he do this? Why create something so evil? He did it because there must be balance in all things, light and dark, black and white. He created men and gave them free will and the ability to choose for themselves. Some men choose the light, others walk the darker path."

"Ursa," Tomas suddenly said.

"Ursa?"

"The name of the girl we fought over. Her name was Ursa."

The old priest laid a hand on his companion's shoulder. "It is time for a new chapter to unfold. Leave here, in the morning. I will see that Aliss does not suffer. I will not leave her until... until the end. Go somewhere far beyond the king's reach. It will not take long for word to reach his ears of how a blacksmith slew the magistrate's guards. He still searches for you, even after all these years.

"We made some bad choices, Tomas. We should have fled south where they would never have found us. Instead we chose a life of villainy. It shames me that my name will be written down by future scholars as a common brigand."

"We were many things, Josh," Tomas grinned, "but never common."

"Will you go?" Joshan asked, his eyes eager for an answer. Tomas simply shook his head. "You mean to stay and take your vows? Live the life of a simple monk?" Again Tomas shook his head.

"If you will not help me, Josh, there is another."

"No, Tomas, you cannot mean to... I won't allow it!" Joshan's eyes glowered.

"You won't allow it? You refuse me aid and now you think to bar me from seeking the help of another?" Tomas stood up then.

"Please, Tomas, allow Aliss to pass over in peace. Do not do what you are contemplating."

"Enough!" Anger contorted Tomas' face. "I will take her from here and travel to the Great Wood. There I shall search out Haera and beseech her to help. She knows me well enough. She owes me."

Joshan's body and spirit visibly deflated. "Well, then I have truly failed your father. If you give Aliss into the care of that witch, then I fear both of your souls are lost."

Duke Normand: Duchy of Lenstir

"No, no, no!" Duke Normand shouted at the boy as he was put through his paces by a grizzled weapon-master. "Move your feet, you look like a lumbering ox." The boy glanced over and quickly turned away again before the duke could see the tears glistening in his eyes.

"Again," the old weapon-master said, dropping into a defensive stance.

The boy swung viciously at the weapon-master's head, but the old warrior calmly parried each swipe with his own blade. The sound of the clashing swords filled the air around the practice ground, as other, far more experienced men were put through an array of drills.

"You are too hard on him. He worships the very earth you walk on."

Normand swung around at the sound of a female voice.

"My lady Isabetha," Normand said, his eyes widening in surprise. "I was not informed of your arrival. Did you send word?"

"No," she answered, her eyes sparkling mischievously. "I thought to catch you unawares."

"How so?" The duke regarded the smiling and pretty face of Lady Isabetha, in consternation. His eyes wandered from the elaborate mountain of blonde curls on top of her head, down across the soft line of her exposed neck and shoulders, to the plunging neckline of the gown, most unsuitable to be wearing on a parade ground full of leering warriors. "You look…"

"Wretched? Travel-worn?" She arched an eyebrow.

"Lovely… beautiful as ever," Normand stammered and was rewarded with a throaty laugh.

"Ooh, I really have surprised you, to have you tripping over your own tongue. Let's expose those dirty little secrets you are hiding."

Normand's face went pale. "Secrets? I assure you I have none. I…"

"I'm jesting, Erik. You are always too serious. It is your greatest fault."

"I'm sorry. You just… I… you caught me by surprise."

"Well, that was my intention." She smiled.

Just then, something caught Normand's attention and he swung back to the practice field. "Get up! Before you make an even bigger fool of yourself." He turned away from the boy then, who had tripped and fallen face first into the muddy field. The ten-year-old boy looked tiny beside the imposing figure of the weapon-master. Even so, he stood stoically before him, his mouth firmly fixed in a grim line in an obvious attempt to stiffen his trembling lip.

"Erik, please. He is your son, not one of your soldiers. Have a care," Lady Isabetha said.

Duke Normand swung around to her, his eyes blazing. "Yes. He is my son, and one day he will be duke. This is not Rothberry Castle where his greatest care will be which coat to choose for the king's feast. Here, we are surrounded by enemies. To the south only a mountain range separates us from barbarian hordes only too eager to plunder our lands. Those mountains are filled with brigands, spies and the gods know what else. Huge white-furred creatures who walk upright like men wander down from the highest peaks and attack travellers, gutting them with claws as big and sharp as daggers. Surrounding us are large, so-called, friendly duchies. Yet, they raid my lands, carrying off whatever they can find, and then attempt to place the blame on each other or marauding brigands. Their aim? To destabilise us until we are so weak that they may walk in and take everything for their own. When I protest to the king, I am met with a wall of silence. Yes, he is only a boy, but in the south boys need to become men very quickly, or they will surely perish."

Lady Isabetha took a step back from the furious onslaught of the duke. Her lip twitched and she instantly regained her composure. "White-haired beasts that walk like men?" She arched an eyebrow. "Bedtime tales for children I think." Two full lips, painted a deep red, parted in a smile. "Often as not they will begin feeding before their victim is even dead. They are particularly fond of the heart and liver." Normand did not return the smile. "Now tell me – why have you come all this way south, from the comforts of the king's court?" His eyes bored into hers.

"Can a lady not visit a... friend?" She ran a painted fingernail up the centre of his chest and let it trail off when it reached his chin.

Normand snatched her hand squeezing it until she flinched. "No," he answered before bringing the hand up to his lips and kissing it tenderly. She laughed then and stood on the tips of her toes, reaching up to kiss him passionately. He crushed her against the stable wall. He breathed heavily in her ear, "I want you. Now."

"Here? In front of all your men?" He could feel her hot breath on his face.

He grabbed her by the hand and marched back towards the castle, dragging her with him. She giggled as she tried to keep pace with his long strides.

After their lovemaking they lay side by side on his fur-covered bed, both staring at the ceiling.

"Why did you never marry again, after... after your wife died?" she asked him.

He turned to regard her, pausing to drink in the sight of her lying naked beside him, assessing every curve as he would a theatre of war on the eve of battle. "Are you interested in the role?" His answer elicited a laugh from her.

"Gods no. One of us would not see the end of the year if you and I were to marry. I would end up as food for one of your mountain beasts, if I hadn't poisoned your soup first." She laughed again. "Your boy's eyes look so sad. He has never known the love of a mother, has he?"

"He is cared for well enough by the servants."

"It is not the same," she said, a note of melancholy in her voice.

"It is enough for me, and it is enough for him. Now tell me why you have come. I enjoy our trysts, somehow though, I doubt you have travelled all this way because you yearned to be with me." He pushed himself off the bed and began pulling on his breeches. He felt her eyes on him as she cast an appraising eye over his lean and muscular form. "Fetch me some wine," she said.

"Fetch it yourself. I have much to do," he barked

"Typical man. Satisfy your needs on a woman and then abandon her, wineless and cheerless."

"Why are you here, Isa? You arrive unannounced, like a surprise storm blown down from the mountains. You make love to me while you tell me I do not know how to raise my son correctly. Do you wish to take the boy from me and teach him the ways of the king's court?" He flung his arms out in exasperation.

"That would be no bad thing. You teach him to ride and fight well enough, but there are other skills a man… a future duke needs to know."

"Enough! Tell me what you are doing here."

"Very well. The king sent me."

"To spy on me?"

"Yes," she answered, her eyes locked on his. Was there an edge of doubt… of fear in her voice?

"Why?" he asked.

"Why did the King send me? Or why have I admitted it to you?"

"Both," he answered before walking across the room where a jug and two goblets sat on a table. He filled both cups with dark red wine and handed one to Isabetha.

"Would there have been any point denying it? You are no fool, Erik. You knew why I was here the moment you set eyes on me."

"As spies go, you are not without benefits." He smirked.

"Could any other get so close to you?" She smiled back.

"No," he answered. "So, tell me why His Majesty has sent you to ingratiate yourself with me."

"The king is concerned with your action on the Thieves Citadel. He is worried that you went to war and invaded another nation without consulting him first. Your aggression has put him in an awkward position."

"Another nation?" he spluttered, spitting wine across the floor. "A nest of villains and cutthroats. The only thing saving that wretched place for all these years was that cursed dream cult – which I'm happy to say no longer exists."

"Yes, the Temple of Eor. You desecrated it and murdered all of the priestesses…"

"They were not murdered. They took their own lives."

She arched her shapely eyebrows at his answer before saying, "Erik, his majesty has been asked for your head."

"My head? By who?" he snarled.

"Never mind that. The other dukes are nervous."

"Tell me who has petitioned the king for my death," he said in a low, even voice.

Isabetha ignored him. "There are others who are not happy. The high priestess has influence in the Sunsai Empire, and other lands have worshippers of Eor. They all bring pressure to bear on his majesty." She paused to sip some wine before continuing. "You'll be pleased to hear he has refused those requests."

"I am happy his majesty has finally found his own voice. His father would never…"

"His father is dead and not the king," Lady Isabetha interrupted him. "Listen to me, Erik. his majesty could change his mind on a whim. Today he has sent me, tomorrow it may be the axe-man with an army at his back."

The clay goblet suddenly exploded in Normand's hand. Blood and wine trickled between his fingers. "Were you also instructed to fuck me, to soften me up?" he said through a clenched jaw.

"No. That was for me," she answered.

"So what does he expect of me, if he does not want my head?"

"In public he is demanding that you withdraw from Eorotia."

"No," he said, not allowing her to finish. "I will not return the rats to their nest. I will not have my lands plagued by hordes of brigands and thieves."

Isabetha spoke calmly. "In private he wants fifty percent of everything. He knows well that those mountains are bulging with stolen gold."

"No."

"Then you will die, Erik. The king values many things, but none so high as gold."

Lady Rosinnio – Jarl Crawulf: Wind Isle

Lady Rosinnio, wife of Crawulf, jarl of Wind Isle and all of the surrounding seas, sat in her sturdy, oak chair at the head of the feasting hall. In front of her, her husband's chosen men sat around on long benches, drinking ale and squabbling amongst themselves. Beside her, Crawulf's carved chair remained empty. The flames from torches sitting in sconces on the walls flickered from the wind sweeping though the stone corridors of the castle. Outside, beyond the safety and disputable comfort of stout walls, a storm raged, an icy wind whipping down freezing rain from the north.

It had been three days since they had defeated the invader. Three more days that Crawulf had not returned. In that time, although they had nodded respectfully, acknowledging her role in the victory, her husband's chief men had refused to take orders from Rosinnio.

'*They will not be commanded by a woman, even less an outlander,*' Brandlor, Crawulf's chief advisor had explained. Yes, respect for her since the battle had grown in their eyes, but she was not the jarl of Wind Isle, merely his wife. As a result, nothing had been done, as the chosen men argued amongst themselves. The gates to Wind Isle Castle had remained barred – no one went in and no one left. Rosinnio had attempted to argue that men should be sent forth to ensure any surviving raiders were captured or had returned to their ships. She had wanted search parties to look for

Crawulf, for surely he must be in serious peril, or worse, to have been missing for so long, and at such a time.

They are nervous. They have been attacked at the very heart of their power and their jarl is missing. They are frightened, but will not admit it to each other or themselves. Brandlor's words echoed in her mind.

"What must I do?" she had asked.

"For now, wait."

She was sick of waiting. She felt the presence behind her of the giant warrior, Rothgar. He had not left her side since the battle, glowering at all and any who approached her, even sleeping outside her door at night. She could do little else but picture him as a faithful hound. The thought brought a smile to her lips, even if she was puzzled by the huge warrior; a man she had wanted put to death for insulting and threatening her. *I will never understand these Nortmen—never be one of them.* "I wish to retire. I am weary and still feeling the effects of the poison," she said to the grey-haired counsellor who hovered nearby. Always, it seemed, on hand to offer a word of advice. She could not help but wonder how much of it she should listen to.

"Yes, my lady. Bed-rest will aid your recovery."

She nodded and gingerly extracted herself from the hard, uncomfortable chair. It was no lie that she still felt aches and cramps, the after-effects of being poisoned, but she had another reason for wishing to leave the hall and the watching eyes of her husband's warriors. As she expected, Rothgar slipped into step behind her and her handmaiden as they made their way silently down draughty hallways. When they reached her chamber, Rothgar took up position outside of her door.

"Come," she beckoned to him, biting her lip at the confused expression on his face. "I wish to speak to you," she added.

He nodded and stepped into the room, clearly uncomfortable being inside his lord and lady's bedchamber. Rosinnio poured wine into two cups and handed one to him.

"My lady, I…"

"It does not sit well with you, being served by your jarl's lady?" she asked, finding herself enjoying his discomfort. "Come sit." She sat on a wooden bench, inviting him to join her. He rested the great Nort-axe he carried against the wall, shifted his sword around his waist and sat, cup in hand, his eyes shifting from Rosinnio to her handmaiden and back again. "We did not make a good start, you and I..." she began. Rothgar shifted uncomfortably. "The fault was mine. It is taking me time to become used to the ways of Nortland and its people. It will likely take me a lifetime to even scratch the surface, but I will try."

Rothgar nodded, a growl rattling in his throat Rosinnio could not decipher.

"You are loyal to your jarl, and quite possibly the bravest man I have ever known." She meant the words. She had been awestruck by not just his courage at facing his enemies, even though they had far superior numbers, but by the sheer brutality of the encounter. It was her first and only battle. Rothgar had been by her side for the duration of it, as she strode into the courtyard—some would say stupidly, others inspired—he had circled around her, beating back all who approached; killing in a wild frenzy, until the invader had fled. "I would ask a favour of you."

"My lady, I..."

"Crawulf must be found. His battle-chiefs will take no action without him. They have sat in that hall, bickering and drinking with no decisions being made. I am his wife, but they will not listen to me... will not take orders from a woman. So I am begging you." She slid off the bench and onto her knees. "Go find him for me, bring him back."

"And if he is dead?"

"Well, at least we will know."

"I am thinking that may not be a good situation for you. Your life will be in the hands of a new jarl," the big warrior said.

Rosinnio's head bowed. She had assumed that if her husband was dead then they would just return her to her father. Was it possible that a new jarl would wish to end any possible threat to his position by ensuring Crawulf's line ended with him... but they had no children. She would never understand the ways of the Nortmen.

She looked up fiercely then. "Well, then so be it."

Rothgar stood up and nodded once. It was as much of an answer as Rosinnio would get. He reached a hand down to her to help her up off her knees, and then turned and walked briskly from the room, snatching his great, two-handed axe from the wall by the door.

"These Nortmen are a mystery to me and that one above them all," Rosinnio's handmaiden said.

"Yes, I agree, he is a strange one. I think though, he will do as I asked. He has a peculiar sense of honour, but one made of iron."

"Or love."

Rosinnio swung around to face her handmaiden at that. "Love?"

"Do you not think him a little in love with you? The way he has followed you, snarling at any who approach you."

"No." The former princess laughed. "Not that one. The loyalty he has shown me is merely an extension of the esteem in which he holds his jarl. If only the rest would act more like him."

"I'm not so sure that would be a good thing," the servant girl answered, before both of them began to laugh.

***

The black sea boiled beneath him and crashed over his head as Crawulf rode each tumultuous wave sending his flimsy craft high into the air and crashing down again. The wind whipped at his sodden beard and hair, icy cold on his skin and eyes. All around him the screeches of the Death Riders—dark dwarves riding black hounds with wings and red glowing eyes—hunted for the souls of lost seamen in order to enslave them in the dark caverns of the Nacht Realm.

He was alone as he fought the rage of Baltagor, Lord of the Sea and the servants of Boda, Mistress of the Shadow World— the Nacht Realm—as they stood united against him. He roared his defiance at all of them, even as salt water clogged his throat and stung his eyes. The howling wind along with the demons borne on it competed with the roaring sea to deafen him, and still he shouted back his defiance from the prow of his ship. He clung to the serpent's head, knowing that his crew had all been washed overboard, the blood-red square sail hung in ribbons from the single mast, with strands of rigging whipping in the air. The strong odour of brine clung to his nostrils as each wave deposited more and more water into the boat. White horses, riding mountain-high waves, snarled biting and kicking as they washed over the jarl of Wind Isle.

A loud crack behind him told him that the mast was gone, as the planks of the deck snapped and splintered beneath his feet. A round shield flew past his head, wrenched free from where it had been secured to the side of the boat, with those belonging to the other crewmen. Crawulf raised his sword and laughed.

"He's waking!" Words drifted on the wind, floating past and into his consciousness.

He opened his eyes and saw the woman of the house jump back when she saw him stir. She had felt the grip of his fingers around her throat once before and was wary to get too close ever since. He growled and nodded, and then shifted himself so that he could sit up. The woman handed him a bowl of boiled oats before hurrying away.

"I was dreaming," Crawulf said. His head spun as he regarded the bowl in front of him.

"Aye, we heard," the fisherman answered. A younger man chuckled as he looked up from his own bowl of porridge. "You cried out," he explained with a smile on his face. "I am thinking it was not such a pleasant dream."

"The black dwarves of Boda were tearing my flesh with their claws searching for my soul," he answered grimly.

"Did they find it?" the boy asked.

"That which is not there will never be found," Crawulf snarled.

"Everybody has a soul," the fisherman answered. "Just some are blacker than others."

Crawulf spooned the porridge into his mouth. "I am feeling much rested, although my leg is still useless," he said between mouthfuls. "Can you take me somewhere? You will be paid well for your trouble." He could still taste the salty seawater, smell the brine and kelp over the earthier aroma of the reed-thatch above his head and the wattle-and-daub walls surrounding him.

He shivered at the memory of the dream, despite the heat thrown off from the fire at the centre of the room.

"Aye, if you wish." The fisherman dug something out from beneath him then. Whatever it was, it was wrapped in cloth. He handled it as if its contents would bite him at any moment. He stood up and approached Crawulf. "This belongs to you I'm thinking. We found it in the cave."

Crawulf took it from the fisherman's hands, snatching back the cloth. A smile crept across his lips at the sight of his sword. The weapon handed down to him from his father, and to he from his. "Aye, this belongs to me."

"We want no trouble," the fisherman said.

"You will have none," Crawulf answered. "You saved my life, where others would have left me to die. You could have looted my carcass and waited for the tide to fill the cave again and wash me out to sea. Instead you brought me into your home and cared for me. I am in your debt, and you will be well rewarded."

"You didn't come off no shipwreck, did you?"

"No, no I did not." Crawulf said, his mouth set in a grim line.

"Father! Father, come quick!" they were interrupted by the cries of the man's second son.

Suddenly the small hut was awash in light as the main door was flung open. A young man stood in the entryway, panting and heaving. The skin of his face was covered in a sheen of sweat, which stuck his hair to his forehead. "Father…" he began again before stopping abruptly. His back stiffened as thick, red liquid bubbled out of his mouth.

Crawulf watched open-mouthed as a blade erupted from his chest. Time froze for an instant, before reality crashed in with violent intensity. The fisherman screamed, "Noooo…" His second son, sat, rooted to his chair, his mind clearly not comprehending what his eyes were telling him. A high-pitched wail of a grieving mother pierced the air, shaking Crawulf out of his reverie.

The dead boy's body was flung aside as pandemonium erupted inside the house. A man, wearing mail armour under his heavy cloak and an iron helmet on his head, burst into the room.

The blade he carried in his hand shone crimson in the firelight as he jabbed it at the fisherman's head. Another followed behind. Crawulf could hear others shouting and roaring behind them. The wailing of the fisherwoman was suddenly cut off abruptly. Crawulf barely registered her body slumping to the earthen floor, her blood splattering the rushes.

As quickly as he could, Crawulf shook the cloth off his sword and swung his legs off the bed. Agony lanced through him from his shin and all the way up his back. With gritted teeth and watering eyes, he ignored the pain, to stand awkwardly on one foot. The first of the intruders, his weapon now dripping crimson from the blood of the father as well as the son, swung towards him. Crawulf blocked the arcing blade with his own and stabbed with a sharp vicious jab at the man's face. The blade caved in his cheekbone and pierced his brain, killing him before he had time to cry out. Crawulf wrenched his weapon free, letting the man slide to the ground. A second snarled a curse at him as he raised his sword to strike. Crawulf lost his balance as he attempted to take a defensive posture with only one good leg. The stumble saved his life. He felt a tide of air as the warrior's sword flew past him.

Another scream snapped his attention away from his opponent for the briefest of instants. The fisherman's second son lunged at the warrior with a spiked hook on a pole, catching him unawares. He drove the fishing implement into his chest, the ferocity of the blow driving through his boiled leather armour, to pierce soft flesh and grind bone. The warrior fell with a look of shock on his face.

More crowded into the small hut, beating down the fisherman's son by weight of numbers, although a number took sore hurts from the enraged boy as they dragged him down. Crawulf found himself hoping the boy lived through the ordeal. He stood impassively, waiting, while the men formed a line in front of him, hard men, men who had seen battle and death. If he was to die this day, it was better to greet the gods with a sword in his hand and the blood of his enemies on the blade. *Far better than shivering to death in a dank cave.*

"So who wants to die first?" he snarled. The effect he had hoped for was somewhat lost when he accidentally put weight on his bad leg and an involuntary grimace wracked his body.

"Well, well, well, look at what just washed up into our nets."

Crawulf squinted at a newcomer, framed by sunlight as he stood in the open doorway. "Well met, Jarl Crawulf," he said, a humourless smile formed on his lips. "Take him!"

Crawulf's sword was useless to him as he was bundled to the ground. He roared in agony as he was manhandled by at least four men. Fire erupted in his leg until he blacked out from the pain.

Tomas: The Great Wood

The Great Wood loomed in the distance as the first flush of dawn bled a crimson glow into the sky. Tomas kicked his horse on, requisitioned from the monk's stables, towards the dark wall of trees. Cradled in his arms was Aliss, appearing to sleep soundly, thanks to the healing charm placed on her by Brother Joshan. Appearances were not all they seemed, and he knew somewhere, deep inside her subconscious, that she suffered greatly. Joshan, his old friend and one time mentor had said she was beyond help, her injuries too severe. He also knew that there were other ways of accomplishing things, darker paths that men like Joshan feared to travel.

The wood stretched across the countryside for hundreds of leagues, as long as it was wide. Its hidden depths harboured many secrets few men had even heard tell of, let alone seen. Rumours and stories abounded about what lived in the very darkest places of the forest; occasional sightings of malformed creatures and beasts to terrify a man's soul added to the mystery and power of the place. It was a place to be avoided by folk if at all possible. Apart from the demons and ghosts who lay in wait for unwary travellers, it was also home to some of the worst kind of men in the Duchies, brigands and villains using its reputation to hide themselves from honest folk. Tomas knew this well – he was once one of them.

There was a time of darkness, shortly after he had fled from the anger and spite of the king, whose relative he had slain in a duel, when he was forced to leave behind the king's Royal Guard, his family for the previous years, his home. He hated to dwell upon it; memories of those days shamed him, and yet, those reflections constantly seeped into his mind, like a mist drifting through the forest, unstoppable, a constant thing, always all around, yet untouchable. He and Joshan had taken up with a gang of brigands. They were waylaid by them one summer morning as they journeyed through the Great Wood, farther east to the place he now found himself. They were rough and nasty, and robbing travellers was no strange thing to them. Yet, they were no match for an outlawed knight and fighting champion of the Royal Guard. Tomas and Joshan had fought them off easily, but instead of killing them or even leaving them somewhere to be found by the local magistrate's men, they forced them to take them to their camp, deep into the forest, and they joined them.

Tomas had been full of anger at the time. He wanted vengeance, he wanted to hurt the king who had robbed him of a life he had fought harder than most for. He had not realised how much he loved being honoured and feted as a part of the Royal Guard, how much the camaraderie of his sworn sword brothers meant to him, until it was snatched from him. They were known as the Shields of the Realm; sworn to defend the king with their lives, honour-bound to each other.

Well, he was born a commoner, the son of a blacksmith, and when push came to shove, his brothers abandoned him. His king declared him outlaw, because he had fought and killed a member of the aristocracy. The bitterness was a vile-tasting thing in the back of his throat. He knew not how to fight back, but marshalling a gang of cutthroats and rapists seemed like one way to strike a blow at the time. Joshan had argued against it, of course, but Tomas was too hot-headed, too angry, and so they had become part of the folklore of the Great Wood. How life had twisted and turned in on itself for a simple blacksmith's son.

By the time he reached the unending line of trees, the sun had broken over the horizon, bathing the valley in a bright golden glow. Tomas knew that even the sun's brilliant white light, and warmth would find it hard to penetrate to the very depths of the forest, to where he knew he must journey. He freed a small bag of provisions he had tied to the saddle and slung it over his shoulder. Hanging across his back was his sword, cleaned now of the blood of the men he had killed, yet the stain of the deed would linger for much, much longer. Once he had Aliss securely cradled in his arms, he slapped the horse's rump and let out a sharp cry, trusting the beast would find its own way home. It would be of no use to him deeper into the forest, where the foliage became thick, along with the dank, cool air.

Aliss had not made a sound since he had fled the monastery. He knew Joshan had put a charm on her, to ease her suffering and put her into a deep sleep. He could not help but wonder if she would ever wake from it. Joshan said she was beyond his help. The old monk had a great gift for healing Tomas knew well—it was a bitter irony that the only other he knew capable of helping Aliss was herself. Magic was a rare thing in the world—if he could not help her, was she beyond all aid? Such thoughts had plagued him the entire journey. He was tired, his body ached, and he couldn't remember the last time he had slept. Was he just prolonging her agony? He didn't want to lose her, couldn't lose her. Was it so selfish to desire to save the woman he loved? Joshan had said he would ease her journey into the afterlife. Was Tomas wrong to deprive her of this? Or should he do all in his power to help her live?

He warred with himself incessantly as he walked, his burden growing heavier with each step. On more than one occasion he stumbled over an unseen root or trailing vine. The damp, musky odours of the surrounding vegetation and rich earthy smells of the forest floor were like an opiate, seducing him into an overwhelming tiredness. He yearned to stop and rest, to sleep. Perhaps when he woke, he would realise it had all been a dream; a dark, terrible nightmare.

When he finally did allow himself to rest—either that or he would fall down where he stood—his dreams were dark and terrible. A blood-lusting monster attacked the village in the valley, slaying all in its path. Only, he was the monster.

His head throbbed from lack of sleep; his traitorous mind sent him thoughts and feelings of doubt and shame. He held his wife close to him. He didn't want her to die. She had saved him, saved him from himself, and a life of villainy and infamy. He thought he had blocked out much of his past, certainly some of the more heinous deeds he perpetrated, but it was Aliss who had done that. She had given him a chance at a better life. He was once a hero, then branded traitor—unfairly in his eyes—then turned outlaw. He was many things in the eyes of men. She saw past that; she drew out the blacksmith's son, accepting him, and all his faults, for who he was. To lose her would mean losing himself.

His attention snapped back to the present at the sound of a footstep on a fallen branch. He remained motionless, head bowed as if still in a slumber. Whispering voices drifted on the wind, making him tense. His instincts urged him to flee, to leap up and run from any approaching danger. He fought that desire with cold determination and waited.

Like shadows they melted from the darkness of the forest and into his makeshift camp. One by one they edged closer, sensing easy prey. The first approached, dagger in hand, as the others made to surround Tomas and Aliss. Two sleeping travellers, lost in the Great Wood, easy pickings – not so. In a heartbeat Tomas was up, with a twist of his wrist the would-be thief's dagger dropped to the forest floor and he was launched across the small clearing. The others, all wearing dark, hooded cloaks, stepped in closer. They paused when Tomas unslung the sword from his back.

"Take me to Haera."

The first brigand picked himself up while massaging his jaw. The others shuffled nervously. Two of them carried bows and drew the strings back, both aiming arrows at Tomas. Another was armed with an axe, and the final one carried a stout, wooden staff.

"And who are you, to know that name?" the injured bandit asked as he cautiously stepped closer.

"She will know who I am," he answered.

The axe-man suddenly lurched forward, aiming a swinging blow at Tomas. If he thought to catch the blacksmith off guard and distracted, he was mistaken. He ran straight into a mail-clad elbow as his axe flew through the air.

"What's wrong with the girl?" the first brigand asked.

"She has suffered severe injuries. If she dies here, she will not journey to the All Father alone."

"What sort of injuries," the bandit ignored the threat, and his unconscious friend. "A witch?" There was no accusation in his question, simply a request for information. Tomas made no answer. The man paused, glancing from Aliss to his companions, until his gaze fell, once again, on Tomas. "Put this on," he finally said, pulling a long strip of dark cloth from inside his cloak. Tomas studied his partially hidden face and found it unreadable. He shook his head. "I will not lead you to the crone if you do not. I will not take the risk of you using the same path to lead a posse of men the same way."

Tomas suddenly crouched down beside the unconscious man, placing his naked blade at the brigand's throat. "I could kill him now," he said. "Then you." He indicated the lead bandit with a hard stare. "Then all of them."

"Aye, or perhaps Leon here will stick your lady with an arrow before you do. Then we all lose." He smiled a humourless smile from beneath the dark hood.

"Only a fool would turn his back on the bandits of Great Wood and allow them to blindfold him."

"Aye," the bandit responded.

"I am no fool," Tomas said. The bandit shrugged, and waited.

Light had already begun to seep from the overhead sky. Soon it would be dark again, and Aliss would be closer to death. Already, he suspected, the All Father had one hand on her. He could feel the air begin to chill. She would not survive another night.

"Leon," the brigand broke the silence. "Pick up Roree. It is time to go." He spoke to his companion but his eyes never left Tomas. Two of the bandits picked up the injured man before melting into the darkness of the forest, the second bowman kept his notched arrow trained on the blacksmith. "Leave this place and do not return. The next time you will not see from where your death will come." Slowly the rest of the band backed away from the night shrouded clearing.

"Wait!" Tomas barked. The lead bandit halted. "I will wear the blindfold."

"Drop the sword and turn around."

Tomas did as he was bid. His exposed back tingled and itched, as if a thousand and more white, creeping maggots crawled across his flesh, as the brigand approached. He did not like the feeling of defencelessness one bit. One quick stab and both he and Aliss would die. *Only a fool turns his back on the bandits of Great Wood.* He could smell the garlic from the bandit's breath, hear his short, sharp intake of breath as he reached around to cover Tomas's eyes with the blindfold. "I know you, king's man. Welcome home."

Tomas wrenched the blindfold free and started to turn around. Too late. Pain exploded inside his head. In a heartbeat, his legs went numb, his arms dropped limply to his sides. Then he fell, crashing headlong into the darkness. *Fool.*

Djangra Roe: Woodvale Monastery

Djangra Roe stared at the dark, stone building sitting on top of the hill. His horse whinnied and stomped its hoof into the spongy earth of the forest floor as a resonant chime echoed from the monastery. Rain misted in the air around him forcing him to drag the hood of his cloak up over his head. With a gentle kick he urged his horse up the narrow track leading to the stout wooden doors. His three men-at-arms followed in single file.

He could not put his finger on why he desired to find this witch so much. There was just something about the way she was rescued from the flames by the mysterious blacksmith that appealed to him. Was she less or more likely to accept his proposal because of it? They were both on the run now; they would be hunted by that fool of a magistrate. It was something he could use as a bargaining tool; offer them enough coin to flee and remain hidden in some sanctuary or other, once they had completed the mission he wished to assign to them. Would they be even capable of tracking and killing the High Priestess of Eor? The dream-witch was a powerful practitioner of magic, in her own subtle way. Her ability to enter a man's dreams and kill him while he slept certainly had Duke Normand on tender hooks, frightened as a small boy of the monsters hiding beneath his bed – sometimes those monsters were real enough.

Either way, if he was to find them he would need to do it soon, before the trail went cold, or even dead altogether. His tracker, Horace had tracked them to this remote monastery. Djangra could not help but marvel at the man's skill. His ability must be born of some form of magic. Even so, he had not the time to puzzle out the way of it. He stopped his horse at the end of the narrow path where it led to the wooden doors of the monastery. There were no symbols or markings that would adorn many temples, in other lands, to denote which of the many deities worshipped across the world this one belonged to. In the Duchies they worshipped the All Father above all other gods. With a simple nod he instructed one of his men to rap on the door.

The door creaked open, pulled back by two grey-robed monks who bowed low, offering respect to an obviously wealthy visitor, to be mounted on such a fine horse and accompanied by three armed men.

"I would speak with whoever holds the highest office here," Djangra said.

"I will fetch the brother abbot immediately, lord," the monk answered.

More monks appeared as if from nowhere with gifts of bread and water, meagre fare, but welcome after hard riding on a long road. Others took the horses off to the stables, while Djangra and his men were led inside the main building. *The god worshipped here is a poor one*, he thought as he was led down a sparsely decorated corridor. He compared it to some of the temples he had been in, *nay*, all of the temples he had been in across the world, and this one was sorely lacking in any appearance or trappings of wealth normally associated with organised religion. Of course, there were many gods in many lands, even those without an appetite for gold, he supposed.

"We are searching for a man and a woman, the woman possibly injured, who came here in the past day or two," he said to the abbot. Again, he could not help but recognise the complete absence of any sign of wealth from the priest. In fact, he could be mistaken for any of his brothers, so similar was the garb he wore to the others. No pomp and ceremony Djangra would normally associate with the head of an order.

Djangra was nothing if not a good reader of men, and the small, bent man in front of him was nervous of his questioning. He fidgeted uneasily in his chair, his eyes darting between the armed men and the mage. His hands gripped the wooden table between them, as if to reinforce the barrier.

"There were two people here, answering that description, but they left soon after their arrival, the night before last," the abbot answered.

"Why did they leave? Was the girl not hurt? And more importantly, where did they go?"

"I do not know. I did not speak with them. Brother Josh..." He stopped suddenly, suspicion clouding his eyes. "Why are you so keen to find them?"

"Brother Josh?" Djangra ignored the monk's question. "What were you about to say about him?" Djangra leaned forward, across the small wooden desk between them. The abbot was a small man, with ill fitting skin wrapped about a thin frame, folds of it gathered at his throat and beneath sunken eyes. His hair sat in thin strands, barely covering the top of his head. He leaned back from the encroaching mage.

The door creaked open, causing the men-at-arms to instinctively reach for the swords strapped to their sides. They relaxed when another monk stepped into the room, his sandals making scuffing noises along the well worn wooden floorboards. "He was about to say they saw me briefly before I sent them along their way."

"Brother Josh?" Djangra stood to greet the newcomer.

"Joshan. I am Brother Joshan." Joshan inclined his head respectfully, even as his eyes took in all four men in a single sweep.

"Where did they go?" Djangra asked, his voice low but laced with unmistakable steel. Joshan standing before him with his arms tucked into the sleeves of his robe simply shrugged. "Tell me, priest. You would not like to see my anger."

"I do not know," Joshan answered.

Djangra began rolling his hands one over the other, the air shifting around him as if his actions were manipulating it. All the while, his eyes never left those of the monk. Suddenly he stretched out an arm towards the abbot who began moving, as if he were being pushed by an invisible hand. When his back was up against the wall behind him he started shifting upwards until his feet were dangling off the ground as he struggled against the unseen force. If Djangra expected to see, fear and awe, astonishment, even a touch of surprise, in the eyes of the other priest, he saw only anger and defiance. If anything, this irritated him more. He raised his other hand and the abbot began choking.

"I can pull his eyes from his head from here," he said.

Anger blazed in the eyes of Joshan as his head snapped up, taking Djangra by surprise. The air in the small room began to crackle and swirl around the priest. The three men-at-arms shifted uneasily where they stood. *Magic!* Djangra realised suddenly. *The old priest is conjuring magic.*

"You dare come here with your threats and demonstrations of power!" Joshan roared above a sound of rushing wind. The noise made Djangra's ears pop, breaking his concentration and the hold he had on the abbot. The old monk slid to the floor, landing in a heap.

Djangra felt a wave of energy hit him, lifting him off his feet and sending him crashing against the wall, to land beside the abbot. The magic-using priest stepped towards him. "I will show you the meaning of power!" he snarled, his eyes blazing. The mage felt the air around begin to heat, becoming uncomfortably hot within a few heartbeats. He tried to summon his own powers. However, magic is often as difficult to grasp as a silver fish swimming in a stream and can be impossible to catch with a bare hand alone. Panic welled inside him. *How could this simple monk possess magic in such strength?* The thought slid into his mind even as he attempted to fight the unseen force pinning him to the wall. He heard a scream then, and realised it was his own, as his skin began to burn. The monk's fingers danced in the air before him as words of power flowed from his mouth. Djangra understood some, but most were incompressible to him. *Who in the name of all the gods is this priest?*

The duke's soldiers circled the priest with swords drawn. The first approached cautiously on the balls of his feet, like a serpent ready to pounce. The monk, who moments before had appeared harmless and frail, snapped around to face the warrior, and with a flick of his wrist hit him with a rippling wave of energy so fierce that the air flashed bright white around him. The warrior slammed against the wall.

Djangra had once used an overhead storm to summon lightning bolts powerful enough to crack the base of an ancient oak tree. He could turn a man into a quivering heap with a word or a thought. He could command flames to leap from a hearth and lash out like a cat o' nine tails. But magic is never an exact science, and requires patience and concentration. At least, that was how it was for him. He knew he was no match for the priest. Even so, he struggled, fought to shake off the energy pinning him to the wall, even as the very air around him burned and cracked.

A second soldier picked up a chair and flung it at the monk, but the missile stopped in mid-air and suddenly burst into flames, before turning and flying back to where it had come from, striking the man-at-arms squarely in the chest. Djangra clawed at the skin on his face as the air around him made him feel as if his eyes were boiling and his flesh were beginning to melt. He screamed, for there was nothing else to do.

And then, his torment stopped. The pain subsided and the roaring in his ears eased. The words of power had ceased and been replaced by another voice.

"Stop! Brother Joshan, cease this madness!" the abbot was shouting at the monk. And the monk listened, and the agony stopped. "Please, Joshan, do not do this." Tears streamed down the abbot's cheeks as he pleaded.

Joshan dropped his hands to his sides and bowed his head. The two men-at-arms rose gingerly to their feet, as Djangra gulped in deep breaths while examining his hands and arms, and gently probing his face. He had never felt such terror in his life. He was sure he would die an agonising death. *It might yet happen,* he thought. Horace, the tracker clearly had similar thoughts going through his mind, as he leapt, dagger in hand, towards the priest. The grey-robed figure didn't move as Horace plunged the blade into his back.

"No!!!" the abbot cried, and rushed to the falling monk. Horace pulled the dagger free and jumped back.

"Fool!" Djangra snarled at the tracker. No one moved.

"Why?" The abbot cradled Joshan's head in his arms as a dark stain swelled across the monk's robe. "He could have killed you all, but he stopped. There was no need."

"I'll make sure," Horace said hesitantly, as if waiting for confirmation.

"No!" the abbot roared. "Go to the valley if you wish to find the people you seek. The man is the blacksmith from a village called Woodvale, and the woman his wife. Go to the valley, you will find no more answers here."

Djangra struggled to his feet and limped over to the monks. "What manner of order are you?" He waved away Horace. "And who is that priest?"

"He is no one," the abbot answered, looking up into Djangra's eyes. The mage simply nodded and led his men out of the abbot's small room, stepping over the stricken Joshan.

Jarl Crawulf: Wind Isle

Crawulf had passed out from the pain pulsing through his injured leg and up his spine. It was not long, however, before he was conscious again. He could feel the harsh bite of driven rain lashing down on him as he was carried between two warriors over the hilly landscape. Each awkward step of the two men sent fresh waves of pain washing over him. He bit his lip hard, tasting blood in his mouth, to prevent himself from crying out, lest he give away that he had returned to consciousness. His captors numbered barely above a dozen, as far as he could tell, and they were in a hurry. It gave him some satisfaction that his dead weight would be slowing them down considerably from whomever they fled. *So why have they not killed me?* It was one of many questions swirling around his brain in a thick fog. He recognised the men for what they were, lordless men, men who placed themselves outside the protection of the law and sold their swords to the highest bidder.

As he sought solace from the pain wracking his body, Crawulf's mind wandered back to the past, to a fair-haired warrior towering over a small, dark-haired boy. To his older brother laughing good-naturedly at his younger sibling as a young Crawulf attempted to look fierce in an over-sized leather byrnie and an iron helmet slipping over his eyes. He had worshipped his older brother, even later when both had grown into manhood and Crawulf was almost a rival to him in all things... almost. His brother had always been the better warrior, the better seaman, but he was impulsive and headstrong. Crawulf had always had a better head for tactics, for politics. His brother

Blood Of Kings: The Shadow Mage 133

inspired men around him, filled their hearts with fierce pride making them want to follow him. Crawulf was a better judge of those hearts and the deceitfulness often as not hidden there. *I would make a better king, brother,* he thought, *but what I would give to have you as one of my jarls.* His older brother was the rightful heir to Wind Isle, and if he yet lived, the closest relative to the king of Nortland, making Crawulf's wish redundant. *What does it matter now anyway?* he thought. For surely he was a dead man.

Shortly after midday they stopped to rest, hidden from sight in a copse of trees. The two men carrying Crawulf set him down none too gently, forcing an involuntary groan from him. Both men cursed the jarl comparing his weight to a number of domesticated farm animals.

"I know you are awake," someone said, speaking in the harsh Nortland tongue.

Crawulf opened one eye to see a face lined with deep crevices, covered in a thick wiry, grey beard. Stains of rust bled into the grey.

"I thought you dead, Erild Kleggsson, yet here you are, alive and hearty," Crawulf answered.

"You know me?" the man asked.

"Aye, well enough. You served on my brother's crew for long enough." Crawulf grimaced as he shifted. Pain shot up his leg.

Erild regarded him with a measure of sympathy in his eyes. "I thought you dead also. We were told you fell from a cliff and were drowned. You were always lucky, Crawulf, favoured by the gods. Wulfgar himself always said it."

Crawulf's eyes narrowed at the sound of his brother's name. "So you have turned traitor and led wolves to my door?" He waited while the other man regarded him with those dark world-weary eyes.

"You think I owe you, or your brother, Crawulf? That I am somehow honour bound to your house?"

"So what then, have you come to claim Wind Isle for yourself?"

"Gods no!" Erild suddenly laughed. "The lure of Nortland has long since lost its appeal for me. These wet, windswept islands can crumble and sink into the sea for all I care. My bones crave sunnier climes with less rain and ice."

"Why then have you brought war to your own people? Why have you returned here with armed men? Do you now hate us also?"

"No, Crawulf, I don't hate you. I loved your brother, even though his pride and arrogance led many men to their doom. Me included. For six years I rotted in a dark dungeon. Six years I did not feel the sun's rays on my face or the gentle touch of a summer's breeze. Six years in the dark with only rats for company. Can you imagine?"

"I don't understand. Where was this dungeon? And what does this have to do with poisoning my wife?" Crawulf's anger began to rise. Was his wife dead as a result of one man's need for vengeance? "This explains nothing."

"They set me free, Crawulf. They opened the door and told me I was free to go. But where could I go after so long? I don't know if they pitied me, or just felt a broken man they'd tortured daily for six years was no longer a threat to them. The rest of the crew, including your brother, had long since abandoned me, leaving me to rot. I asked them to kill me. I did not even care if they put a sword in my hand. I was not thinking of Alweise's feasting halls. I just wanted an end to my miserable existence. But they didn't kill me. They gave me bread, and a new cloak and boots. They spoke to me of their god and bade me embrace him. And do you know what, Crawulf? I did. I opened my heart to the All Father and turned my back on our own gods." He smiled then, even as he wiped tears from his cheek. "And none have struck me down since, even here, where their powers are strongest. What does that tell you?"

"Where... where did my brother lead you?" Crawulf asked through gritted teeth as he felt his rage building inside him.

"The Duchies. That is where my brothers of the sea abandoned me."

"So this," Crawulf spread out his arm to encompass the other men, "is an attack from the Duchies? They have used you to bring war to my home?"

"No, Crawulf." Erild leered as he spoke. "You have enemies from far further afield than the Duchies, powerful enemies with gold. I walked away from that land too, even though they offered me a home and a new god to prostrate myself before. But there were too many bad memories of long days and nights in the dark, deprived of food and water. I had to leave. My travels took me south. I've seen things you wouldn't believe, some I scarce believe myself…"

Crawulf suddenly roared and lunged at Erild. His fist rammed into the face of the other man sending him sprawling backwards, but when Crawulf attempted to follow, his leg gave away, and he fell screaming to the earth. Within moments he was dragged up by the two men who had earlier carried him. They forced him back down with fists and kicks from booted feet. Crawulf snarled and screamed, but injured as he was, was no match for them. "You dishonour my brother's memory!" he roared, even though his wounded leg now felt as if it was aflame. "You are a coward and a traitor, Erild Kleggsson!"

"Your brother led three score men to their doom because he thought he was an equal to the gods, who could not be defeated in battle no matter the odds. Men followed him because they believed it too!" Erild roared back as he picked himself up. Spittle sprayed from his mouth as he lashed Crawulf with his words. "And you… you are far too clever for your own good, Crawulf! Want to know why I'm here? Why I paid men gold to poison your food and storm your castle? Do you want to know why your life is now forfeit and why your body will be dumped into the sea once we've escaped this cursed island?" Crawulf glared at the man, but remained silent. "You are as arrogant as your brother, only his foolhardiness led a crew and its ship to a fate worse than death, yours will destroy an entire land." Erild dropped to his knees to be on a level with Crawulf, their faces inches apart. "The Duchies were ever wary of us, frightened of when we might raid their costal towns or attack a lone trading vessel. They'd wipe us out if they could, but an all-out war would be far too costly for them. So, they patrol their seas with warships and build garrison around the coast to look out for when we raid. It has become a game for both of us. Sometimes we will slip by their defences and carry of whatever spoils we can lay our hands on, and sometimes they will catch us, as happened with me. But you, you are not playing the game by the accepted rules. You want to make up your own game. You married the daughter of the Emperor of Sunsai. The Duchies' greatest rival and their worst fear. They can barely sleep at night for fear that hordes of desert warriors will one day rampage from the south and pour over the mountains. And now, you, the most likely heir to the throne of all Nortland have made their nightmares come true. Your son will be the emperor's grandson. You have changed this game forever. You have stumbled into a nest of vipers you did not even know were there." He sat back onto his haunches then, breathing in deep breaths.

"Is my brother dead?" Crawulf asked, meeting the hard stare of the other man.

"Had they cut off his head and fed his body to their pigs, it would have been a kinder fate. You will not find him feasting with the gods in Alweise's hall when you go there. I will see that you do not suffer the same fate, Crawulf. When you die it will be with a sword in your hands. I'll do that in memory of your brother."

"I will kill you first," Crawulf said with icy steel in his words.

"I can understand your hatred, Crawulf. You see my actions as a betrayal. It is, but it is nothing personal. With me it is just about the gold," Erild answered as he pushed himself to his feet.

"Oh but it is, Erild. It is very personal, for you, for these men you hired to ransack my home, to kill my wife, and those who paid you. I will rain down fire on them like they have never known. Blood will flow like rivers."

"Big words, Crawulf, but you will see no vengeance, least not in this lifetime. It saddens me that your brother will not be in the feasting halls of the gods to greet you when you die, but die you will."

"Aye, all men die," Crawulf answered, "but I will not die this day."

Erild smiled then. "You really are arrogant bastards, your family."

"Look," Crawulf said, indicating with a nod the crest of a hill in the distance, barely visible as rain misted the atmosphere. Suddenly men were scrambling to their feet. Crawulf smiled as the rattle of weapons and armour and men barking orders filled the air. A second, smaller man and horse appeared behind the first.

"Riders," one man announced needlessly and received a scornful look from Erild who had seen them himself already.

"How many men have you here, Erild? Little more than a dozen," he answered his own question. "Barely enough to crew a single ship. There were many, many more in your raiding party. I saw them for myself. Where are they now? Scattered throughout Wind Isle? Fleeing from my men? Or are they dead, Erild?"

"What of it? We have what we came for," he answered irritably, his eyes remaining on the riders on the hill. "Your death, Crawulf, and that of your wife, that is my prize." He swung around towards the jarl of Wind Isle.

"That you have not killed me thus far tells me that you are scared, scared of being hunted and caught. You're keeping me alive to bargain with. You have wasted your time. Do you know who that is out there?"

"Tell me, Crawulf. Tell me who those two lone men are out there who you think will save you."

Crawulf pushed himself up, aware that the two men standing over him stepped back as he did so. When he stood he was a full head taller than the other man. "That is Rothgar Rothsson. I doubt there is a man among you who has not heard his name, or heard tales of his deeds. I've seen him split men in two with a single blow from that axe he carries." Crawulf smiled without humour.

"He is still only one man, Crawulf."

"You think where Rothgar Rothsson is my war-band is not far behind?" He could feel the tension rise in the men around him. "And you will call me jarl!" He raised his voice, causing Erild to take a step backwards.

"You know what? You are right," he said, turning to one of his men. "Kill him. He is slowing us down. Take his head and we'll make a run for the ship." The familiar rasping sound of a sword sliding from a sheath made Crawulf turn his attention to the warrior, before swinging back to face Erild.

"Rothgar Rothsson is not the one who will save me this day, although I dare say he would cut a bloody path through your bedraggled band."

"I tire of this, Crawulf." He indicated to his man to proceed.

Crawulf continued as if Erild had not spoken. "These men here, this not so loyal band of cutthroats and swords-for-hire will save me. Because that is exactly what they are, swords for sale to the highest bidder, and I have plenty of coin. Can you read the hearts of men such as these?" He turned then to face the two men who had carried him from the fisherman's cottage. "None of you will leave Wind Isle alive... unless..."

"Kill him!" Erild raised his voice, but his words fell on deaf ears as nobody moved. Erild spat a curse at them and drew his sword.

Crawulf didn't move as the shorter man raised his sword and swung towards his head. Nor did he flinch as the blade arced through the air towards him. He would have no man tell a tale of how the great Crawulf of Wind Isle backed down in the face of his death. He tensed as he braced for the impact... that never came. With a ringing clang another blade deflected the one aimed at his head. Suddenly there was a scuffle and Erild was jostled to the ground by his own men. He screamed and cursed as he was forced to his knees before Crawulf.

One of the men who had carried the jarl bowed his head and handed him a sword, Crawulf's own sword. "Jarl Crawulf," he said as he extended the weapon, hilt first.

"For the sake of my brother whose crew you were once a part of, Erild, I will allow you to die with honour and a sword in your hand, even if you have turned your back on your gods. Let the All Wise judge you."

"You don't know who your enemies are, Crawulf, or how powerful they are."

"So tell me, redeem yourself before you die," the jarl said.

Erild shook his head and laughed bitterly. "I'd sooner die here than betray that one. The day you married, Crawulf, you invited a very dark guest into your life. You will know soon enough."

And die he did. He took no joy in the death, nor in Erild's betrayal by his own men, mercenaries whose loyalty was so easily bought. The payment they would receive would be one fitting to their double betrayal and not the reward they envisaged in their greedy hearts. When Rothgar rode up to the clutch of trees Crawulf saw that his companion was the fisherman's youngest son. His heart was gladdened that the boy had survived, even if his life was now forever changed.

He nodded a greeting to his giant housecarl, aware at the ripple of anxiety coming from the waiting mercenaries. "My wife?"

"She lives," Rothgar answered as he clambered down from his horse to help Crawulf. He did not comment on his jarl's smile as he helped him up onto his own horse and took the reins to lead the injured jarl back to his castle. The fisherboy and Erild's unreliable men followed in their wake.

Tomas: The Great Wood

Tomas woke disorientated and with a pounding head and a nauseous stomach. An orange glow coming from a firepit in the centre of a small hut threw out a faint light filling the small space with thick smoke. An involuntary groan escaped his lips as he sat up, pain washing over his throbbing head. His first thought was for Aliss.

In the gloom he could make out walls made from mud daubed over a wooden frame. Loose reeds coated the floor, and, bound tightly together formed a thatch over the low roof above him. He noticed his sword lying on the ground beside him. This surprised him, but made him no less wary. He was alone. A piercing wail made him pause, a shriek from some sort of animal, a cat perhaps. As he listened intently, the main door of the dwelling suddenly swung inwards, making him jump and fumble for his sword.

The bandit who had hit him over the head stepped in, carrying a plate of what looked like bread and roast meat. The smells drifting towards him and the involuntary rumble from his stomach confirmed his suspicion. "Relax. I've brought you some food," the man said.

"Where is my woman?"

"She is with Haera," the brigand replied, and offered the plate of food to Tomas. "Sit. Eat. She will summon you when she is ready."

With the door open, Tomas could see that night had fallen and outside was a blanket of darkness. He could also hear the wailing of the animal more clearly now. An animal of sorts, he realised, for surely what he was hearing were the cries of a baby. Confusion reigned as he cautiously took the plate from the outstretched hand. "If she has come to any harm…"

"She's in no worse condition than when you brought her here, leastwise, not by any hand of ours. She's not far from death as it is." Tomas scowled at the brigand as he sat back down and began tearing chunks off the bread. "No hard feelings about, eh…" The brigand indicated Tomas' head. "We couldn't just let you walk in here. I remember you. I knew Haera would want me to bring you to her."

The meat was venison, succulent and delicious. Tomas mopped the grease with the bread. "You have other women here?" he enquired as he crammed the food into his mouth.

"Just Haera."

"But I heard a baby crying," Tomas said.

The brigand shrugged. "Haera often has… requests."

Realisation dawned as Tomas remembered the missing baby from the village. "What need would the old crone have for a baby?"

"If you know her, and I think you do, then you know that some questions are better off not voiced."

There were numerous bandit gangs using the Great Wood as a base, Tomas knew, but all of them would seek out Haera, the Forest Witch, as she was known, if they were in need of her unique abilities, oft as not looking for a potion or unction to kill as well as heal. His band of villains, long disbanded, were no different.

"I don't know you. How is it you know me?"

"I've been with Haera a long time now. You were ever one of her favourites."

"Hmmm," Tomas snorted, "she had a strange way of showing it."

"Aye well, she has her own ways." He turned and walked to the entrance then. "Rest, she will send for you when she is ready. She is with your woman now." With that he was gone.

Tomas finished his meal and lay back on the wooden-framed cot. From his recollections of the old woman he knew there was little point in forcing the issue, as he was told, when she was ready she would send for him. It was unwise to antagonise or press her. She possessed a power he did not understand; even Joshan had been wary of her and the dark magic she was capable of. Sleep did not come, however, as both his mind and heart ached to be with Aliss.

Later that night the brigand returned and indicated for Tomas to follow him. No words were necessary, and the blacksmith leapt up eagerly. He was led to another dwelling, much like the one he had just left. The two men entered slowly. A thick pungent odour hung heavily in the air, so thick he could feel it cloying the back of his throat, while the sound of an infant crying pierced his hearing. The strong scent was both sickly and intoxicating at the same time, making his head swim the moment the door was closed behind him. A fire burned in a pit at the centre of the dwelling, adding its own peaty fragrance to the mix. Tomas blinked away the grogginess threatening to overwhelm his senses.

"I did not think to see you again," a voice cackled from the gloom of the hut.

Tomas saw a pile of fur and vegetation move from the shadows to stand erect in the centre of the room. He realised the apparition was the old woman dressed in animal hides and wearing a crown of leaves on her head of long grey hair. The flames from the fire spread her flickering shadow across the floor and up the wall. He quickly scanned the rest of the dark room and located Aliss, almost hidden beneath a shaggy fleece. He ran to her side, while the old woman cooed and clucked at the wailing baby.

"Your woman has not long left in this world; she will soon join her baby."

"Baby?" Tomas swung around to look at the old woman who had now picked up the infant from its crib.

"You didn't know? She was with child, but there is no life left in that which is inside her. The torment suffered by the mother was too much for the unborn babe to bear."

Tomas felt a lump rising in his throat as he turned back to his horribly injured woman. He shook his head; his words came out broken and cracked, "No... I didn't know."

"What is it you want of me?"

"Help her," he simply answered.

She turned her back on him as she bounced the baby in her arms, whispering soothing words into its small ear. Tomas waited for her to answer. She said nothing for a long while until she finally turned back to face him, absent-mindedly stroking the baby's hand. "Do you know what you ask?"

"Yes."

"I do not think you do." He followed her gaze towards the babe in her arms. "She is beyond the help of man. There is only one way to save your woman now, blood magic, the darkest of all arts, and it comes with a price. Are you capable of bearing that price?"

Tomas looked into her dark eyes as the fire steamed and hissed beside her. The baby began crying again, adding to the noise of a beating drum banging inside his head. His eyes watered from the heavy, spicy air in the hut and knowledge that he may lose the lives of two and not just the one. The old witch's words reverberated through his mind. *'She was with child – the babe no longer lives…'* "Yes," he answered.

"And what are you willing to pay?" she cackled as she stroked the baby's cheek with a long, bony finger.

"Anything. Including my life, if it is your wish to take it."

"It may be that it will be the price I ask, young knight." She displayed blackened teeth as her mouth formed a smile.

"So be it," he answered, refusing to rise to her taunt. It was a long time since he served in the Royal Guard, making him neither a knight nor the young man he once was.

"You may keep it for now." Her smile widened, looking more like a grimace in her worn, wrinkled face. "Do not deny my prize for an instant when I do call or I will seek the return of the gift I bestow." Tomas nodded his agreement. "Now leave me!" She turned her back to him then and returned to clucking at the baby.

As Tomas reached for the door the infant began wailing once again, a terrible high-pitched screech. Tomas stopped and tensed as the cry was suddenly cut off. He exited the dwelling without looking back. The old woman's words echoed in his mind as he stepped outside into the darkness and the earthy smell of the forest, in contrast to the suffocating stuffiness of the old woman's hut. *'Are you capable of bearing that price?'* An image of Marjeri's face came unbidden to him then, as she pleaded with the men of the village to find her baby, supposedly snatched by wolves. *Aye, kidnapped by wolves right enough, but wolves walking on two feet, and far more dangerous than any wild animal.* Overhead a light flashed across the sky followed by a thunderclap signalling the coming rain. Tomas barely felt the downpour even as it became torrential in an instant. He forced down his guilt and shame, and focused on his woman, Aliss, but a scar etched into a soul is not so easily dismissed.

"Hey, you there! Is your mind addled? Come out of the rain." It was the brigand. Tomas turned to the sound of his voice and realised his vision was blurred. He had not noticed when his own tears began. "Why are you just standing there? Have your wits deserted you?" The forest outlaw took his arm and led him back to the hut he had woken in. "Wait here," he said and ducked out of the entrance. Moments later he returned carrying, under his arm, a small wooden keg with a tap at one end. "Mandarian Brandy!" He beamed, also producing two pewter goblets. "We confiscated a wagonload of this stuff last winter when a convoy passed through the wood. A fair tax to allow the rest of them through." He laughed.

Tomas just looked at him blankly. His body was shivering now; he knew it was not just from the cold and the drenching. He could hear the rain assaulting the thatch overhead. The bandit banked up the fire and then poured two generous goblets of brandy, handing one to the blacksmith.

"Is it true then?"

"Is what true?" Tomas said irritably, before downing a good swallow of the brandy. It burned as it slid down, warming him from the inside, almost melting the knot of dread gripping his stomach.

"Oh by the gods this stuff is good, like honey with the kick of a mule." The brigand laughed. "Is it true that you were once a knight in the Royal Guard? I'm Rolf by the way." He beamed a grin at Tomas.

"I was never a knight, but it's true. I served in the Royal Guard... once upon a time. My name is Tomas."

"Pleased to make your acquaintance, Tomas." Rolf stood and bowed theatrically before offering his hand. Tomas took it, with little enthusiasm and shook limply.

"So how did you end up here? You were quite notorious for a while. Even the other gangs operating in the wood feared you. To be honest, we thought you were dead when you disappeared."

"The gods like their jests, and when my path through life was predestined it came with more than one twist."

"So it would seem, my friend. Here, drink. I'll warrant you'd not find as good as this even in the king's hall."

It was very fine brandy, Tomas grudgingly accepted, and held out his cup for a refill. Rolf continued to chatter, and with the drink to ease his burden, Tomas found the brigand an amiable enough companion, even if he did hit him over the head on their first meeting. He spoke of the harsh realities of life as a commoner raised to a king's chosen warrior, though made no mention of Joshan's involvement there, and how quickly the aristocracy are prepared to snatch back gifts they bestow when it comes to protecting their own. He laughed with Rolf as he talked about his brief career as a bandit of the Great Wood, and some of the characters known mutually to the two men. He talked a lot more than he would have liked had the brandy not flowed so freely and had Rolf not made an entertaining drinking companion.

When he woke, his head pounded and his stomach churned. Rolf was passed out on a mattress stuffed with leaves on the other side of the dwelling, the empty cask discarded on the floor beside him. Tomas swore and pushed himself up. His mouth and throat were parched, and each movement sent a fresh wave of pain through his head. Silently, he cursed the drunken bandit and himself for being an idiot with a loose tongue. Outside, spears of sunlight broke through the trees dappling the clearing with bright light. Tomas could see now that there were several similar sized dwellings huddled together and ringed with a defensive ditch, although he doubted any sort of determined attack would be even remotely delayed by the not-so-deep moat.

As he squinted in the direction of the old witch's hut, using his hand to shade his eyes, a figure emerged from the darkness. Tomas froze, a lump rose in his throat. *Aliss*, her name formed on his lips but was snatched away by the early morning breeze before he could voice it. She saw him then and started to run towards him. He wanted to meet her, but his legs would not move. All of her hair had been burned off by the pyre, her skin horribly burned and scarred. Now though, although her hair had still not grown back, all of her other injuries appeared healed. There was not a blemish on her skin. Tears ran down his cheeks as she leapt at him. Encircling her with his arms, he buried his head in her shoulder muffling his sobs.

"Tomas!"

"Am I dreaming?" he finally said. "You are well and whole again." He started to laugh uncontrollably. She just smiled back, a curious look on her face.

"What has happened, Tomas? I have no memory of how we come to be here. Why are we not at home?"

"Oh, love, it is as well you do not remember. I pray those memories never return."

Suddenly she cried out in pain and doubled over. When Tomas looked down he saw a swelling stain of red spread across her dress. She screamed and collapsed into his arms as Haera hobbled up to them. "The babe," the old witch said. "Bring her inside."

Tomas was ushered back outside by the old crone once he laid her on the bed. As he left, his eyes lingered on the empty cradle. He waited at the entrance for most of the morning, listening to the tortured cries of his woman coming from within. Eventually Haera beckoned him in. "All is done," she said, nodding her head up and down. "She no longer carries the dead child."

"Our baby," Aliss whispered weakly.

Tomas knelt by her side, "I know." They were the only words he could bring himself to say. He stroked her forehead and cheek, marvelling at the transformation. The gods only had one miracle to bestow that day.

"I wish to return home," Aliss said after two days of rest.

Tomas stared at her, unsure how to proceed. He took her hand in his own, much bigger one. "We cannot, love. We can never return there." She made no reply, simply dropped her head, sadness evident in her eyes. A barely perceptible nod told him that she had already accepted this, even if she still had no memory of the reasons why.

"Where shall we go?"

Tomas shrugged and shook his head. "I know not."

"I know," Haera, who had been hovering behind the blacksmith, cackled. "I know, I know, I know."

Suddenly light pooled at the entrance as the door was flung open. A well dressed, middle-aged man with a trimmed beard and shoulder length grey hair stood there. "My name is Djangra Roe, and I am in need of a witch!"

"That is no business of mine," Tomas answered, glancing at Haera.

"A young one, capable of following a trail of magic," Djangra said as he walked into the hut, "with a protector by her side." He walked up to Aliss, who struggled into a sitting position, smiled before taking her hand and brushing his lips against it. "I can sense a darkness in your soul," he said to her, his smile broadening. "Perfect."

"What is it you would have us do?" Tomas asked.

"Find somebody for me, and kill them." Djangra turned to face the blacksmith.

"Begone from here. I am nobody's assassin!" Tomas responded angrily.

"This is my price!" Haera interjected suddenly. "You swore! Pay the price or the blood magic will unravel." Her eyes glowed in the firelight.

Tomas rubbed at his temples, aware of Aliss staring at him in confusion. He felt like a hare stuck in the hunter's snare. "Who is it you would have us kill?"

"You have heard of the Priestess of Eor?" Djangra smiled.

"Have you lost your wits? The dream witch?" Tomas glared at Djangra.

"I see that you have. This task requires somebody with magic in their blood to find her, and the heart of a killer to complete the deed. I think I have found them."

"This is my price! This is my price!" The old witch hopped on two feet behind Djangra.

"And then what?" Aliss spoke for the first time.

"What would you like?" The mage turned back to face her.

"We have no home, no place to go…"

"I have powerful friends who can help you build a new life, away from any transgressions of the past."

"No," Tomas stated resolutely.

"I can do it," Aliss said.

"Yes, yes, yes." Haera beamed from behind them.

"My three men-at-arms will accompany you and offer any assistance necessary."

"Begone from here now," Tomas growled at Djangra.

Aliss' eyes narrowed as she appeared to look off into the distance. "Yes," she simply said.

PART II

Jarl Crawulf: Seafort, the Duchies

The folk living near the costal town of Seafort had become used to raids from the Nortland pirates over the years. Countless generations had suffered at the hands of the Nortmen. They had learned to build a stout wall of stone around their town, and when the dark, sleek ships emerged from the morning mist, they would sound the alarm and flee, with whatever possessions they could carry, to the fortified town. There they would wait out the storm of pillaging Nortmen until they grew tired of torching empty farmsteads, or the duke arrived with his men-at-arms and chased them back to the sea. Never would the raiders attempt to attack the garrisoned town, with high walls and reinforced doors made from the strongest oak… until now.

Crawulf had a fire raging inside him, fuelled by the thirst for vengeance, a need to lash out at those who had sent warriors to his door and poison into his wife's food. But he did not know who they were or where they came from. He did not even know why they had attacked him. He cursed himself over and over for rashly killing Erild without bleeding him dry of whatever he knew. In the meantime the company of lordless men who had attacked his stronghold after luring him from the safety of its walls had weakened his position in the race to succeed his uncle as king. The men of Nortland were hard, uncompromising men. They would never follow a leader who was weak, and allowing a bunch of swords-for-hire to assault your castle and almost murder your wife was not a sign of strength. So, he needed a big gesture. He needed to reassert his claim as the best man to become king of Nortland when his uncle died.

When the men of Nortland went raiding, it was usually in small groups, with three or four ships. With their shallow hulls they could run right up onto the beach having traversed vast oceans or sail up a river to penetrate deep into the territory of their victims. Raiders were what they were, getting in and out quickly, often leaving devastated communities in their wake.

The fleet that darkened the early morning horizon, emerging out of the huge emptiness of the Nort Sea, as the sun first cast its rays into an equally vast, empty sky, was a hundred and more ships in strength. Far too many for the shepherds, who first spied them from their vantage point on a cliff rising out of the sea, to count on all of their fingers even if they put them together. Those ships carried hard men, hungry for war and spoils, and supplies to mount a lengthy campaign. Crawulf was going to war, and his men were a tempest feeding off his hatred and anger. They laid waste to the surrounding countryside, burning isolated homes and poorly defended settlements— usually abandoned by the time they got there—torching the fields and homes of the fleeing folk. Any slow-moving refugees or brave folk willing to put up a fight they killed or raped before moving on destroying and devouring all in their path.

Every Nortman dreamed of a glorious death in battle, for without such there would be no eternal afterlife feasting in the halls of the gods; no glory at Alweise's side in his eternal struggle against his enemies. Each man took to raiding and warring with relish.

"It will take time to bring down that gate," a man clad in mail and holding a double-bladed axe in one hand said to Crawulf as they watched a group of warriors assault the reinforced wooden door with a crudely made battering ram, while others did their best to protect them with upraised shields from a selection of missiles raining down on them from the walls. Crawulf's own archers sent wave after wave of arrows at the defenders to deter them and make them duck for cover. Meanwhile more warriors used wooden ladders and ropes with grapple hooks to attack the wall in various locations, an effort to spread thin the defences inside. He watched as one man was bludgeoned by a heavy piece of masonry thrown two-handed from the top of the wall. The assailant, in turn, toppled from his lofty perch, pierced in the chest by three arrows. A warrior rushed from the waiting ranks to take up the place of the downed man.

"There!" another man shouted, pointing to a section of the wall where several Nortmen had made it to the top and were now fighting hand to hand on the rampart.

"Send more men to help them," Crawulf growled, as he watched his warriors clamber like ants up rickety ladders. At the same time a loud crack came from the direction of the wooden door. A flicker of a smile touched the corner of Crawulf's mouth before he pulled his iron helmet on and drew his sword from its leather scabbard. A satisfying crash and a cloud of dust signalled the destruction of the main door into the town. All the while more and more snarling Nortmen made the top of the wall.

As Crawulf advanced on the town, with the vast majority of his war-band formed into ranks, with their round wooden shields held before them, they were met by a much smaller shield-wall. This is where the men of Nortland excelled, in the butchery of hand-to-hand combat. They were not comfortable at laying siege to towns or assaulting castles, but with a sword or axe in hand and an enemy before them their hearts sang. And why wouldn't it when waiting for them, after they fell in battle, was the eternal reward of The All Wise. The jarl of Wind Isle was no different to the rest of his men. He had a formidable reputation as a fighter and relished the rush each new battle gave him. *Was there a better way to feel alive but in the midst of the savagery of battle?*

Locking shields with the men either side of him, he signalled for the line to move forward, the gates to the town now hung from broken hinges, leaving a yawning gap for the Nortmen to go through. Waiting beyond the thick cloud of dust was treasure, and women. Once the defence had been beaten into submission the real pain would begin. Arrows and stones fired from slingshots bounced off his shield and mail armour, not all were as lucky, the screams hanging in the air were testament to the skill of the archers on the wall. Each gap was quickly filled by another though, and the line moved steadily toward the town.

The defenders, made up of townsfolk, farmers from the surrounding countryside and a poorly trained militia, emerged slowly from the town. The Nortmen banged their wooden shields with their swords and axes while they hurled insults at the wavering line before them. As valiant and defiant the townsfolk were, they were not trained warriors; even if they were, the sight of so many snarling, fearsome Nortmen baying for their blood, would likely as not ended in the same result. Barely had the attack begun when the enemy line broke and ran. Crawulf led the advance, cutting down with a single stroke, a boy barely old enough to shave. His sightless eyes stared blankly at the sky as his body was trampled into the mud by the heavy boots of the men following their jarl. Crawulf slashed at another as the frightened defender turned from the advancing Nortmen. He screamed as he too fell forward into the dirt, his killer barely registering his existence.

Once they passed through the gate and into the town all was chaos. The raiders who had already made it over the wall had begun setting fire to the thatched roofs and dwellings made from wood. Thick, choking smoke hung heavy over the town while the stench of blood and worse filled the air. The heat from the burning buildings made breathing unbearable as people screamed and ran this way and that seeking an escape. There would be none for most of the folk of Seafort, who had wrongly thought themselves safe behind their stout walls of stone. The cries of women rang out, hauled to the ground and violated where they lay, while their men were butchered wherever they were found. Small children stood amidst the carnage, blank expressions on their faces as their young minds grappled with the destruction around them. Once the fight was gone from the townsfolk the real suffering began. For them their town had become The Hag's fiery Pit, where The All Father had abandoned them. The raider's blood was afire with lust for women and violence, having fought their way into the town, watched many of their brethren fall beneath the walls, now was the time of retribution on the defenders.

Crawulf stood by a well at the centre of the town square. Cupping his hands, he dipped them into the cool water and brought them to his lips. Fighting in a shield-wall was thirsty business, even without the raging fires all around him. Even to trained fighting men, carrying a heavy wooden shield on one arm and swinging or stabbing with axe or blade in the other, was tiring work. After a few mere heartbeats the muscles of arm and back would begin to burn, as the mail-clad warrior hacked his way through battle. His legs would ache, his head throb from the rush of blood and the fear of dying. Men had their own way of coping with the pain and fear, Crawulf knew. Some drank before a battle to dull the senses and give them courage, others prayed to their gods. Some, though they were rare, became consumed with battle-rage, often seeming to grow physically, would attack with devastating savagery, and with no thought to their own defence. These men both instilled fear in the enemy and inspired their own brothers. *Rare is it to see a man succumb to the rage of a berserker.*

"Jarl Crawulf." A Nortman approached Crawulf, his face darkened by dirt and dried blood, splashes of crimson covered his mail shirt and drawn sword. "Here are what's left of the town elders. They attempted to escape through a hidden door in the wall as we broke through the main gate. They would have made good their escape had they not been so laden down with boxes of treasure." The warrior dumped several wooden boxes onto the earth, to emphasise his point. Crawulf saw silver coins and trinkets of gold spill onto the ground.

He regarded a sorry collection of townsfolk with narrowed eyes. "Nail them to the walls so that all who pass this town will bear witness to their cowardice," he said coldly, ignoring the pleas for mercy, and when none came, the sobbing.

Crawulf gave his men full rein to make the citizens of Seafort suffer through the night, before calling a halt once the sun began to rise over the still burning town. Any who were still left alive, mainly young women and children, were chained together in a long line and marched slowly back towards the fleet of ships waiting beyond the beach.

"How long before they arrive do you think?" a chosen man called Olf asked Crawulf as they stood watching the weeping line of new slaves, linked by chain around their necks.

"If he comes with just his knights and men-at-arms, tomorrow or the day after."

"But he will not come with just his warriors," Olf replied.

"No. He will not. He will gather an army to face us, it will take time to call in the peasants from the fields." Crawulf looked inland towards the rolling hills and patchwork fields of tended crops stretching into the distance.

"They will be too many for us when they do come."

"Yes," Crawulf agreed.

"Perhaps we could mend the gates…"

"You would fight behind those walls, Olf?" Crawulf asked, a hint of amusement in his eyes.

"No, of course not!" The Nortman was aghast. Crawulf laughed.

"Once the treasure and thralls are loaded, give the order for the ships to pull back from the coast, out of harm's way. In the meantime we'll see if we can't force Duke Elsward's hand." Crawulf grinned.

Duke Normand: Mountains of Eor

Duke Normand absent-mindedly soothed his horse by cooing in its ear and patting the beast's muscular neck. He was rewarded with a snort and the stomping of hooves on the cobbled street as a caravan of traders, compiled of ox-drawn carts filed past. It gave him enormous pleasure to see the wagons, piled high with goods from the south, pass through the gates of Eorotia. Now that the mountain passes had been made safe and cleared of brigands, just as Djangra Roe had predicted, the traffic travelling between the Duchies and the lands to the south had begun to trickle through. In time it would increase and generate substantial wealth for the small duchy of Lenstir – assuming Normand could hold onto it.

"This is the third caravan in a week," Djangra Roe said.

"The taxes they bring in barely cover the upkeep of guarding the road," Normand grumbled, unwilling to concede acknowledgment to Djangra's foresight. The mage simply shrugged and made no further comment.

The past months had been busy for Normand. The taking of Eorotia had made a lot of people around him nervous. The king fretted that it would be seen as an act of aggression by the lands south of the mountain range all the way to the Sunsai Empire, although Duke Normand thought it none of their damn business. His neighbouring nobles were anxious that he was becoming too ambitious and were wary of him encroaching on their own territory. They were right. Lenstir was one of the smallest duchies in the kingdom. Normand was intent on overseeing its growth, and the potential wealth of Eorotia becoming a trade hub between north and south would aid him greatly in this desire.

First he needed to rebuild the walls he himself had knocked down with his siege engines, fend off those who would have the Thieves Citadel returned to a so-called neutral faction and become a buffer between north and south, calm the insecurities of a nervous monarch—one lacking in ambition as far as Normand was concerned—root out whatever brigands still using the mountain as a haven, and wipe out the threat from the man-like beasts who, supposedly, inhabited the higher regions of the mountains. Normand had never seen these monsters himself and doubted their existence, but there were many sightings of them wandering down from the colder regions in search of food, including a reported attack on a caravan three days previously. A wagon driver was supposedly ripped limb from limb before the beast was chased away by the convoy's guards. Waiting with the Duke and his men were his hunting hounds, huge shaggy creatures capable of great bursts of speed and jaws seemingly made from iron.

"What news, Mage of your witch?"

Djangra's smile wilted. "Nothing, my lord, these past months. I am thinking that is not such a bad thing though."

"Your thoughts could cost us everything… cost *me* everything!"

"They are on her trail. Had they been thwarted and killed I would have heard. Trust me, my lord, the dream-witch is no threat to you while she is being hunted halfway to the empire."

"I hope you are right. I do not trust your witch and her rogue knight, but at least they have three of my men with them to keep their minds focused."

"He was never a knight, my lord."

"Whatever he was, I hope you chose well."

"Oh yes, they are all well suited to the job." Djangra met Normand's stern gaze. "Happy hunting, my lord."

"It is not too late for you to come," Normand said.

"No, my lord, these old bones are no longer suited to such an arduous expedition." The mage looked up, beyond the walls of Eorotia and towards the snow-capped peaks of the jagged mountains, to where the spring thaw never touched and one misplaced step could send a man tumbling to a cold, lonely death. "Besides there is work that must be done here to rid the city of any remaining charms and curses left by the witches of Eor."

"Very well, Mage, happy hunting to you also." Normand led a line of a dozen mounted, fighting-men, riding two abreast, their red cloaks fluttering in the breeze, followed by half a score of the great shaggy hunting hounds, barely contained by their handlers, and in turn by a small group of lightly armoured archers. Among them were men who had lived and hunted, much of their lives, in the mountains. They would lead Normand towards the high peaks, where travellers rarely ventured, and any with half an ounce of sense steered well clear of, as any man who lived in the shadow of the great mountain range knew well, there were things best left undisturbed where man rarely travelled.

Normand glanced back at the city he was now master of, with its walls gleaming in autumnal light, and the mountains rising up behind it, a ragged line shading a clear blue sky, his thoughts racing from one idea to the next on how best to build and fortify his new possession, and indeed, how to add to it. The small column was soon swallowed up by trees cloaked in orange and plum coloured leaves. Twice as many again lay in clumps on the worn track, used as a road through the forest, or swirled about their feet, blown in a chill wind.

There were few travellers passing through the forest, but there were some, which pleased Normand to see. They scurried off the road to make way for mounted warriors, but the duke could read little resentment on their faces, and some even smiled at the sight of armed men appearing to patrol the woods. It would mean a safer journey for them, making them more than happy to give way if it meant a visible deterrent to the bandits who once claimed the forest for their own.

"We should make camp up at Widow's Keep, my lord," one of the foresters accompanying the duke and his men suggested. "If you don't mind havin' her ghost for company that is." He grinned.

Normand turned away from the sight of blackened teeth leering in a dirt-covered face. The wind sent a chill through him at that moment, making him pull his cloak tighter about him. He noticed the air had become colder the higher they got, and the deeper into the forest the steeper the winding road became. He had even seen flakes of snow drift down between the trees only to dissolve on impact. "This Widow's Keep is an old ruin, is it not?"

"Aye, my lord, a castle belongin' to those who disappeared long ago," the scout answered.

"Very well, it will give us shelter for the night." He motioned with a wave of his hand for the forester to lead on.

Light was already fading from the sky when they approached the ruin. Widow's Keep was in fact a tower castle with only three remaining walls. The fourth had collapsed long before, with the stone harvested by local folk to build walls and small cottages. A stone staircase spiralled up the side of one wall, the steps uneven and different sizes, an old trick to make life difficult for any would-be invaders. All interior walls and any wooden features, such as floors or rafters were long gone. Normand looked up at the ragged line on top of the three remaining walls, a dark scar in the twilit sky.

They made campfires in the shadow of the ruin, using the walls to shield them from the cold winds blowing down from the ice-capped mountains. They sat around the fires according to class and hierarchy, the dog-handlers huddled together with the big shaggy hounds close by. The archers made sure their strings were dry and protected as they settled in for the night, humming a tune known only to themselves. The warriors sat together checking their weapons and gear, sharpening swords and axes. Normand stared into the flames of a fire he shared with the two most senior men he had brought on the expedition, their words drifting over his consciousness as he felt the glow of the flames warming his face, and the inner fire garnered from the fortified wine he swigged from a flask. Only the woodsmen seemed at ease as they laughed and shared stories, passing skins of wine between them to chase away the night chill. The duke wrapped his fur-trimmed cloak tightly around his shoulders, listening to their tales.

"She were a maid, wed and widowed all in one day," one such story began. "It were a time long before the Duchies were called the Duchies, a time when folk were different... wilder. It is said a great king ruled these mountains and beyond, and his castle were Widow's Keep, only it weren't called Widow's Keep then.

"Her beauty was beyond compare. Thick curls, dark as a raven's wing fell down to her waist, and skin so fair it was almost translucent. Her eyes were the colour of a mountain spring in morning sunlight, her lips like ruby red wine. Some said she had ensnared the king with dark magic, others, that her beauty alone was enough to trap any man. The morning of her wedding, when she was presented to the king, dressed in an ivory gown and with her hair tied up in a crown of flowers, every man present at the feast felt a pang of envy, their thoughts turning to the luck of the king and the night he would look forward to, for what man would not wish to spend a night with such a beauty?

"It were the king's ill luck to cross a powerful witch he had lain with and uttered false promises to after he'd met his lady. He were no noble lord this king, and took his pleasures where he willed; the witch cursed him, for it were her desire to be his bride, and not some foreign beauty from beyond the mountain. She put a hex on him that his line would end with him. And that it did, for as he lay on top of his new bride in their wedding bed he suddenly began to choke. The more he struggled for air the more his face bulged. He died while still inside his queen with a swollen head and a swollen cock, and not a drop of seed spilt.

"The new queen was dragged naked from her wedding bed and hanged from a tree – the king's folk believing she were responsible for his death. Before she breathed her last breath they cut her down and burned her in a huge pyre in front of the castle. It's said her screams can still be heard at night when her ghost drifts on the wind searching for her killers. With the death of the king, invaders were soon at their gates seeking easy plunder. Whatever curses the queen spat at her killers worked, as the memory of those folk was wiped from the mountains."

"I heard tell it were dragons what laid waste to the keep," a young archer interjected.

"Ain't no such thing as dragons, boy," the woodsman shot back, his words barbed with scorn. There were low chuckles from more than just the scouts silencing the boy archer.

"Enough," Normand growled. "Get some rest, all of you."

He inched closer to the fire, willing the warmth towards him as the weariness of the road bore down on his eyelids and aching muscles. He cursed himself silently for growing soft as he yearned for a feather-filled mattress and the security of intact castle walls around him. When his head finally drooped and he fell into a restless slumber his dreams were troubled.

She screeched a blood-freezing wail as she swirled about the camp and the sleeping warriors at an impossible rate. She approached each one in turn, reaching out with a long bony finger searching for their heart. Her icy touch was death, her breath poison, her eyes gates to everlasting torment. She was the Soul-Stealer, a harbinger of doom. Her thirst for vengeance on the men who slew her was unquenchable. Her search for the husband, who had betrayed her with another woman and brought a witch's curse into their marriage bed, would never cease.

And yet, her beauty would fill any man with a yearning that would bring tears to his eyes. It would fill him with desire while at the same time empty his heart and soul, leaving him a shell of frustration and lust. To gaze upon her face was to know both joy and pain beyond any ever before imagined.

She was no longer a blur, screeching from the high walls of the keep, but a maiden of immense beauty and innocence, dressed in an ivory wedding gown, her deep red lips parted slightly as she seemed to float through the camp. Normand wanted to reach out to her, longed to touch. Longing became lust then torment as he struggled with the bonds of sleep. All he wanted was to be with her, forever. Her mouth opened wider as soft, snow-white skin began dripping from her face. Her eyes burned; smoke drifted from her hair and clothes, her features contorted into a hideous mask, and she screamed. A harsh, bestial noise, so filled with pain and fear it made him want to cover his ears, but he could not. Her skin began to blister and melt away making his own eyes burn as he watched, feeling the heat touch his own skin. And then she reached for him, a long skeletal finger pushed through his chest, followed by another and another until her whole hand was reaching for his heart. He screamed then.

"My lord?"

His eyes flashed open. He took in the grime-covered face of the man standing over him. "The sun will be up shortly, my lord. It's almost morning."

Wind wailed through the ruined castle, making Normand flinch. He swallowed hard and nodded at the warrior who had woken him. He glanced over at the campfire occupied by the scouts, it was snowing and flakes whirled about them, gusting in the wind. The storyteller was staring right at him as wind whistled through the tower.

"The widow's searchin' tonight," he said. "She'll not rest 'til she's tasted blood."

The duke turned away from his leering glare as a man-at-arms handed him a skin of water and a chunk of hard, black bread. He'd not admit it to any man present, but he had to suppress a wish that his steward was with them. A tisane flavoured with honey and lemon would be most welcome to chase away the cold and screeching wind.

"How is it possible to be so damn cold up here?" he grumbled.

"The higher you go the colder it gets, my lord," the man-at-arms offered helpfully. Normand glared at him.

"I am not an idiot."

"No, my lord... sorry." He quickly found some packs that needed urgent attention.

By midday they had reached the site of the attack on the trader's caravan. Despite a clear blue sky overhead, Duke Normand still pulled his fur cloak tightly around his shoulders. All that was left to mark the death of the wagoner was some splintered wood from a broken wheel and a collection of stones heaped on top of the hard earth he had been buried beneath.

"Probably best to leave the road from here, my lord," a woodsman suggested before hawking and spitting at the duke's feet. Normand followed the trajectory of the spittle to where it landed beside his boots and then back up at the scout.

"The horses?"

"Leave 'em here with a couple o' yer lads to guard 'em. If ye want to catch the beast it'll be best if we leave the road now an' go straight up." He turned and looked up.

Normand followed his gaze. Massive trees cloaked in dark green needles shimmered in the bright sunlight. The heady scent of pine filled the air, as he looked at the steep climb. Even though he could not see from where he stood, the enormity of the snow-covered jagged peaks beyond the tree line suddenly made him feel quite small. He remembered the tale of the widow, and wondered what ghosts and demons awaited them higher up.

Warriors and scouts alike strapped as much gear as they could carry to their backs, leaving two of the duke's guards to remain behind with the mounts. The big shaggy hounds milled around, sniffing the ground around the makeshift grave of the wagon driver, their handlers hauled on leather leashes and yelled curses at dogs as big as ponies.

"Them's is clever puppies," the storyteller from the previous night said. "They knows when to be scared."

Normand checked his sword in its scabbard before giving the man a nod. "Lead on!"

Tomas: Alka-Roha

Tomas swirled a mouthful of warm water before spitting it into the dust. He then upended the waterskin over his head, letting the liquid flow down the back of his neck. It was a moment's respite from the heat and dust of the road. In the distance the walls of the city Alka-Roha shimmered red, making it stand out from the hard, barren landscape.

"The walls look as if they are bleeding," Aliss said. Tomas regarded his woman. They had been wed two years previously in the sacred grove beyond the Valley. The entire village turned out to bear witness to the joining of the new blacksmith and the village girl who had a knack for healing sick animals and the children of local folk. She was beautiful that day, her long golden curls tied up in a circlet of flowers. She wore a pale green gown to her ankles, giving the impression that she was one with the forest, sunlight pooled at her feet as birds sang a chorus in union to her… or so it seemed to an awestruck blacksmith. And now, he never felt so distant from her in all the time they had been together as he watched her squinting towards the crimson walls of the desert city.

"Tis the haze of the sun playing tricks with your eyesight," Horace, the weasel-faced tracker said.

She turned towards Tomas and smiled, an unguarded moment quickly concealed when he looked away from her eyes. Her eyes were the worst of the changes she had gone through since the witch Haera had brought her back from the brink of death with dark magic and the blood of an infant. Where once they had been the bright blue of a mountain spring, now they

Blood Of Kings: The Shadow Mage

were like a storm-filled sky, with dark grey clouds constantly shifting, depending on her mood. Her hair too had changed once it grew back. Her golden locks were gone, replaced by straight white hair, the colour of purest snow. Her skin had healed without a blemish, and for that he was eternally grateful, even if he found it odd for there not to be a single mark on her soft, white skin – so very white. He could not help but wonder, time after time, if the witchcraft used to heal her had not in fact replaced her with a different woman. A ridiculous notion of course, even so… The scars she bore inside though, would take longer to heal. Often she would wake at night screaming, begging for the flames to be put out. He would cradle her in his arms, hold her close, yet unable to look into her eyes for fear he would become lost in some dark portal to a place where chaos and black magic reigned.

"I care not if the bitch is standing at the gates waiting to greet us. For this one night I would forget about the dream-witch in favour of a hot bath, a skin of wine and a whore to warm my bed," the warrior Horald said. He was one of the three men including Horace the tracker and Ronwald another soldier in the service of Duke Normand, Djangra Roe the mage, had sent along with Tomas and Aliss to hunt down the Priestess of Eor. "Beggin' your pardon of course," he added the last part for the benefit of Aliss.

She simply dismissed him and the leering look from the smaller, Horace, with a wave of her hand, and kicked her horse towards the city. Tomas waited until the three men had fallen in behind her before he followed. Two of them wore mail armour and swords strapped to their waists. The tracker wore a lighter padded leather jerkin. All three had removed tunics bearing the duke's crest, a red dragon on a green background, while they travelled through other lands, each one becoming more exotic and stranger than the last. A cloud of dust quickly enveloped the small group of riders as they bore down on Alka-Roha, often called the City of Blood on account of the walls and how they appeared to bleed when reflected by the sun.

Horace led them through narrow streets teeming with life. Often they were forced to steer their horses around some cart laden with goods or wait for throngs of people to make way. More often they just rode through them. The smells wafting through the hot air were a mixture of exotic spicy food being cooked by a variety of vendors on the roadside and the waste left by a huge amount of people living cheek by jowl, flowing freely down hard-baked streets.

Tomas felt sweat trickle down his forehead and sting his eyes, it rolled down his spine and pooled at the small of his back. The further south they had travelled the hotter it got and the heat more oppressive. At first his skin had burned red raw and broke out into painful blisters, until Aliss had ground some leaves into a paste and spread it over his skin. The salve cooled and soothed his burning skin. She made another that seemed to reflect the worst of the stinging rays of the sun. He had quickly decided he preferred the cooler climes of the north.

"You have been to this place before? This city I mean?" Aliss asked the tracker as he guided them to an inn.

"I've been to many places, girl." He hawked and spat before grinning a gap-toothed grin in her direction. She looked away and followed Tomas into the inn.

'I don't trust that one,' Aliss had confided to Tomas at the start of their journey south. 'I don't trust any of them,' he had replied. They had chased rumours and followed where the tracker led, hunting the Priestess of Eor, as the seasons changed and the moon cycled through its phases over and over. Their participation was the payment asked by Haera for giving Aliss back her life. No price was too much to pay to have his woman by his side, whole and well, but Tomas was growing mighty weary of the hunt.

They huddled together at a table in the corner of the inn, ignoring the curious glances of the other patrons. Tomas was grateful for the respite from the blazing sun, enjoying the coolness of the building as much as the jug of wine placed before them. The innkeeper provided them with rounds of flat bread and stew comprising of hunks of some undetermined meat floating in bowls of grease, flavoured with some spice or other that burned as it went down.

"So you think you are capable of finding her?" Tomas said pushing away his empty bowl. "Yet she has eluded us for months. I am becoming sick of this chase."

"I found you, didn't I? For his lordship," Horace replied, crossing his arms over his chest in a defensive posture.

"I think she is close this time I can feel... something," Aliss interjected. She placed her hand gently on Tomas's arm.

"The All Father curse the bitch!" Horald suddenly stood up. "I promised myself a whore, and a whore I aim to have."

"I know just such a place," Horace said, a smile creeping across his face. "Perhaps I will join you and find a nice little dark-haired beauty. Or perhaps one with skin as soft and pale as a new-born lamb." His grin became a leer as his gaze fell on Aliss.

"It is not wise for us to split up if the dream-witch is close," Tomas said.

"We don't all have the comforts of our own woman to warm our beds and..."

"Do not continue speaking or I'll gut you where you stand." Tomas's eyes narrowed, his hand dropped to the hilt of his sword.

Horace's grin grew wider. "Come on, lads. Let's find us a dark-skinned harlot we can show what men of the Duchies are made of."

Tomas only realised that Aliss' hand was still on his arm when she squeezed it tighter. *Let them go*, that simple gesture said. He relaxed as the duke's three men left on their quest to find a woman prepared to lie with them for silver.

"Let's leave here now. You and I, we can be miles away before they come back. This task Haera set us is nonsense. What is the dream-witch to us? Nothing."

Aliss smiled sadly and shook her head. "Haera gave me life. With magic there is always a price to pay, and this is what she asked of us. It would be unwise not to settle our debt to her."

"I do not fear Haera," Tomas said.

"You should."

He smiled at that, but there was no humour in it, for he knew the truth when he heard it. It was never wise to cross a witch.

"And then what? What about them?" He flicked his head in the direction of the door, where their companions had just left. "When this is over what were they instructed to do? What will they do?"

"When this is over the Duke Normand will be in our debt. It would be unwise for *him* not to settle *his* debt," Aliss answered.

Tomas looked into her eyes then, the clouds swirled as if a tempest brewed somewhere deep inside her.

"The rich are most adept at forgetting debts owed," Tomas said bitterly.

Aliss placed her hand on his. "You walked into the fire for me. You carried me from the flames and bore me until I was made whole again. If we were not joined by the gods in the sacred grove, surely we are now. My body and soul were stripped bare, burned to the core by the inferno, and I was remade by Haera in the Great Wood. I know not the how or the why of it, but I am not the same person they tied to a post and condemned to die. I will never submit to such torment again. We will never suffer such injustices at the hands of people such as them ever again. Upon my soul, and the love I bear for you, I swear it."

Tomas felt himself drawn into her stormy eyes as the clouds shifted and darkened. The knowledge he bore weighed as heavy as the anvil in his workshop on his heart and soul. He had not found the courage inside himself to tell Aliss of the infant... of the sacrifice borne by Marjeri's baby. Did that make him a hero or a coward? To shield Aliss from the dark cloud shadowing all of their souls. He knew the anguish it would bring her. What is one life weighed against another? Does innocence trump injustice? What is the worth of the love felt by a man for a woman compared to the bond between mother and child?

She rested her head on his shoulder and squeezed his hand tightly. "We will kill this witch, and we will be free of Haera, Djangra and all the rest. If Horace and the others have plans to stand in our way, then that will be ill judged on their part."

"You would kill them?"

Aliss shrugged. "If needs be."

He looked deep into her eyes again, into the storm. He imagined a girl with golden hair so concerned for the welfare of a crippled bird that she nursed it back to health, crying herself to sleep every night, until its wing had mended.

He could not find her in those storm clouds.

Later as she lay beside him in the sparsely furnished room upstairs in the inn, her breath coming slow and easy, he too drifted off to sleep.

He knew he was dreaming for her hair was once again the colour of a field of wheat just before harvest. She was kneeling beside him as he lay back on the bed they shared. Her lips broke into a mischievous smile, her eyes shining. She was naked. His eyes drank in the sight of her, drawn to her full breasts and the curve of her hips. He felt a movement on the other side. Turning, he saw another woman appear in his vision. She too was naked, but that is not what Tomas's gaze focused on; painted onto her forehead, between two clear, emerald eyes, was a third eye, freakishly lifelike. Fear's icy touch made him gasp. He struggled to leap up. Aliss placed a comforting hand on his chest, pinning him in place. She used her other hand to trace a line over the breasts and belly of the other woman. He heard her moan as her head fell back and her eyes closed. He felt her warm hand on his body then, sliding across him. Long, slender fingers encircled him, fondling and stroking him. He exhaled; it came out in a groan. Aliss leaned in towards the other woman, her lips finding the soft skin of the other's neck.

Tomas had seen the dream-witch once before, although it was from a distance. It was when he had thrown his lot in with the brigands of the Great Wood. The Thieves Citadel was the best place, by far, for a group of bandits to sell the booty built up over months of waylaying travellers and robbing caravans. To many of them it had become a pilgrimage to be made once their need to convert their ill-gotten treasure into coin became greater than the risk of travelling outside their own sphere of power. Even though he had only spied her from afar, he was certain that she was the same woman who was now holding him in her hand, giving him exquisite pleasure, even as his woman kissed her neck while sliding her hand down her body.

Both women knelt over him as they leaned into each other. He overcame his fear… or at least his desire and lust was the stronger, and he reached out to both of them. They both looked at him at the same time, smiling conspiratorially between themselves. He watched mesmerised as Elandrial, High Priestess of Eor, commonly called the dream-witch, lowered her head towards him and took him in her mouth. His body shuddered at the pleasure. Aliss was watching him, smiling as she curled her tongue between her teeth, before running it along the spine of Elandrial. He closed his eyes, succumbing completely to the ecstasy of the moment, surrendering his body and soul to both women, somehow it seemed only right. They three would forge a bond, a link that would become an eternal triangle where each would depend on the other and each would both feed and be sated by each other. He felt a surge of emotion well inside him. He yearned for the climax, for his seed to be shared by both women. For wasn't it right they three should share in the moment?

"Tomas." A female voice called to him, yet neither of the women had spoken, too engrossed, as they were, in their activities. "Tomas…" He ignored the voice and slid his hand into Elandrial's hair, letting the dark strands twine around his fingers even as her head slowly and methodically rose up and down. "Tomas!"

"Leave me be," he gasped.

"Tomas, wake up now!"

His eyes flashed open. Aliss was leaning over him, her white hair reflecting in the moonlight coming through the window. "I…" He was disorientated as he slowly became aware of his surroundings, of the ache of his swollen loins. "I was dreaming."

"Yes, I know, love. She is close, I can sense her. She was in your dreams."

His face flushed. How did one explain such a dream to the love of their life? "Yes," he simply answered.

She stroked his brow and cheek. "She is gone now. I was not sure how to fight her, or if I even could. But now I know. Now that I have tasted her power, I can combat it. And I can follow its trail."

"She didn't try to kill me."

Aliss shrugged, not understanding his meaning.

"She could have killed me. She knows we are hunting her, but she did not. Why?"

Before Aliss could answer they heard a scream. They both looked at each other and realisation dawned at the same time. Horace.

They ran from the room and down the corridor. Tomas put his shoulder to the door, which gave way easily and both burst into the room. The tracker struggled alone in his bed, his hands gripping his throat as if he were trying to prise fingers from it. His eyes bulged in their sockets as he gasped for air. Aliss ran to his side and placed her hands on his head. She put her own head back and drew in breaths in a slow easy rhythm. Horace instantly calmed. Her eyes were open wide. Storms raged there as even the whites of her eyes filled with swirling, dark clouds. Although Tomas was looking straight into them, he knew she could not see him.

Horace suddenly bolted upright, gulping down air. "It's horrible! Horrible! It's after me, it won't stop." He began sobbing then. "Please help me," he squeaked in a pitiful voice.

Aliss blinked and then regarded Tomas. "Now it begins."

Jarl Crawulf: Northern Duchies

Crawulf rubbed tired eyes as he pored over the maps spread out before him. Gathered around him were his chosen men. Ulf Soulgarde, also known as Ulf the Red, built like an ox with a shaggy grey beard stained with rust. His red hair was tied in a single plait that trailed down his back. Torngor Blakhar, as tall as Ulf, though not as wide—in truth few men were as wide as Ulf the Red—his hair was dark brown and hung loose over a face that may once have been handsome but for a crooked and scarred nose broken too many times. Olf Skarnjak, known as One Eye, the other lost in battle along with two fingers of his left hand. He wore a leather patch to cover the loss, and snarled at any who looked too closely at him. Honbar Dolfson, blond-haired and with pale blue eyes, and unlike most Nortmen, clean-shaven, he had often been called pretty as a girl. None who did so lived long enough to repeat the insult. These men were Crawulf's battle leaders, his most trusted advisors. Each man was sworn to him, an oath of blood taken in the sight of the gods. They would do his bidding and they would die for him if needs be.

"We will wait for him here where we will have the higher ground." Crawulf pointed a dagger at a location on the map. "If what the scouts say is true, then he should be at this point by now. He will be upon us before the sun reaches its highest point in the sky." They all looked to the east where the sun shimmered in a clear blue sky, two fingers' width above the horizon.

"Will he come? Has he the stomach to do battle?" the blond-haired Honbar asked, idly cleaning dirt from beneath his fingernails with a thin-bladed dagger.

"He'll come. He has no choice. We have burnt his crops and torched his villages. We have killed countless and taken as thralls even more. He will come," Crawulf answered.

"Aye, we've done well. This has been a mighty raid that will be sung about for a long time." Olf Skarnjak began, his words greeted with nods of approval. "This is our way, how it has always been. We raid and take what we want. All that can be plundered from the weak is rightfully ours." He paused and drank from a wineskin.

Crawulf's eyes narrowed. "Go on, One Eye."

"We hit, and then we return to the ships, leaving a trail of havoc in our wake. We are the bringers of death. No one knows when or where we will appear, and then we are gone as quick."

"You do not wish to fight this fight?"

"It is not our way."

"Our way is how I say it is," Crawulf snarled.

"They have twice the men we do."

"Less than half are trained warriors. The rest are peasants summoned in from the fields."

"Our ships are laden with treasure. There are so many captives on board we'll barely have enough room for ourselves. This..." Olf gestured expansively with his arms, "is a needless risk."

"Are you afraid to die, One Eye?" Crawulf took a step towards his chosen man, but Olf did not flinch.

"No! I embrace death like a lost love... as all Nortmen do. I do not see the need to throw away all that we have gained when we have no reason."

"I have brought pain and fire to the people we count as enemies. You say this is not our way. When was honour not our way? When was vengeance not our way?"

"A lot of men will die for your honour," Olf answered.

"Yes." Crawulf's eyes shone with the sun reflected there. Olf looked away, his shoulders slumped in defeat.

Honbar clapped him on the back and snatched the wineskin from his hand. "Come, One Eye, let's drink to a glorious death." All of them, including Olf smiled their agreement.

Crawulf watched the morning creep in, bringing with it dark clouds rolling from the ocean. Below him men dug trenches around the side of the hill and sharpened long stakes before hammering them into the soft earth turning the crest of the hill into a prickly hedgehog.

"They'll not ride armoured horses up that rise too easily once we've finished," Torngor Blakhar said, standing beside his jarl, hands on hips. "A storm'll be upon us soon enough," he added looking into the distance at the dark blanket of cloud swallowing up the sapphire sky.

"Aye. Rain is good. Rain adds to the confusion," Crawulf answered.

"How many dead will satisfy your honour and sate the gods' thirst for blood?" the big Nortman with the crooked face asked.

Crawulf levelled his gaze on him. "All of them."

"I hear thunder." Olf One Eye approached them from behind. All three listened while staring at the distant clouds.

"Not thunder," Crawulf said.

"Drums," Torngor added.

"Aye. Gather the men."

Moments later two blasts of a horn rang through the valley, signalling for the men to gather on top of the hill. Like a pack of some dark-furred predators, they lifted their heads and quickly grabbed their weapons in unison and scrambled up to where Crawulf and his chosen men waited.

The jarl of Wind Isle felt his blood race as nervous energy coursed through him. There was no feeling like it; the anticipation of battle. No matter how many times he stood, sword in hand, standing toe to toe, eyeball to eyeball with an enemy, he would never tire of the rush he felt, the combination of elation and dread. No matter what they say, no man lives without fear, for what is courage without terror? They are two edges of the same sword.

Hundreds of Nortmen raced to stand behind him, checking weapons and armour, chattering noisily and raucously as each of them summoned their own well of courage and tried not to think about the many painful ways a man can die in battle. Swords, axes, spears will do terrible things to soft flesh, even that encased in mail. Archers readied their arrows and checked that their strings were dry, knowing that from a distance they were relatively safe, unless the men standing in front of them were to fall; in which case their deaths would be just as, if not more horrible than the men-at-arms.

The tree line in the distance appeared to move as men sent to defend their land and thwart the invader melted from the forest. Crawulf glanced left and right of him, although he knew he had no need to check on the stoutness of heart of his own men.

In the distance a line of horsemen made their way, in single file, to the front of the growing ranks. Crawulf could see the banners now fluttering in the wind held proudly above the swell of men as their numbers grew, like a dark pool melting from the forest. He felt the first drops of rain on his face and looked up at the darkening sky. Archers hurried past him, stringing their bows and placing arrows into the ground before them. They would rain death down on the advancing army as it charged up the hill. Once the attackers were close they would slip behind the line of shields and men strung out across the rise. Then, the real butchery would begin; hand-to-hand, blade-to-blade.

The drums continued to beat as the men of the Duchies formed lines and readied themselves for battle. It occurred to Crawulf to attack at that moment with a thousand raging Nortmen into the disorganised ranks of the enemy, but he had the higher ground and was reluctant to give it up. The Duchies had strength of numbers and knew the lay of the land. With such an advantage often came arrogance and over confidence. Mounted men dressed in mail and carrying shields and lances formed a line at the base of the hill. Some struggled to control their horses as the animals stomped and fought the rein. The sound of curses, along with the snorting of horses and rattling of weapons and mail, carried up the hill to the waiting Nortmen, who jeered and flung insults at the men waiting to advance on them.

The rain and wind picked up as fighting men waited to be unleashed; to begin the killing and maiming. It was a time when doubts and fears were given life; a time when men soiled themselves or sought courage at the end of a wineskin; a time when the real fear was showing lack of courage to the men around them or the chosen men barracking them to fight or hold.

At the sound of a horn the line of horsemen began to advance up the hill. Crawulf felt a ripple of nervous tension wash over his men. It was no easy thing to hold a line against the advance of armoured horsemen, even those with the disadvantage of a hill to climb. He drew his own sword then and tightened his grip on his shield. Flinging his arms in the air and with a theatrical grin on his face, he joined the front ranks of his army. His chosen men disappeared, taking up positions along the line where they would goad, encourage and curse men into giving their lives for their jarl.

About halfway up the hill the front line of horses found the ditches and potholes hastily dug by the Nortmen. With a squeal, a horse went down, breaking its leg and collapsing onto its side. It took out two others following behind. The Nortmen jeered and snarled insults at each flailing mount and rider. A few casualties, though, were not enough to halt the advance as most of the riders avoided the traps dotted about the hill by the Nortmen. Crawulf heard a barked order from his Master Archer, followed by a 'twang'. A dark cloud whistled into the air from his own ranks, arcing, like a swarm of stinging insects, towards the line of horsemen. Many arrows found their mark, most bounced off expensive armour, but some found gaps or weakened points, knocking knights from their mounts. Still more took down the more lightly-armoured horses. The sound of dying men and beasts drifted upwards.

Still they came, hard, determined men eager to reach their enemy and deal out some pain of their own. Rain dripped from Crawulf's helmet, blurring his vision, as the sky overhead darkened some more from the rainclouds moving over them. He felt the icy grip of fear clutch his heart as the mounted knights of the Duchies kicked their warhorses onwards, despite the stinging onslaught of arrows. His archers fell back when the charge shook the ground and the air was filled with the sound of grunting horses and riders barracking them on with curses and roars of encouragement. The Nortmen responded with their own war-cries, calling down the names of their gods and heroes of the past, hoping their own hearts would be filled with the courage of legends of old.

They gripped the sharpened stakes they'd cut from trees earlier that morning and held them out inviting the horsemen to their deaths. Some of the mounted men baulked at the prickly wall of wood, flesh and iron, others crashed through bringing death from lance and the weight of a charging warhorse on the defensive wall. Men screamed in pain as they were crushed beneath the hooves of horses or pierced savagely; a charging horse adding weight to the thrust of a lance. Along the line, horses stumbled or faltered and the riders were dragged from their lofty perches to be hacked to death, their screams joining the cacophony of battle.

A massive Nortman stepped out of the line of shields and stakes to swing a great Nort-axe at a charging horse. The animal bellowed in agony as the axe bit deep into its neck and collapsed onto the ground, trapping the rider beneath it. Ignoring pleas for mercy, the Nortman advanced on the stricken rider, raised the axe, and with a single swing removed his head. A great cheer went up from the line of defenders close enough to witness the act of bravery, and the killing stroke. Crawulf allowed himself a quiet smile.

Most of the casualties suffered by the horsemen were when their charge had run out of steam and they attempted to disengage themselves. Nortmen lashed out at the mounts, pulling riders from their horses. The bodies of men and beasts littered the crest of the hill, a good number of them his own men, Crawulf noted. The knights untangled themselves from the melee, urging their horses to carry them to safety. A good deal fewer of them would make it off the hill. The Nortmen had little time to catch their breaths, following closely behind. In tightly packed ranks was the bulk of the Duchies army. Leading from the front were the hard, experienced men. Crawulf wiped rain from his face and set his boots into the churned earth at his feet, his mouth set in a grim line. The smell of turned earth and the metallic scent of blood filled the air.

The advancing army closed so that Crawulf could see the faces of the men coming to die. To die or deliver a savage death to their enemies filled the minds of men on both sides, battle lust overriding fear now that the enemy was within smelling distance. Crawulf heard his men roaring all around him, and realised he was shouting, as if he were intent on bursting a lung, along with them. He dug his heels into the softening ground as rain came down in great sheets of water. A flash lit up the sky, quickly followed by a crack of thunder. *The All Wise bears witness*, Crawulf thought, pleased that Alweise, king of the gods was there to accept his gift of blood. "We will feast with the gods tonight!" he roared over the din. The men around him cheered back, welcoming a glorious death in battle.

The distance between the two lines closed in a heartbeat as the Duchies army ate up the ground. Two lines of flesh and iron crashed together with wooden shields clashing as if thunder rippled along the line. A warrior with a mouthful of black teeth and stumps snarled at Crawulf as he thrust a spear over his shield, aiming the point at the jarl's face. Crawulf caught it on his own and stabbed with his sword at the man's neck. The warrior fell back as a crimson spray erupted, like the geysers dotted all over Fire Isle, drenching the men around him. Another stepped forward to take his place and Crawulf jabbed out with the iron boss of his shield before he had time to settle into place. Beside him, a Nortman hammered at an upraised shield in front of him with an axe, sending splinters of wood into the air. The relentless assault stopped abruptly when a spear snaked out from the opposite wall of iron and wood, stabbing him just below the eye. The man slumped onto Crawulf's shoulder as the jarl attempted to swing his sword, breaking the momentum of the arc. With a curse he shrugged the dead Nortman off and quickly raised his shield just in time to block the strike from a short-sword.

He was beginning to regret carrying his own sword into battle and not opting for a shorter blade or a spear to stab with. His sword, gifted to him by his father, and by his father before him was a fine length of killing steel, but perhaps not the best weapon in such close quarters. He was close enough to feel the splash of spittle from his attacker wash over his face when the man screamed a war-cry. He drew his head back and then launched it forward, the man's nose disintegrated from the iron helmet smashed into his face, and he fell back screaming. Crawulf stepped forward as the man fell, grinding the heel of his boot into the man's head, crushing his skull like a thick-skinned fruit brought to Wind Isle by the merchants of the empire.

Rain water ran down the hill, dyed a reddy-brown, equal parts mud and blood. He glanced back and realised the line of Nortmen had steadily pushed the Duchies from the top of the hill and were inching them back to where they had come from. It was good that they were pushing the enemy back, but he did not want his men moving from the top of the hill. He would need to stop their advance.

As he was thinking on how best to stop the steady advance of his men, he caught sight of Duke Elsward's banner, a prancing lion on a green field—Crawulf had never seen a real lion before and doubted if Elsward had either. It could just as easily be an exotic chicken as a ferocious predator—it was moving fast behind the line of men-at-arms, and peasants making up his army. Cold dread dripped into his bowels when he realised why the duke was moving so fast. He was rallying the scattered horsemen and forming them to attack the Nortland left flank. Crawulf scanned the line until his eyes found the chosen man commanding the left: Olf Skarnjak – One Eye. He caught a glimpse of him barracking the men around him. Had he spotted the danger? Crawulf needed to get a message to him.

Before the thought could form properly a surge from the lines behind him propelled him forward. The dull thud of a weapon bouncing off his mail armour reminded him that he was in the midst of a battle. He lashed out at the man in front of him, so close that he could smell his sour breath and the sweat of a hundred and more men all around him. The man went down, lost beneath a forest of legs and likely crushed into the sticky earth at their feet. He took a step back reaching out to find the man behind him and haul him in to take his place. He had to stop his men from pushing forward and giving up the crest of the hill, and he had to get word to One Eye.

Pain exploded in his head and travelled like a lightning strike to the base of his spine. White light flashed before him then turned red. He staggered back trying to focus on the man in front of him. No easy thing with his sight blurred. He saw two men, hazy as if they were emerging from a fog... no, not two, just one. The man raised a weapon. To Crawulf it was just a blur, it could have been an axe, or hammer... it could have been a lump of wood for all he could tell. His mind told him he needed to raise his shield, but his arms refused to respond. In the distance Elsward's banner rippled in the wind as the lion stood on two legs roaring its defiance at the Nortmen and the gale blowing across the battlefield. He waited, dumbly, for the killing blow.

He felt hands grabbing him then. He imagined the bone-white fingers of the Soul Reapers lifting him into the air. "My sword," he mumbled. He would greet his gods with his father's sword in his hands. Rain landed icy kisses on his face. All else was numb.

Duke Normand: Mountains of Eor

Mist clung to the trees in silky threads and blanketed the forest floor as Duke Normand led his warriors in pursuit of the hunting hounds and their handlers. He could hear the great shaggy beasts barking and yelping in the distance as they picked up the scent of their prey. *Was that prey some hapless forest animal, or the mythical man-like monsters purportedly roaming the high and almost inaccessible parts of the mountains?* he wondered. He pulled his fur-trimmed cloak tight around his shoulders, yet still the cold penetrated through to his bones. It was becoming harder to breathe the higher they climbed. Countless times that day he cursed himself for undertaking this expedition personally; he had men for this sort of thing. What was he trying to prove?

"My lord, up ahead, the hounds have caught something," a mail-clad warrior said. Normand simply nodded to the man as he sucked in ragged breaths.

The pack of hounds were being held back on strained leashes by their handlers, he pushed past the circle of woodsmen examining what the hunting dogs had found.

"What is it?" he demanded.

"Deer, my lord. A large stag," a woodsman answered, as he leaned on his unstrung bow, examining the carcass.

"I can see that." Normand made no effort to hide his irritation. "Is this what has dragged me..." Before he could finish, a loud, throaty growl rent the mountain air, sending a shiver down his spine. "What is that?" Normand scanned around him, but all he saw were trees covered in gossamer strands of mist. Another loud snarl answered the first. The hounds barked and snarled back, straining at their leashes as they pranced and jumped excitedly. A third, then fourth roar called out in the distance.

"Sabre lions," a woodsman answered. "Sounds like a pack, hunting. He hawked and spat on the ground.

"Lions?" Normand groaned.

"Bigger'n lions, my lord. Big as ponies they grow, with two long fangs thick as yer arm and sharp as that dagger on yer belt. They like the cold so they does, and stay up here high in the mountains."

"Will they attack? Surely not."

"Aye, maybe, depends how hungry they is, and how big the pack is. There's not much they's afeared of, especially when you're in their territory. You cross into their lands, that makes you their prey." He grinned and then spat again.

"And none of you thought it wise to share this before we left?"

"We wasn't huntin' lions, my lord."

Normand drew in a breath to castigate the man for his insolence, but then realised he would most likely only waste his time. The agitated dogs distracted his thoughts as he tried to picture a lion as big as a pony with dagger-like fangs. He shivered again, but not from the cold this time. "So this deer is theirs? Can't we just leave it to them and go?"

"Not sure about that, my lord. This animal's had its skull caved in. Sabre lions don't kill like that. They'll either hold their prey down and strangle it with their jaws or slice its throat with their fangs and wait for it to bleed to death."

"Thank you for the graphic description," Normand answered. The woodsman tipped his finger to his forehead, ignoring or not sensing the sarcasm in the duke's words.

"So they would attack a group such as ourselves?" Normand's eyebrows rose in incredulity. The woodsman just shrugged.

"If they see us as a rival pack encroaching on their territory they'd likely feel a need to," another woodsman said. Normand looked from one man to the other then back to the dead stag, noticing now the bloodied head and broken antler.

"And this deer was killed by some other beast?"

"Aye, my lord. Somethin' powerful by the looks of it."

Normand paced back and forth, his hand idly stroking his trimmed beard. "Very well," he came to a decision, "you two roam ahead and search for signs of the monster we seek…"

"My lord, there's a pack of sabre lions huntin'.…" the first woodsman interrupted.

"You would prefer for us all to remain packed tightly together, with no eyes or ears scanning ahead?" The idea of pushing into unknown terrain without scouts probing ahead was completely at odds with his military training.

"I would prefer if we left the mountain, leastwise the territory of the pack."

"What is your name?"

"Olaf, my lord."

"Well, Olaf, take your friend here and lead the way." Normand kept his voice even and calm, but a twitch in his cheek and the reddish colouring around his eyes told the woodsmen they had crossed a line. "We came here to hunt and kill a beast, who you and your fellows assured me exists, and this we shall do. If these lions are upset by us crossing their hunting ground, well I have news for them… I have news for all of you." He suddenly raised his voice high enough for the entire group of fighting men, dog-handlers and woodsmen to hear. "This is my land. These are my mountains. No man, nor beast shall tell me where I can or cannot go. Eorotia is my city. My word is law here. Let these beasts come and we shall all wear lion hide coats this winter."

The men-at-arms nodded their approval while rattling their weapons and slamming their fists off their mail-clad chests. The dog handlers continued to struggle with their charges as the hounds reacted to the distant call of the lions. The scouts slunk away, melting into the forest and disappearing from sight. Without another word the rest of the troop followed the woodsmen, every man looking nervously at the mist-shrouded trees surrounding them.

By midday the terrain remained unchanged. The mist, at least, had lifted, but despite a clear blue sky, it remained cold. The ragged mountains still rose high above them, cutting a dark, jagged line in the sky, the peaks seeming no closer than when they set out from Eorotia. Normand reflected on the vastness of his new lands, wild lands, previously the preserve of bandit gangs and beasts such as the lions who still tracked them, judging by the calls back and forth, sometimes seeming so close as to be right on top of them, then other times when the roars and snarls seemed leagues away. All of the men were on edge, with weapons at the ready, the hum of jovial banter heard the previous day silent now.

Normand called a halt when the hounds became even more noisy and animated than they had previously been. The fearsome, shaggy hounds snarled and growled, pulling their handlers along as the hapless men tried to control them. Finally one leather leash snapped. For an instant the animal froze, as if its disbelief at being freed overrode its desire to answer the challenge from the forest. And then it was gone. Great bounding strides ate up the ground as it became a grey blur and headed into the trees. The rest of the pack became uncontrollable as they yearned to answer the call of their brother and follow after into the woods.

"Release them!" Normand bellowed. "We'll follow."

The entire pack of hounds raced from their handler's grip, and the men followed the cacophony of barks and snarls as they disappeared from sight. The armed men hurried after, crashing through the woods like a huge, iron-clad monster, setting to flight any small animals brave and curious enough to still be in the vicinity.

The massive hounds were no ordinary hunting dogs, as Normand knew well, they were bred and used throughout the Duchies for hunting wolves, even bears. He had never known a wild predator to be a match for them. They could range for hundreds of leagues with their great loping stride, if need be, also capable of huge bursts of speed over short distance. Their bite was fearsome and relentless. In many ways they were the perfect hunter. A hugely intelligent animal, and fiercely loyal to their masters. They were a breed of hound only found in the Duchies, although they were much prized and sought after far beyond those borders. Which is why Normand failed to hide the utter shock from his face when they came upon a bloody scene, what seemed like moments after the pursuit had begun. Two of the huge hounds lay in a clearing, their grey, shaggy fur matted in blood. Both of them had had their throats ripped out. Their bodies bore evidence of further wounds.

"The All Father preserve us," a warrior muttered.

One of the dog handlers, a boy of about twelve, rushed over and knelt by the corpses of the hounds, his eyes glistening with the visible evidence of his grief as he cautiously reached out a hand and placed it on the flank of one hound.

"Quiet!" Normand snapped, as he strained to listen. The faint sounds of violent struggle between animals drifted through the forest.

A woodsman pointed. "There!"

"I've never seen them hounds take such a maulin' before," a gruff voice said.

Men glanced about anxiously as the forest seemed to come alive; the trees rustled and swayed. Dark shapes flashed at the corner of the eye and disappeared as quickly when men swung around to catch a better view of whatever it was. Up ahead, beyond sight, where the narrow trail disappeared among the trees, Normand heard a high-pitched yelp and then all went silent.

"The hounds, my lord..." a warrior began but was silenced by Normand flapping his hand irritably. The forest went still, deathly quiet... and then erupted into a wall of noise.

Bursting through the trees, leaping through the air, snarling wicked smiles of terror were the sabre lions. Normand barely had time to see the wickedly sharp fangs dominating the gaping maws of the leaping beasts. The enraged animals slammed into his warriors, knocking them to the ground before slashing at them with sharp claws and reaching for exposed throats with their deadly fangs. The mail-clad warriors were lucky as their armour offered protection against the vicious bite of the lions, whereas the houndless dog handlers and the lightly armoured archers and woodsmen fared a lot worse. The weight and strength of the beasts was colossal as they forced screaming men to the ground, where they were savaged with dagger-like teeth. Normand stood, disbelieving as his troop of warriors was overwhelmed by the sudden onslaught of massive predators defending their territory from what they saw as an intruding pack. He had fought in many battles, both been ambushed and laid surprise attacks on his enemy, yet he'd never felt so helpless by an onslaught. He fumbled for the sword strapped to his waist barely able to tear his eyes from the sight of a huge lion ripping out the throat of an archer with a twist of its massive head. The beast looked up and regarded Normand with yellow eyes, its maw bloodied red.

"My lord, this way." Hands pushed the duke leading him from the slaughter. Frightened men ran in all directions, while those unlucky enough to be the target of a brown, mottled lion fought desperately for their lives.

Normand followed the back of a warrior as he pushed his way through the foliage, blindly running from the melee with the lions. Behind him, those who had survived the attack followed, confusion and terror plainly visible on their faces. They ran as the sounds of men dying horrific deaths faded into the distance, as the blood-freezing roars of the terrifying beasts grew dimmer. They ran, although they knew not where to, or how to return to the trail. They ran with fear twisting in their guts.

The lead warrior stopped abruptly at the edge of a clearing. Normand dropped his hands to his knees as he gulped air into his burning lungs. He yearned to unbuckle his mail shirt, but feared to do so having seen what the claws and jaws of the lions were capable of doing to un-armoured flesh. Men all around him wheezed and coughed as their chests heaved. A wave of shame washed over Normand as he thought about the men he'd left behind and how he had run from the fight. He wanted to blame the men who ushered him from the scene and led him in a blind flight. Yet, he knew that was unfair. Blind terror had gripped him at the sight of the slaughter. He had stood mesmerised as men became meat; prey to the apex predators of the mountains. He looked around him, half a dozen or so, mail-clad warriors, and a handful of archers gathered about him, each of them bearing a haunted look in their eyes. He empathised with each one of them. He knew what he had to do. He had to take charge once again and lead his men back. To round up those who were left alive. Shame burned within him as he thought of the left dead and dying.

"My lord..." Normand turned around to see why he had stopped so abruptly.

"What is that?" Normand asked as his gaze followed to where the warrior was pointing.

"That is a man wedged in a tree," the warrior said quietly.

Normand could make out the shape now. "Where is his...?"

The warrior pointed at the ground at the base of the tree. Normand's eyes widened as he took in the sight of a head and arm. The trunk of the tree looked as if someone had painted a wide line the length of it with red paint. The duke felt bile rise in his throat.

"The lions did that?" His voice cracked.

"I don't think so, my lord." Neither man could tear their gaze from the horrific scene.

A realisation came to Normand. "That is Olaf... the woodsman I ordered to scout ahead."

"What's left of him at least."

Normand shook of the trance and took a step closer to the tree housing the decapitated scout. "How did he get up there?"

"Looks as if he were flung there, my lord."

"What could have done that?" Normand moved closer. He could see tear-shaped drips of blood hanging from branches before falling to the forest floor. His gaze wandered up, to where Olaf's remains hung ten feet off the ground, wedged between two branches, the headless corpse coating them, and the surrounding leaves, in red gore. Hot bile rose to his throat, making him wretch. His men remained silent and motionless around him.

"My lord..." the warrior reached out a tentative hand, which Normand brushed aside.

"For the sake of the All Father, get him down from there," he instructed as he wiped his mouth with the back of his hand.

The warrior gave a nod to two others and they quickly moved to make an attempt at climbing the tree. No easy thing with the trunk slick and greasy with gore. Eventually one of them made it up and clambered out onto one of the branches supporting the body of the scout. Gingerly, on hands and knees the armoured man made his way to the corpse. The others watched in grim silence as he tugged and heaved until finally Olaf crashed to the earth. Normand flinched at both sight and sound of the body landing with a sickening squelch.

Normand had no time to gather his thoughts as a spine-chilling roar erupted from the forest, shattering the silence of the clearing. A flock of birds who had been observing from a lofty perch took flight, rustling the treetops all around the men. *Lions,* was Normand's first thought, although somewhere deep down in his subconscious he knew that the roar he had just heard was not the same. A primeval instinct yelled at him to run. This time, though, he fought his fear.

"Form a line!" he barked at his men. The warriors quickly formed a small shield-wall as the sound of snapping branches told them something heavy was moving quickly towards them. He could taste the fear in the air, as he suppressed the almost overwhelming urge to turn and run as fast as he could in any direction away from what was crashing through the forest. A second roar made him flinch and the world turned to chaos.

A massive shape smashed into the clearing. Running upright, on two legs, just like a man, was a colossal beast, its entire body covered in white and grey fur. Twice the size of any man in both height and width, it crashed into the clearing in a whirlwind of violence and terror. Arrows flew over Normand's head, fired by the archers standing behind the shield-wall.

"Hold!" a man yelled from the end of the line.

The beast bellowed a fear-inducing screech as a hail of arrows hit it. Enraged, it swatted two massive hands at the line of warriors, ripping their shields from their hands, before it smashed through them, flinging men into the air. Normand swung his sword at the mountain of fur, not even knowing if he connected. The man-beast swatted at him, backhanded, sending him sprawling into the trees. He landed hard on his back and smashed his head off a tree. He could hear the cries of terror, but try as he might he could not move. When he tried to focus on his surroundings, all he could make out was a blurred image of colours.

As he fought down panic, he suddenly felt hands upon him, and realised he was being dragged. Urgent voices filled the air around him, voices of strangers, both men and women. They spoke in whispers in a sing-song accent he did not recognise. He tried to fight them, to even focus on them, but they were just blurred shapes in a sea of blues and greens.

"The Dragon Lord has returned," they whispered.

"Kill him now. He is the bringer of doom."

"No! That is not how it is written."

"He will wake the dragon and bathe the world in blood, so it is written" they said in unison, an edge of panic and awe to their voices.

"Kill him!" a female voice insisted.

"No! The Lord of Shadows forbids it."

Panic welled inside Normand. He had no feeling other than the sensation of being dragged. He could see nothing but blurred shapes.

"The Dragon Lord is among us." The voices trailed off and Normand drifted into blackness.

"My lord... my lord!"

He flinched and a whimper of fear escaped from him as he gazed into the grizzled face of his man-at-arms.

"Are you well, my lord?"

He swallowed hard before pulling himself into a sitting position. "The beast?"

"Fled, my lord. Do you wish to pursue it?"

"No, Malachi, I do not."

Tomas: Alka-Roha

Tomas dragged a whetstone down the length of his blade. Stone rasping on steel was the only sound in the small room. He watched Aliss, her face hidden by strands of long white hair hanging over a wide wooden bowl filled with water. She held her hands either side of the bowl, gently moving them through the air in slow, short movements, as if she were parting the water held in the wooden vessel she was so intent on.

"It has been three days now, and nothing," Tomas complained.

Aliss looked up, regarding him with storm-grey eyes. He looked away from the shifting clouds. "Patience, my love. I can feel the power growing within me, getting stronger every day. Haera not only saved me, but she has awoken a deeper well of magic. I don't understand it, but I feel it."

Tomas sighed and shook his head. "What are you doing there anyway? You haven't stopped staring into that bowl of water all morning."

"Searching." Aliss smiled, her eyes shining.

"In a bowl?" Tomas arched an eyebrow.

"I have heard of mages and powerful witches with the power to scry the past and future using various devices. I never realised before that I too had the power." Her smile widened.

"And what do you see?" Tomas asked somewhat sceptically.

"I see a temple, in the desert. Its walls are crumbling and its gates have long since turned to dust. To any who would pass it by, or even stop to rest in the shade of the ruin, it looks as if it has not been inhabited for a hundred years or more."

"What is this place?"

"It is a temple to a god long forgotten by the folk here, worshipped by their ancestors in a different time. A charm has been placed upon it to make it look so." She grinned and Tomas would swear a bolt of light flashed across her eyes.

"So it is not in ruins? How is that even possible?"

"Magic, as I am realising more and more, can be a very powerful force."

"You think the dream-witch is there?"

"Oh yes," Aliss answered.

"Where is it?" Tomas asked.

Aliss dropped her head. "I do not know."

Tomas sighed and dragged the whetstone down the length of his sword once again, while Aliss returned to scrying.

Suddenly she cried out and jumped back away from the bowl. Horror twisted her face into a mask of fear. Tomas leapt up and ran to her side.

"What is it?" he asked urgently, as he looked mystified at the bowl. Aliss lashed out and knocked it from the table. Water splashed onto the floor as the bowl landed upside down on the floorboards. "What did you see?" he asked again as Aliss slowly composed herself.

"Blood. I saw blood," she panted.

"Blood?"

"She knows we are searching for her. We must be careful and we must find her quickly."

"How can we do that if we do not know where she is?"

"She is in the temple," Aliss answered.

"But you already said you do not know where that is." Tomas's face creased in consternation.

"No, but we know what we are looking for, and it is likely known well enough. We just have to ask."

"Horace is the tracker. I'll tell him to ask around. He may even have heard of such a place himself. If he can tear himself from the whores and wine that is." Tomas strapped on his sword belt.

"I'll come too. I need to leave this room and fill my lungs with fresh air."

"You'll do well to find a clear breath of air anywhere in this stinking town. By the All Father, I've never been anywhere so hot." Tomas wiped sweat from his forehead with the back of his hand before opening the door and standing back to allow Aliss to leave the room first.

Below, in the common room of the inn they quickly spied their three travelling companions. Horace the tracker sat with a dark-skinned girl on his knee while he quaffed a jug of wine.

"Must you bring your... entertainments here?" Tomas asked, his lip curled in disgust.

"Listen to the lord high and mighty, king of the fucking swamp," Horace shot back before draining the jug. "More wine!"

Tomas tensed, balling his fists. He felt a hand on his arm and glanced at Aliss.

"He's drunk, let it pass," she said. He looked to the other two men, all warriors of Duke Normand. They shrugged before returning their attention to their own wine.

"We need to find a temple," Aliss said to Horace. "It is likely in ruin, with crumbling walls, long abandoned. Can you ask around, Horace?"

"I know of such a place," the whore spoke up, her interest suddenly piqued.

"You do?"

"Yes," she answered, quickly looking away from the swirling clouds examining her intently. She slapped away Horace's wandering hand as it slid inside the brightly coloured dress she wore. "I can take you there... for gold," she added.

"Is it far from here?" Aliss asked, stepping aside to allow the landlord through to deliver a clay jug. Red liquid sloshed over the sides making small puddles on the table when Horace snatched it from his hand.

"Two days' ride," she answered, fighting off another assault from the drunken tracker.

"Very good," Aliss' full lips curled into a smile. "You will be paid well if you speak true."

She nodded and beamed a smile in return. Horace grabbed her as she attempted to stand up, pulling at her skirts. She swung on him and punched him hard in the face. "I am no longer your whore. Now I am your guide," she spat, her exotic accent, rolling the words as she spoke, lacing them with venom.

Horace drew back his fist as his face clouded with anger, only for Tomas to catch his wrist, using his great blacksmith's strength to immobilise the arm of the much smaller man. "Enough," he said, his voice calm and soft, yet his meaning was clear enough.

Horace shot each of them dark, dangerous looks, but pushed the issue no further.

"We will leave before first light," Aliss said, before turning to the woman. "What is your name?"

"Ivannia," she answered.

"Meet us here before the sun has risen, Ivannia." The girl nodded and left, shooting a look of daggers at the tracker as she passed.

Tomas followed Aliss back up the narrow wooden stairs to the upper floor of the inn. Floorboards creaked in protest as the two walked through the cramped corridor to their room at the end. "I do not trust her," he said as he closed the door behind them.

"You trust no one, my love," Aliss answered.

"It is a wise policy."

"We are so far from home, in this strange place where people look different and sound odd to our ears. Those who can even speak the common trading tongue do so with a queer accent. The heat is oppressive and relentless—what I would not give for a gentle shower of rain—it is hard not to mistrust everything and everyone. And yes, wise too, but we are desperate, love. We need her."

"I am tired of this place. I am sick of the heat stifling every breath. My heart aches to return home," Tomas said, closing his eyes, his mouth set in a grim line.

"I also," Aliss moved into Tomas's reach, moulding into his shoulder when he encircled her with his arm, "but we can never go back."

"I know," he whispered into her hair.

"We will find a new home. We have been promised much gold for this task and our debt to Haera will be paid. We will start a new life, even better than the old."

"Yes, you are right. There is nothing left for us back there now. Our home is in ashes and if the magistrate's soldiers spy either of us they will kill us instantly. This is a dangerous task though – hunting a witch – I do not know why I ever agreed to such folly."

"All will be well, love. Perhaps the duke will allow us to settle somewhere on his lands," Aliss answered.

"No. It would be unwise to stay anywhere in the Duchies."

"You're right of course. The duke would likely give us up easily enough. Perhaps we…" Tomas felt her flinch then as her words trailed off. She cried out and staggered back, bending over as she wrapped her hands protectively about herself.

"Aliss, what is the matter?" Worry lines wrinkled his forehead.

"Wine, get me some wine," she gasped.

Tomas quickly filled a cup with the ruby liquid and held it out for her. She took small, urgent sips.

"What is happening?"

"I do not know," she answered, "but it is passing."

"Sit," he instructed as he led her to the bed.

"I think I may have been using too much magic, too quickly. My body suddenly ached all over and I felt a burning hunger like I've never felt before, but I do not know what will sate the hunger. I just need to rest." She lay back on the bed and closed her eyes.

Tomas sat back in a wooden chair and watched her as her even breaths told him she had fallen asleep. He made an oath to himself then that when their task was completed, they would find a place to settle, and there they would remain for the rest of their days. He had experienced too many upheavals in his life already. Too many changes, from blacksmith's son, to orphan, to Royal Guard, to outlaw. He thought he had completed the circle when he met and wed Aliss and became a village blacksmith. He was sure that was to be the final leg of an overlong and complicated journey. Not so it would seem.

He would have to get word to Joshan. The old priest was the one constant in his life. The presence of the old man gave him a sense of assurance, a comfort knowing that if he fell, someone at least would pick up the broken pieces and put them back together. With these thoughts on his mind he drifted off to sleep.

A short while later he opened his eyes and Aliss was gone. His neck and back ached from falling asleep in the chair. He stretched and massaged his muscles as he shook off his sleep. He looked at the empty bed, bathed in the ghostly light of the moon. Surely he had not overslept, and if he had Aliss would have woken him. His glance fell on his sword hanging from the back of the chair, as he tried to dampen his feelings of anxiety. He heard a high-pitched wail then. Snatching his sheathed sword he ran to the window. By the time he got there, the cry had been stifled. Fear formed a knot in his stomach rising through him in a wave of frosty panic. *Aliss,* her name formed on his lips.

Beyond the second-storey window moonlight liquefied silver in the street below, but he could see naught. He had fallen asleep fully dressed, even wearing his boots. He contemplated climbing out of the window and dropping onto the street below. It would be quicker than using the more traditional exit. It was a good size drop though, and he was unsure whether Aliss was even outside. Perhaps she had simply gone down to the common room of the inn in search of food. He would look a fine fool if he broke his leg in the fall only to discover Aliss standing there brandishing a loaf of bread. He scanned the street below as best he could from his vantage point, listening for the sounds of crying again. Perhaps it was just a cat hunting, or fighting over territory.

In the three days they had been in the strange city Alka-Roha, with its bleeding walls, they had encountered no hostility—some curious glances perhaps—but that was not to say there were none about who would visit harm upon them. Aliss herself had said that the dream-witch knew they were hunting her. He knew very little about the High Priestess of Eor—or indeed about her god—she would undoubtedly have the resources to have a witch snatched from beneath the nose of a fool of a brigand and even worse blacksmith.

He strapped his sword-belt around his waist, resolving to go in search of his woman. He had thought her lost once already, when he snatched her from the magistrate's pyre. He would not lose her a second time. As he walked towards the door, his boots echoing on the wooden floorboards, seeming far louder in the still of night, he heard scratching coming from outside the window. Before he could move to go and investigate, Aliss suddenly sprung through the frame, landing with feline grace before him. Her storm-cloud eyes were a swirling maelstrom with bolts of energy lightening them into a fervour before him. She glared at him with such intensity and hunger he took an involuntary step back.

"Aliss..." he began but was silenced by her passion as she clamped her mouth to his, snatching the wind from him. She tasted strongly of iron.... overwhelmingly so. He staggered back as she pushed him against the wall, her tongue probing his mouth, her hands pulling at his clothes.

Through the roaring in his ears he heard a pitiful cry coming from outside, the words stirring memories as they echoed from the past. "My baby!"

He pushed her away, having to use all of his strength to do so, despite the difference in their size. He saw then, in the pale light of the moon, the crimson streaks on her face, her hands bathed in red... her clothes. "Aliss, what have you done?" His voice cracked as the words came out in a whisper. Above all was the sound of the woman keening from the street.

"You gave me new life." She smiled and he flinched at the sight of her bloody teeth. "I was reborn through blood magic, and I will ever hunger for it."

"Nooo!" he gasped, covering his eyes from what he had done.

When he opened them again Aliss was still asleep in the bed, moonlight pooling around her. *Just a dream.* His eyes watered for the memory of what he bade the old witch Haera do back in the Great Wood, and how someday he would have to tell his woman, what price her life had cost. He tried to shrug off the image of Aliss covered in blood, her eyes gleaming in the moonlight. The image blackened his soul. *It was a dream*, he told himself. A really vivid dream brought on by guilt and shame. He glanced at his woman again, lying peacefully on the bed.

Jarl Crawulf: Northern Duchies

His eyes opened slowly, allowing in a crack of light. He was looking up at a dark stormy sky. He could feel the rain on his face, he could smell the churned up, soaking earth, hear the sound of fighting men milling about; the rattle of weapons and armour, the raucous boasts of men glad to be still alive, the cries for help of those too injured to help themselves. Pain washed over him then, from his head all the way down to his feet. *At least I can still feel them*, he thought. Someone had taken his helmet off and rolled up a cloak for him to rest his head on. He raised a hand to where it hurt the most, and felt a bandage of sorts wrapped around his skull. He could taste blood—his own he assumed—as the incessant rain fell on him, almost soothing... almost. He could not summon the will to move anymore, or to tear away his gaze from the overhead clouds as they raced across the sky. It had taken him thus long to remember where he was. *Am I to die rolling in muck, in a field so far from home?* he wondered. He was not ready to die. The face of his wife with her olive skin and nut-brown eyes flashed before him. Curious, he was not usually one for sentimentality, but he found her image a comfort. She was a piece in a game, a game of kings played by powerful men she did not understand. *As am I*, he thought. Her father would not be best pleased to learn of his son-in-law bleeding to death on a sodden hillside. Crawulf knew that he too was merely a piece moved around the board by the real players, men like the emperor who gave their daughters to men far from home to ensure a favourable union, and to seek advantage in the game. The emperor was gambling that Crawulf

Blood Of Kings: The Shadow Mage

would one day become a king... a king of a rocky collection of windswept isles far from the empire. *What must it be like to possess such long arms that they reach around the world?*

"Jarl Crawulf, you yet live then?" The handsome face of Honbar Dolfson appeared in his vision, if a little blurred.

The jarl of Wind Isle suddenly sat bolt upright, remembering... remembering what? There was something urgent he needed to attend to, it was just on the edge of his memory.

"Easy now," Ulf the Red said. Crawulf stared past the shaggy beard and into the concerned eyes.

"The left!" he suddenly blurted. "Defend the left."

"All is well," Dolfson spoke in soothing tones. "Old One-eye saw the danger. His one good one twice the worth of most men's two." The clean-shaven Nortman grinned. "The battle is won."

Crawulf tried to push himself up, but a wave of dizziness and nausea swept over him. "Help me," he growled, and his two chosen men grabbed an arm each and hauled him to his feet. His vision swam. His head felt as if Boda's dark dwarves were using their hammers to mine into his skull. He stood on top of the hillside he had been so determined to hold; everywhere was carnage. Bodies of men and horses littered the ground, huge divots of churned-up earth scarred the hill. It gave him a sense of satisfaction to see that the dead of the Duchies far outweighed the deaths of his own men. He glanced over to the left, to where Duke Elsward had regrouped his mounted warriors and threatened the flank. He could make out the distant figure of One-eye as he strode about the aftermath of battle, clapping men on the back, or sharing a joke Crawulf could not hear. The scene was replicated everywhere on the battlefield.

"And what of Elsward?" he asked.

"Fled with a handful of mounted hoursecarls. The rest of his army is broken. Even now we hunt them down."

Crawulf nodded in grim satisfaction. Annoyed with himself for missing the end of the battle. Not that he had much choice. "Separate those men who are uninjured from the rest." Crawulf glanced over at a small group of Duchies warriors corralled together and surrounded by guards. They all wore the same look of fear and hopelessness on their faces. He searched for any sign of defiance and found none.

"We will hardly have enough room on the boats for ourselves if we take all those we have taken captive today," Dolfson said.

"They will not be boarding our ships. I am going to sell them. Jari-Vin will be here soon."

"Jari-Vin the slaver from the Deadlands?" Dolfson asked.

"Aye, skin as dark as coal and a black heart to match. I don't envy these men their future lives," Crawulf answered.

"So what now?" one of the men asked.

"Elsward will run to his castle, thinking himself safe there. He will send out for help from the surrounding lords, perhaps even his king. He will hope that we will take our plunder and return to the sea."

"Aye, it is what we do."

"Not this time," Crawulf said. "We will march on his castle and we will take it."

The sky grew darker still, the wind and rain increasing in pace. All around him, Nortmen ignored the weather as they herded prisoners together. The dead and dying were stripped of their valuables and anything useful they had on their person. Crawulf stared into the distance, consumed by an urgency and overwhelming need to conquer the lands around him and bring pain to the people who live there, a desire born from the humiliation of having his own lands defiled by an invader and a need to prove that he was still a man of strength.

"Jarl Crawulf." A warrior approached him, his face covered in dried blood and mud. "A... man wishes to see you," he said

Crawulf smiled; the pause from the warrior told him exactly who it was who wished to see him. He and many of his warriors had travelled far and wide in their sleek longboats, seen many strange things in distant lands, even so, the sight of a man with skin the colour of charred leather still gave them pause, and had them reaching for one of the many charms they carried about their person to ward off evil spirits.

"By the gods, he doesn't waste much time." Crawulf turned to see a channel open amongst his men as a huge figure strode imperialistically through the gap. Behind him lackeys strained under the baggage strapped to their backs, while either side two huge, dark-skinned warriors watched with steel-eyed coldness any they deemed to be encroaching too close.

"Not when there is coin to be made," Dolfson answered straight-faced.

"Aye." Crawulf grinned as he waited for the retinue to approach.

Rain beat down on the heads of both noble and lowborn, victor and captive, as a hush settled over the battlefield.

"He makes a fine entrance, I'll give him that," Ulf the Red said in his thick gravelly voice.

"My lord, Crawulf," the massive dark-skinned man beamed a smile as he bowed expansively before the jarl of Wind Isle. He wore bright, loose-fitting clothing, making him appear even more strange to the gathered Nortmen, as if his height and the colour of his skin were not enough. Strapped to his waist was a sword which curved at the end, its hilt possessing a large, green gemstone set into the pommel. Crawulf also noted a bright gem in each of his ears. *He dresses and wears jewellery like a woman,* the Nortman thought, but was under no illusion of how dangerous the man could be. Crawulf knew that he did not carry the peculiar-looking sword as a decoration. And certainly the two warriors at his side looked like killers. "It has been many, many moons since last we met. Far too long a gap for such friends as ourselves." The newcomer's mouth dropped into an exaggerated frown.

"Jari-Vin, it is good to see you too," Crawulf answered with a smile. He turned towards Dolfson then. "Find some wine for my guest. I also have a parched throat." The handsome Nortman nodded once and hurried to do his jarl's bidding.

"Even amongst all this blood and death, it is nice to see the laws of hospitality observed." Jari-Vin beamed a smile, the contrast of dark skin and ivory teeth startling in the gloom of the weather and morbidity of the surroundings.

"I am sure you have a thirst after a long and speedy journey."

"What else could I do when a good friend requests my presence?"

"Aye, I'm sure you have longed to be in my company again, and your almost unfathomable haste has nothing to do with the prospect of cheaply bought bodies for you to auction in the slave markets of the empire."

"You wound me." Jari-Vin clutched his chest.

"Aye, no doubt, but come. I have not the time to tarry. There are several hundred warriors here. You may have them all for ten gold crowns a head."

"Ten? And all I see are defeated herdsmen."

"You will sell them for five times the price."

"I will have to feed them. Many may not even make the journey, and you greatly overestimate any profit."

"Jari-Vin, you're a rogue and a thief." Crawulf smiled as he took a cup offered to him from his chosen man and passed it over to the slaver. They settled on seven gold crowns and sealed the deal with more wine and clasped hands.

"Where are your ships?" he asked the slaver, watching the tall, dark man grimace as he swallowed the wine. *A man with expensive tastes and used to getting them*, he thought as he savoured and swallowed his own drink.

"There is a small fishing village to the north and west of here. I have anchored there. I would like to make the next tide and begone from these excessively damp shores."

Crawulf looked up at the dark sky and the sheets of rain coming down from the black clouds. "You should come north to Nortland. *Then* you will see real rain." He grinned.

"Someday perhaps, but I am a man who prefers the feel of sunshine on his face. Not that I doubt the beauty of your magnificent home." Jari-Vin bowed.

"Aye, you're a sweet-tongued demon, Jari-Vin," Crawulf said. The big slaver simply bowed again, before turning to his guards and speaking to them in a language the jarl of Wind Isle did not understand. Immediately the two men bellowed instructions to the rest of Jari-Vin's followers. The rattle of chains followed as iron cuffs were, none to gently, slapped onto the wrists of the captive Duchies men.

"Honbar," Crawulf called his chosen man to him. "Take what men you need and escort Jari-Vin to his ships." The clean-shaven Nortmen nodded and began rounding up some warriors.

"Many thanks, my friend. May you travel calm waters under the favourable gaze of the gods," the slaver said before leading a much larger column of men from the hill than he first arrived with.

"Aye," Crawulf simply answered before hawking and spitting.

"They will hate you for this," Ulf the Red said as they watched the line of men snake over the hill and into the gloom of the misty rain.

"Yes, Ulf, they will," Crawulf answered as he turned his back on the men he sold into slavery, "but they will fear me more."

"What now?" a gruff voice demanded from behind. Crawulf turned to Olf Skarnjak marching up the hill, taking great bounding strides through the mud.

"One-Eye." Crawulf grinned. "They tell me you fought like a man possessed by the rage of a berserk."

One-Eye waved off the compliment with a scowl as he dropped his battle-axe into the ground and leaned on the upturned handle. Crawulf noticed the double blades were still thick with blood. "If they wish to come in nice straight lines to be killed, then so be it."

Crawulf laughed, feeling a little of the tension of leadership melt away. "Elsward's castle is less than a day's march from here, with very few defenders. I would have us take that castle." He waited as he watched One-Eye digest the information. It was never good to hurry Olf Skarnjak.

Eventually he hawked and spat before scratching his red beard and answering in his gruff voice, all the while his one good eye intent on his jarl. "You know my feeling on this. We are raiders, we hit and we go. Besieging castles is not what we do. We have not the knowledge or the skill for it. We cannot hope to hold the castle. We have beaten well the lord of these lands and softened them up for raiding for years to come, but there are other lords and their king who will hit back and hit back hard if we linger over long. However you are my jarl, and as I have always done for you, your brother and your father before that, I will follow where you lead."

Crawulf turned towards Ulf the Red. "Why do I keep poets and bards to sing songs and tell tales of our deeds when I have One-Eye?" He turned back to the big one-eyed Nortman. "Eloquently spoken, One-Eye." Then clapped him on the back.

As it happened, there was no need for a siege. The army of Nortmen emerged out of the mist the following morning and slowly encircled the castle. As Crawulf was examining its high stone walls and crenellated towers, the heavy wooden doors swung open. The jarl watched, with his chosen men alongside him, as a small column of six horsemen emerged through the archway, beneath the banner of Duke Elsward. *The dancing chicken.* Crawulf allowed himself a smile. The Duke himself led the group. The riders rode right up to where Crawulf waited.

"I am Duke Sorbatine Elsward, master of these lands you have invaded." The duke wore a long coat of mail; beneath a round helmet, blue eyes that may once have sparkled bore dark rings and heavy clouds, his beard was white and well trimmed. His jaw trembled slightly as he spoke, a muscle twitching in his face.

Crawulf stepped forward until he was a hand's length from the duke's grey, dappled mount. The horse stomped and snorted nervously as the Nortman approached. "I am…"

"I know who you are," the duke stammered before Crawulf could finish. "What do you hope to accomplish by this display of savagery? Does your king wish to go to war with the Duchies? Because I assure you, my king and fellow dukes will not stand by while you attempt to forge out a new kingdom for yourself. It is enough that we suffer incessant raids from you and your ilk… savages! Every last one of you!" Spittle formed at the corner of his mouth, his cheeks burning red. "Go back to the Pirate Isles, before you are all driven into the sea!" He paused then, his shoulders slumped as he turned and pointed at a line of carts trundling from the castle gates. "There, there is all the gold and silver we possess. Take it. Take it and go. You cannot hope to hold this castle from the king's army. I offer you my wealth in exchange for the lives of my people. What remains of them. It will make you a rich man and impoverish my family for generations. Take it and go back to the sea."

It was not what Crawulf had expected to hear. Yet he heard the truth in Elsward's words. They would never hold the castle from a determined assault from a large Duchies army. He looked to where Elsward was pointing at the line of carts rattling towards them along the muddy road. With a simple nod he took possession of Elsward's treasure and left behind a broken duchy, a far richer man than when he landed on its shores.

Lady Rosinnio: Wind Isle

"My lady, it is time," Crawulf's grey-haired counsellor said to her.

Rosinnio nodded and rose from her chair. Her handmaiden and the giant warrior, Rothgar, fell in behind her as she followed Brandlor from the empty hall. Normally the hall would be packed with warriors feasting or sleeping off hangovers at such an early hour, but since Crawulf had left to raid the Duchies, those men who had been left behind avoided the feasting hall of the dark castle. *Or is it me they avoid?* she could not help wondering.

A huge log fire blazed in the hearth at one end of the hall, but even so, she shivered as she walked across the flagstones. Two hounds worried at bones in front of the fire, crushing them with their sharp teeth, only pausing to look up briefly before retuning to their search for the marrow hidden inside the bones. Wooden shields and all manner of weapons adorned the stone walls of the jarl's feasting hall, eerily quiet without the raucous chatter of scores of Nortmen.

Outside, a groom held her horse for her while Rothgar helped her into the saddle. She had been shocked when the giant warrior had requested he be left behind when Crawulf took the majority of his men on the raid. There had been talk of little else leading up to their departure and ever since. It was to be a raid that would go down in legend among the Nortmen. So many men and ships assembled for a single assault on the Duchies, a raid needed to reaffirm the strength of Crawulf's claim on the crown once his uncle travelled his final journey to the All Wise's feasting hall. And Rothgar had chosen to miss the opportunity to have his name immortalised, in order to stay and guard her. It touched her heart that he felt such concern, especially when she thought most of Crawulf's other men would have preferred if the poisoner had been more successful. True, she had gone up in many of their estimations after she had roused the men to fight off the attempted coup. Yet, it seemed to her that, in their eyes anyway, nothing had changed. She was still and always would be an outsider. Rothgar had been good to his word in not mentioning to Crawulf the were-beast in her chamber or the blue flame she had somehow conjured to defeat the monster. She needed time to work out what was happening to her before she involved the jarl. In truth she was half concerned they would cast her out, or worse throw her into the grey sea when they heard the tale. She was grateful to the big warrior for keeping her secret, although a little surprised. Was it not, in a way, a small betrayal of his jarl after all?

She shivered again as she climbed aboard her mount and pulled her cloak tightly around her shoulders. The sun had not yet risen and in the gloom of night, when the only light came from the overhead stars and the flickering torches held by the grooms, every sound seemed to magnify tenfold.

They rode in darkness, with Brandlor leading the way. Rothgar rode by his side with Rosinnio and her servant behind them, two more warriors brought up the rear. She was an excellent rider, having grown up around horses in her father's palace. They were a different breed of animal to the larger, shaggier mounts used by the Nortmen. The stables in the palace were full of sleek, statuesque horses, bred for speed, as opposed to the sturdier beasts of Nortland. The conditions were a lot different too. Wind blew in the salty taste of the sea, dampness in the air reaching her bones, so that she felt as if she would never feel warmth again.

Brandlor brought them to a halt above a cliff as a crack of orange appeared on the horizon. She could hear a bird call out a long mournful note from the darkness.

"We will have to leave the horses here and climb down to the shore. It would be best to wait until the sun has risen. I would not like to be responsible for my jarl's lady falling to her death in the dark." He regarded her with a penetrating stare, making her turn away and watch as the light slowly spilled out from the horizon, turning the sea into liquid gold.

When he deemed it light enough to see what they were doing, Brandlor instructed the two warriors to remain with the horses, while Rosinnio gave the same instruction to a much relieved handmaiden. Rothgar, of course, would not leave his mistress's side. *I demanded this man's death when first we met*, she mused, once again unable to fathom how these strange men think. It was a stark reminder of how different they were and how much of an outsider she seemed to them. *I can see the beauty here*, she thought as she looked over the sea, the white caps visible now, the sound of waves breaking against the shore. *It is wild and rugged, so different to home... as different as I am to them.* The lone seabird called out again, leaving Rosinnio with a feeling of empathy with the small, lonely creature.

"Mind your step, my lady. It is quite steep." Brandlor led the way, as Rosinnio followed, half climbing, half sliding down the rocky incline. When they reached the bottom an apron of rocks stretched towards the ocean. Brine hung thick in the air as waves sprayed salty water over the rocks leaving a border of dampness along the boulders closest to the edge.

Beyond that vast ocean lies my home, she thought. *No, this is my home now.* "How can somebody live down here?" she asked the counsellor.

"Maolach is no ordinary man, my lady. He is both revered and feared by the folk. As one so close to the gods ought to be," he answered. "There!" He pointed at a dark opening cut into the cliff face by the power of the sea.

Rosinnio swallowed hard and felt a knot of fear form in her stomach at the sight of the cave. She could not help but wonder what would happen to Maolach if the tide were ever to rise over the shoreline and fill the cave with water. "Yes," was all she could manage as the muscles in her jaw clenched it tight and set her mouth in a grim line.

"You do not have to do this, my lady," Brandlor said, offering her his hand as she clambered over the rocks, silently cursing herself for wearing a dress, even if it was plain and spun from wool, unlike the elaborate silk gowns she wore in her father's palace. It would have been unseemly for her to wear the coloured breeches the men of Nortland wore, even if they would be more practical.

"Yes, yes I do," she answered as the salty wind snatched her breath. "If I were a noble lady of Nortland, born on one of the other islands and married to Jarl Crawulf, would I not be expected to visit the seer of Wind Isle?"

Brandlor nodded his agreement but remained silent. She felt the comforting presence of the giant warrior Rothgar behind her as she stood at the mouth of the cave. She regarded the black, gaping opening as she would the widening maw of a giant serpent intent on swallowing her whole. The thought made her shiver.

"Do not fear Maolach, as I said, he is not like other men." He handed her a torch and struck a flint to ignite a small flame. "Just follow the passage. Oh, and one other thing. Maolach will expect a gift, something of value."

Rosinnio nodded and took the torch. The flame danced frantically in the wind, forcing her to hurry inside the cave before it was blown out altogether. She hesitated at the mouth, perched on the border of light and dark, her fear paralysing her muscles. Hers had been a privileged upbringing. Youngest daughter of the emperor, her every desire and whim catered for by an army of attendants. Never before had she known such fear, not even when her father informed her that she was to be wed to a Nortman and shipped off to the Pirate Isles—although that had been bad enough—not even when she walked, holding aloft a sword, into the midst of a battle in the courtyard of the castle. But this, this brought terror to a whole new level for her.

Tentatively she placed one foot in front of the other. The passage was damp and smelled of rotting seaweed and dead fish. The deeper she went the stranger were the noises made by the wind, like ghosts wailing in the dark. Every sound made her jump and whirl around, the flickering torch making monsters of her own shadow and that of slimy rocks. Her mind searched for an anchor and conjured an image of the palace gardens, she imagined the colour and the heady perfume of the flowers, but the vision only made her realise that she could not find a place in the world any more removed from those gardens than where she was. *What would Crawulf think of her fear? Or Rothgar?* They would simply laugh at her and march boldly into the darkness.

She saw a glow up ahead, gently pulsating, inviting, a haven from the dark; yet now she feared to move into the light. *A gift.* Brandlor had said the seer would expect a gift. She pulled a silver comb from her hair, hoping he would deem it suitable. Then she walked towards the light.

The passage opened up into a wider chamber. At its centre a fire burned, the dancing flames casting eerie shadows on the damp walls. The rocky floor was littered with animal and fish bones, and stank so much of waste and rot that it made her gag. She resisted the urge to cover her mouth and nose from the foul odours. She held her breath, afraid to make a sound, fighting the urge to turn and run. Up against one wall, what looked like a bundle of oily rags, stirred.

"Who disturbs the rest of Maolach?" a voice hissed from the rags, dragging out each S, putting Rosinnio in mind of a serpent from some child's story she had once seen acted out. Only, no performer had ever sounded so sinister.

"Lady Rosinnio, wife to Crawulf, Jarl of Wind Isle," she said, hoping her voice did not quiver as much as her heart. "I bring a gift," she added and held out the silver comb.

The bundle shuffled forward into the orange light cast by the fire. A stooped figure wrapped in a cloak made from, what appeared to be, the feathers of gulls and other seabirds, stepped towards her. Lank, greasy hair hung in strands over his shoulders. He reached out with bony fingers, the nails crusted with dirt, and snatched the comb from her outstretched hand. "And what does the Lady Rosinnio wish from Maolach?" the voice hissed.

"I wish to see what Maolach sees," she said, taking an involuntary step back when he regarded her with dark eyes, before turning them on the comb.

"Maolach sees much," he said, reaching out to touch her belly and then screwing his eyes up to look at her quizzically.

"Even that others do not wish him to see. Like a womb that should be full, yet remains empty."

The small vial of the bitter liquid her handmaiden had procured for her sprang into Rosinnio's mind. *How could he know of this?* she wondered.

"What do you suppose would happen to the childless wife of Crawulf should he fall in battle on some distant shore?" he asked, stepping into Rosinnio's comfort zone. The smell of him standing so close made her gag again, but she hid it well—at least, she hoped so. Her answer was a shrug. It was all she could manage. "They would tear such a delicate summer flower into little pieces." His hands roamed over her body while she stood stiff-backed, daring not to move. "But the mother of Crawulf's child, they would fight for." He turned away from her then and shuffled over to sit on a rock by the fire, inviting her, with a gesture of a pale-white hand, to take the one opposite.

She sat on the rock, glad to have the fire as a barrier between them. He said nothing, nor even seemed to notice her as his head slumped forward. She waited. *He's fallen asleep,* she thought, *or died.* Her uneasiness only grew more intense as the silence continued. She pulled her cloak tightly around her as her mind recoiled from the memory of his touch. The sound of the sea drifted to her as her eyes were drawn to the hypnotic dance of the twisting flames. She allowed herself to be drawn there until she could see dark shapes forming at its heart. Figures from the past began to reveal themselves in the flames, lost memories of her childhood. Happy memories she was sure she would cherish forever, yet she had forgotten so many, she realised. When she looked up from the flames he was watching her.

"What do you see?"

"Nothing. I was just remembering some old friends," she answered, wondering how long he had been watching her.

"Tell me," he insisted.

"My sisters, there was an orange grove in the palace grounds. We would play there as children..." She trailed off as the memory brought a smile to her lips.

"Look again."

She returned her gaze to the flames, feeling the warmth of the fire on her face. A clear image of Crawulf suddenly appeared to her. He was standing on a hill surrounded by his warriors. Rain lashed down on them, turning the ground into a treacherous quagmire. She could see him bellowing orders, though she could not hear the words. He bore a sword in one hand, a round wooden shield in the other. She grimaced at the sight of the savageness of battle, flinching as each blow was struck, as blood flowed freely down the hillside turning the ground crimson. Crawulf gritted his teeth as he fended off a sword strike with his shield before stabbing his attacker in the chest. She did not want to look, but she could not tear her eyes away from the images in the flames, as clear as if she were watching through a window. "Why? Why do men fight and kill each other? How can they boast and sing songs about valour… about this… slaughter?" She wrenched her eyes from the scene and looked up at Maolach who was staring at her intently.

"Eat," he said, handing her a bowl of watery broth. The scent of the food wafted over to her, making her mouth water. She had not realised how hungry she was. She took the bowl hesitantly, fearful of what it might contain. She did not want to offend the seer of Wind Isle by refusing his hospitality. She brought the bowl, slowly, to her lips. Surprisingly, it was delicious. When she was done she handed back the bowl, very conscious of Maolach's unrelenting stare. It was as if his eyes were drawn to her every movement, linked with some invisible thread.

"Look again," he said.

She did as she was bid and returned her gaze to the blaze one more time. The flames parted to reveal Crawulf once again. This time he was alone. He was standing beside a massive tree. Its branches were bare of leaves; bark came away in thick strips from the gnarled trunk. The ground beneath his feet was covered in snow – Rosinnio had never seen the ground covered in a blanket of white before. Her eyes opened wide as the snow began to stir behind him, and a grey and bloodied hand reached out. She saw Crawulf's face turn to fear as he stepped back from the emerging arm, then a head, followed by a torso, until finally a full body leaking fluids and maggots rose. She wanted to cry out, but was paralysed with terror. Skin peeled from the corpse's head as it leered a lipless grin at Crawulf. The jarl raised his sword and cut it down. The dead thing—she could think of no other way to describe it—crumpled back to the earth. Crawulf stood with his back to the tree as the snow parted all around him, and more corpses rose from the ground. Rosinnio screamed then and tore her eyes away. Her lip trembled as her whole body shook.

"What did you see?"

Although it pained her greatly to relive the scene she told Maolach exactly what she saw. He regarded her for a long time before speaking. "You have been gifted with the hidden eye. Why would the gods bestow such a gift on a foreign harlot, unless they wish to mock me?"

Rosinnio's jaw dropped. Never in her life had anyone dared call her such a thing. Outrage boiled inside her. Yet, her desire to receive an explanation of her vision overrode her anger. "What does it mean?"

He looked at her with those dark, cold eyes. She felt as if she were looking into twin holes in the cold earth. "You have seen the past, the present, and what has yet to pass." His voice quivered, and Rosinnio thought she detected a hint of fear there.

"I do not understand. How can the dead rise from the ground?"

"A shadow looms over you. It bathes you in darkness. Even as I gaze upon it I can feel it trying to hurt me as it will cause pain to all who are close to you."

Rosinnio dropped her eyes to the ground. "I..."

"No!" he bellowed, interrupting her. "Speak no more of it. The more you do the closer you bring it. It is an evil thing I do not understand, yet I sense that it knows you only too well. Leave me now."

Rosinnio felt the compulsion in his words and yearned to leave. She fought that feeling. "If you can see the shadow then you know you must help me," she persisted, even as she moved away from Maolach and the fire.

"Go!" he commanded.

Her legs, almost of their own accord, carried her to the entrance of the cavern. "Can it be stopped? If it has not yet come to pass, can there be a different future?"

"Perhaps," he answered, and then walked slowly back to the cot by the wall and slunk down into it.

Rosinnio ran from the cave then, heedless to the dangers of running through the rocky passageway in the dark. Outside, Brandlor and Rothgar waited for her.

"My lady, we feared greatly for your safety. Thank the gods you have returned," the counsellor greeted her.

"You did? How so?" She looked out towards the horizon, the sun had barely moved in the sky.

"You have been gone a day and a night, my lady," the giant warrior Rothgar said.

Duke Normand: Eorotia

Duke Normand sat beside a roaring blaze, letting the heat from the fire wash over him. He had commandeered the largest dwelling in Eorotia for himself while he resided in the mountain citadel. The closest thing to a keep was the Temple of Eor and he had no desire to sleep beneath its roof. One priestess still remained at large, Elandrial, the most dangerous of all. He would never rest easy while she still lived, even if Djangra Roe insisted that he was beyond her power. He did not believe it.

He watched in silence as the mage walked towards him, his boots echoing off the polished flagstones. He could feel his face flush as he downed another mouthful of brandy, the fiery spirit warming his insides even as the flames heated his outer body. Djangra dragged a wooden chair over to the fire and sat opposite Normand, he carried in his arms a collection of leather bound books. Even before he opened them, Normand could see that they were old, by the tops of the yellow pages and worn bindings.

"Are you rested, my lord?" Djangra asked.

"Well enough." He still had a lump on his head the size of an egg where he smacked it against a tree and bruises aplenty from the mauling he had received from the giant beast.

"I've been searching the temple, seeking clues about this Dragon Lord. There are not a lot of books stored there, a lot less than you would expect. Most religious are pretty good at keeping archives. It's possible they destroyed them while you were besieging the city I suppose."

"And what did you find?"

"Tell me again, my lord, do you know who these people were? Or where they disappeared to after they dragged you away from your men?"

"It is as I already said," Normand began irritably. "I was thrown by the beast and hit my head. I felt hands on me and voices whispering all around me."

"And they called you the Dragon Lord?"

"Yes. No. Maybe. I don't know. They said something about a Dragon Lord returning or some such nonsense."

"So this Dragon Lord is a thing of worship for these people?"

Normand closed his eyes tight, his face twisting in pain. His head ached, and not just from trying to recall the events on the mountain. "The Dragon Lord will raise the dragon and bathe the world in blood," he intoned the words he heard. A log split in the blazing hearth, flashing sparks into the air.

"Do you think it a coincidence that your own crest is that of a red dragon, my lord?"

Normand shrugged. "Have you discovered who lives in the mountains?"

"I'm told there are a number of hamlets populated by wild folk who keep to themselves. Even the brigands who occupied the city stayed away from them, and know little enough about them."

"Are they followers of Eor, these wild folk?"

"Aye, perhaps."

"How is it these people have lived on the borders of my family's lands and we know nothing of them?"

"The same reason none of your predecessors were prepared to confront the problem of this city and its inhabitants. It takes a brave man to poke a hornet's nest."

"Or a stupid one," Normand added.

Djangra Roe shrugged. "The writings I have found are mostly gibberish intoning the great virtues of the goddess Eor. Some psalms about her grace and all-consuming power, and some warnings to her followers to eschew false prophets, and so on, and so on." He opened one of the volumes in his lap.

Normand could hear the crackling of the pages as the mage searched for a marked passage. "I thought this might interest you." He began to read. *"The goddess did walk among her folk, and all bowed before her, giving great cheer, with much gladness in their hearts to have her shadow fall upon them. Where the soles of her feet touched the ground, many jewels of different colours sprung like wildflowers from the earth, or veins of gold threaded the bare rock around her, fanning out like arms of the sun, with She at its centre, the source of all light. 'Gather these treasures and keep them safe from all who would seek them. One will come, he will rise from the chaos, you will know him and you will follow him. He is my Lord of Light.' As her eyes fell upon them, bathing them in her radiance they fell to their knees and wept, for they knew they had borne witness to the eternal light and all else would seem dim in comparison. Her people gathered her treasures then and retreated to the dark places of the world. Waiting for Him, the Lord of Light."*

"So? You read me a story for children and expect me to be impressed?" Normand said.

"Myth and rumour all have a whiff of truth to them, my lord."

"And you think, some disciple of the goddess Eor is going to come down from the heavens, and rid the world of all darkness, is that it?"

"No, my lord. I think there are those who believe this will happen and are watching for a sign, folk hidden in the dark places... and the *high* places, anywhere hidden from sight. These people are possibly sitting on a vast treasure. They are waiting for their lord to come and take it from them."

Normand paused, swirling the brandy in his mouth. "And if these mysterious people were sitting on a vast treasure how do you suppose we might convince them to part with it?"

Djangra set aside one book for another musty tome, before leafing through the crispy pages. *"The great king of the east, Jalen brought blood and fire to all realms. His was a reign of death and suffering, ushering in an age of darkness. From the midst of the storm rises the light, and none shine so bright as the Dragon Lord of Eor. From astride his great winged beast he casts down the Lord of Suffering and all who serve him in the world of man, even the mighty King Jalen who thought himself an immortal."*

"Dragon Lord, Lord of Light... you are giving me a headache, Mage. What do these stories have to do with me?"

"These books are written in different eras, by different authors. I believe they speak of the same man... entity... whatever. They are speaking of some kind of demigod made flesh who arrives into the world in times of great strife. Not once, but many times."

"Well, thank you for the lesson in obscure theologies, but you are talking about a man riding a dragon, more children's tales, more nonsense." Normand drained his goblet and refilled it from a decanter sitting on a table by his side. He did not offer any refreshment to the mage.

"My lord, it is not important that you believe in the Lord of Light, or Dragon Lord, whatever he calls himself. Merely that the guardians of Eor's treasure believe it, and believe that *you* are the Dragon Lord incarnate. Thereby making the entire hoard your birthright."

"Assuming it even exists."

"I think it does, my lord. Why else build this," he circled his hands to encompass their surroundings, "a city in the middle of an inhospitable mountain range, for no apparent reason?"

"This place has been called the Thieves Citadel for a reason. It has been home to brigands and pirates for hundreds of years. That is the reason for its existence. That it was not raised to the ground years ago is a shame on my predecessors. The power of the bandits and their witch has been broken. Broken by me," Normand answered.

"I'm sorry, my lord, but I believe there is more to it than that. This city may be hundreds of years old, but that temple is older still. It is at the heart of the city's past. You believe the brigands brought the priestesses of Eor to their city, gave them a home and worshipped their god in exchange for their protection against those with larger and stronger armies. Well, I say it was the other way round. I believe the city built up around the temple and the priestesses allowed its reputation as a den of iniquity to spread, in order to mask its real purpose. As guardian of the treasure of Eor."

Normand shook his head, clearly not convinced.

"These mountains are sacred to the followers of Eor," Djangra continued. "They have other temples scattered about the Sunsai Empire and even some small ones secreted about the Duchies, and beyond. But this is where they believe their goddess walked among them. This is where her treasure is hidden." His eyes blazed as he finished the last sentence.

"And how is it you've become such an expert on Eor, all of a sudden, Mage?" Normand demanded.

"As I said, my lord, I've been investigating their histories while you were hunting the mountain beast."

"Even if what you say is true, how does one become a Dragon Lord?"

"By acting like one, my lord."

"And I suppose you will conjure up a dragon to act as mine own steed." Normand allowed himself a smile at his own joke.

"Who knows what may be found in the higher peaks of these mountains, my lord."

"Do not talk nonsense. There are no dragons."

"Perhaps, my lord."

"My lord," a stiff-backed servant interrupted the conversation. "A royal messenger awaits your pleasure."

Normand's eyebrows rose, as he threw a quizzical glance towards Djangra. "Send him in." The servant bowed and beckoned with a raised hand.

The messenger hurried into the room, his tunic bearing the king's coat of arms. His family's crest was a boar's head, in the upper half was the crest of the Duchies, three grey castles on a sky blue background. Topping this was a crown. He handed a rolled scroll to the duke, and waited to be dismissed. Normand did so with a wave of his hand before breaking the king's wax seal and unrolling the parchment.

"His majesty," Normand spat, making the title sound like an insult, "has called a council of nobles. He has requested all title holders present themselves by a new phase of the moon."

"Less than two weeks away," Djangra said. "Does he say why?"

"Yes." Normand read through the royal message. "That old fool Elsward has had Nortmen overrun his duchy. The king is calling all dukes to a council of war to plan a strategy to protect the realm. In other words he's looking for gold and men from each of us."

"But surely, the north coast is constantly harassed by raids from the Pirate Isles. This is nothing new."

Normand shrugged. "The king is calling it the greatest threat to the Duchies since his reign began. It would seem that this was more than the normal raid on a fishing village to snatch a few slaves and loot a few monasteries."

"Will you go?" Djangra asked.

"I have no choice. Doubtless the king merely wishes to puff out his chest and scrape more taxes from already over burdened nobles."

"With your leave, I would remain here to continue my research."

Normand made an anxious face. "I am not altogether happy with so much distance between us, while the dream-witch yet roams free."

Djangra quickly rummaged inside his tunic and pulled out a small silver chain. He held it up for the duke's inspection. At one end dangled a small locket, a closer look and Normand could see the shape of a dragon embossed on the silver disc. The mage then pulled it open, two halves connected by a hinge. "I require a drop of your blood, my lord," he said, holding out the locket.

Normand hesitated as he inspected the proffered locket and chain. "You wish me to bleed into this?" His iron glare—often enough to make men tremble—fixed on the mage.

"Yes, my lord. It is a ward. It will keep your dreams… your own," he answered without flinching.

The duke drew a dagger from his belt and dragged it across the palm of his hand, ignoring the stinging pain he held up his hand and allowed his blood to drip into the locket. "Do not play me for a fool. I am not a patient man."

"No, my lord," Djangra answered, as he snapped the two halves together, before handing the locket and chain to the duke. "Wear it about your neck at all time. It will protect you from any attempts by Elandrial to enter your dreams."

Normand put the chain around his neck and fastened the clasp, his hand still dripping blood.

One week later: on a cold damp morning, Normand was greeted at the main gates of the citadel by Djangra. "What's all this?" the mage asked, surveying a line of mounted warriors lined up behind the duke. All wore blood red cloaks over their shoulders and identical helmets adorned with white horsehair plumes.

Normand had not seen the mage in the week since he had given him the locket. He was curious to know what news Djangra had about Eor and the mythical treasure he was convinced was hidden somewhere in the mountains, maybe even in the citadel. It would have to wait until he returned from the king's council. "One must look one's best for the king."

Normand led his Dragon Knights, two score of the best fighting men in his army, through the gates of The Thieves Citadel, their red cloaks billowing behind them.

Tomas: The wild lands beyond Alka-Roha

Tomas packed all of their gear—which didn't amount to much—threw it over his shoulder and followed Aliss down the stairs. The common room of the inn was shrouded in darkness, save for a single wax candle held by the innkeeper as he waited for them to leave. It was the happiest Tomas had seen him since they arrived. Harbouring armed foreigners under his roof evidently made him nervous. The duke's three men waited on top of their mounts, as did Ivannia, courtesan and guide. All four appeared spectral in the pooled moonlight, Aliss even more so. She looked pale, sickly even, yet her spirits seemed bright enough.

Ivannia had told them it would take two days at a steady pace to reach the temple. Tomas hoped fervently that they would find the dream-witch there, and would be done with this dangerous quest once and for all. As they set out on their trek, leaving the red walls of Alka-Roha behind, the sun bled crimson light into the horizon, turning the barren landscape into a bed of fiery waste.

Aliss smiled when she caught Tomas's eye. "It's beautiful," she said.

"Aye, it has a certain charm, for a bleak wasteland," he answered. She shook her head at his cynical attitude, but kept on smiling regardless.

The heat of the day quickly overwhelmed the cool morning as the sun rose steadily into an azure sky. Tomas cast his mind to the valley and the village of Woodvale where autumn would be turning the woods around the village into a magical kingdom of orange, yellow and plum leaves, where cool breezes would carry the musky perfume of the forest to his workshop. There would be a chill in the air most mornings, with a mist covering the fields and wrapping gossamer strands around the spindly branches of trees. He snuck a glance at his woman then, her straight hair the colour of a fresh snowfall, where once it had been like a field of wheat in summertime, her constantly shifting, storm cloud eyes a dark reminder of events past. The dark magic used by the old witch Haera had changed her physically, he could see that, but how much had she changed on the inside. It was her right to know what Haera had done... what he had agreed to; that dark, evil deed; using one life to save another. Yet, how could he tell her?

They took a break, shortly after the sun reached its highest point in the sky, at a small watering hole, where tall skinny trees, capped with long green leaves, towered over them. Tomas was glad of the rest even if the trees offered little shade from the heat of the burning sun. The water at least was cool and fresh. They refilled their waterskins and splashed water onto the backs of their necks and heads, before passing around loaves of flat bread they had bought from the innkeeper before leaving.

Horace sat down beside Ivannia leering at her as he did so. When she got up to sit elsewhere he made to follow until Aliss intervened. "Leave her be." The tracker shot her a dark look but stayed where he was.

"I wish for my payment now," Ivannia blurted out.

"No," Horace said. "Pay her now and the whore will sneak away at the first opportunity."

Tomas watched each of them in turn, sensing something was going on, but not knowing what it was. He could see by her eyes that Aliss was thinking the same. "Why do you wish to be paid now?" she asked the courtesan.

"I do not trust you to pay me once I've shown you the way. That one least of all." She nodded in the direction of the tracker.

"And what if you are lying and know of no such temple?" Aliss met the dark eyes of Ivannia without flinching. "What if you take our gold and abandon us somewhere in the desert?"

"I do not lie!" she spat. "Pay me now or I will return to Alka-Roha and you can wander out here until the skin falls off your bones."

Horace stood up, sliding his dagger from its sheath on his belt. Tomas stepped between them. "Give her half," he said.

"Don't be a fool," Horace snapped.

"It is the duke's coin, what do you care? Give her half."

Horald and Ronwald were both on their feet now, their meal forgotten. Ivannia stared defiantly at the tracker and held out her hand.

"If she runs…"

"Just give her some coin, and let's be done with it," Horald said.

Horace pulled out a small purse of coins and tossed out five silver coins.

"Gold, I was told I would be paid gold." The tracker fished out three gold crowns and slapped them into her hand. The coins quickly disappeared into her tunic. "Hey," she called after him as he began to walk away. When he turned she waggled her little finger at him.

Horald and Ronwald both guffawed. "Well, she should know," Horald said and laughed some more.

With the tension eased they all returned to their meal, Ivannia sitting beside Aliss. "Have you always lived in Alka-Roha?" she asked.

"No, not always. My village lies to the south, but I have lived in the Red City since I was a girl."

"Why did you leave your family?"

"I was left with little choice. There were too many mouths to feed and not enough food. My father took me to Alka-Roha. He exchanged me for enough coin to feed the rest of them for another year."

"Your father sold you to the brothel?" Aliss failed to conceal the shock from her face. Ivannia simply nodded before tearing a chunk of bread and stuffing it into her mouth.

"I..." she began.

"I do not need your sympathy," Ivannia cut her off. Aliss simply nodded and pursued the issue no further.

Shortly before nightfall, when the dying sun bled a crimson trail into the sky, they passed through a small village of squat, whitewashed huts. Women ushered small children indoors as the armed strangers rode through the town, their horses kicking up dust and leaving a billowing cloud in their wake. Men eyed them suspiciously, but none approached them or barred their way, nor were they given invitation or welcome to stay.

"Friendly bunch," Horald commented as they rode the length of the main street.

"They are frightened of strangers. Especially strangers with weapons. They are usually bandits and only come into the villages to rob what little they have," Ivannia quickly answered.

"Just like home then," the man-at-arms answered, grinning.

"We should stop here for the night, it will be dark soon," Tomas said.

"No," Ivannia answered. "We are not welcome here. I know a place where we can camp for the night. It is not far."

Tomas's gaze found hers, her dark eyes unreadable. "Don't they have an inn? Or even a stable we could bed down in?"

"Leave it be," Aliss interjected. "We will go with Ivannia."

Their guide led on without another word and soon the town disappeared into dust. She led them towards a small group of hills. Visibility became very poor as light drained from the sky. Riding in the dark over foreign terrain was a treacherous thing to do, and Tomas was becoming anxious they stop for the night. As the hills loomed closer, he could just make out an opening between them. Ivannia suddenly kicked her horse towards the gap, quickly leaving the rest behind.

"What's that fool of a girl doing? She'll break hers and her horse's neck," Horace spat, his contempt clear in his voice.

"Follow her, or we'll lose her in the dark," Aliss said and urged her horse after Ivannia's.

"No, wait!" Tomas called her back. He loosened his sword in its scabbard. Aliss arched her eyebrows. "This doesn't feel right," he answered her unspoken question. Even as he spoke dark shapes emerged from between the hills.

"Riders!" Ronwald barked, drawing his sword, the steel glinting in the receding light.

Tomas could make out a dozen or so riders coming at them fast. "Horace, get Aliss to safety," he commanded the weasel-faced tracker.

"No," Aliss said defiantly. "There's no time."

Within moments the riders were upon them, the robes they wore as protection from the sun billowed as they rode. They all bore weapons – scimitars, spears.

"Bandits," Tomas snarled. Behind him Horace had drawn his bow and nocked an arrow. Horald and Ronwald waited with swords drawn. "Aim for the one at the head," he instructed the tracker. Horace took aim and fired. The arrow looped into the air, missing his intended target, but finding a mark in one of the riders behind. A dark shape was punched from a horse, rolled in the dust and was quickly left behind.

The three swordsmen kicked their mounts into action and went to meet the charge head-on. Tomas swung his sword at the first bandit as his momentum took him through the group. The sound of hoof beats on the hard ground was quickly replaced by the noise of clashing steel and the screams of men dying. The maelstrom of mounted fighting men quickly became a swirling mass of dust. Horses screamed in protest as their riders fought to control them and swing their weapons at the same time. Tomas stabbed out at a dark-robed assailant, even as others lashed at him. A scimitar flashed by his head, the man behind it disappeared into the storm, dragged from his horse by Ronwald. He saw Horald gritting his teeth as he brought his sword down onto the head of a bandit. An arrow thumped a rider in the chest and he slumped onto his horse's neck before falling off altogether. Still there were too many.

Then he saw Aliss. She was at the edge of the melee, her eyes blazing as she made circular motions with her hands. He parried a spear thrust and swung at the neck of the spearman. A black cloud began to form in the palm of her hand. He could see her lips moving as she silently worded some incantation. The dark cloud grew to the size of a head, and she thrust it from her. A swirling mass of darkness enveloped the head of the lead bandit, cutting off his scream, energy crackled in tiny flashes, dancing from the first rider to men either side of him. All three suddenly burst into flames.

Tomas parried a half-hearted blow from an opponent before the man turned and fled, along with those brigands left alive. What was left of the three burning men lay still, their remains charred husks. He leapt from his horse, as Aliss dropped to her knees, and ran to catch her before she toppled over.

"Aliss... what did you do?" He felt her weight falling into his arms. Her eyes were closed, and when she opened them he could see the swirling grey clouds pulsing with energy.

"I drew heat from the air and below the surface of the ground and directed it towards those men," she answered.

"But how?" Tomas's voice trembled.

"I just knew," she answered quietly.

"Witch!" a female voice cried in accusation. Horace dragged Ivannia by her long dark hair and pushed her to the ground. "Sorceress!" she spat as she looked in the direction of the three scorched corpses. "You killed my brother with witchcraft." She began to sob then.

Horace unsympathetically shoved his hand into her tunic and retrieved the coins he had earlier given her. His rummaging took longer than was necessary, but Tomas was in no mood to chastise him for tormenting the woman who had just betrayed them.

"You led us here to be ambushed," he said.

With the aid of Tomas's arm, Aliss pulled herself to her feet. She walked slowly towards the woman, who would have backed away if not for Horace's hold on her. "Do you even know where the temple is?"

Ivannia nodded in answer, tears streaming down her face, her lip trembling in fear. "Don't burn me," she pleaded.

Horace leered and put his hand inside her tunic again. Ivannia didn't even notice, she was so intent on Aliss.

"Leave her be," Aliss said to Horace. The tracker shot her a defiant look but pushed the woman away and joined the other men. She then turned her full attention back to Ivannia. The courtesan flinched away from the hard gaze of Aliss. "You will take us to the temple. No more tricks."

"And you will let me live?"

"I don't know. Maybe," Aliss answered.

Tomas turned away from the scene, no longer able to watch the terrified harlot or the hard, pitiless look on his woman's face, nor the grey swirling eyes, flecked with tiny silver bolts, set so coldly on Ivannia. This journey had changed her beyond all recognition, he thought. The magic wrought by Haera, in the Great Wood, to bring her back from the threshold of death, had changed her. *What has become of his Aliss?* he wondered. *Will she ever return?*

Lady Rosinnio: Wind Isle

Rosinnio stood on the quayside, with what seemed like the entire population of Wind Isle, or at least its main town: Osfeld... her home. The people had turned out to greet the return of their jarl, she was there to welcome home her husband. Cheers and cries of greeting rang out as the flotilla of longboats manoeuvred into harbour. She remembered her own arrival, what seemed a lifetime ago, on board one of her father's ponderous sailing ships, nothing like the sleek longboats of the Nortmen. Beside her was Crawulf's counsellor, Brandlor, and as always, her shadow, the giant warrior Rothgar.

"Many ships return, and riding low in the water. A good sign they are full of treasure," Brandlor said.

To the outside world, the islands of Nortland were known as the Pirate Isles, inhabited by fierce sea raiders. Rosinnio had heard many tales, both as a child and a grown woman, of the horrific deeds perpetrated by these pirates all along coastal towns, even sailing their sleek longboats as far as the empire, to snatch and grab what they could before disappearing into the mist. The irony that she was now cheering home one such raid was not lost on her. She spotted Crawulf in the lead ship, one hand resting on the serpent-head prow. *Even from distance he looks relaxed,* she thought. His eyes searched the crowd until he spotted her, then he waved. She raised her hand in greeting as a horde of butterflies colonised her insides. She knew what would be expected of her, as a wife, later that night. It was a duty she accepted, perhaps not willingly, but she would perform and play the role the gods fated for her. Perhaps it would not be so bad if he drank a little less... a lot less, but she knew there was a feast planned and the hall would be awash with Nortmen quaffing ale, wine and honey mead. Their jarl would be a willing leader in the festivities.

Her father had sent her north, to the Pirate Isles, to become the wife of a Nortman. As a princess it was her duty to obey her emperor and accept her betrothal to whomever he deigned. Even so, the prospect of life on the damp and misty isles of Nortland had terrified her, even more the thought of being wed to one and living among them. They were still a mystery to her, but she would like to think she had grown up a lot in her short time on Wind Isle. She had accepted her fate with as much grace as she could muster and was determined to make the most of what she had been fated with. Did she miss the feel of warm sunshine on her face? Or inhaling the heady aroma of jasmine in the night air? Of course. Did she still cry herself to sleep every night at the prospect of never seeing her homeland again? Yes and most likely would for a very long time. The sound of gulls shrieking in the air as they sought to steal an easy meal from a fishing boat, or the feel of damp mist on her skin every time she stepped outside would never compare with the lush and colourful gardens of her father's palace. Yet, for all their wild ways, and harsh guttural language, the people of Nortland had an honesty about them. She may not understand it, or them, but if they smiled they were happy, if they scowled they were angry. Simple, honest folk... who robbed and slaughtered their way through life. *I will never understand them.* She smiled then.

Crawulf leapt across a yawning gap between ship and dock and landed firmly on both feet. A cheer erupted from the assembled crowd at his show of bravado. They were rewarded with a grin from their jarl. He spotted Rosinnio and headed straight for her. Her nerves were set on edge. She had quickly become used to life without him the weeks he had been away raiding. Now she would have to grow accustomed to being a married woman once again.

"My lady," he greeted her with a grin. She dipped her head demurely. "I have a gift," he said and held out a necklace towards her.

She took the gold chain, a large emerald wrapped in gold wire hung from the end. It was a pretty thing—she'd worn far more valuable baubles in her life as a princess of the Sunsai Empire—yet this gift touched something in her heart. "It is beautiful, my lord," she said.

Crawulf smiled, clearly pleased she liked his gift. He looked almost boyish, she thought, with his impish grin. She smiled then, surprising herself to discover she was, in some ways, actually pleased to see her husband. His was a familiar face in a land of strangers.

"Jarl Crawulf," Brandlor interrupted the meeting between husband and wife. "Welcome home, my jarl. I trust the raid was rewarding and eventful and you will have many tales of heroism and mighty deeds to enthral us with later."

"Oh aye," he answered with a grin. "And how have you looked after my wife and home?"

"There are some matters I would like to address with you," the counsellor answered, his expression stern. "There has been some trouble with wolves in the northern pastures of Halock's Feld, and the castle roof has sprung another leak…" And so the returning hero was barraged with all of the mundane problems a jarl is duty-bound to face. Rosinnio could only shake her head as Crawulf was ushered off the quayside by Brandlor, with the older man listing the many problems the jarl would now have to deal with.

"It is good that they have returned safely, my lady," Rosinnio's handmaiden said.

"Yes, Marta, it is," she answered, turning towards her servant. The other woman's attention was elsewhere however. Rosinnio followed her line of sight and her gaze fell on a tall warrior walking up the quay, a heavy chest over one shoulder a battleaxe in his other hand. He was glancing their way with a grin on his face. "Marta!"

Marta's cheeks reddened and she turned her head to hide her embarrassment. "Yes, my lady?" she answered with as much decorum as she could muster.

"He's handsome… for a Nortman." Both women tried and failed to suppress giggles. "Come, there will be a feast tonight.

I'm sure you wish to look your best." Marta's eyes opened wide and her face turned crimson once again.

Back in her chambers Rosinnio prepared herself for the night's festivities. As she sat at a small table, allowing Marta to drag a silver comb through her wet hair, the door suddenly burst open. Both women jumped with fright at the sudden intrusion. Crawulf stood in the opening, hands on hips.

"Leave us," he instructed Marta. The handmaiden quickly stood up, bowed and hurried past him. He waited impassively for her to leave before turning his hungry gaze on Rosinnio. "It has been too long." He closed the door to the outside world then and paced across the room.

Rosinnio let out a squeal as he pulled her up and began planting lust-filled kisses on her neck while pulling at the simple shift she wore. She tried to squirm out of his grasp but he was far too strong for her, the leather byrnie he wore over his tunic felt hard and rough against her simple silk garment.

"Stop!" she suddenly let out a roar, catching Crawulf off guard. A quizzical look formed across his face. "Please," she said then, more gently. She pointed towards the corner of the room where a curved copper trough sat, steam drifting up from its contents.

"What's this?" he asked, more curious than angry.

"A bath, lord. It is quite soothing," she said, taking his hand and walking towards the tub. "It will ease any aches and hurts you have suffered on your long trip." Crawulf allowed himself to be led. His nose wrinkled at the scent of roses and sweet perfume.

Rosinnio began unlacing his leather cuirass while he stood there regarding her. Next she pulled his tunic over his raised arms, marvelling at the hardness of his sculpted body, imagining the raw power contained in those muscles. She traced her finger along a jagged white line across his chest. "You have many scars."

"Marks of a warrior," he answered, still not moving, but for his eyes. She dropped to her knees and began pulling off his hard leather boots, he lifted his legs just enough for her to do so.

Her hands moved, nervously to his breeches, as if she were trying to coax some wild animal to eat a berry from her hand. He moved then, covering hers with his own, much larger hands. "I can do it," he said.

Stripped naked he stood before her, still watching her with a mixture of curiosity and amusement. Then he stepped into the copper tub and sat down in the steaming water.

"How does it feel?" she asked.

"As you said, soothing," he answered and lay back, closing his eyes.

Rosinnio took a cloth and began washing his battle-hardened and scarred body. He allowed her to scour out weeks of dried mud, blood and worse. She washed his hair and beard before combing scented oil through both. All the while Crawulf remained still, at first curious then contented. Once she'd finished to her satisfaction, and the once clean and sweet smelling water had turned dark and oily, she stood back while he watched her. With a deft movement she reached behind her and tugged at the lace on her shift, it fell to the floor in a puddle of silk, leaving her naked. Crawulf did not have to be asked twice to get out of the bath.

The feasting hall of Wind Isle Castle was stuffed to bursting point, a sight not lost on Rosinnio. While her husband had been away raiding the Duchies she was left to dine with none but the servants and her husband's hounds. Those men who had not gone on the voyage had chosen to dine by themselves and drink their own ale rather than their jarl's while he was away. Now he had returned. A great feast had been prepared, the large wooden tables were piled high with roast mutton, fish, and fowl, and bowls of steaming vegetables: turnips, leaks and a few other Rosinnio did not recognise. Servants squeezed past warriors, filling their cups with wine and ale. Those women with a comely face and shapely walk fought off the straying hands and admiring glances of warriors who had been away from home for too long.

Crawulf, every inch of him a lord of the north, handed out rewards to both those men who had fought bravely—an arm ring or a prized weapon—and gifts to others who remained behind to stand guard while the vast bulk of the fighting men were abroad. To the giant warrior Rothgar he presented an ornately decorated shield that had come from the pile of treasure Duke Elsward had paid him to leave his shores. "For the man who stood as defender to my wife and home, forsaking his chance at fame and wealth, in order to do so."

As the night wore on the feast became more and more boisterous as men who had become used to sleeping under the stars with one eye open, waiting for an attack from an enemy, who had spent weeks in hostile lands where every person from peasant to lord was a foe, one who hated them, were now once again home. Even Rothgar had relaxed his stiffness and sat with his lord, eating and drinking his fill. Rosinnio, however, was wary of strong alcohol and sipped in moderation from a single goblet of wine. She had given her handmaiden, Marta, permission to have the night to herself. She had spotted her earlier in the evening sitting at a long bench with the young warrior she had seen on the quayside. Both had long since disappeared though, and Rosinnio frowned in consternation. "I hope that fool girl knows what she is doing."

"What's that, my love?" Crawulf slurred his speech as he turned towards her. She had not even realised she had spoken aloud.

"Nothing, my lord. The celebration is going well," she answered.

"Aye, that it is." He suddenly reached for her and pulled her towards him, planting a wet kiss on her face. He smelled of ale, and of the sea, and of rose-scented water, she noted with satisfaction. "It is good to be home," he said with a grin.

Rosinnio's stomach lurched. She was not used to such shows of affection, even between man and wife, and it made her feel uncomfortable. She remembered the words of the old seer in the cave by the sea, and wondered how long it would be before Crawulf began to question her childless state. Thinking of Maolach sent a shiver down her spine, making her jumpy, so much so that she thought she spotted a shadow flittering between the bodies of the warriors. *Don't be a fool. You are acting like a frightened child,* she chastised herself. Even so she craned her neck in an effort to see beyond the revellers.

She soon realised her imagination was not playing tricks on her, when a stooped figure slowly walked towards the head table. Warriors and servants alike stumbled over each other to get out of the way and a path quickly formed. Rosinnio recognised the bird-feather cloak. The musicians trailed off the tune they were playing and the raucous din of the feast fell silent. Crawulf tensed beside her, before standing tall. Even when she stood beside him he made her feel small, being seated while he stood made him feel like a giant from the stories of her childhood.

"Welcome, Maolach. It is long since you honoured us with your presence."

Rosinnio noticed an edge to his words, and when she looked up into his eyes she saw something there she had never seen in him before: Fear.

"Aye, tis long since your father passed into the halls of the gods," Maolach said in the low, rasping voice Rosinnio remembered.

"You do us great honour. Come sit at my table and feast with us. The gods have granted us a great victory. There is much to celebrate." Crawulf waved at a servant to clear a place for the seer.

"You were ever the great warrior, Crawulf," Maolach answered with a sneer. "Destined to become king someday."

"With the help of the All Wise," Crawulf answered.

"Oh no, not with the help of Alweise, Crawulf, in spite of him!" Maolach sprayed those closest to him with a spray of spittle.

Rosinnio could sense Crawulf's unease. She was confused herself. Had Maolach just said that Crawulf was not favoured by the gods? She knew little of the ways of her new people, but one thing she did know was that a jarl without the god's favour was likely to have little luck.

The big Nortman smiled—it did not reach his eyes—and pounded on the table. "Some food for noble Maolach," he shouted out.

"I will not dine at your table this night, perhaps another." He edged closer until he stood directly in front of Crawulf and Rosinnio.

"Have you come seeking a boon? Whatever it is, if it's in my power I shall grant it." Crawulf fidgeted with his eating knife. Rosinnio had never felt such nervous energy from him before. The mysteries of the gods turn men into children the world over.

"Remember you spoke those words, Crawulf." Maolach regarded all those around him before turning his glare on Crawulf. "I had a dream. I dreamt that Feergor was caught by Irgard and devoured by his mate." Murmurs rippled through the feasting hall at Maolach's words. Rosinnio was doing her utmost to learn the ways of the Nortlanders and their gods. Only recently, Brandlor, the jarl's counsellor had spoken to her of the fire dragon who brings light to the sky each morning and the silver dragon whose icy breath quenches his flames each night. The two mighty beasts engaged in a constant struggle, eternally chasing one another's tail through the sky, giving the world day and night. Clearly Maolach's dream was seen as an ill omen. "Without Feergor there can be no sunrise. Ice and darkness will creep over the land, and all men and beasts will die." Rosinnio swallowed hard as Maolach's dream was met with silence.

"What can we do about this, Maolach? We have made offerings to the gods, should we make more?"

"No!" the seer snapped. "The gods do not want your offerings."

"Then what?"

"You have brought a shadow under your roof. All of the land will be shrouded in darkness because of your actions. You must journey to the land of the Frost People. You are the mighty warrior Crawulf, famed throughout Nortland for bravery and the knowledge of war. One day you will be king, but a king who rules the dead is no king at all."

"You're speaking in riddles, Maolach," Crawulf said.

"Ask her!" The seer flung up his hand and pointed a long, bony finger at Rosinnio. "She has seen it. The dead will walk and Feergor will not rise again!"

Rosinnio felt the eyes of the hall turn towards her. She looked up into the questioning glare of Crawulf. "I too had a dream," she began, "when I went to see Maolach in his cave. I dreamt of you. You were fighting men who were once dead and had risen again."

"Where?" Maolach interrupted with a roar, making Rosinnio jump.

"By a tree..."

"The Tree of Souls! You saw the Tree of Souls."

"I don't know." Rosinnio shrugged. The intense scrutiny of the entire hall was unsettling she could feel tears welling inside her.

"Find the Tree of Souls, Crawulf. It is in the land of the Frost People. She will guide you." He pointed a dirt-encrusted finger at Rosinnio once again. She wanted to shake her head, to deny any knowledge of the so called Tree of Souls, but no words would form. Instead she could picture in her mind a clear image of a dark, withered tree, its naked, spindly branches reaching skyward towards the heavens. She did not understand why or how, but she knew she would find a path through the ice to the tree.

"I cannot take my wife on such a hazardous voyage north. There must be another way, Maolach." Crawulf's eyes reluctantly left those of Rosinnio's and searched out the seer. "And what do we do once we've found the tree?"

"Take the Horn of Galen."

"Galen, who stands sentinel at the gates of Eiru, home of the gods?"

Maolach nodded vigorously. "She will know the way." Once again, Rosinnio felt the full weight of the seer's glare.

Duke Normand: Rothberry Castle

Duke Normand sat at a long, heavy oak table, along with the thirty-one other dukes who made up the most senior nobility of the Duchies. As the ruler of one of the smallest duchies he was seated farthest but one from the king, the duke with the dubious honour of sitting in that position was Duke Elsward, whose lands had recently been ransacked by the invaders from Nortland. That he had been so far removed from the king spoke loudly of his monarch's displeasure with him. The grey-haired duke sat with his head bowed, his shame clearly evident in his bearing. Normand sat restlessly beside him, eager to be as far removed from the dishonoured duke as possible.

Behind the king in a large open hearth, a blazing fire burned high against ancient scorch marks blackening the stone. Weapons adorned the walls of the high-ceilinged chamber, and at one end a large banner depicting the royal coat of arms hung over the fireplace. A large shield bearing the king's family crest was positioned just below the banner. The king was a powerfully built man, with a neatly trimmed grey beard and dark hair streaked with silver, tied back with a leather chord. His very presence dominated the room as cold, grey eyes regarded each of the nobles in turn, finally falling scornfully on Elsward. Normand felt the king's gaze wash over him briefly.

"Duke Elsward," the king began, immediately silencing the din of chatter in the room, all eyes turned on the hapless duke. "You have a tale to tell, do you not?"

"Aye, Highness. A tale and a warning," Elsward began nervously, ignoring the looks of scorn and whispered insults. "For generations we have suffered raids along the coast from the Pirate Isles. They appear out of the mist, run their longboats up our beaches and strike fast, carrying off loot, women and children, who are sold into slavery. We have always done what we can to protect our folk from these wolves of the sea. Usually by the time any force of men arrive they have gone."

"Not this time," the king interrupted.

"No, Highness, not this time. I am told the king of Nortland is weak and dying. He has no direct heir. His jarls are jostling for position, trying to outdo one another and prove that they are the strongest challenger to take up the throne. The one who led the attack on my lands was one such jarl. His name is Crawulf and he is nephew to the king. He landed on my shores with an army of battle-hardened pirates. It was no raid, it was an invasion force. He began by sacking the town of Seacliffe…"

Normand's concentration lapsed as Elsward began the whole litany of every farmstead burned, every rape and murder committed by the Nortmen. His gaze wandered around the walls, focusing on the many weapons: spears, maces, axes and swords hanging from the walls, and to the king's banner hanging high over the fireplace. He noticed a small balcony half concealed by the banner, and a figure standing there watching the council. *A woman.* He recognised her, memories of her bringing a smile to his lips: Lady Isabetha; as ever the king's spy.

"And how do you, my lords, think we should defend our land against these… pirates?" The king spat out the last word as if it left a bad taste in his mouth.

"We should build a fleet and invade the Pirate Isles and put the devils to the sword for once and for all," Duke Boromond said, a large man with a bald head. Normand knew that his lands and Elsward's bordered each other, and that the two were close allies, a friendship cemented with a union of marriage between his daughter and Elsward's son.

"Don't be ridiculous. The cost of building such a fleet would be astronomical," Duke Gregorn, a man with a bushy black beard and black hair hanging down to his shoulder, replied.

Normand closed his eyes as a row broke out between the nobles, those in favour and those against raising an invasion force. Several dukes took to their feet to press home a point, while others threw curses and threats around the room. Finally the king called the room to order.

"Enough!" his booming voice filled the chamber. "It is not practical to launch an attack on Nortland. The seas around the islands are treacherous. We would likely lose half the fleet on the journey. Then there is the matter of the islands themselves. Each one would have to be taken individually before putting to sea again to move on the next one… and for what? They are not a wealthy nation. There are few natural resources to exploit."

"But they must be taught a lesson!" Boromond interrupted his monarch. He was quickly silenced with a withering look from the king.

"That lesson you wish to teach would be a most expensive one for my treasury." The king turned back to the assembly. "This is what I propose to do. I will collect a tithe of ten percent on the annual levy. Each of you shall contribute this sum immediately. With this coin I shall increase the costal defences and form a standing militia to be garrisoned in the north. A professionally trained body of men who will be ready to answer any threat coming from the sea. In the meantime…" The chamber erupted into uproar as the nobles realised that they would now have to pay increased taxes. "Silence!" the king roared. "In the meantime I shall send representation to the king of Nortland and demand payment and the head of this Crawulf."

"Highness," Duke Elsward made himself heard. "I would assume I will be exempt from any increased taxes. The Nortmen rampaged through my lands and the cost of paying them to leave has impoverished me."

Once again the assembled dukes were on their feet, hurling insults at Elsward. The king regarded him coldly. "You think you should be exempt from paying the levy? The land you allowed the Nortmen to burn was granted to your family by the crown… my ancestor to yours," his voice began low and steadily rose. "The folk you allowed to be taken into slavery were my subjects. Better you had given your life in defence of the realm than to have taken the coward's road! You are lucky your head is not adorning a spike on the outer wall. It may yet. You, Duke Elsward," he spat, "have disgraced us all."

"It was not my fault," Elsward pleaded. The king suddenly launched up from his seat. He ran around the table, grabbing Elsward by the collar.

"Don't you dare!" he roared before drawing back his fist and punching the duke repeatedly in the face. Elsward sprawled against the flagstones. When he dragged himself into a seated position his face was bloody. He groaned as his eyes rolled into the back of his head. "Get him out of my sight," the king instructed two guards who were quickly on the scene. He was dragged from a chamber in stony silence.

Normand paid few visits to court, the distance to Rothberry Castle being too far for social visits, nor was he well known to the king and his courtiers. He had, however, heard enough tales of the king's temper. Even so, the sudden explosion of violence against Duke Elsward came as somewhat of a surprise. He wiped blood, sprayed from the hapless duke's broken nose, from his boots as the king marched from the chamber, his guards and lackeys quickly falling in behind him.

"So now we have to pay for that fool's mess." Normand turned to the man who spoke, but before he could respond a movement on the balcony above caught his attention. A swirl of skirts disappeared behind the banner as Lady Isabetha swiftly took her leave. Normand shrugged at the complaining duke and hurried out of the chamber.

Once outside in the corridor he caught sight of her hurrying down a wooden staircase and heading for the large wooden doors open to the courtyard and the sunlight beyond.

"My lady," he called after her as he pushed his way through the crowds that always accompanied a king's assembly, scribes carrying bundles of scrolls and feather quills, merchants dressed sombrely with respectful expressions as they looked for royal favours, and finely dressed nobles just posing and waiting to be seen. "Isabetha!"

She turned when she heard her name called and waited just beyond wide open, oak doors. Sun bathed her in golden light as her light blue dress matched the clear sky overhead.

"Erik," she greeted him with a smile. "It is such a rare surprise to see you this far north."

He ignored her feigned surprise, secure in the knowledge that moments earlier she had been watching him from a concealed balcony. "A pleasant one I hope," he answered.

"Of course," she smiled. "I assume you did not travel all this way to see me... although I would be most flattered if it were the case." Amusement sparkled in her eyes.

"Indeed, it would be reason enough, my lady."

"But..."

"But sadly, no. A duke must obey a king's summons."

"I hope the journey was worthwhile," she said.

"Three days in the saddle to have my taxes raised... I've had better."

"Oh, I'm sorry." Her eyes met his. If he did not know her better he would have been almost convinced that she meant it.

"Share a jug of wine with me," he said.

"I can think of no pleasanter way to waste an evening," she answered.

"Ah, so now I'm a waste?"

"Oh, Erik. You've always been my favourite waste of time."

"I will need some time to work out if I'm being flattered or insulted," he said, a frown creasing his face.

"Isabetha," the voice of a young woman interrupted their conversation.

"Highness," Lady Isabetha greeted the newcomer, inclining her head and curtseying respectfully.

A young woman with dark brown hair tied up in curls and waves stood before them. Her low cut gown exposed a long neck and ample bosom of cream-coloured skin. Blue eyes sparkled mischievously as she brazenly looked Normand up and down, lingering on his broad shoulders before her full, pink lips parted in a smile. "And who have we here? How naughty of you to be hiding him from the rest of us, Isabetha."

"Your Highness, may I introduced Duke Erik Normand of Lenstir."

"Oh, the mysterious Duke Normand. You do not disappoint, my lord."

"Duke Normand, this is, Her Majesty Princess Cordalia."

The king's youngest daughter, Normand suddenly realised. The last time he saw her, her hair was in pigtails and she was playing with a wooden doll. "It is a pleasure to meet you again, Highness," he answered. "A very great pleasure to see the woman you have grown into."

"Oh, he is a feisty one, Isabetha. Don't you dare keep him to yourself." Princess Cordalia smiled. "Alas, I cannot tarry. Don't you dare return to Lenstir without first coming to visit me." As suddenly as she arrived she'd gone.

"She seems… nice," Normand said, turning his attention back to Isabetha.

"She'd eat you raw." She laughed. "And then the king would feed your balls to his hounds." She slid her arm into the loop of his elbow then. "Come on. Didn't you promise me a jug of wine?"

They made it through half the jug before ending up on Isabetha's feather-filled mattress. Normand lay on top of her, driving into her as she arched her back to meet his thrusts. He held her wrists over her head as she wrapped her legs around his waist, urging him on with moans of pleasure. All the while it was not the face of Lady Isabetha he saw beneath him, but the mischievous eyes of Princess Cordalia. Even as Isabetha sunk her teeth into his shoulder he was picturing the track of freckles across the princess's nose, her creamy skin soft and tight over her collarbone. Isabetha screamed as she reached a climax. Normand heard Cordalia's voice as he spilled his seed into the writhing Isabetha. He rolled off her then and both of them lay on their backs, gulping in air.

"Oh, Erik, you really must visit Rothberry more often."

Normand rolled off the bed and walked naked to a table by the window. He poured wine from the unfinished jug into a goblet and drained it in one go, before refilling. "I was just having similar thoughts," he said.

"When do you leave for Lenstir?"

"Right away." He finished the second cup.

"So soon?"

Normand fingered the amulet at his throat, gifted to him by Djangra Roe, as a ward against the dream-witch. "That fool of a mage I have in my employ is convinced the mountains are filled with hidden treasure, the hoard of a god, no less. I must return before he pulls my new city and those mountains down."

"Djangra Roe?"

"Yes, do you know him?"

"We've met. You should listen to him. He is a most resourceful and insightful man."

Normand did not quite know what to make of that… but then again, he never quite knew what to make of Lady Isabetha. She was ever the enigma, a beautiful one, and a most dangerous one. "I'll bear that in mind," he said as he scooped his clothes up from the floor and began pulling on his breeches.

Isabetha called to him as he was about to leave her chambers. "Princesses are not meant for minor dukes, Erik. I would not like to see your head adorning a spike above the castle entrance."

Normand didn't answer and closed the heavy wooden door behind him.

Tomas: Temple ruins, wild lands of Alka-Roha

Tomas led the small group of riders towards the temple. When they saw it first, it was little more than a dark shadow in the distance, a smudge against the clear blue sky. "There! There is your temple," Ivannia shouted excitedly. They approached the ruin in silence, weary from the long journey over the hard, parched land, wary of what they might encounter, the least of which being a further attack from bandits.

"This is the place we seek?" Horace asked, incredulity and scorn lacing his words.

Tomas took in the crumbling walls and collapsed buildings within those walls, any building material other than stone long since rotted away. As he approached the area that would have once been the main gate, his horse shied, forcing him to pull hard on the reins. The animal's unease spread quickly to the other mounts and they too began to struggle with their riders. Tomas dismounted and handed the reins to Horace.

"This is a cursed place. Even the animals know better," Ivannia spat.

Aliss sat on top of her mount in stony silence, all colour drained from her complexion. She'd spoken little since the fight with the bandits, only to answer direct questions, and then with single words or nods. To Tomas it almost felt as if she were draining away, even though she had reassured him of her health countless times.

"There's no one hiding here," Horace said, also dismounting and passing the reins of both his and Tomas's horse to Horald.

"Only ghosts," Ivannia said.

"We can leave here and return to Djangra Roe and tell him we failed if you wish," Tomas answered the tracker.

Horace spat into the hard-baked earth, clearly weighing up the options, balancing which he feared most, mage or the temple ghosts. "This place has a queer feel to it," he said.

"It is the magic used to conceal what is really here," Aliss spoke, her voice barely above a whisper.

"Magic..." Horace said and spat again.

"Let me go now. I have brought you where you asked," Ivannia said.

"No, she will bring more bandits and attack us while we sleep," Horace said.

"You want to drag her with us all the way back to the Duchies?" Tomas asked.

"No. She's right about one thing. She's done what we asked of her. She is no longer of any use to us," Horace answered. "Kill her."

Ronwald, who was closest to her, drew his sword.

"No, wait!" Tomas cried, but too late. Ivannia's eyes suddenly opened wide in surprise as Ronwald's sword exited through her chest. "What have you done? You bloodthirsty curs!" He ran to catch her as she toppled from her horse, but even as she fell into his arms he could see that she was dead.

"It's better this way." Horace shrugged.

"Murder is the better way?" the blacksmith said, fighting to control the emotion in his voice.

"She would have left our bodies in the desert after robbing us and not given it a second thought. Do not act the child, blacksmith," Horace answered before turning towards the ruined temple.

Tomas felt his rage build inside him, the flames of anger fanned to white hot. His hand dropped to his sword.

"No, Tomas. Horace is right. We could not let her go." He heard Aliss' words in his mind, and then a calming wave covering him

like a blanket. He shrugged off the emotion and turned to his woman, who was still sitting on her horse, her lips not moving.

"You're putting words and thoughts in my mind now," he accused. "Who are you?" he spat when she didn't answer. Her eyes slid away from his accusing glare and dropped to the earth. He loosened his sword in its sheath then and followed Horace into the temple.

Broken columns and pillars littered the courtyard, giving the impression of what once may have been a very grand place. A statue of a woman, its nose chipped away and one arm missing, caught Tomas's eye. "The goddess Eor," Aliss said, coming up behind him.

"You're speaking to me now… with actual words," he shot back.

"I'm sorry, Tomas. My ability to control magic is growing. I don't know where this power is coming from, or how I'm supposed to use it. Most of the time I don't even know what I've done, or how I did it. I feel so tired," she said.

"When you two are quite finished whispering love poems to one another…" Horace called out. Tomas looked over to where the three Duke's men stood waiting. A dark chasm beckoned behind them, the entrance to the only building still standing. The door was long since gone, pillars at either side chipped and broken. A shiver ran down his spine as he looked into the dark portal of gloom.

"You say magic is being used to cloak what is really here," Tomas said. Aliss nodded in response. "So what I'm looking at is not real?"

Aliss shrugged. "I don't know anymore. I thought I saw something in the scrying bowl, a shifting image of what we see now and a temple in perfect repair. I was sure I was seeing through a magical screen… but now we are here it looks real enough."

Tomas frowned. "If you are right then there are most likely eyes upon us right now." He glanced at the three men, waiting, weapons in hand, and then to the body of the girl lying just beyond the enclosing wall. "We can leave here now. We don't have to do this."

Aliss' back stiffened; her eyes became more alert. "She knows we're here," she said.

"So this is the place?"

She nodded and pointed towards the dark doorway. "In there." Tomas's eyes followed to where she was pointing, his feeling of unease growing even stronger. "When we leave this place life will have changed," she said, turning her grey shifting eyes on him.

He looked into the swirling clouds gathered there. "Life has already changed." He drew his sword then and joined Duke Normand's warriors.

Once he stepped into the darkness he felt as if a curtain had been drawn. No longer was the temple an ancient, dusty ruin. A long stone-flagged passageway yawned before him. Flickering torches bathed the corridor in an orange glow. The walls were covered in drawings depicting images of animals and people supplicating to a female deity. The two warriors, Ronwald and Horald, led the way, placing each step cautiously in front of the next.

"How is this even possible?" Tomas whispered, as he gawked in awe at the artwork illuminated by the glowing torches.

"Magic," Aliss answered back.

"How can I tell what is real and what his not?"

"Trust nothing," she said.

Even though the passageway was clearly still in use Tomas could detect an underlying mustiness to the place—the thought of a tomb springing an unwelcome image to mind.

"The passage widens," Horald said.

Up ahead, the corridor widened into a circular chamber, at its centre a large statue, not unlike the one Tomas had seen outside, only this one was not in disrepair. With sapphires for eyes and ringlets of gold through its hair, the idol was worth a fortune. Other precious stones were used as decorative buttons on her carved garments. Horace could not contain himself and ran to the base of the statue, where he immediately began prying loose a ruby decorating the goddess's foot.

"This place is more crypt than temple," Horald voiced Tomas's concern. The blacksmith and the two warriors circled the statue seeking another passageway or door.

"Look at the walls," Aliss said, her words coming out in a whispered croak.

The chamber was a circle only broken by the passage they had entered by. The walls, illuminated by the flickering glow of torches, were covered from floor to high ceiling with a painting of a vast mountain range. The closer Tomas inspected the mural the more detailed he realised it was.

"Mountains," Aliss said.

"There is some script here," Horald said from the far side of the chamber, forcing Tomas to peer around the statue. "The lettering is in gold."

"Gold?" Horace looked up from his excavation work.

"What does it say?" Tomas asked.

"I cannot tell. It is in no language I know how to read," the man-at-arms answered.

'The return of the Dragon Lord shall herald the dawn of a new era for man. Only when the world is plunged into darkness will the light of Eor shine bright again.' A female voice intoned. Tomas whirled around. Standing just beyond him, between he and Aliss was a woman, who could only be Elandrial High Priestess of Eor. *'Only the purifying flames of the dragon can cleanse the world and bring about a new beginning,'* she continued. Tomas raised his sword two-handed before him. The three warriors formed a semi-circle behind him, all with their weapons drawn. *'When the Dragon Lord ignites the fire, he shall call forth the servants of Eor, summon them even from death to purge the world.'*

"Don't move," Tomas said.

Elandrial parted red lips in a smile. Hair so black to be almost blue hung over pale shoulders, exposed by a low cut gown of sky blue silk, green eyes sparkling in a face of almost impossibly white skin. The very sight of her was mesmerising to the blacksmith, none more than the incredibly lifelike tattoo of a third eye printed onto her forehead.

"Welcome, Tomas," she said, continuing to smile warmly, as if she were hosting old friends for dinner. She turned full around to face Aliss. "And welcome, Aliss... sister." She turned back around then. "These three are not so welcome," she added, her smile falling from her lips as she turned her eyes on Duke Normand's men.

They had spent long months hunting their quarry, travelling hundreds of leagues from home in their quest. Now that they'd found her, Tomas did not know what to do.

Horace raised his bow and drew back the string. The arrow shot forward towards the priestess, an easy target from such a short distance for the experienced tracker. For an instant her eyes appeared to glow, an emerald radiance in the dull light of the chamber. The arrow turned to shadow and passed through her before clattering against the wall.

The grating sound of shifting stone filled the air around them as black-robed men suddenly appeared from the walls, surrounding them. Aliss quickly slipped past the priestess to join Tomas, while their three companions formed a small circle, back to back as they eyed the robed men warily.

"We have been waiting on you, Tomas," the priestess said, the smile returning to her lips.

"You knew we were coming?" An uneasy thought that the mission had been doomed from the start began to gnaw at him.

She simply smiled warmly and opened her arms as if to invite him into an embrace.

"I don't understand."

"Don't trust her," Aliss whispered in his ear. The priestess turned her gaze on the young witch.

"And you, dear one, I know what it is that you crave." She took a step closer. Tomas raised his sword in warning. "I can help you." The sound of a babe crying in the distance drifted across the chamber.

"No..." Tomas gasped.

"The old witch in the woods cursed you when she brought you back from the dead."

"I..." Aliss began, but then trailed off, her brow wrinkling in confusion.

"Haera healed her. She was sorely wounded, but Haera concocted an elixir to repair her hurts," Tomas insisted.

"I know what the witch did." Elandrial took another step closer, and turned her gaze on Aliss. "The blood of an innocent is what you desire. You can feel it deep inside you. You will always lust after it... even if you don't understand why."

"No," Tomas said without conviction.

"What does she mean, Tomas? What did the witch do?"

Tomas turned towards his woman, but he could not meet her eyes. "The babe, the missing babe..."

"Marjeri's child? The infant you searched for in the woods? You said it was snatched by wolves."

Tomas didn't answer, as his mind returned to that night in the Great Wood. *A life for a life.*

"She never told you it wouldn't end there, that it would never end. Dark, dark magic brought you back into this world, and without it you will return to the realm of night." The sound of the baby crying became louder. Tomas could see the strain and despair in Aliss' eyes. Her hands were balled into tight fists as she faced the reality of the life she was gifted when she ought to have died. He knew she would consider the price paid to be too high. That she would sacrifice herself that the babe would breathe life once again. *Too late.*

"And you, Tomas, you find yourself in league with the murderers of your mentor and long time friend." Tomas's eyes narrowed. "The priest," she added, noting his confusion.

"Josh?"

"They killed him when they searched for you."

Tomas turned towards the three duke's men. He could see the fear in their eyes. "You killed Joshan?" he asked, his voice low and even.

"It were the mage, Djangra Row what killed the priest," Horace said, his voice edged with hysteria.

"Joshan is dead?" He turned back towards the priestess. She nodded sombrely.

"He took on the role of father when your own passed," she said.

"I..." Tomas stumbled over his words as confusion clouded his mind.

"He was a good man. Men call me the dream-witch. They say I can turn their nightmares on them and kill with a thought."

"That is why we are here. Duke Normand..."

"Duke Normand is a fool!" Elandrial's emerald eyes flared. "He and that pet mage he thinks can protect him. He thinks he defies me with his tricks and wards... yet he cannot see who it is who guides his hand. Where did the thought come from that he needed a witch to hunt me down? Why would he seek out a blacksmith and the woman he walked into the flames for?"

"You?" Tomas asked hesitantly.

"Yes," she simply answered.

"But why?"

Once again Elandrial smiled her enigmatic smile "Look at them," Elandrial said, pointing at the duke's men. "Read the guilt in their faces. Kill Joshan's murderers, join me and together we will redesign your destiny. Yours and that of your love."

Tomas looked again at the three men. He saw Horace as a twisted, craven thing, always looking to see how he could best profit from any situation. He remembered how Ronwald had coldly rammed his sword through the back of the courtesan, a life taken without a second thought... and Horald, was he the one who struck down Joshan?

The black-robed disciples of Elandrial produced scimitars with wickedly curved blades, from beneath their robes. Only their eyes were visible beneath the head scarves they wore.

"Kill her, kill the bitch!" Horace bellowed an instruction at Tomas.

The blacksmith blinked, and suddenly the priestess was inches away from him, close enough for him to inhale her scent of exotic fruits. She placed a hand on his chest. He felt his heart beating rapidly. Just one push and he could skewer her with his blade; end it all there and then.

"They are not your friends," she said, leaning in closer. He could feel her breath caressing his cheek.

"Tomas..." Aliss called a warning. He ignored her as he focused on the cherry-red lips of the priestess.

"They killed the priest simply because he would not give up your whereabouts. Join with me now. We belong together." She turned towards Aliss. "All of us."

"Let the Hag's Pit take you then!" Ronwald suddenly roared and ran at the priestess, swinging his sword in an arc towards her head.

Tomas's own blade came up to meet the blow. Sparks flew as the swords met. Ronwald glared at him with wide open eyes, his jaw dropping in surprise. Horald let out a roar and hefted his weapon, but before he had time to move he was assaulted from all sides by the black-robed disciples. Curved blades flashed in the orange light of the chamber, slashing down and coming up red, the duke's man-at-arms cried out sharply as he was forced down by the relentless attack of multiple whirring blades. In moments he was silent.

"No!" Horace cried and turned to flee. He was grabbed and dragged back, screaming.

"I can remove the curse afflicting your woman," Elandrial purred into Tomas's ear. "Or would you rather feed her the blood of innocent babes that she may continue to live?"

"Who killed Joshan?" Tomas asked Ronwald, his stare cold and hard as he regarded the warrior.

"Like he says." He nodded towards Horace. "It were the mage."

"And you were with him," Tomas spat. Ronwald flinched but had no more time to react as Tomas drove his sword into his chest, memories of the old priest burning into his mind. Ronwald dropped to his knees, his eyes wide. He tried to raise a hand towards Tomas, but failed and slumped forward onto the ground, blood seeped into the flagstones as he lay still.

"The All Father protect me," Horace whimpered.

"You will make Aliss well again?" He turned towards the priestess. She nodded as her lips curled into a smile. "The mage... Djangra Roe?"

"I will take you to him, and you can do as you will."

Tomas nodded and flicked his wrist. The tip of his sword drew a thin red line across the throat of Horace. The tracker gasped and then made a choking sound, bringing his hands up to his throat, a spray of blood drenched those closest to him.

"Stay true to your word and we will have no quarrel," Tomas said, turning back to the priestess. Beside him Aliss coughed and swayed. He caught her before she fell.

"Oh I will keep my promises, Tomas, I will fulfil your every desire." Emerald eyes sparkled in the torch light.

Aknell: The house of Lorian

Aknell raised the hood of his robe, and bade Rolfgot do the same with a slight inclination of his head as he approached the wider, quieter streets of the nobles and merchants quarter of the city. The road rose gently as the houses became steadily bigger and grander until he reached the final tier. Even the air was cleaner higher up, none of the constant cloud of choking dust, along with the sounds and smells of so many people living closely together. Nothing of the palatial homes of the richest men in the city was visible beyond a solid wall fronting the street. Aknell was well aware of the type of residents hidden behind those dour facades; these were the homes of men to whom money was no object, no luxury too fine. Stout wooden doors were all that marked them as homes, until one stepped across the threshold. Only then was the fabulous wealth of these most powerful of men put on display. Spy holes, where suspicious eyes kept a constant vigil on the street below, dotted each wall. *They're a cautious lot, the nobles of Alcraz,* Aknell thought to himself. *And why wouldn't they guard their riches jealously?*

"This way," he said to the giant Nortman, pointing at an ornately carved oak door. "The house of Lorian Olmet." He read aloud the script etched into the wall in gold leaf.

He looked farther up the hill to where the emperor's palace dominated the skyline, sitting beyond the houses of the wealthy citizens of Alcraz. Its towers and domes dwarfing every building around it. *Like a fat hen sitting on her clutch of eggs,* Aknell thought.

He knocked on the door with the edge of his fist, pounding on the heavy, solid wood until a small shutter was pulled back.

The doorman wordlessly slammed the peephole back into place and moments later the door creaked open. Aknell and the massive Nortman Rolfgot stepped through the archway into an open courtyard. Several guards, armed with spears and short swords by their sides, lined the walls.

"It would seem our friend, Lorian, has upped his security," Aknell said, as much to himself as to his companion. Two guards approached, blocking them from proceeding through the house.

"Your weapons," a third said.

"I am unarmed," Aknell said, a pleasant smile on his face. "You can search me if you wish," he added as he opened out his arms.

"That won't be necessary, but I'll need to take your bodyguard's sword."

Aknell's smile grew wider. The sight of these house guards attempting to disarm the giant Nortman would be most entertaining. He was almost tempted to let them. Instead he nodded towards Rolfgot and the Nortman unstrapped his weapon and handed it over, sheath and all, while his face remained neutral and unreadable. Aknell revelled in the guards discomfort as he took the weapon from the Nortman.

The gatekeeper led them through the small courtyard towards the main door of the house. Once he stepped onto the tiled-floor of the hallway, the real wealth of the owner was revealed. Artworks adorned the walls of the spacious entranceway, huge pillars propped up the high ceiling. Overhead skylights allowed sunshine to flood the room. Standing in a pool of light was their host, Lorian Olmet. The fat nobleman spread his arms wide in greeting, before clapping his hands together twice in quick succession. Servants hurried to attend him, bearing trays of drinks and bowls of water for his guests to wash their hands.

"Welcome, welcome to my home, my friend." He grinned. His chins moved as he nodded his head jovially. *A little too good-natured,* Aknell thought. He noted, once again, the increased guards hovering, trying to remain out of sight, and how Lorian glanced once at the big Nortman before quickly looking away. His fear of Rolfgot was evident enough. "Come, sit with me on the balcony. It is a beautiful day and there is a wonderful view of the city from there." He led his guests towards the back of the house without waiting for a reply.

There was indeed a fine view overlooking the city, likely only bettered by the view from the palace one level higher up. Aknell sat on a cushioned couch, while Rolfgot took up position behind him, standing statue-still, his arms folded across his chest. A small table set before the couches was piled high with various fruits of the empire, as well as breads and cold meats. Lorian dropped into a couch opposite and immediately plucked a duck leg from a platter on the table.

"Eat," he said and began gnawing on the drumstick. Aknell noticed how his hand trembled ever so slightly as he reached for the food.

He smiled graciously and reached for a small loaf of bread, tore off a chunk and bit into it. "Thank you, it is most welcome," he said. "We have not spoken in many months, my friend. It has been too long."

The fat man shrugged, his eyes darting between Aknell and the Nortman standing behind him. "Life has been busy... difficult," he said, his eyes dropping away from Aknell.

"Oh, how so? Is there trouble at the palace?"

Lorian's eyes shot back up. "Always questions about the emperor, Aknell. Your fishing makes me worry I have allowed a spy into my house." The fat man smiled at his own joke, although the humour did not reach his eyes.

"Now I know something is troubling you, Lorian. Are we not friends?"

"Yes, yes of course, I'm sorry. A cloud of suspicion hovers over the palace. It is as contagious as a plague."

"It must have been seismic to have you so nervous, my friend, he who is normally the very essence of calm and foresightedness." *Peddler in rumours and gossip more like*, Aknell smiled reassuringly at the fat man.

"Some months ago, assassins made an attempt on the Princess Rosinnio's life."

"On Rosinnio's life?" Aknell's smile remained in place.

"So I'm led to believe. It was made to look like a coup and attempt on the life of her husband, but I'm told by my sources, the emperor and his closest advisors believe that was a rouse to mask the real reason, that being to murder the princess."

"But why?"

Lorian leaned in closer, glancing around him, as if there were eavesdroppers all around him. "Rumour has it the reason Rosinnio was sent north to marry was to remove her as far away as possible from the palace. The emperor feared so strongly for her that he sent her to Nortland, where he thought she would be safer. Imagine... safer in the Pirate Isles!"

"But that makes no sense." Aknell sat back into his couch and looked beyond his host at the city yawning below the balcony.

"Somebody in this city has the emperor scared enough for his daughter's safety that he sent her as far away as he could imagine. Who has the power to frighten an emperor?"

"There are higher orders than that of an emperor," Aknell said.

"Higher than an emperor? I don't follow you," the fat man said.

"Are the gods not infinitely higher?"

"I suppose, but the gods have their own places and rarely interfere directly with affairs of mortals."

"That is where you are wrong. The gods take a very great interest in what men are doing. A god is only as powerful as his followers make him... or her."

"Anyway it is a moot point. It was men who poisoned the princess, not a god," Lorian said. "Somebody with enough wealth to hire a company of swords, and enough power to frighten an emperor. Who has that power over an emperor? And why Rosinnio?"

"Sadly, all things must end, my friend," Aknell said.

"What are you talking about?" The fat noble fidgeted nervously on his couch, glancing over to where his guards stood silently just inside the house.

"The time has come for change, Lorian, for the world to be remade."

"Aknell?" Lorian smiled unconvincingly.

"It has been quite some time since your friend Aknell walked among the living, I'm afraid."

"I don't understand."

"His likeness has served me well, these past years, but now I think it is time to move on. I can sense him finally departing. He was most strong, stronger, I think than you will ever be. Alas, I have a long journey to undertake now, Lorian, and I need something from you."

"What is that?" The fat man's words came out in barely a whisper.

"Your soul."

"No!" Lorian backed away from the man he thought his friend. A movement caught his attention as the giant Nortman started towards him. "Guards! Guards, kill them!"

Guards armed with spears and short swords suddenly materialised, rushing the balcony. The one nearest Lorian stood between the fat noble and the Nortman, his spear raised. Rolfgot snarled and advanced on the guard, snatching the weapon from his hands and turning it on its previous owner. Lorian backed to the edge of the balcony until he felt the balustrade behind him. He watched in mounting terror as the Nortman lifted a charging guard into the air and flung him from the balcony. Another swung a sword at him, but he simply caught his wrist, twisted and the sword fell to the ground with a clatter. The huge warrior grappled the man then, twisting his neck until a sickening crack made him go limp.

The Nortman turned towards another advancing guard only to have a sabre driven into his chest, running him through until it protruded out of his back. The captain of the guard stood back then, a smirk on his face as he assessed his handiwork. The smile quickly faded.

Without taking his eyes from him, Rolfgot, with both hands on the hilt, pulled the sabre slowly from his own body. Where a dead man ought to be lying stood an angry warrior with a bloody blade in his hand. The captain of the guard ran.

Lorian wretched. "What in the name of the gods are you?" Words choked out from a constricted throat as tears watered his eyes. He slid down onto his knees as Aknell approached him, shaking his head as he blubbered out words, begging for mercy. The jewel Aknell had gifted him all those months before fell out from beneath his tunic, a silver light pulsed veins of light from deep within the unblemished stone. Lorian gasped for air as he clawed at his throat.

"Your body is weak and pitiful," Aknell said with disgust clear in his voice.

"Help me." Lorian choked on his words.

"Help you? I despise you. It pains me that I will be stuck within your weak flesh until I find a more suitable host, but your face will open doors for me another could not."

"What...?" Lorian gasped, as tears streamed from his eyes

Aknell revelled in the pain and fear of his victim, just as he had done when he stole the body of a merchant as if it were a new cloak. The soul of the merchant had cried out in agony and anguish from somewhere deep inside for a long, long time. He fed on the exquisite pain of Lorian as he melded his emotions with the fat noble. It was an easy matter to push aside the essence of the man and assume his body as if changing his coat. Deep down he felt Lorian struggle, he fed on his fear and desperation. The power of the ancient jewel aided his own, but it was he who possessed the magic to transfer his essence into the body of another. He who could usurp the soul of another.

Rolfgot stood over them, his shadow falling on the fat nobleman. All the while the Nortman's expression remained emotionless.

Lady Rosinnio: Wind Isle

Mist swirled around her feet clinging to the dark, naked trees barely visible in the moonlight. She felt the chill of night creeping into her bones, making tiny bumps rise on her skin... or perhaps it was not the cold making her feel so. Fear instilled the iciness of winter into the blood, as every shadow became a monster stalking its prey. She knew terror's freezing touch well enough, and the hooded creature who haunted her dreams. She turned about in a full circle, slowly, taking in her surroundings. The forest was impenetrable, an army of dead trees with jagged thorns and leafless branches sharpened into spears; a single touch from one of the poisonous tips would be death. Filtering into the air around her were noxious gases exhaled from the dying bark and stinking earth where the trees sunk decaying roots, corrupting the soil with their wrongness. There was no escape from the haunted wood, no escape from him.

The sound of snapping branches and snarls of an angry beast fighting against its incarceration in the wood caught her attention. Fear filled her soul as she redoubled her efforts to find an escape route. All the while, the hooded man laughed silently, mocking her, from just beyond her vision, seen but unseen, hidden from view and her inner sight.

Her heart leapt and stomach lurched as the fur-clad creature burst into the small clearing. He looked up, fierce anger burning in his eyes, and something deeper... hunger – Crawulf. She raised a hand, nervously, in greeting. He drew his sword. She could feel the heat of his fury burning the air around her as he regarded her with the eyes of an untamed forest creature. A wolf wrapped in fur and with the sharpest of teeth, forged from the strongest steel. She felt the mixture of awe and fear she always felt when he was near her, like being caged with a wild and unpredictable beast.

"Husband?" Her single-word question floated on the air, a barely felt breeze on a hot day. In the distance she could hear laughter, not good-natured jolliness, but cold, mocking laughter. Another shape emerged from the trees. Crawulf snapped his attention towards the newcomer. She gasped as a mirror image of her husband stalked from the forest. The laughter intensified, coming from all around her now.

The two Crawulfs ran at each other, swords raised. Thunder erupted from their meeting, lighting flashed from the clang of blades. The earth beneath her feet rolled, knocking her to the ground as her husband fought with his mirror image. They roared and swiped with savage cuts of their blades, each aiming for the killing blow, both evenly matched. Blood gushed through the air in crimson sprays, splashing greedy, black soil, as both combatants found a mark. They whirled about the clearing fighting a deadly duel until she could no longer tell which was which. Still the laughter drifted across the forest, its source just out of sight. Fear and frustration warred within her as she watched the ongoing battle, increasing in its ferocity, knowing that her fate was entwined with the outcome.

Thunder raged and wind howled as she opened her eyes into darkness. The room was suddenly illuminated as Alweise hurled lightning spears across the sky, doing battle with the dark elves of Boda who eternally besiege Eiru – home of the gods. Her heart raced as the memories of the dream overwhelmed her. She realised then that her first thoughts on waking were of the gods of her new home and not those she worshipped since a girl. Shivering, she pulled the heavy furs covering her bed up around her neck. She was alone in the bed. There was a feast, she remembered… there was always a feast. She could hear the muffled sounds of drunken warriors carousing, singing their battle hymns, and bragging about their feats of bravery to each other.

A flash of lightning quickly followed by a clap of thunder shook the walls of her chamber, the stark, stone walls and narrow windows doing little to keep out the wind and sound of The All Wise's eternal struggle with the minions of the wife he cast out. She threw off the furs and jumped out of bed, quickly lighting an oil lamp. Elongated shapes crept up the walls as the orange glow of the lamp chased away the darkness, consigning any demons hidden there to the shadows. She dressed quickly in her warmest clothes and flung a heavy woollen cape over her shoulders, and hurried from the room. A spiral staircase led downwards, its steps uneven and awkward. She put her hand on the wall to ease her passage down, feeling the dampness seeping into the stone. The noise became much louder, the light brighter as she reached the bottom of the staircase. She could hear men guffawing at some joke or other, while others called to the servants to bring more ale. She hurried past the feasting hall, not waiting to see if she had been noticed.

Once she was outside in the courtyard, she could see how the weather besieged the castle, as rain was driven in from the sea by roaring winds. A wooden pail skipped and bounced across the cobbled ground, rolling past her at speed. Within seconds she was soaked as the icy rain froze any exposed skin. She ignored the howl assaulting her ears and ran to the stables, disturbing a stable boy from his slumber on a bed of straw in one corner.

"My lady..." he stammered, caught off guard by the late-night visitor.

"Help me," she simply said as she pulled at a saddle from the rack. The boy was quickly on hand to lift it down for her while she selected the mount she wished to use.

"The weather, my lady..." he said, it was not his place to question a noble born even if it did appear she'd lost her wits.

"Saddle this horse for me. Quickly now," she instructed, ignoring his concern. Spears of light lit up the sky, allowing her to see his grime-covered face clearly and the questioning look he gave her. Moments later thunder roared, making them both jump.

"It's not a good night for riding, if you don't mind me sayin' so, my lady."

"Never mind that. Here, help me up."

He cupped his hands and lifted her aboard. "I can come with you," he said.

"No," she replied, "but thank you. Open the door."

The horse was reluctant to leave the warm, dry stable, but a sharp kick to the flanks from Rosinnio had it moving with a jolt. She was almost flung from the animal's back as it reared on hind legs, protesting with loud snorts. "Open the gates and close them behind me," she roared over the wind. The boy quickly ran across the courtyard to the heavy wooden gates, dipping his head against the howling gale sending sheets of rain over the castle wall. She calmed the horse with soothing words while she waited for the main gate to ponderously creep open. "Ha!" she roared at her mount. Even the loud echo of hooves on cobbled stone was drowned out by the wind.

Any folk mad enough to be abroad on such a night who caught a glimpse of her riding recklessly along the coast road, with cloak and hair streaming behind her as waves crashed against the shore, sending salty spray high up the cliff face, would swear they'd seen a ghost atop a dark horse driven by the wind.

Lightning streaking across the sky lit her way, showing her the outline of the road, worn into the ground from years of use. One slip or a misplaced hoof and she'd be thrown from the horse, with no one to find her broken body until morning. Still she urged the beast on faster. She knew where she was going, and although she'd only been there once before she knew she would find it, even in the dark. She would find it if she had to crawl all the way blindfolded.

When she reached the spot she had last been with Brandlor and the warrior Rothgar she dragged sharply on the reins, bringing her mount to a skidding halt. She leapt from its back, a flash of lightning revealed the small track that led down the cliff. She could hear the sea crashing against the shore, smell the brine in the air. Without a backward glance she began her descent, pulling up her hood against the biting rain and the spray of seawater as she climbed down closer to the shore. It occurred to her that the sea may have already invaded the cave with its violent assault on the shores of Wind Isle. Still she pressed on. When she reached the bottom she could feel the spray of salt water on her face as waves battered the rocky ledge, below that the stone beach had already been reclaimed by the sea. Without thinking she ran towards the dark entrance to the cave, a black portal to the realm of Maolach.

Wind howled through the tunnel, like the roars of some great sea monster. Each wave crashing over the ledge sent water racing up the dark passageway. She splashed her way on until she finally spotted a dim glow up ahead.

She walked slowly into the light, each breath a struggle. The wind and roar of the sea became a faint din in the background, almost forgotten. A mound of feathers stirred from before a fire, a grizzled head of white tufts looked up. "You are late," Maolach said without looking at her. He poked at the fire with a stick sending sparks spiralling into the air.

"I don't understand," she answered.

"You should have come a lifetime ago," the seer answered.

Rosinnio ignored the answer and sat on a rock opposite him. "I dreamt of Crawulf again. This time he battled a warrior with his own likeness."

"What else?"

"The hooded man… I could not see him, but he was there."

"How do you know he is real?" Maolach looked up, regarding her with dark, hooded eyes.

"Because he haunts my dreams," she answered. The fire crackled as the old man jabbed it with his stick, one end blackened the other slick and green. "And I haunt his."

"Yes, I see him. I have always seen him," the old seer hissed. "He cloaks himself in shadow. He has crossed the bridge that cannot be crossed. He has sparked a light where there can only ever be darkness." He glared at her then, his stare reflected in the firelight, intense and frightening, so much so that she felt an urge to flee from him as fast as she could. "He has walked among the dead and brought them back."

The fire between them suddenly began to dance wildly as flames grew and took on the dark shape of a tormented face, writhing at the heart of the fire. Its widening mouth formed an 'O' as it opened in silent agony.

Rosinnio leapt back in alarm. "What's happening?"

Maolach threw what looked like a handful of sand into the fire. Flames momentarily flared to several times their size, with burning tongues stretching outwards. The fiery face loomed over them with flaming arms reaching for them. Then the fire quickly returned to normal. "He will bring shadow to the world of light."

Rosinnio scrutinised the fire before returning to her seat. The face was gone. "It was him... the hooded man."

"Yes," Maolach answered. "The ghost of your dreams."

"He will come for me." Terror laced her words.

"Perhaps. Or you could go to him," the seer answered.

"I..." Rosinnio regarded the old man as if he were truly insane... perhaps he was. "I would never go to him. Why would I do such a thing?"

"Because you must. You must stop him before he drowns the light from the world."

"Do you know who he is?" she asked.

"No. But you do."

"He knows you are here now," Rosinnio said, her lip trembling.

A choking sound came from Maolach's throat. An icy thrill of fear ran down her spine as she wondered if the hooded man had cast some enchantment on the seer, until she realised the noise was laughter.

"I am just an old man in a cave at the end of the world." Maolach cackled. "The sun has risen and the storm has died. Crawulf searches for you outside."

"I should go to him," Rosinnio answered, surprised at the feeling of comfort she felt at the thought of her husband's protection.

"Yes."

"Please, Maolach. Tell me what I must do."

Maolach looked up as she stood over him, his eyes opening in surprise. "I have told you once already. You must take the Horn of Galen from the Tree of Souls."

Before she could answer, voices drifted into the chamber from outside, her name drifting on the wind over the noise of the ocean. She turned from the seer then and fled back down the tunnel, towards Crawulf.

Duke Normand: Duchy of Lenstir

"How was your trip to Rothberry Castle, a worthwhile journey, my lord?" Djangra Roe asked as he walked across the polished flagstones of the great hall.

Normand looked up sharply as he poured wine from a jug into a silver goblet. "The king's solution to all things is to raise taxes, so no, Master Mage, it was not a worthwhile journey." He returned his attention to the red liquid filling his cup. "Help yourself." He indicated the jug to Djangra once he'd finished with it.

"Thank you, my lord." The mage took a cup and poured a measure of wine. Both men then took their drinks to sit in chairs by a roaring fire. "These old bones feel the autumn chill more each year," he said as he stretched out his hands to warm them. "Did the amulet serve you well?" he asked, gesturing with his head towards the chain hanging from Normand's neck.

"I had no witches attempting to kill me in my dreams, if that's what you mean. Perhaps she's already dead. Have you heard from the men sent after her yet?"

"Perhaps, my lord, but no, I have not heard from them."

Normand sighed, his impatience evident in the thin line of his mouth and his furrowed brow. "So why are you here, Mage? I would have thought the temple in Eorotia was a better place to search for clues to the location of the dream-witch."

"Ah yes. I have taken the liberty of questioning some of the wild mountain folk regarding the hoards of treasure secreted by the followers of Eor."

"Those people are now citizens of Lenstir… my people," Normand interrupted.

"I was most gentle, my lord," Djangra responded without losing a breath. Normand shook his head and regarded the mage coolly. "They were not very cooperative, but I did manage to discover from some texts in the temple that they have a sacred place, a hidden valley high in the mountains, a place where the goddess Eor supposedly first walked among men. Of course none of them were prepared to reveal its location." Djangra's face widened into a smile. "But I have found a map. It's very old and I've ordered it to be copied lest it fall to pieces under our touch, but…"

"A map? To a hidden valley and a god's treasure? I have a duchy to rule, increased taxes to raise. I have no time for such idle foolishness."

"But you were most enthusiastic when last we spoke," Djangra said.

"Perhaps the mountain air has addled my wits."

"Come back to Eorotia with me. Let's find this pass before the winter blocks off the high places. If nothing else it will give you a chance to eradicate the cult of Eor. Those mountain folk may well be your subjects now, but as far as they are concerned their loyalties are bound to the goddess Eor and her servants, including the dream-witch."

Normand's brow wrinkled then, and the cup he had raised to his lips fell away. "You don't suppose they are hiding her in those mountains? Could she have been under our noses all this time?"

"Who can say, my lord?"

The following morning, Duke Normand led his Dragon Knights out through the castle gates, with their red cloaks billowing behind them. From a distance they looked like a stream of blood flowing through the countryside.

"So you can find this hidden valley?" Normand turned towards Djangra as they sat wrapped in cloaks, warming themselves by a campfire.

"I think so, my lord."

"Do not expect a mountain of hidden treasure."

"Perhaps if you read the texts from the temple yourself, I have done little else since you left Eorotia."

"I have no interest in reading any texts," Normand snarled, "let alone nonsense from some anonymous, ancient author. If it were not for the very real possibility of the witch hiding somewhere in my mountains I would not be making this trip. Get some sleep. We have a long hard ride tomorrow." Normand turned away from Djangra Roe and stared into the flames. His mind wandered back to previous conversations he had had with the mage regarding the mythical hidden treasure of Eor. True, he had become caught up in the mage's enthusiasm for treasure hunting, yet events had overtaken his desire for finding an easy fortune on his doorstep. Other plans were formulating inside his mind, plans which need a seed to be planted before they would take fruition. A smile played at the corner of his mouth as he pictured the sparkling eyes of a princess, and the words of warning from Lady Isabetha, *'princesses are not for minor dukes'*. *We shall see*, he thought. *We shall see*.

He could feel the heat of the fire on his face as the sound of armed men drifted over him; the chatter and rattle of weapons and armour, the neighing and stomping of horses. Flames danced before him, writhing hypnotically. His mind wandered to far-off places and imagined delights of a princess's bed—and the power and privileges that would come with it—*she'd eat you raw*, Isabetha had said. Normand smiled at that as his eyes grew heavier. *Wine*. Had he thought it or said it? *A jug would be most welcome*. His eyes closed and his head drooped forward.

When he opened them he was disorientated and confused. He was sitting in a chair on a raised platform in the audience hall of the temple to Eor in Eorotia. He knew it well enough having only recently taken the city from the thieves and brigands who occupied it with the help of the dream-witch – the High Priestess of Eor.

"Your wine, my lord," a female voice interrupted his thoughts.

"Wine? How am I here?" he asked. The woman simply smiled and walked towards him, bearing a large jug in both hands. She looked familiar to him. She wore a simple, ankle-length white dress. Her dark hair was scraped back and tied on top of her head in a pony-tail. *Pretty*, he thought and felt his desire rising.

"You ordered wine, lord," she said as she approached the platform, three steps separating them. Emerald eyes shone in the lamplight.

"I have seen you before," he said. He stood then, sensing the wrongness of his situation. His movements were slow, his thoughts clouded and confused. Yet, he felt a burning need for the woman before him. He could imagine throwing her down on the steps and taking her there and then. She smiled, as if reading his thoughts, biting her lower lip. *She wants it too.* He walked off the first step. She bowed her head demurely, offering the jug.

"I know you want it, lord," she said, a distinctly seductive tone creeping into her voice. He did not think she was talking about the wine. And she was right—he did want her, his need and desire for her growing by the second.

He knocked the jug out of her outstretched hands. It fell to the floor, shattering into shards, wine spilled over the mosaic floor—he had never noticed the image in the tiled floor before—from the steps he realised the image was of a dragon in the coloured tiles. He grabbed her shoulders roughly and tore the dress off them, exposing her creamy breasts. She made small sounds of protest which only enflamed his desire more. His need was raw, pulsing through him as he pulled her garment free of her body, leaving her naked before him. Spilled wine pooled at his feet – wait – not wine, blood, he'd seen enough of both spilled in the past to know the difference. His mind told him there was something very wrong with a girl bringing a jug of blood to him, but his body overrode the logical workings of his brain. He pulled at his own breeches, aching to be released, while he held her with his other hand.

He felt a sudden pain in his chest. He pulled his tunic aside and felt a burning sensation where the amulet, gifted to him by Djangra Roe, was touching his exposed skin. His mind cleared.

"I know you," he said to the girl, noticing for the first time the eye tattooed on her forehead. Somehow the blood on the floor had smeared her body, as if she'd been rolling in it. He realised then that more than blood had spilled from the broken jug. There were three heads lying on the floor, pained expressions etched on their faces. He looked at the blank eyes and open mouth of Horace the tracker and shivered. "Witch!" he cried while pointing accusingly at the naked girl. She just smiled, her cheeks painted red with blood.

Suddenly she leapt at him with a sharp piece of pottery. She slashed a line across his cheek with the broken shard, drawing blood. He hit her hard with the back of his hand, pushing her away and knocking her to the floor.

"Come, lord. Take me now," she said while laughing. She lay on her back in the spilled blood, with her arms stretched out either side of her.

He still wanted her... even more so. "Curse you and your spells," he snarled, fighting hard to resist the temptation to join her on the floor and take her while sliding in the blood of his warriors. Desire and disgust warred inside him.

The smile suddenly dropped from her face. "You desecrated my temple. I will haunt you forever," she said. Her face turned into a hideous bestial mask as she launched up from the floor and flew at him.

He closed his eyes and flung his hands up before him, bracing for an impact. None came. When he opened his eyes the bright orange flames of the campfire flickered before him. "Mage!" he bellowed as he tore the amulet from around his neck and flung it in the fire. "Mage! Find me that witch!"

Tomas: Temple of Eor, wild lands of Alka-Roha

Tomas watched from behind the thin veil of a gauze curtain as the dream-witch caressed Aliss' snow-white hair. He could see his wife swaying as if she were caught between the dream and waking worlds. Both women were dressed in similar pale-cream silk shifts. The words of the priestess drifted towards him as a musky aroma of incense made him light-headed.

"See how your eyes change with your emotions," the priestess purred, as she stared into Aliss' stormy, grey eyes. "Truly they are windows to your soul."

Tomas had barely had time to think about his actions. Horace's face, twisted in agony, flashed into his mind. He had killed the tracker, but Normand's men had killed Joshan. Grief flooded his senses again when he pictured the old priest. In truth his mind had felt clouded ever since, as if he was seeing everything from behind a silk curtain. Elandrial had told him she had been waiting on him. Did he believe her? Did he not have the tip of his sword at her throat at the time? Perhaps she would have said anything to save her life. More importantly though, she had said she could lift the curse afflicting Aliss. If it were possible that she could remove the taint of dark magic... well then he cared not what yarns she would spin.

"I know what you need," the dream-witch leaned in closer to Aliss until her lips brushed her cheek. Aliss appeared unresponsive. Tomas's mind suddenly became alert when he saw a thin-bladed dagger in Elandrial's hand. He took a step forward but stopped when the priestess dragged the blade across her own palm and flung the knife onto the floor. "This will sustain you for now," she said and brought her hand up to Aliss' lips.

Tomas watched in horrified fascination as his woman greedily drank the dream-witch's blood from the open wound. Elandrial threw her head back. Tomas could see her eyes smouldering in ecstasy. The eerily realistic tattoo on her forehead remained unblinking, as if it remained ever watchful. She then turned her emerald gaze on him. Their eyes locked.

"We three complete a circle. A witch and a king joined with me." Her lips parted in a smile.

"I'm no king," Tomas answered.

"I could make you a king," Elandrial smiled before taking a silver goblet from a nearby table. A drop of wine rolled down her chin when she took the cup away, reminding Tomas of Aliss' blood-covered lips. "When we return to the mountains I will make you a king, and Aliss a queen."

"I have no desire to be a king, only for you to lift the curse the old witch put on Aliss, and to find and kill the mage Djangra Roe."

"Both of these things I have promised you, and I shall live up to those promises. But first you will lead my army and together we will take back what was stolen from me."

"Army?" Tomas's eyebrows rose.

"When we return to Eorotia the people of the mountain will rise up and join with my warriors who have travelled from the far south."

"The hooded tribesmen?"

"Disciples of Eor."

"I know nothing about leading armies. I'm a blacksmith and onetime common soldier, nothing more."

"There is one who comes who will help us all fulfil our destinies." Elandrial's eyes widened as her words tumbled out with fervour. "He who has transcended the boundaries that could not be crossed. He who has the power of life and death in his hand. He who has the power to wake a god from slumber. They call him the Shadow Mage."

He turned away then, from her to Aliss. His woman lay on the silk-covered bed with her back to him. He put his hand on her shoulder, only for her to move away. "Aliss," he whispered into her ear, so close to her that he could feel the heat rising from her body.

"Prepare yourselves. We will ride the moment he arrives." She swept out of the chamber then, leaving Tomas alone with Aliss.

"You should have told me." She turned to face him.

"I know. I couldn't." Tomas's eyes slid away from her and dropped to the floor.

"An innocent life was taken that I could live." Tears fell from her eyes. "I would never have agreed."

"I know," his words cracked even as he tried to speak them. "The decision was mine. I didn't want to lose you."

"You have set us both on a dark path, Tomas. I'm not sure if we can step aside."

"She." He indicated Elandrial with a nod of his head at the door the dream-witch had just left through. "She can help us."

"How many lives have we taken since you carried me from the flames? How many more must we take? I never wanted any of this. It would have been better if you'd left me to burn."

"No! Don't speak such words. Never!" He grabbed her shoulders then, looking into the swirling grey clouds of her eyes, and pulled her into his chest. "Joshan took me in when my father died. The man who had raised me from a child and taught me his trade had left me alone. I have no memory of my mother. In truth, the one who I always felt more akin to was Brother Joshan. If anyone could lay claim to that role it was him."

"What does that have to do with anything?" Aliss asked.

"Don't you see? I have no idea who I am. Joshan was like a father to me. Now he's dead too. All my life I've been passed from one post to another. It doesn't matter who I am, or who I was."

"I know who you are," Aliss answered, reaching out to touch his shoulder.

"You are, and forever will be, my husband. My loyal, fierce man."

"That's all I ever want to be," he answered.
"How did we end up here?"
Tomas could see tears pooling in her eyes. He had no answer for her.

***

Elandrial took in the fat man seated before her and the huge Nortman standing behind him with a long stare, before blinking long, dark lashes. She regarded the big warrior with curiosity. "That one has no emotion," she said, looking into his eyes.

"You'll not find his dreams a welcoming place for you," the fat nobleman said, a smile parting his thick lips.

"No, I think not," she agreed. Although the appearance of the man before her had changed utterly from the last time she saw him, she could sense the power behind the façade. This was the Shadow Mage, so called because of both his ability to steal and discard the identities of other men, and more importantly, because of his mythic status. His name was whispered in fear by those who had heard the tales of him. Very few believed he even existed. "This is not the most pleasing form I've seen you take," she said.

"It will suffice for now." He shrugged. "You have acquired some new playmates since last we met."

"They will be of use to us when the time comes."

"Do not play games, Elandrial. Not now, when we are so close. Is he strong?"

Memories of glimpses caught of a toned, hard body made her smile. "Strong enough."

"Perhaps I should take a new form. The one I currently have has... limitations."

"No!" Elandrial gasped. "That one is not for you. You will have a powerful host soon enough."

"And the witch. Is she powerful?" he asked.

"She has raw talent, but it is growing. I can feel it dripping from her, wild and unharnessed." The priestess's lips curled into a smile.

The fat man frowned, reading her smile. "Make whatever witch's magic you like, Elandrial, but be wary of that one. It is no easy thing to escape the realm of the dead. And what do you think he will do when he discovers that you are leeching her power, that she will be ultimately left an empty husk?"

"Let me worry about a blacksmith and a village girl. I have told him he will lead my army. Every man wants to believe he has greatness in him."

"Play your games, Elandrial, just remember, you promised me the duke, he must be taken alive."

"Once you have crushed his spirit you will become the Dragon Lord and together we will bask in the greatness of Eor."

The fat man smiled then, a hungry sneer creeping across his face. "I will help you raise your god and pray you have eternal happiness together. But I have debts to repay, and will use the power and influence of a duke to bring vengeance to mine own enemies and his line."

"We're all after something." She glanced into the hooded eyes of the Nortman, sensing no life there at all, and shivered.

Jarl Crawulf: Wind Isle

"Leave us," Crawulf instructed, as his warriors dripped rain water onto the stone floor of the great hall. The long benches were full of half-eaten meals and unfinished tankards of ale and mead. "You too," he said to the giant warrior Rothgar, his words brooking no argument. When the hall was empty he turned to the small figure huddled by the fire. Her hair hung in wet strands as she shivered beneath a heavy woollen cloak. She looked tiny, frail and vulnerable. She looked up at him then with her brown eyes, her pitiful expression making him bite back the angry words he was of a mind to unleash.

"I'm sorry." Words spilled out in a whisper, before she looked away and into the fire.

"You're sorry? Men are still out there, scouring the island looking for you. Not the best of nights for an aimless ride into the countryside," he answered. A muscle in his cheek twitched.

"I had a dream..." she answered by way of explanation.

"So have your girl fetch you some warm milk. You do not ride out into a storm, such as the one raging beyond these walls, alone," Crawulf snarled.

"I had a dream," she continued, her words barely audible, "only a seer would know the meaning of. I needed to speak with Maolach."

"By the gods' crusty beards, girl, I will never understand you. Are all women just so...?"

"My lord?" She raised her eyes again.

"Unfathomable." He shook his head and sat on a wooden stool opposite her. Her eyes followed him.

"When I was a little girl, my father told me a story. A story that scared me then and still scares me today. It was about his grandfather who had been emperor many years before. His name was Hahmed-Tor. Many call him Hahmed the Great. He was a warrior emperor and expanded the empire greatly during his reign. He had a trusted advisor... his most trusted, a mage called Harren Suilomon. Some even said that Suilomon was the real reason behind my grandfather's power. Many times, often on the eve of battle, his enemies would mysteriously fall ill or die. Sometimes their hearts would turn and they would bend the knee to the emperor when it seemed most unlikely they would ever submit. It was said that he used dark magic to influence those he could and kill those he could not.

"Unfortunately for Suilomon, my grandfather was a jealous man and not very trusting. When no heir was born to the emperor and his wives, or his concubines—each pregnancy ending with the death of the unborn—a rumour began that the mage had laid a curse on him, that his line would end after his death.

"My grandfather sentenced him to death and ordered the entire city to witness the execution. A huge pyre was built on the steps of the great temple in Alcraz, and there Suilomon was burned. Even as his flesh melted from his bones he shouted out curses, swearing vengeance on Hahmed-Tor and all his line." Rosinnio paused then and looked into Crawulf's eyes.

"The existence of your father and subsequently you is proof of the mage's guilt, is it not? I mean, at least one of the women bore your grandfather a child after the death of the mage."

"Yes, it's true. He went on to sire many children afterwards. Perhaps this does prove Suilomon's guilt and that he had designs on the throne for himself."

"A fine fireside tale for a night such as this," Crawulf said, "but it does not explain why you forced me to send out half my men in the middle of the night to search for you."

"I am daughter to the Emperor of Sunsai. It is my duty to obey my emperor and father in all that he bids me do. If my father wishes to form an alliance with a far-off kingdom and I am to be the glue to bind that agreement then I will honour that duty. But my father did not send me to you in order to form a union between you and he. He sent me here because he could think of no where farther away for me to go." Rosinnio paused to wait for Crawulf's reaction. When none came a realisation dawned on her. "You knew!" she gasped.

"Aye... well, when the emperor of the most powerful empire this side of the setting sun asks you a favour, and that boon is to take his daughter in wedlock, it is always well to accept such a proposal."

"Did he tell you why?"

"No, that he did not."

"Some members of my family are gifted... or cursed with an inner sight, an ability to see things that may come to pass or have already passed, although interpretation can be difficult when visions are often clouded in riddle and mystery. Those of us with this gift are more susceptible to magic and any with the power to wield it... including Harren Suilomon."

"You are speaking of a man burned alive in your grandfather's time?"

"Yes, his body was destroyed. But many believe he escaped his burning flesh and the death he was sentenced to."

"How so?" Crawulf's brow wrinkled in confusion.

"Somehow he had the power to project his spirit out of his body and escape the bonds of death, perhaps even time."

"You're saying he somehow catapulted his soul into another body?"

Rosinnio nodded. "It is believed he is responsible for the deaths of several members of my family, including my father's older brother who was in line to succeed my grandfather. Both my father and grandfather have employed many men of great power to find him. None have come close. Few believe he even exists, but those who do call him the Shadow Mage."

Crawulf scratched his beard and sighed. "No harm will come to you while you are here among my warriors."

Rosinnio reached across and placed her hand on top of his much bigger hand. "Your men are brave beyond compare... *you* are brave beyond compare. I can think of nowhere I would feel safer than among them against any mortal foe, but they cannot fight a shadow.

"I can see him, albeit in my dreams, even then he is just a shadow, but I can see him and he can see me. He fears me because I can find him where no other can. For this reason he will try to kill me."

"The attack on the castle... the poison, you think it was him?"

"Without a doubt."

Crawulf frowned, his mouth forming a tight line as his eyes narrowed. "What would you have me do?"

"Maolach has told me of the Tree of Souls and the Horn of Galen. Galen is the guardian of souls, he who stands sentry between this world and Eiru home of the gods. The horn will gather those souls who have crossed back and should not reside here."

"You seek to lecture me about my own gods?" Crawulf's eyes sparkled with amusement while Rosinnio dropped hers in embarrassment.

"I - I mean no offence," she stammered.

The jarl rubbed at tired eyes. He had been drinking and feasting for most of the night before being forced into a wild ride across the country in a raging storm to find his missing wife. Talk of magic and dark mysteries he did not understand made his head hurt even more. "Tell me what you want of me?"

"The Tree of Souls is..."

"Yes, I know the myths. The Tree of Souls is among the Frost People. They are a savage race and no friend to any Nortman."

"I understand, but I must go there. Lend me one ship and a crew of men willing to take me."

Crawulf stood up and paced the floor, every so often turning to glance at his wife. He cast his mind back to the day the emissary had arrived from the emperor. He had listened with growing incredulity and not a little scepticism as the messenger, dressed in bright clothes of silk and uncomfortable-looking shoes, read out a letter from the most powerful man in the known world, offering him the hand of his daughter in marriage and a shipload of gold as a dowry, not to mention the eternal gratitude and friendship of such a powerful man. What would the emperor think of him now if he knew he contemplated sending his daughter off in a ship towards the frozen north.

"There is more at stake here than just me and an old family grudge. The souls of dead men do not belong among the living. It is a corruption that can only grow and spread vileness throughout the land."

"Have you seen this?" He swung around to face her. "You can see things, things most men cannot. Have you seen a dark future for all of us?"

"I cannot say." She shook her head. "My dreams and visions are so difficult to interpret. Often they say one thing but mean another. Usually they only concern those close to me."

"And afterwards, what then?"

"Afterwards?"

"When it's over? When you have the horn and this… Shadow Mage is no more, what then?"

"I am your wife," she answered as she stood up. "When this is over I will still be your wife. I will bear you the sons you desire and do all I can to be the best wife any jarl could desire."

"Or a king," he answered.

"Or a king," she agreed.

***

Rosinnio's stomach lurched each time the boat shifted from the swell of the sea. And they had yet to leave the harbour! Despite assurances from Crawulf that the ship was perfectly seaworthy, she looked with scepticism at the small craft, tiny compared to the large galleons in her father's fleet. Even her time spent on one such had not been a pleasant one. She had bid her handmaiden stay behind, finding amusement in the relief evident on her face. Both women had already been to sea once on one of Crawulf's longboats. It had not been a pleasant experience for her, even less so for her servant. Marta was loyal though, and Rosinnio could see how it pained her to abandon her mistress.

Somehow she doubted the crew would tolerate two women on the voyage they were about to undertake.

The crew was Crawulf's own. The jarl insisted on accompanying his wife if she wished to persist with *'this foolish quest'*. The big warrior Rothgar was there too, his great axe never far from him. All of the men were armed well, with swords, axes and spears. Each man also had a brightly painted round, wooden shield, which he hung from the side of the boat beside his own rowing bench. All wore armour of interlocked chainmail or hard leather.

"Do they not worry they will sink to the bottom of the sea if they end up overboard?" she had asked, concerned at the weight of the armour they wore.

"If you end up in that sea, it is better to go straight down," Rothgar had answered. She did not pursue the conversation.

Despite being assured that the seas were calm and the voyage uneventful, Rosinnio suffered two days and nights of misery. She was cold, soaked to the skin, the contents of her stomach well emptied after the first few hours into the voyage. Men looked at her with amusement, some even with concern and pity in their eyes, but none mocked or chided her. She didn't care if they did. Then there was the terror of seeing nothing but sea, occasionally not even that when a thick mist would descend. This was the worst time when she imagined all manner of sea monsters lurking in the impenetrable fog, waiting to ambush them and drag the ship to a very deep and cold grave. She had heard the stories of Baltagor's mischievous daughters who never tired of trying to tempt men into the sea and to a watery end. She wondered if the sea god's daughters targeted women also. The sight of land midway into the third morning brought great relief to her, even if the frowns of the men spoke loudly of their own concerns.

In the distance she could see how the land rose up, with snow-capped hills rolling back from the shore. The closer they got the more she could see that most of the land was covered in a thick white carpet of snow. "What are the Frost People like?" she asked Crawulf as the men around her pulled down the heavy square sail from the single mast, and began heaving on oars as they approached the shore.

"They are just men," the jarl answered. "Not fire-breathing giants as some of the stories are told?"

"Only to those who have never met them." Crawulf laughed.

"But they are to be feared?" Rosinnio asked.

"Oh yes, fear them. Byorne, come here," he called to one of his men then.

"Aye?" an older crewman made his way to the front, with a long grizzled mane and weather-beaten skin of old leather.

"Show her," Crawulf simply said.

The man pushed back his hair. Rosinnio flinched at the sight of two pink slits where his ears should be. "The Frost People did this?" she asked, aghast but unable to look away.

"Aye," Crawulf answered and gave a nod to the man to return to his rowing bench. "Had he not been rescued in time, next would have been his nose, then his tongue, his eyes, and after that his fingers and toes. I've seen men with stumps up to their knees and elbows left to die in the snow. If they were lucky the cold would claim them and give them a quick death."

Rosinnio turned away then, suddenly fearing and hating the feelings welling inside her. Unwilling to display any emotion in front of Crawulf and the crew, she let her tears fall silently into the sea.

The flat-bottomed ship ran up the black pebble beach as men jumped overboard and hauled her out of the water.

Immediately she stepped ashore, feeling eyes upon her, a prickly sensation in the back of her neck. "We're being watched," she said, alarm making her words tremble.

"Aye," Crawulf simply answered as he hauled his weapons and gear over the side and began marching onto the beach. All around them men were doing the same.

"I will go alone," Rosinnio said.

Crawulf swung around to face her. "Did you crack your head off the side of the boat?"

"No. Alone I am no threat to them, but all of you bring the trappings of war to their land. Will they not act accordingly?"

"I'll tell you what they will do. They will bury your body somewhere in those mountains after they have taken all they want from you if you walk out there alone," Crawulf snarled.

"I can sense their fear."

"You are a strange one," he answered while scratching his head.

"I will go alone."

"No. A small guard of four of us, lightly armed, will pose no threat to them."

Rosinnio thought about this and then nodded her agreement. "Very well."

"Rothgar, leave the axe," he said to the big warrior before turning to two others and motioning for them to fall in behind. "Let's get this done and be away as soon as possible." He led the small group up the dark beach and over black rocks until they were climbing a dirt track stretching upwards.

It was not long before their path was blocked by a group of very pale-skinned warriors carrying spears, and bows with arrows and spearheads made from flint. They stood still while pointing their weapons at the small group, their meaning clear enough. Rosinnio noticed how impossibly blue their eyes were, like sapphires sunk into a fresh fall of snow. They were all dressed in furs and the hides of animals. Crawulf pulled a dagger from his belt, making the group of Frost People jump back and gesture wildly with their weapons. Crawulf calmly approached them and held out the dagger to the nearest one, hilt first. It was snatched, wordlessly from his hand. All of them turned then and quickly disappeared over the hills.

"They have not the knowledge of smelting iron. They crave all weapons of steel." Crawulf grinned.

"Where have they gone?" Rosinnio asked, but Crawulf just shrugged and pressed on.

It was not long before they reached a village of hide tents and wooden cabins. "I've heard it said that deep in the Frozen Waste, the Frost People build houses made from bricks of ice." Rothgar leaned into her and told her.

"Perhaps that is where the fire-breathing ones live," she answered with a smile.

"Do not be quick to dismiss such mysteries," Crawulf said. "I know of a shepherd who once found the entire skeleton of a whale deep in a cave, high up on a mountain. How did a whale get up there? Perhaps there was once such a thing as flying whales." He laughed then, with the other men joining in. Rosinnio could not help feeling she was the butt of some joke, but simply dismissed them with a wave of her hand.

"Look!" One of Crawulf's men pointed towards the settlement. A much larger group of men than the one they'd already encountered waited for them.

"I did not think my death would come at the hands of the Frost People, but if that is the will of the gods then so be it," Crawulf said, drawing his sword.

"No, wait," Rosinnio answered. "See there? The old woman, I will go to her." Without waiting for an answer, she started down the hill towards the village.

"Wait..." Crawulf called, but she ignored him and started towards the group waiting at the edge of the small village.

As she approached them the old woman made her way to the front, the line of spears before her lowered as the warriors parted to let her through. She could sense their tension as Crawulf and his men slowly followed behind her.

"Perhaps your men should wait here. They are making the folk nervous." Although she heard the words spoken by the old woman, in the common trading tongue, Rosinnio did not see her lips move. Her eyes opened a little wider in surprise as she realised the words had been heard in her head. She nodded to the woman before turning to Crawulf.

"Wait here. I do not think they will harm you if you do."

"You don't think?" Crawulf sounded sceptical, but reluctantly agreed.

The old woman beckoned her with the same deep blue eyes of the other Frost People. Rosinnio followed her through the crowd, very aware of the tension in the air and the eyes on her. The woman led her to a low structure made from a frame of huge tusks covered in hides. She could not fathom what animal could produce such massive lengths of ivory. Even the great bull elephants that roamed the jungles far to the south of the empire could not have borne such enormous tusks. The dwelling was warm with an overbearing muskiness in the air. The woman handed her a small cup of water and a plate of dried fish.

"I thank you for your hospitality, Old Mother." She was not sure where she got the title from, but it somehow seemed to fit. The old woman didn't seem to mind and smiled warmly, before taking a seat on a cot covered in furs. She bade Rosinnio sit on the hide-covered ground before her, which she quickly did, sitting cross-legged at her feet.

"I know why you have come." The words echoed inside her head. It was a strange sensation to hear her and yet see how her lips did not move.

"Can you help me?" Rosinnio asked. The woman nodded.

"I can see the darkness that surrounds you, the corruption that has seeped into the world."

"I mean you no harm, Old Mother." Rosinnio felt a knot of anxiety balling in her chest.

"I know that, child. I too have dreamt dark and strange dreams. I have also dreamt of one who would travel here from very, very far away. One with a good heart who would come to me for help. Your journey has been most long thus far, my child." She reached out and took the younger woman's hand in her own. "And it has not ended yet."

"Do you know what I must do? What road I must travel?" Rosinnio asked.

"Take what you have come for and let it guide you, for who am I to know the ways of the gods? Sometimes they speak to me, but do I understand what they say? No." Rosinnio heard a chuckle in her head then, it made her smile.

"How do I find the Horn of Galen?"

"If you are worthy, you just have to reach out and the Guardian of Souls will..." The old woman's words trailed off as Rosinnio suddenly felt overwhelmingly tired, her eyes growing unbearably heavy.

"The Guardian?" She struggled against the desire to sleep and forced her eyes open.

The woman was gone, the hide tent, village and everybody in it were gone. She stood on a rocky mountain top. In the background she could see the sea stretching out to the horizon where it joined and became one with the grey sky. On top of the mountain, growing out of the rock, was a single black tree, its branches stark in their bareness and harsh, sharpened ends. The smell of rot emanated from it in waves of dank foulness. Lying at the foot of the tree, nestled between gnarled roots protruding from the rock, was a curved horn made of bone. She reached towards it and stopped as her fingers hovered over it. *Am I worthy?*

Her fingers closed around the horn. Its touch was like ice. Like everything around her, the mountain, the tree. It felt like death. *How else would his realm feel?* she thought. *The Guardian of Souls – Sentinel to the Underworld. The Reaper of Souls to the Nortlanders.*

Her eyes snapped open and the woman was in front of her once again.

"You should leave now. The wolves you have brought to our door are filling the folk with fear."

"They fear you too," Rosinnio said a little more defensively than she intended.

"You have a kind heart and they will gain immeasurably from your radiance shining on them."

"Perhaps someday the Frost People and the Nortlanders can live together in peace, without fear or hate," she said.

"When the great cats who hunt the woolly bison of the north learn to live off grass, perhaps that day will come."

Rosinnio made her way back through the crowd. Crawulf and his three men sat facing each other around a small campfire, seemingly relaxed and simply warming themselves, but she knew each man watched the back of the other and any perceived threat would be met with a sudden explosion of violence. The thought saddened her.

"Did you get what you came for?" Crawulf asked when she joined them. She displayed the simple bone horn to them.

"Then let us be gone from here."

Rosinnio nodded her agreement. "We have a long voyage ahead of us and none of you are going to like it."

Duke Normand: Eorotia

Duke Normand paced the tiled floor of the audience chamber in the Temple of Eor, his mind focusing on the image of the dragon made up from hundreds of small tiles at his feet.

"My lord, you summoned me." Djangra Roe walked into the room. Normand watched him enter, saw him note the presence of warriors in the room.

"Have you heard, Mage?"

"Heard, my lord?" A confused look spread across Roe's face.

"Those cursed mountain people have risen up in rebellion against me. They dare to challenge me!"

"This is the first I've heard of it, my lord. But then I've been locked away in the library, studying the old texts. I'm becoming quite the scholar on Eor."

"Curse you and that damnable goddess. May she and that witch of a priestess be swallowed into The Hag's Pit."

"What has happened?"

Normand turned to one of his warriors, a man with dirt and dried blood smeared across his face. When he moved he did so stiffly and with obvious pain. "A caravan travelling from the Duchies going south with tin and wool was attacked in the mountains two days ago."

"Bandits?"

"Bandits would have stolen the cargo to sell themselves, but the only thing taken was the lives of the traders and their drivers... every last one of them. I sent a score of men into the mountains to track down whoever had done this. This man is the only survivor of that patrol. They were attacked by a large force who knew the terrain, who knew exactly where to set an ambush."

"What will you do?" Djangra asked, his face set in grave lines.

"What I always do. I will take the fight to them."

"Is that wise, my lord? If what you say is true, you do not know the numbers you will face or even where to find them. The mountains are vast and treacherous. You could wander around there for months without knowing where you are going. Then of course you have another problem; they are most likely among us even now, cooking our food, emptying our chamber pots, right under our noses, yet invisible."

"I have tried the road of patience once already and that has failed."

"If you speak of the priestess, do not be so sure, my lord. We have yet to hear from the men sent to hunt her down."

"They are dead. She taunted me with them in my dream, brought their heads to me in a jug. All three men I gave to you. Think on that." Normand spat the words out bitterly. "Your charms and petty, inadequate spells have failed. You have failed." Normand could see fear creep into Djangra Roe's eyes. It was well known the duke was not a patient man and did not tolerate failure.

"I will send others, better men, a more powerful witch…"

"No, from this day on you will stay by my side until that witch is dead. Heed my words, Mage. If she violates my dreams one more time I will have your head."

"Yes, my lord, I understand." Colour drained from Djangra Roe's face.

"Now make ready. We ride out immediately."

"I would make one suggestion, my lord."

"Speak," Normand said irritably.

"The valley – Perhaps you should take your warriors there."

"This is not a treasure hunt, Mage."

"No, my lord," Djangra Roe answered, "but it is a sacred place to the people of the mountain… to the goddess Eor. Perhaps if they fear we will desecrate it they will show themselves to us."

"Very well, if nothing else I will have the satisfaction of destroying something of value to the dream-witch."

They marched out of Eorotia on foot, with an honour guard of grim-faced peasants and frightened traders lining the narrow road. There was little point in taking mounts into the mountains where the paths were little more than animal trails, often ending abruptly or needing a steep climb to continue. Duke Normand led them out followed by his Dragon Knights, above them his banner bearing the image of a red dragon on a green field billowed in the wind. Following behind were an array of men-at-arms, archers and crossbowmen, scouts and woodsmen. All in all a force of close to ten score armed, fighting men marched through the gates and into the morning mist clinging to the mountains.

Normand's mood was buoyant. He was nothing if not a warrior, and the thrill of leading hard, fighting men into battle was the one thing that made him feel he was where he belonged. The intrigues of the king's court were not something he enjoyed, probably why he stayed away from Rothberry Castle. The ways of the gods and their priests, the dark arts of witches and mages made him nervous. He was not comfortable with things he did not understand. Put a sword in his hand, though, and an enemy before him and he would revel.

Such a large body of fighting men was unlikely to encounter any trouble on the road and they made it to Widow's Keep without incident. By then light was draining from the sky as night eased its dark mantle across the heavens. The men built fires and wrapped themselves in their cloaks as the first touches of winter stole the heat from their bones. There were no stories of ghosts and murdered brides this time, only the rattle of weapons and armour as men, feeling the tension of going into the unknown, kept their thoughts and fears to themselves.

They suffered their first casualty that night. Normand was woken to the cries for help and the barked orders of sergeants calling men to arms. A man-at-arms making his way to take up sentry duty found one of his fellows slumped against a tree. At first he thought the man had fallen asleep at his post, but when he kicked his legs to wake him the body had toppled over, revealing a bloodied throat and a gash from ear to ear.

Normand rubbed the tiredness from his eyes, catching his breath as the icy air caught in his throat. Underfoot the ground had hardened as a coat of frost painted the land white. It was still well off sunrise, but there would be no more sleep for that night. Normand sat before a fire reflecting on the last time he had led a party of men into the mountains, and the beast that had almost claimed his life. *What else is in these mountains?* he wondered.

Three more men lost their lives the following day, all of them scouts who had run foul of traps set to catch woodsmen wandering ahead of the main body of Normand's small army. It made the going even slower as each step was taken with caution and no little fear. A wooden stake triggered by stepping on a crude mechanism buried under a cover of brown leaves and broken twigs, was not a nice way to die.

Djangra Roe scratched his beard nervously when they stopped at midday to rest and take on water. "They're out there. I can feel their eyes on me," he said, his eyes darting in different directions.

"Good," Normand snapped.

"Good?" the mage asked with incredulity.

"I want them close. They will have to face us soon enough." Normand lay back and closed his eyes, allowing himself a smile at the thought of the flabbergasted look on the mage's face.

The drums started later that night. Normand had already ordered the guard doubled, with no man to be left out of sight of another as he stood sentinel. For those not on sentry duty there was very little sleep to be had, as a constant thrumming filled the air, leaving each man in no doubt that his enemy was close by, and though he could not see them, they could see him. Later in the night the air was punctuated by a scream. A guard who had stepped away from his post to relieve himself was found face down with an arrow in the back of his neck and his breeches down around his knees.

The early morning sun, though bright and sitting low in a clear blue sky, carried little heat in its rays and less cheer in the hearts of the men. Tired from lack of sleep, anxious of facing the unknown in a strange place to them, they packed up and headed deeper into the mountains. Normand had been told that there were scores of villages hidden all over the mountain range, populated by people who offered no allegiance to crown or monarch, a wild, lawless folk. He would tame them. If he had to kill half of them first then so be it.

The first village they found was, unsurprisingly, deserted, although, still warm embers, and steaming cooking pots over hearths told of the speedy and recent evacuation of the village folk. Even so, it gave the men a focus to vent their fear and anger. It was a squalid little place, the wattle-and-daub walls practically one with the forest that covered this part of the mountains. By the time they pressed on, not a building remained standing.

Camouflaged pits with fire-hardened stakes at the bottom made the force move warily as it snaked its way along hunting trails through the woods. Arrows and stones fired from slingshots were a constant threat from the darkness around them, until finally they climbed high enough to leave the tree line behind. Even though they looked down on the vast carpet of green, and with the air becoming harder to breathe, snow-clad peeks still towered over them in all directions.

"How much farther?" Normand asked irritably as dark clouds rolled in from behind the mountains, bringing wisps of snow floating down from the heavens.

"There! Beyond that peek, there should be a path down," Djangra answered breathlessly. Normand made no reply, simply waving his men on in the direction the mage had indicated.

The valley they looked down on was bordered on both sides by steep banks of rock as if some ancient giant had carved a path through the mountain. A stream flowed through its centre, water gurgling over rocks back down towards the forest below. Normand sucked in a breath as he regarded the gorge stretching out before him. "There could be an army hidden down there," he mused, looking down as a thick mist shrouded the far end of the valley.

"See those stones, near the centre?" Djangra Roe asked, pointing into the valley at a group of massive boulders circling a rocky plinth just beyond the wispy touch of the mist. Even from a distance they could see the giant rocks had been smoothed and shaped. "That must be their sacred place."

A narrow and treacherous path led down into the valley. More than one man slipped on the loose stones and hard earth, often knocking one or more men in front tumbling also. Once they reached the bottom, Normand signalled for his men to fan out and form two separate lines, five men deep and twenty wide. Then he slowly marched them towards the circle of stones, constantly wary of an unseen enemy. Normand was confident his trained warriors would easily overcome a force of mountain folk many times its size, in a pitched battle. So far though, none had been offered.

As they approached the sacred place, swirling designs and intricate carvings etched into the rock could be made out on the massive stones. The closer they got, the more imposing the stones appeared, each one twice the height of a man.

"A strange place to erect such a thing. How long do you suppose they are here?" Normand turned to the mage as they approached the circle. The raised area the rocks circled had also been carved and smoothed to give an even surface. More designs, reminding Normand of huge snail trails decorated the stone floor.

"I think..."

Normand swung around towards Djangra Roe when the mage stopped speaking. "Go on."

"I think this may have been a mistake."

"How so?" Normand scanned the valley for any sign of mountain folk. In truth he had a rising sense of anxiety. It annoyed him to even have those thoughts. *These mountains are mine. These people are mine.*

"Can you not feel it? There is real power here. I can sense it emanating from the stones and in the air all around us."

"Do not act the fool now, Mage," Normand snarled. "We'll pull these down and put an end to it."

"No!" Djangra Roe leapt in front of the duke. "I beg you, do not do that."

"Have you lost your senses?"

"I can feel it here." The mage thumped his chest. Normand couldn't help but notice the ashen colour of his complexion. "Vibrating through me, I feel as if I'm swimming in a lake of tar."

Normand shook his head in disgust and turned away from the mage. Just then the drums started again, only louder. They echoed across the valley bouncing from one wall to the next. He watched as his sergeants barked orders, bullying and cajoling the men into organised ranks, facing out from the circle. "Now, at last." He punched his palm with the opposite hand.

Green and grey clad mountain folk appeared, as if magically conjured from the mountain, armed with bows, spears, clubs, even a few axes and swords. There were easily three times the number of the duke's men. "This will be a slaughter." Normand grinned.

"Look!" He wasn't sure who said it, but all eyes turned towards the end of the gorge where the stream disappeared of the edge to the forest below; the mist had lifted. Dark shapes began materialising. "There must be a hidden path up from that end also." The men climbing into view, wore black robes, their faces and heads covered by scarves of the same hue. Even from a distance he could see that they were proper fighting men. They organised themselves quickly into rows, moving with catlike grace. Most of them carried small round shields and the curved blades of the south.

"Wheel right!" a sergeant bellowed at his squad to face the new threat.

Djangra Roe's face was sweating, his jaw clenched in a grimace. Normand had no time to deal with the fool of a mage now. The black-garbed warriors parted allowing a force of two score, or so, Nortmen through.

"Nortmen? And Tribesmen from beyond the empire? These mountain folk have strange allies."

"The witch..." Djangra Roe gasped, clearly in pain.

"What is the matter with you?" Normand asked impatiently.

"Choking..." The mage held two hands to his throat as he tried to gulp in air.

"Somebody help him!" Normand barked. He was quickly distracted from the mage's fate by a further disturbance in the opposing ranks.

A huge Nortman walked out of the crowd. Normand wondered if he was about to issue a challenge, but he was followed by a short, fat man, a tall warrior dressed in ornate armour and two women.

"Witch!" Normand gasped. "She's here!"

The two women joined hands and raised their arms. Words that made his skin tingle and heart race began drifting towards the duke and his men. Mist formed in the circle of stones, making his warriors restless as they glanced towards it.

"I need you, Mage," Normand said through gritted teeth as he tried to keep the panic from his voice. "I cannot fight magic." But Djangra Roe was on his knees, mumbling incoherently as he fought his own battle with some unseen force.

A more familiar sound filled the air then, the thrum of drawn bows released and the whistle of arrows taking flight.

"Shields!" The cry went up as the instincts of trained fighting men took over.

Tomas: Temple of Eor

Tomas felt an icy grip of dread in his stomach when he watched the Nortmen lined up in the courtyard of the temple. All of them bore the same blank expression and the same hooded eyes. From a distance they looked just like any group of fighting raiders from the north—he'd seen enough of them while in the Royal Guard to be wary of them—a frightening and intimidating enough sight as it was, but up close they were terror personified. The big one, who was permanently at the Shadow Mage's side, Rolfgot, alone would fill the dreams of any man with horror.

"What's wrong with them?" he asked Elandrial.

The priestess shrugged. "Harren Suilomon has bound their souls to him with invisible bonds of dark magic. No one else has ever commanded such power." Tomas was struck by the awe in her voice.

"Who is he? He looks like any fat noble."

"It is not his true appearance. His body was destroyed many years ago and now he changes bodies as you would a cloak, discarding them when they become worn or outlive their usefulness. The weaker the spirit of the host the quicker he crushes it from within, so he is forced to change it for a new one as the body begins to decay. The fighters last longer."

Tomas shivered at the thought and not for the first time wondered how he had become caught up with the priestess he was supposed to be hunting. He turned to Aliss who was by his side, her own appearance utterly changed from the yellow-haired village girl he had married. Dark clouds swirled in her unsettling, storm-filled eyes, her complexion drained of the healthy glow she once possessed.

Beside the Nortmen were Elandrial's black-robed warriors. Tomas could see how they too were uneasy and wary of the soulless northern warriors; even the horses stomped nervously around them.

"We will ride swiftly and prepare a warm welcome for the duke," her mouth dropped in distaste, "he who has usurped my lands and the mountains most sacred to Eor."

"How can you be sure he will be there?"

"I've told you before, Tomas. They do not call me the dream-witch for no reason. I can influence a man's thoughts while he sleeps, even a foolish mage or arrogant lord. They will come, because their greed and lust for gold and power will drive them to it. They will come because it is what I wish them to do." Her lips curled into a smile and she trailed her hand across Tomas's cheek and down his chest before turning back to the men assembled in the courtyard, waiting and ready to do battle for her.

Tomas flinched and shied away from her touch. Even after a week of waiting on the Shadow Mage's arrival he was uncomfortable around her. Aliss stood beside him, her expression blank and unreadable as she stared down at the courtyard. Tomas was unsure if she was actually looking at the warriors assembled below or just staring into space.

The Nortmen had arrived the previous day with Suilomon and barracked themselves away immediately. Tomas was glad they had kept themselves to themselves and he had had few up close encounters with them. Even from a distance he could sense there was something not right about them. And he was not the one with the intuition for such things.

"What do you make of them?" He turned to Aliss when Elandrial left them standing alone on the balcony.

"They have no souls, no life-force." She dropped her head then. "They are a corruption... like me."

"Don't talk nonsense. You are the woman I love, will always love."

"You should have let me die. An innocent child would not have had the life stolen from her. I do not want it." Tomas reached out a hand, but she shrugged him off and stepped away. "It is time to leave," she said.

He was not looking forward to the many days he would spend on the road in the company of the Nortmen and the dream-witch. "We don't have to go. We could just leave. Let The Hag take them all."

"And will you bring innocent babes from the arms of their mothers for me, Tomas? When my need is so great that the dark magic consumes me?"

"We can find another way," he said through gritted teeth, knowing in his heart that there was no other way. Elandrial had promised she could lift whatever dark desire Aliss craved to feed the black magic within her, and to keep her alive. "When this is over I'm going to kill that old witch in the wood."

"More death, Tomas. What has become of us?" Aliss brushed past him as she walked from the balcony and followed Elandrial down the stairs and out into the courtyard.

Mounted on the horses they arrived on, they left the temple without a backward glance.

The journey back to the Duchies was a long one, although quicker than the trip in the opposite direction, when they were hunting the dream-witch, always searching for clues and following rumours. Tomas marvelled at how the terrain and weather changed as they rode north, becoming colder, the vegetation much thicker on the ground even in the bitter grip of an oncoming winter. The lands and people they passed on the way were unknown to him, a simple blacksmith—albeit one with a diverse past—had little use for knowing the ways of the world. He was surprised they encountered no resistance with what was effectively an army at their backs. When he asked Elandrial why no lord attempted to stop so many armed warriors passing through their land she simply shrugged and said, "We are no threat to them." Not much of an answer but it was all he was going to get. They steered well clear of Suilomon's company of Nortmen, and the black-robed warriors also kept to themselves, huddling together around campfires and talking quietly whenever they stopped for the night. Even Aliss had little to say to him. So passed long days and nights he lost count of, until they came within sight of the large mountain range Elandrial called home and Duke Normand had usurped from her. Tomas almost felt sorry for the duke when he learned of the fate awaiting him, but he was just another noble of the Duchies and Tomas got over it quickly enough. *Let him suffer at the hands of the Shadow Mage. Let him feel what it is like to be enslaved by one vastly more powerful.*

They began a steady climb up the mountain even as flakes of snow drifted all around them. Tomas wondered how the hooded warriors of the south were dealing with the cold. It was hard to tell when all they ever revealed of themselves were their dark eyes. They left their horses behind at the foot of the mountains before they began their ascent, following guides who had come to their camp hours after they arrived.

"This is nearly over," he said to Aliss as they passed beneath a waterfall to a hidden passage through the mountain. He could see that Elandrial was becoming more excited and urging them to greater speed, even though all were exhausted from the seemingly endless journey.

Drums reverberated all around them as they climbed steadily, hidden from view by the narrow waterfall gushing over the cliff above them. "The people of the mountain," Elandrial answered the unasked question with a smile. "My people."

"Where are they?" Tomas asked. "I have seen no one other than those who came to guide us."

"They are all around us. These people have inhabited the mountains when the Duchies was just a vast wild land. Their traditions are joined with the mountain as one. They flow through the trails and pathways as blood flows through a body, bringing life to the heart."

"You?" Tomas raised a sceptical eyebrow.

"Not me, but the majesty of Eor."

Tomas waited for Elandrial to move ahead of him before he offered a helping hand to Aliss. "I do not trust her, or that so called Shadow Mage," he said as Aliss gripped his bigger hand with her own.

She shrugged. "We have made our choice. We cannot turn from the path now."

As they filed over the cliff edge to stand at one end of a large valley, a thick mist descended on them, obscuring their view of the rest of the gorge. The drums were louder now, echoing off the valley walls. Black-robed warriors formed ranks as each man hauled himself up from the steep climb, followed by the Nortmen. The sea-raiders ignored all as they stood, expressionless behind the Shadow Mage, led by the giant Rolfgot.

"Tomas," Elandrial said excitedly, her eyes gleaming as she spoke to him. "Lead my warriors and strike down my enemies." She turned to Aliss then. "Can you feel the power? Open your heart to the source. Let if flow through you. Take my hand."

Tomas watched in silence as the two women joined hands. Even he could feel the raw energy pulsing through the valley. He was dressed now in an ornately engraved breast plate and plumed helmet given to him by Elandrial. From his shoulders hung a gold cloak. He looked every bit the warrior general he claimed not to be. The mist began to clear and he saw the ranks of Normand's men gathered in a defensive ring around a circle of large standing stones.

"The duke," Tomas said needlessly. Above the men a banner of a red dragon on a green background billowed in the breeze. It was then that he recognised the mage Djangra Roe, on his knees clutching his head in his hands. "What's wrong with the mage?" he asked.

"He has opened his mind to the power of the stones," Harren Suilomon answered, his voice dripping with scorn. "It is a far greater power than he could ever hope to understand. His feeble mind will explode like an overheated melon."

"No!" Tomas snarled. "He must atone for the death of Joshan." Even as he spoke the words he knew he was being foolish, but it was one of the reasons that swayed him to change sides. What did he care of the power struggles of nobles and their pet wizards. Life was what was important to him, the loss of Joshan's, the saving of Aliss'.

"Do not lose sight of what is important, Tomas," Elandrial rebuked him softly.

A cry went up around him and black-robed archers pushed their way to the front. They released a volley of arrows into the air, leaving their re-curved bows of horn and wood like a swarm of buzzing insects. Before the first flight hit its mark, a second was already in the air. The cries of men dying floated down the valley. The men packed tightly around the cairn were subjected to further attacks from their flanks as the mountain folk also fired an array of missile weapons in their direction.

"Gather the power. Hold it within you until the pressure makes you feel as if you will burst open. Then release it!" Elandrial's words were filled with excitement and joy as she addressed Aliss. Tomas watched mesmerised as he felt the air being sucked from around him, his skin tingling and making it impossible to breathe. Although the mist had cleared from the valley, it gathered in a swirling mass at the centre of the stone circle. Suddenly a bolt of energy crackled to life around the two witches. With a cry of unbridled joy from Elandrial the women redirected the energy towards the ranks of Normand's men. Lightning fizzled randomly across the men standing there, thumping three men from their feet. Tomas could not see what happened to them once they went down. What he did see was the look of pure ecstasy on the face of Aliss as she wielded such terrifying power.

"Now!" Elandrial cried. "Kill the invader. Remove their stain from our lands!"

"For the glory of Eor!" a cry went up from the mountain folk off to their right.

"Elandrial! Elandrial! Elandrial!"

The black-robed warriors were moving then too, a surge pulsing through their ranks. The men of the mountain were already charging out from their hidey holes and pre-dug bunkers. Caught up in the euphoria of the moment, Tomas drew his sword and let out a roar. He could still deliver the finishing blow to Joshan's murderer.

A restraining hand gripped his shoulder. "Secure the duke. See that no harm comes to him. Kill the rest." Tomas was uneasy about taking a direct order from the Shadow Mage, but he nodded his assent. A cold shadow passed over his soul as he regarded Rolfgot and the men standing behind him, each of them with the same black eyes and blank expression. Many men have been called evil, defined by the deeds they perpetrate, but even the cruellest of tyrants is capable of love for his children or for another. Does that negate the pure blackness of their soul? At that moment Tomas felt as if he were in the presence of something purely evil. The Shadow Mage regarded him coldly, daring defiance. Tomas got the impression that he would welcome it.

"Kill them all!" The words echoed in his mind, even as he felt his legs carry him across the valley that had become a bloody battlefield.

Jarl Crawulf – Lady Rosinnio: The Duchies

Crawulf moved with the swell of the sea, his feet firmly planted on the wooden boards of the longboat. All around him men slept slumped on their rowing benches as their work was done for them by the square sail catching Baltagor's breath, driving them ever closer to the unknown over a white-capped, grey sea. Sitting at the prow, looking tiny, wrapped in an over-sized fur cloak was his young wife, an exotic creature far from home. He reflected on times past, to a distant memory. A fair-haired girl with sparkling blue eyes full of mischief and joy—his first wife, Agathea—she had died bearing him a son, the babe had perished that day also. He swore he would never take another woman, a foolish promise, for a jarl must have an heir, but back then he was young and the second son of the jarl of Wind Isle. It was never supposed to be he who would inherit his father's seat; the Fates have strange ways indeed. Spur-of-the-moment vows made by an unthinking young noble are quickly set aside when important alliances and the improved state of coffers are at stake. He had accepted the Emperor of Sunsai's offer without a second thought when the proposal was put to him. It had helped greatly when he first met his young bride and her soft olive skin and round dark eyes had lit a flame of desire in him. Truly, he thought, the gods had favoured him with such a match. *Yet*, he thought, *there was more, much more to this young girl from the far south than first realised.*

He walked up behind her and felt her tremble beneath the fur. The voyage had been hard on her. Anything she ate or drank was immediately lost over the side. She looked small and frail to start with. Soon she would be nothing but bone covered in a thin layer of skin. "The men are becoming anxious, we have sailed almost the length of the Duchies. If we encounter any of their warships they will think we are raiding and attack us," he said. His heart ached when he saw how weak and pale her complexion had become from the lengthy voyage on a rolling sea. At least whatever gods were watching over them… watching over her had favoured them with a relatively calm sea and no sight of storm clouds on the horizon.

"I know," she said, her voice cracking. "I will know it when I see it." He noticed that she still clutched the horn close to her chest.

"How is it the gods of the north are speaking to you? Do not your own gods favour you anymore?"

She shrugged and looked into his eyes. "The gods use whatever tools they deem fit, northern or southern," she answered before her head slumped forward.

He crouched down beside her. "Lay your head on my shoulder and rest for a while," he said. She smiled but shook her head.

"There!" she suddenly cried, becoming animated.

Crawulf peered into the distance and saw a small fishing village, sheltered in a natural cove, in the distance. A wooden jetty stretched out from the beach along which small craft were moored.

"If nothing else, this should be entertaining." Crawulf grinned before he began bellowing orders to wake his slumbering men. Some folk were set to get a surprise this cold winter morning.

By the time they docked and began clambering onto the pier, a greeting party of armed villagers were awaiting them.

"We will need to buy horses and food enough for a long ride, several days," Rosinnio said as Crawulf helped her off the boat.

The jarl of Wind Isle went to meet the hostile fisher folk with a grin on his lips and a pouch of silver coin in his hand. There was nothing like silver to reassure folk that they came in peace and only wanted to trade. The villagers quickly overcame their fear and agreed to sell them supplies and horses, but insisted they must then leave. Even a wolf bearing silver would not be permitted to spend the night in the sheep pen. In truth Crawulf was happier to have his ship retreat back to sea and out of sight once he and a dozen of his men mounted their overpriced horses and followed a foreign princess, guided by the gods, into the unknown.

***

They made camp in a forest nestled at the foot of a large mountain range after two days hard riding. Light drained from the overcast sky as they tethered their horses in a small clearing, a safe distance from the road, and lit a fire to chase away the chill of night. Although not as cold as the harsh north, there was still the sting of ice in the air making their breaths mist when they spoke. Rosinnio, although becoming more accustomed to the colder climes of the north, still yearned for the heat of a southern sun. *At least I am on solid ground,* she thought, the horror of a long sea voyage still fresh in her memory. All around her men spoke quietly in their harsh, guttural language. She could pick out a word here or there, but in general it was still a mystery to her. Thankfully when they spoke to her they used the common trading tongue and no longer bellowed at her, using their own words. The sound of men moving in armour rattled in the cold air as she stared into the hypnotic dance of the flames, men who had followed her… *followed Crawulf.* She was still not sure why he had agreed to the journey.

Her eyes searched for her husband. He was standing with a small group of his men, talking and laughing quietly, totally at ease with them, and they him. He still terrified her. They all did, yet he had followed her so far away from his home, simply because she had asked him to. *What did he expect to find at the journey's end?* she wondered. Perhaps he was just pandering to the whims of a spoiled princess from a distant land, allowing her to make a fool of herself. *I will become one of you. I will make you a good wife.*

Her eyes grew heavy as the glow of the writhing dancers warmed the skin of her face. She pulled the fur cloak tight around her shoulders, letting the sounds of the Nortmen and the scent of the forest drift over her until they shifted to the edge of her consciousness. Her breathing settled into a slow steady rhythm as the pull of the flames drew her closer and then beyond into the realms of sleep.

Her eyes snapped open as two small shadows drifted across the blaze. The shadows formed a ring of white around them until she realised two eyes stared back at her from the flames. *Who are you?* she thought, lazily, still in a dream state, sleep weighing heavily on her. Then she heard a sound, a voice whispering on the wind... her name. Someone was calling to her. The eyes in the flames stared at her with pupils made of mist and shadow, dark orbs with the power to touch her soul. *The Shadow Mage!*

An arm of flame suddenly burst from the fire towards her. She could feel its heat, feel its rage as it attempted to engulf her in fire and pain. She was frozen, mesmerised by the eyes narrowing in hate. A face formed at the heart of the fire, a face of orange and yellow flame with two dark shadows for eyes. The mouth opened and she heard a single word – die.

Fear froze her even as the creature's fiery grip burned her, igniting the cloak of fur she wore.

Voices called to her from the forest, her name borne on the breeze. She remembered a previous dream where Crawulf had come to her and fought for her, she focused on that memory. Suddenly the monster in the flames hissed and began to steam. She looked up and Crawulf stood over her, an empty waterskin in his hands from which he'd poured the contents over the fire.

"The fire," he said, confusion on his face. "It attacked you."

She looked down at where her cloak had been burned, the smell of singed hair and flesh lingering in the air. She brought her hand up to her cheek and felt the heat there... pain. "The Shadow Mage," she answered.

"Are you hurt?" he asked, concern in his voice. She was, but she shook her head. A howl rent the air then, followed by another, then another.

"He knows we're coming." Rosinnio tried to fight the fear welling inside her, but could not control her voice from trembling. "He is sending creatures of darkness against us," she said, tears formed in her eyes. "I'm sorry," she added, her voice dropping to a whisper. "I've killed us all."

***

Crawulf stood at arm's length from his woman, seeing the terror in her eyes and how she fought it. Her cheek was red and blistered from where the fire had snaked out a pillar of flame at her. She was talking about things he had no comprehension of. He did not understand the ways of the gods. He sacrificed to Baltagor at the beginning and end of a voyage, leading a goat into the sea where its throat was cut and the blood allowed to flow freely into the waves. He prayed to Alweise that he would one day die with a sword in his hands and journey to The All Wise's hall to feast and make war on the enemies of the gods, the dark elves and dwarves of Boda. He left any other concerns to those with ears and eyes open to the gods, such as Maolach, and now his woman, a princess from a far distant land, who could see things he did not understand, speak the language of the gods.

As the howling increased all around them, he quickly ordered torches lit illuminating the small clearing they were camped in. If this mage wished to send beasts to attack him, demonic or not, let them come into the light. His men formed a ring around him and his woman, shields, mail, flesh and bone, this was what he understood. The forest was alive now with the sound of howling as each call was answered by another and another, then another.

"Wolves," a man said.

"They will not be ordinary wolves," Rosinnio answered, her voice shaking. "Strike their heads."

Crawulf beat his sword off his wooden shield. His men picked up the rhythm, the sound reverberating around the trees, an answer to the beasts howling, a defiance to whatever horror lay beyond the light. Grim-faced Nortmen, hard as the coats of mail they wore, immovable as the mountain looming above them. *Tell your gods and your men, we are of the Isles and we defy you.*

Their eyes shone silver in the darkness, reflecting off the light of the torches and the moon overhead, their howling and yelping closing in around the Nortmen, making them feel as if the very forest was alive, that the trees around them were coming against them. It mattered not.

Silence. Then a fallen branch snapped and chaos erupted from the darkness. Small flashes of grey, brown and black flew through the air, hounds cast from the Nacht Realm, with flesh and fur hanging off them, fangs exposed through blood-filled grins and snarls. They attacked the ring of men attracted by the warm glow of life surrounding them. A dozen swords and shields came up as one throwing back the demonic pack as the beasts attempted to render flesh with teeth and claws. Black blood gushed from wounds inflicted by the hard steel of the Nortmen's swords and axes as the magic that was their life force bled from them with each cut.

A huge beast, decayed flesh hanging from its bones, leapt over the wall of men. With eyes burning and with a maw dripping poisonous bile and blood, it flew through the air towards Rosinnio. Crawulf swung his sword in a wide arc, slicing clean through the neck with one blow. Another followed barely before he could catch a breath. He shoved up his shield, knocking it onto its back before stepping over it, once again decapitating the beast with one blow. Bodies piled in front of the men, yet more came, and from the sound of the howling forest there was no end to them.

Crawulf was knocked from his feet by a leaping wolf. He could smell the death and corruption from its snarling maw as it tried to bite through the arm of his mail. Thankfully he wore the armour of a jarl and the interlocked links held firm. He shoved the hound off, digging deep to find the strength before fumbling for the dagger at his belt. He then drove it hard into its skull. He was close enough to see the black trail of corrupted magic float free into the air and for the animal to drop lifeless to the ground.

Another thumped into him as he climbed to his knees and then another. As he fell he noted that two of his men were down, all of the others were surrounded by monstrous beasts, each man hard-pressed. Then the air began to crackle and shift as if a lightning bolt had hit the ground close by. He could sense the unnatural force around him. The beast on top of him howled in pain as it was engulfed in blue flame. Crawulf, acting on instinct, quickly crawled out from under the body and hauled himself to his feet. Rosinnio's eyes blazed as white and blue flame shot from her fingertips, scorching the beasts even as they emerged from the darkness. All around them the demon-pack perished as the magical fire enveloped them.

Power Crawulf did not understand flowed from his woman's hands, cleansing the clearing of the beasts, ceasing as abruptly as it came. Rosinnio stood at the centre of the clearing, her eyes open wide, staring at her outstretched hands.

"What..." Crawulf began.

"I don't know," Rosinnio answered before he'd finished the question.

The jarl took a step back. "What manner of power do you possess?"

Rosinnio continued shaking her head.

"Have you used this before?" he asked, awe and confusion filling his words.

"Once," she answered hesitantly, glancing at Rothgar, "but not like this."

Crawulf swung around to the big warrior. "You knew she could do this?"

He nodded his head slowly. "Aye, but like she says, not like this."

"The horn," Crawulf said, pointing at the bone horn of Galen. It was glowing white in her hand.

Duke Normand – Tomas: Hidden valley

A green wave rushed across the valley floor as the people of the mountain charged towards the warriors assembled in ranks facing them. Moving like a dark shadow from the far end of the gorge, were the black-robed tribesmen. Archers fired arrows at the rolling horde from behind the protection of the rows of warriors.

"There's only one way out, back the way we came," Malachi said as Normand surveyed the battlefield, his warrior's mind assessing the situation. "We could make a run for it."

"And get slaughtered," the duke answered. "I will not run from peasants."

"Those are not peasants." Malachi pointed towards the advancing tribesmen.

"No," Normand agreed. He was more than confident that his trained men would easily hold against the wild mountain-men, charging towards his flanks, but the warriors approaching from the front were a different matter. He had lined the bulk of his force to face that threat, but the numbers of mountain-men emerging, as if from thin air, was a worry.

Djangra Roe meanwhile was still on his knees, mumbling incoherently before the ring of stones as wisps of mist circled the floor of the cairn, growing steadily thicker. "Get him up! I need him," Normand bellowed at two warriors standing over the mage, as lightning bolts struck three of his men at random.

Though used to holding a line against any odds, men suddenly began to fidget uneasily as the crackle of magic hummed over them.

"We can't stay here," Malachi, normally a level-headed and calm commander of men, said, his words tinged with fear.

"We have no choice."

The first line of mountain-men reached his warriors as the clash of weapons and the cries of dying men filled the air. Normand watched, fighting a battle within to keep calm, the dark shadow of cloaked tribesmen smearing across the valley floor. Pain-filled screams of hate and rage sung out around him as his warriors held their line against the massed assault of the untrained mountain-men who threw themselves onto the naked blades arrayed against them. *If only they were all we fought today,* Normand thought bitterly. Dying an inglorious death in an anonymous valley had not been part of his plan that morning.

The closer the tribesmen got the faster they began to move, until they were charging at a full run at the moment of impact. They slammed into the duke's men who fended them off with shields and cold steel. Normand stood with his Dragon Knights—held back in reserve—the banner fluttering overhead. At the far end of the valley he could see the witches, could sense the charge in the air around him each time they sent forth a surge of power striking down two and three of his men at a time with bolts materialised from out of nowhere. *No wonder the king had ordered the burning of witches throughout the land,* he thought bitterly. His own mage was a useless lump of gibbering mess. He was slowly beginning to realise there was a reason the lands of witches and mages were not generally invaded.

A gap appeared in the line in front of him as the black-clad tribesmen fought like demons. Several of them poured through the opening like dark blood seeping from a wound. Normand cried out and led his Dragon Knights into battle, forgetting all about magic and desires to turn back time. This was a moment to revel in, the juxtaposed emotions of joy and terror. He slammed his sword into the chest of a tribesman, feeling the blade slice into whatever reinforced leather armour he wore beneath his robe, before tearing flesh and smashing bone. Blood sprayed across his face, falling on him like rain. The metallic taste drove him on to find another foe. Wielding his sword two-handed, Normand batted away a blow from a snarling tribesman before reversing a cut across his opponent's neck. The man slumped to the ground and Normand moved on.

In an instant the breach was closed and the duke found himself with no enemies to kill... for now. He wiped sweat and blood from his brow and eyes and reassessed the situation. If it wasn't for those cursed witches he would have been confident his men would easily triumph. That is until another problem presented itself – the Nortmen.

On his flanks the sheer numbers of mountain-men were threatening to overwhelm his own lines, but the trained warriors fought valiantly and bodies began to pile in a heap before them. *How many losses can they take before they break and run?* he wondered. How much longer before the magic buzzing in the air filled his warriors with enough fear to make *them* break?

"My lord." Malachi tapped him on the shoulder and then pointed to their rear.

"What next?" Normand raised his eyes towards the sky as a small group of Nortmen rushed towards them from behind their ranks.

"It is a small enough band, no more than ten."

"I will take half the knights myself and face them. You remain here with the others and plug any more breaches."

"My lord." Malachi inclined his head forward.

Normand took half a score of Dragon Knights and a handful of archers and turned to face the new threat.

***

Tomas trotted along with the Nortmen as the two score raiders with dark, dead eyes followed the giant warrior Rolfgot towards the battle. The black-robed tribesmen had already begun their attack and were pressing hard against the lines of the duke's men. He could not help but be impressed by the resolve of those men as they faced a force much larger than their own. At first he was sure the huge numbers of mountain-men would easily overwhelm them, and if not, surely they would not hold against the added weight of the tribesmen, but hold they did, and Tomas could see the mountain-men begin to waver as a small trickle of them began to break away and return to wherever they had come from. The lightly armed and armoured men of the mountain were not suited to a pitched battle with trained warriors.

Ahead of him Tomas could see the battle between the Tribesmen and the duke's men was fought in a boiling cauldron of ferocity, as men died and fell on both sides suffering horrendous injuries. Beyond them was the circle of stones with the strange mist swirling between the huge boulders. As he got closer he could see swirling designs etched into the stone shining silver as the glint of the winter sun caught the ancient runes. Kneeling before them as if in some sort of homage was the mage – the murderer of his friend.

The Shadow Mage had instructed him to follow the Nortmen and secure the duke. It was his desire to possess the duke's body, crushing his spirit and soul from within. The very thought sent a cold feeling down Tomas's spine. He did not envy Duke Normand. In truth he cared little for what the Shadow Mage wanted. If he wished to become a powerful lord while wearing the body of another, then so be it, but he did not like being in the presence of the unnatural group of Nortmen. He could sense the wrongness about them oozing from them, their look, their smell. They just ignored him—yet he knew they would turn on him in an instant—everything felt of death.

The Nortmen pushed their way through the rows of black-clad warriors, the tribesmen parting to let them through. Those who stood their ground were pushed aside, some trampled under the heavy boots of the sea raiders. Tomas followed. By now the mountain-men had broken and run and the duke's men were reinforcing the line facing their more deadly attackers... facing him. Once the Nortmen reached the front, the slaughter began. They pushed through the line of defenders as if they weren't there. Warriors who had stood their ground valiantly against tribesmen, men of the mountain and even the magic bolts rained down on them from Elandrial and Aliss, crumpled under the assault of the Nortmen. Tomas saw one man deflect an axe blow on his shield and then drive his sword into the chest of a Nortman. What should have been a killing blow had no effect and the duke's man now lay face down in the dirt, his head almost cleaved from his shoulders.

The black-robed tribesmen now flowed around the defensive line of the duke's men as the Nortmen assaulted the front. With the mountain-men now gone, it became one massive brawl. Tomas could see the fear in the eyes of the men he faced as they realised they were facing an enemy they could not kill. They tried to keep their shape and back away in order, but with the tribesman hemming them in where once the men of the mountain were, panic crept into their hearts.

Tomas pushed past them all. He met the eyes of one of the duke's men and saw the terror there, more than simply the fear of dying but the horror of being tainted by the demonic foes they faced. He raised his sword, prepared to cut the man down but he turned and fled. More of his companions were doing the same now. In the distance he could see the duke's banner as he took a small force against a much smaller group of Nortmen coming from the opposite end of the valley. He had not realised there were more of the raiders from the Pirate Isles on the field other than the company he was with. He dismissed the thought from his mind as he approached the kneeling mage.

"Djangra Roe," he said, "you sent me on a quest to track down the dream-witch. I found her and brought her here."

Djangra Roe slowly turned towards him. Blood streamed from his eyes like crimson tears trailing down his cheeks. "Help me," he mouthed.

"You killed the only friend I've ever had in this life, the one man who mattered most to me," Tomas said, but the mage wasn't listening. He spotted something moving out of the corner of his eye. A shape shifted in the swirling mass of mist hemmed in by the stones.

All around him the battle raged as men died beneath the swords and axes of the Nortmen. Those smart enough to get out of the way survived... only to face the tribesmen.

Suddenly the mage's head jerked up. Tomas jumped back into a defensive position, raising his sword, as Djangra Roe slowly climbed to his feet. The Nortmen all around him pushed past, the smell of blood and death cloying in the air around them.

The mage's face bore a haunted expression, his eyes dark and wild as blood still streamed from the corners. "Something is coming," he said softly.

"Why did you kill Joshan? What purpose could the death of a priest serve you?" Tomas asked ignoring the mage, too caught up in his own need for vengeance.

"We have to run!" Djangra Roe's eyes took on a fevered look as he staggered forward.

Something shifted between the stones, a dark shape seen from the corner of his eye. Tomas turned to look closer as a formless shape shimmered in the mist. His blood turned to ice as fear took a hold of his heart. "It is the priestess. She is calling to her god."

"No. It is something else," the mage answered, suddenly becoming lucid, fear written all over his face. "The stones, they are a gateway, the markings are enchantments meant to keep it closed... to keep whatever is behind there out."

"It means nothing to me," Thomas spat the words out, although he glanced anxiously over the mage's shoulder. "You will atone for the death of an innocent priest." He raised his sword, ready to strike a blow before the mage escaped or had time to conjure a magical defence.

"Priest?" Djangra Roe said, puzzled. Tomas took a step closer. "Wait! I know you. The priest from the monastery? You are the blacksmith. I did not kill your friend. It was the tracker. He stabbed him in the back. The priest attacked us with magic, I was powerless. I couldn't even move my arms."

"And you think I will believe you. You are lying to save your life."

"It matters not. We are all dead anyway." Djangra Roe slumped back onto his knees.

"What do you mean?" Tomas held back the killing blow.

"Can you not feel the magic swirling in the air all around us, dark, dark magic? Someone is trying to break the seals of the gate. When they do they will unleash something that does not belong in this world."

"Harren Suilomon," Tomas answered. "He is aiding the priestess to call upon her god. She told me herself."

"No, he is not. And if the dream-witch believes that the goddess Eor is going to walk from those stones then she has been duped too."

Suddenly the mage cried out, regained his feet and lurched forward. Tomas flung up his sword, misinterpreting Djangra's movement and the mage walked straight into the blade. Tomas stared, wide-eyed, as Djangra Roe slid from his sword. Vengeance was his, yet somehow it did not feel that way.

He turned then and ran in the opposite direction, back to where Aliss stood with Elandrial, the Witch-Queen, High Priestess of Eor.

Lady Rosinnio – Tomas: Hidden valley

Rosinnio led the small group of Nortmen down a forest trail. Crawulf had tried to persuade her to return to the ship after the attack of the wolves, but she refused. "It's becoming too dangerous," he had said. But they were close now. She could feel it in every part of her. The Shadow Mage knew where to find her and now that he had scented blood he would not stop. He would send more assassins, more beasts in the night. There was only one way to stop him; to face him and kill him.

She led the men through the mountain and to the crest of the valley, guided by some force she did not understand. Crawulf wondered why the gods of the north would speak to her. In truth she wondered that herself, but something had led her to the horn and now to this mountain at the opposite end of the Duchies, far away from the isles of Nortland, farther still from Sunsai.

The sound of battle carried on the wind towards them. Crawulf was shaking his head when it was reported by the man he sent to investigate. "I'll not take you into a battle," he said.

"But that is exactly where we must go," she answered. "You have shown such faith in me, trusted me to take you this far, followed me when I had no right to ask. Please do not turn aside at the moment we have reached the end."

"Men are dying down there. We all could join them if we go down."

"Yes, we might die, but it is what we must do."

"I'm marching towards certain death on the basis of a foolish girl's dreams and the ravings of a mad hermit who lives in a cave." Crawulf looked skyward. "Can you give me naught but mysticism and talk of dark magic, in order to do this?" Rosinnio just shook her head. "We'll take a look, but that is all," he said then.

When they reached the edge of the valley they looked down from their vantage point. The screams of men dying carried towards them along with the smell of blood and war. The warriors of the Duchies fought in defensive lines repelling a much larger force attacking their flanks. In the centre they were assaulted by black-robed warriors.

"Sukes," Rosinnio gasped, recognising the garb of a nomadic tribe who roamed the plains and deserts of the southern empire.

"There! Do you see?" One of Crawulf's men pointed towards the far end of the valley. Rosinnio looked and saw a group of Nortmen heading towards the battle.

"Is that..." Crawulf began.

"Aye – Rolfgot," the man answered. "I recognise a few others down there too."

Rosinnio looked mystified at them both until the man explained. "They are members of Jarl Crawulf's brother's crew. They disappeared many years ago and were thought lost. The big one at the front is Rolfgot, Wulfgar's chosen man."

"They're alive," Crawulf whispered in awe.

Rosinnio put a hand on his arm then and said quietly, "No, they are not alive."

He turned towards her. "You mean they are like the wolves?"

"No, the wolves were beasts. These are... were men. Now they are soulless shades who cannot be killed by mortal weapons." She dipped her head and continued. "Now I know why I have been drawn to this place."

Crawulf led the way down the steep path while Rothgar helped her down the treacherous trail. Their presence was noted almost straight away as a group of red-cloaked warriors broke away from the Duchies army to face them. They formed a line while several archers made their way out. The jarl barked an order to stop and raise shields as a flight of arrows whistled through the air, they thumped into wooden shields and speared the ground around them, but none, thankfully, found a mark.

"Hold! We are not here to fight you," Crawulf roared across the divide. He was answered with another volley of arrows.

Suddenly, further down the valley, beside the circle of stones the Duchies army broke under the onslaught of Rolfgot's Nortmen and the dark-cloaked warriors. The defensive lines splintered and ran pursued by the southern tribesmen across the valley in every direction. The Nortmen continued towards them.

The small group of red-cloaked warriors beneath a banner displaying a red dragon turned to face the larger force of Nortmen advancing towards them. Arrows peppered the bigger column but had no effect. The raiders did not even raise their shields, simply took the projectiles and ignored them.

"They cannot fight shades such as those," Rosinnio said.

Rosinnio suddenly started running towards the red-cloaked men beneath the banner. Crawulf cursed and ran after her, his own men following. "You've lost your wits," he panted, sucking in breaths when he caught up with her, his mail weighing heavy on his shoulders.

"Wait! I can help," she cried out.

The leader of the red cloaks turned with several of his men, while the rest prepared to meet the advancing Rolfgot and his crew. "And who are you?" he asked, taking up a defensive position, sword raised.

"I am Jarl Crawulf, and we have not come here to fight you," Crawulf answered instead.

"Crawulf? The same Crawulf who raided Elsward's lands?"

"Aye, what of it?"

"We are not friends, Nortman, and as you can see I am a little preoccupied."

"Aye about that. My lady here believes she may aid you."

"You cannot fight them. They are not men," Rosinnio said, sucking in air as she caught her breath.

"They are Nortmen, barely men I'll grant you," Normand answered, adding, "no offence." Crawulf scowled in reply.

"They are shades under the control of a powerful mage. I believe I have a way to stop them."

"Well then you had best do it quickly," the duke replied as the Nortmen bore down on the small group.

Panic suddenly surged through Rosinnio. What if the horn didn't work? What if she'd led them all to their deaths for no reason? Then she began to wonder if the Shadow Mage had drawn her here? Was it all a cunning ruse to get her to travel to him, where he could exact his sworn vengeance on her ancestor by killing her? The clash of swords on shields and sounds of men doing battle brought her back to her senses.

"Hurry, my lady," Rothgar urged as black-eyed Nortmen closed in on them.

She heard a scream and saw a red-cloaked warrior impaled on a sword, another struck down with an axe. She raised the horn to her lips and blew.

***

Tomas marched towards the dream-witch, his mind barely registering what Djangra Roe had told him before he died. Behind him all was chaos as the tribesmen and Nortmen overwhelmed Duke Normand's force of warriors, thanks mainly to the unnatural ability of the sea raiders from the Pirate Isles. What was driving him now was fear, fear of what he'd seen forming in the mist between the standing stones, fear that the mage may have spoken true. He had followed Elandrial in order to gain revenge for the death of his friend and to find a cure for his woman. He had listened to the priestess's plans to call upon her god and to rid her land of the usurper, even agreed to help her in return for her aid with Aliss. Now though he was afraid, and deemed it time to leave. He would seek help elsewhere for Aliss, go back to the Great Wood and confront the witch, let her remove the curse that bade Aliss long for the blood of an innocent.

First though, he was confronted by three black-garbed tribesmen who stood sentinel before the Shadow Mage and the two women. Aliss, he saw, still joined hands with Elandrial, her complexion pale, almost translucent. *How long has she looked so sickly?* he wondered. The mage too stood beside them with his eyes closed. Tomas could feel the power crackling in the air around them, feel the magic pulsing in waves from them, so powerful even one without the gift of magic could sense it.

"Cease this, Elandrial. You don't know what it is you are summoning," he said as he approached. "What are you doing to her?" he added when he saw the pained expression on Aliss' face.

"The glory of Eor shall descend from the heavens and smite our enemies," the priestess answered, opening her eyes.

"No! That is no god you are releasing from those stones. He has led you false." He pointed his sword at Harren Suilomon.

"And who are you, blacksmith, to decide what is and is not a god?" the Shadow Mage answered, malice dripping from his words. "Have you suddenly been blessed with divine powers?"

"I can see that you are killing Aliss. Release her now."

"No, Tomas," Elandrial answered. "We need her, just as she needs us. We are joined, we three. Come. You too are part of the circle." She reached out a hand for him to join them.

He felt a draw on his mind then, an urge to join the three magic wielders. He stepped forward into the embrace of Elandrial.

"He lied to you," he said once he'd stepped past the guards, "whatever promises he made you to help win back your lands and call your god. He used you." He rammed his sword into Elandrial's chest then. He did so with not a little regret, but the only way he could break the connection between the dream-witch and Aliss was to kill her. He had not the time to try persuasion.

Elandrial screamed as the blade smashed through her breast bone and died instantly. Aliss collapsed to the floor as if she were nothing more than a child's toy.

"You fool!" the Shadow Mage shrieked, his fat jowls turning red. "Kill him," he ordered the tribesmen.

The three black-robed tribesmen turned on Tomas. The first two stabs were excruciatingly painful as the curved blades entered his side. The third he didn't feel at all as he dropped onto his knees. He reached out a bloody hand to his woman who was lying on the cold, hard ground, but his vision blurred and he realised he could no longer control the use of his arms. He slumped forward onto the ground. In the distance he heard the sound of a hunting horn, his mind unable to fathom what it could mean. All he heard was a cry of anguish coming from the Shadow Mage at the sound of the horn – that at least made him smile.

Hidden valley, Mountains of Eor

All around her men screeched and wailed as death held sway across the valley. The cursed crew of Wulfgar visited pain and suffering on all who stood in their way; Crawulf's men and the Duke's Dragon Knights. She blew a long blast on the horn as the sound of steel ringing on steel and of men dying filled the air. Rothgar stood over her, alongside Crawulf battling undead Nortmen they were unable to kill. She felt tears welling, blurring her vision as she tried to summon the blue fire that had killed the wolves and the were-beast. On both of those occasions it had just come unbidden to her. Now there was nothing. She watched helplessly as the giant leader of the Nortmen bore down on Crawulf. She heard her husband shout out his name in a challenge, 'Rolfgot'. She'd never seen a warrior look so fierce, not even her husband or the big axeman, Rothgar.

Rolfgot's black eyes held no recognition or any emotion as he launched a fierce attack on the jarl. Crawulf blocked the blows with his shield until there was nothing left of it but splintered wood. He flung it aside and stabbed his own sword at his opponent's head, while Rothgar attacked from the side, swinging his axe in an arc. It plunged into the back of the massive Rolfgot, but the Nortman didn't even flinch. He swung his sword backhanded towards Rothgar, slicing a savage blow across his chest, smashing through the interlocked rings of mail. Rothgar fell back as a crimson spray arced through the air.

"Nooo!!!" Rosinnio screamed as her protector fell down at her feet. Rolfgot meanwhile turned back to Crawulf… and then stopped.

The giant warrior looked down. A shadow seeped into the earth like a stain at his feet. His face took on a quizzical, almost comical expression as the shadow became a cloud submerging his feet and then his ankles. A similar black cloud was swirling around each of the cursed Nortmen. Rosinnio saw the horn in her hand pulse with a bright light, as the undead warriors struggled to free themselves. Translucent, skeletal hands and faces appeared in the clouds, wrapping themselves around the warriors.

"Soul Reapers," Crawulf said as he pulled Rosinnio back. She felt almost sorry for the warriors then as each of them was enveloped by a cloud and dragged, struggling and crying out, into the hard earth.

She fell on her knees then beside the body of her protector, Rothgar. His great chest was still as the heart within it no longer beat. Tears clouded her vision as she reached out to touch him, beseeching her own gods and those of the Nortmen to give her the power to heal him, to bring him back to life.

Crawulf's men—those who remained standing—formed a defensive arc around her as the jarl bent down to touch her shoulder. "He is feasting with The All Wise now."

When Rosinnio looked up she saw the joy on her husband's face as he genuinely revelled in the glory of a warrior's death, happy that his friend met his end with the blood of his enemies on his axe. *I will never understand them*, she thought, unable to find any happiness in the death of a friend. *And he was a friend*, she realised, even though her first wish for him was to have him slain for insulting her. *I have come a long way.*

She took Crawulf's hand and he helped her up. "Was your…"

"No," the jarl continued her line of thought. "My brother was not among them."

"Perhaps he yet lives," she said.

"I hope not," Crawulf answered as he stared at the spot where Rolfgot had been dragged into the hard earth, not a mark or sign remained to give any hint he was ever there – save the bodies he left in his wake.

The black-robed tribesmen withdrew once the Nortmen met their end and Duke Normand's warriors began to rally, drifting back to the battlefield now that the only enemies remaining were those who bled and died as they did. Rosinnio followed the tribesmen with her eyes until she spotted a fat man dressed as a Sunsai noble moving towards them. He was the focal point for the nomadic warriors of the south. *Shadow Mage,* an icy thrill of fear ran down her spine. She could feel his hatred for her burning her mind. And something else… he was afraid. The same dark magic that had bound the cursed crew of Wulfgar also allowed him to exist in the world. If that foul link could be broken, then could not the poisonous glue allowing him to live as a parasite within the bodies of others not be broken too?

"I see you, Harren Suilomon, and I do not fear you, nor the curses you have invoked on my family." She doubted her words would carry across the battlefield, yet she knew he would hear them.

"Something stirs within that strange mist," Crawulf said, pointing with his sword towards the circle of stones. The runes carved into them pulsated a silver light.

"He is calling on some foul power," she answered.

"How is it you know such things?" Crawulf asked. His face was covered in grime and blood, his eyes blazing fiercely, a sight that would have frightened her witless not so long ago, and yet now… feelings stirred within her.

"Madam, you are a most unusual Nortwoman," Duke Normand said, moving beside them.

"This is the Princess Rosinnio, of Sunsai and Wind Isle," Crawulf answered, then added. "And my wife."

Normand's eyebrows shot up. "Well, this is a most interesting development. Doubtless it is an important piece of news worthy of consideration, in the outside world. However, right now there are more pressing matters."

The circle of stones began to rock as the mist shone with an eerie silver light. The dark shape hidden there grew, stretching upwards and outwards. While the remaining tribesmen now formed a line in front of the Shadow Mage and began moving up the valley towards them. She could feel strands of dark magic probing her mind as Suilomon sent out tentacles of power to entrap her. She brought the horn to her lips once again, just as a blood-freezing roar rent the cold valley air. One of the large boulders shattered.

She felt the strong arms of Crawulf pulling her back and away from the stone circle as debris landed at her feet. Six of his men remained alive, all raising their shields over her as small stones and larger chunks of rock shot forward from a second exploding stone.

"I think it would be best to leave now," Crawulf said.

"Agreed," Normand concurred.

"No." Rosinnio shook him off. "Not while Harren Suilomon still lives. He will hunt us down. He will unleash terror unto the world like no other seen before."

"Worse than he has already done?" Normand asked.

"Far worse."

"What must we do?" Crawulf asked, resigned now to following his wife's lead.

"I can feel the grip on whatever monster he is calling loosen. The link has been weakened."

"I saw the dream-witch fall," Normand said. "Perhaps she was aiding him. This was, after all, once her domain."

"Yes, perhaps," Rosinnio answered. "If she possessed power she likely was."

Another stone burst apart, while another bowel-loosening roar came from within.

"What will happen if the link between the two breaks?" Crawulf asked.

"I... don't know," Rosinnio answered before bringing up the horn and blowing a long note, just as before. Only this time, nothing happened.

"Look!" Crawulf gasped. A crack appeared in the horn snaking its way up the centre until the bone instrument fell from her hands and turned to dust. "Well, bollocks to that," he said and hefted his sword once again as another boulder shattered, leaving the circle half broken.

***

Tomas's eyes snapped open. He grimaced and flinched as pain shot through him. "Don't move," Aliss said softly as she laid her hands on his chest. He could feel a soothing warmth emanate from her touch, slowly flowing over his body and easing his hurts.

"You were always a fine healer," he said, his voice cracking. She smiled sadly and took his hand in her own when he reached up to touch her face.

"It's all I ever wanted," she said.

"We can leave this cursed place," he said. He could still sense the charged air as the taint of magic hovered all around. In the background he could hear men cry out in pain, the smell of blood clinging thickly to his nostrils.

"You walked into the flames for me, Tomas," she said gently rubbing his cheek, "and now I'm giving you back your life. Flee from here. There is nothing for you but pain and suffering in this valley. Elandrial is dead, killed by your own hand. But she made false promises to us, Tomas. She was never going to help us, just as Harren Suilomon led her false. She thought she was calling her god, but that was never his intention. He harnessed her power, and through her mine to call upon a beast he means to unleash upon the world. His only desire is to destroy."

"You mean to stop him?"

She shrugged. "I don't know if I can, but I will try."

"I will help," he said, pushing himself up, ignoring the pain.

"No," she said, her strange swirling eyes boring into him. "I need for you to survive... I need that."

"I'm not afraid to die," he said. "If your intention is to sacrifice yourself then we will die together."

"You still don't understand, Tomas. I am already dead. I've been so since you carried me from the flames."

"I won't leave you."

"I can't do this if you are here." Tears streamed down her face. "Please, I need to know you are safe." She leaned in and kissed him then, the saltiness of tears mingled with the metallic taste of blood. "Go."

He shook his head and dragged himself up, pain lancing his side and back where the blades of the tribesmen had pierced him. "I won't leave you," he said, his jaw set in firm determination. She nodded sadly, helping him up.

The Shadow Mage and his tribesmen warriors were advancing on the remnants of the duke's warriors who were lined defensively just beyond the circle of stones. The large boulders began shattering and sending chunks of flying rock outwards, one by one.

"Those stones are inscribed with words of power, charms to seal closed a gateway. The Shadow Mage is trying to break those locks. Elandrial was aiding him. She created a link between herself and me in order to use the magic growing inside of me. I could feel her draining me, using me to boost her own power, but I could touch her mind also and see what she and Suilomon were trying to do. There is another here, who opposes him, whom he fears. This I could also sense when we briefly touched minds through Elandrial."

"Djangra Roe, the mage," Tomas said. "He's dead."

"No, another. A woman. It was she who broke the spell binding the wraiths of the Nortmen to Suilomon."

"Perhaps we may be of some assistance to her then."

"Yes," Aliss answered, smiling weakly. "That is my intention."

***

Barely a score of warriors remained from Normand's and Crawulf's combined men. Together they faced at least five times that number, as the winter sun slowly bled a fierce crimson light into the overhead clouds. Black-robed tribesmen advanced warily once again, one eye on the circle of stones and what was barely held back by their ancient power. The Shadow Mage's words of power could be heard drifting across the valley, stabbing the air around the cairn.

Crawulf picked up an undamaged shield from the body of one of his crew and joined the line of Normand's men facing the tribesmen. There was no need for words; all were drained physically and emotionally. Those men still alive had faced mountain-men, fierce warriors from the south, spears of magic thrown at their ranks and wraiths of men no blade could kill. He caught Normand's eye as the duke clapped his men on the shoulder, encouraging and praising, dispelling fear as a good commander should. The two lords the Fates had thrown together on this battlefield, men who should be enemies but found themselves on the same side, nodded to each other. Then the blood-letting began again.

Like a dark wave they charged across the valley, shouting war-cries in their own language, words that held no meaning for Crawulf, yet somehow he understood; it was not about the words, it was about filling the heart with rage and joy, fierceness and hatred, anything to quell the fear. The impact was loud and savage as men who knew they could kill or die on this day, came together.

Crawulf smashed the iron boss of his shield into the face of a charging man, his own momentum driving the round metal into his cheekbone. The man fell screaming as Crawulf stabbed down with his sword, before turning to face another. Dark eyes full of hatred glowered at him for an instant before life drained from them and he toppled backwards, his lifeless body held up by the snarling warriors coming behind him. Either side of him, Crawulf's men—those few who yet lived—fought, as all Nortmen do, without fear of death, their only concern that the gods witness their bravery and they do not dishonour themselves before man or god. Beyond them, Normand's men fought with a methodical savageness. Every stroke, every movement contained fury.

The sound of a colossal crack rent the air then, and it seemed as if time stopped. Men in mid-blow turned away from their opponent, even those dying on the blood-sodden earth strained to see as the final stone split down the centre and piece by piece fell apart. The mist cleared and Crawulf stood, mouth agape, fear overwhelming him with invisible bonds, restricting all movement.

The sound of Rosinnio screaming snapped him back. He saw her fall onto her back, her body convulsing on the ground. He searched for the fat body of the Shadow Mage. Somehow he had moved through the battle and into the ranks of Normand's men. He held the duke on his knees—seemingly powerless—while he gripped his head in both hands, a jewel dangling from a golden chain between his fingers.

"I am developing an intense dislike for that mage," the jarl of Wind Isle snarled. "Janri, help her. Get her to safety," he instructed one of his few remaining men, while he turned to face the horror that had appeared where the circle of stones once stood.

***

Aliss watched the battle unfold, feeling as if she were waking from a dream. Her last real grip on reality had been when Tomas had left their home in the middle of the night to search for Marjeri's babe, supposedly snatched from her cot by wolves. What had happened since then? *I died, Tomas walked into the flames and carried me out.* The old witch in the Great Wood had brought her back from the embrace of the All Father, but had used dark magic and the blood of an innocent to do it. *That was wrong, and now the debt shall be repaid.*

Elandrial had been fooled by the Shadow Mage who brought her an army of tribesmen and promised to return to her, her realm, the sacred mountain of Eor. But his intention had always been to bring chaos into the world. He was a parasite living off the life-force of others, his own body long since destroyed. Balancing the lives of those whose bodies he stole against his own, prolonging his own existence, exchanging their lives for his own.

Aliss' heart and mind had been exposed to blood magic, the darkest of all powers when the witch swapped one life for another. It had changed her appearance, and planted a black seed within her... yet, that was not her. All she ever wanted was to help people, to ease the suffering of others, and to live her life with Tomas. It was she to whom women unable to conceive visited seeking a charm to aid in the planting of a seed. She who was called when a child or beast of the field fell ill, or a farmer

Blood Of Kings: The Shadow Mage

needed a broken leg splinted. Her reward was to be raped and sent to the pyre, her home torched, her man beaten. Yet they had endured.

The magic she possessed that was at the root of her was not the blood magic of the old witch or the Shadow Mage. It was of the earth, gifted to her by the All Father. She could feel the life of the valley all around her, the seeds in the cold earth waiting for spring, the animals hiding from the beast of man, but all around them, watching, even the patterns of the air, meaningless to most, but a map to the future and the weather it would bring. Above all, she could feel the fear and confusion of that which Suilomon had called from beyond the stones. Tomas had told her he sensed its evil. It was not evil, it was no demon taking shape, even as she watched the Shadow Mage drift, like smoke, through the battlefield until he held his prize in his two hands: Duke Normand poised, albeit unwilling, to become his newest host. It was simply a beast, not unlike those of the forest, but out of place, out of time. It did not belong in the world of men and that is why it seemed evil to all who saw it, all who felt it. Harren Suilomon did not understand this either.

Often, while trying to heal a farm animal, or soothe the hurts of a beast of the forest she would touch its mind, ease its pain and fill it with reassurance, feelings of warmth and calmness. When she touched the mind of the summoned beast it felt like a hammer blow, the sheer weight of its emotions threatening to overwhelm her. She could feel its fear, feel herself being submerged by the depth of its feelings; she could feel herself being absorbed by the creature.

When she looked, she saw through its eyes the creatures running from her, milling in fear, not unlike the hunters, of her own world, she and her kind were wary of, although their skin was lacking the green hue to it, those that sought to ensnare her kind with their nets and long sharp teeth they carried in their hands. When she stretched out her arms, thick leathery wings unfolded. She longed to take to the safety of the sky, where the little creatures with the stinging teeth they threw could not harm her; to float on the air, through the clouds, to feel the heat of the sun warming her. She looked up at the towering, ice-capped peaks around her, that is where she would be safe, that is where she needed to build a nest.

The little creatures ran from her when she began to rise. She could taste their fear as she recognised another feeling – hunger. As she stretched her wings to their full length and floated on the air just above the fleeing creatures she saw one who filled her with a strange sensation of warmth, overriding her instinctive need to hunt. He was kneeling beside a female. She could feel his sorrow, leaving her with a burning ache in her chest.

Tomas.

She felt a sharp tug on her mind then. It jerked her attention away from the two lone creatures. One was calling to her, hurting her. This one wished to possess her. She could feel him tugging on her mind, forcing her to obey his commands. She felt her chest burn as she unleashed all of her rage. Flames engulfed the little running creatures, scorching the earth, before she beat her heavy wings and aimed for the sky. *My name is…* for the briefest of moments an image of a blonde-haired girl filled her mind… and was gone. The open skies and the lofty heights of the mountains waited.

Jarl Crawulf – Tomas: Hidden valley

Crawulf stood to face the terror emerging from where the stones once stood. A massive creature unfurled leathery wings, the skin of its body reddish-black scales. When it opened its mouth to roar, the noise rooted him to the spot, freezing the blood in his veins. "Feergor!" he gasped. "Is this the end of time?" A smile snaked across his lips. "I thank thee, All Wise, for granting me a death beyond all deaths!" he roared above the noise of the dragon. He flung away his shield and gripped his sword two-handed ready to die a glorious death at the hands of a god.

But the dragon did not attack him. Instead it flew over his head. All around him men from opposing sides dropped their weapons and ran, the fear of the beast overriding all others. Crawulf alone stood his ground, shouting words of defiance. A huge shadow passed over him as the dragon beat its wings and took to the air. The jarl swung around to follow its flight and caught sight of the Shadow Mage. The fat Sunsai noble had flung Normand aside as he stretched out his arms towards the dragon, calling to it. The beast turned around and flew over their heads again, only this time he raked the ground with fire. Flames engulfed men from both sides including the Shadow Mage. He screamed in pain as his scorched body fell down by the still body of the duke.

"Strike him down before he can transfer his life force into another!" Rosinnio cried out. Crawulf allowed himself a brief moment of satisfaction that his woman still lived before he ran towards the mage. He hauled the badly burnt body away from the duke.

The Shadow Mage met his eyes, and Crawulf saw the fear there.

"Now you die," he said before cleaving his head from his body with a single blow.

Rosinnio stood by Crawulf's side. "You did it. You have killed him."

"Aye," Crawulf said and staggered back. He could feel his legs buckling beneath him as pain from a score of wounds washed over him. All around them the earth was scorched black. He could feel the heat in the air as he tried to take in deep breaths. Suddenly his woman was propping him up, lending her support to his bulkier frame. "And you?" He forced out the words.

"I am well." She smiled. "I am tougher than I look."

"And the dragon?" Crawulf looked up to the sky, where there was no sign of the great winged beast.

"I think that is Duke Normand's problem now," she answered.

"What is my problem?" Normand staggered up to them, grimacing as he brought both hands up to his head.

"The dragon, my lord," the duke's man, Malachi answered.

Normand gave him a withering look. "There are no such things as dragons," he said.

"Did you miss the whole battle?" Crawulf asked while Rosinnio stifled a grin.

"When we meet again, Nortman, it will be as enemies," Normand said.

"Aye, likely as not," Crawulf answered.

The duke held out his hand and Crawulf took his wrist in the warrior's grip.

"What of them?" Malachi asked, pointing towards a large blond man who walked towards them, carrying the limp body of the white-haired witch.

"It was he who killed the dream-witch, and I don't know what she did, but somehow she wrested control of the dragon from the Shadow Mage," Rosinnio said.

Crawulf gazed around the battlefield, amazed at how few men were still standing. Of his own men he had led to the valley, all but two were now dead, his friend Rothgar included. "I think any who have survived this day thus far deserve to live," he said. "What now?" he directed towards Rosinnio.

"Now we should go home."

***

Tomas carried the lifeless body of his woman from the valley, not caring if he was struck down by the duke's men as he passed, or scorched with dragon fire as he'd seen others fall. Aliss weighed almost nothing in his arms, yet the burden on his heart was heavier than any he'd ever borne. She gave her life in the saving of others. That would have pleased her.

MORE FROM PAUL FREEMAN:

TRIBESMAN

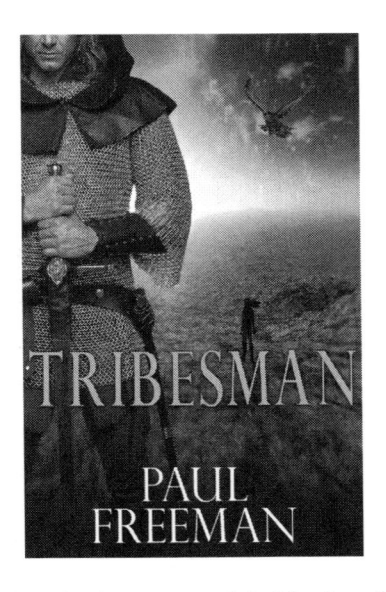

Banished from his homeland, a warrior of the Northern Clans grows weary of life in a harsh alien land. With the dark god Morrigu haunting his dreams, the warrior and champion Culainn journeys north in search of a merchant's daughter abducted by clansmen. With a desert princess as a companion he will travel through a land baked by a scorching sun, where bandits roam free and dark beasts stalk the night.

An ancient evil is rising from the desert. A Benouin myth of a ghost city inhabited by the souls of their ancestors, a bridge to the Underworld is unleashing demonic creatures on an unsuspecting world. Culainn and Persha, warrior and mage, stand alone against a tide of darkness. All the while the dark war god of the north seeks to use Culainn as her own tool, her own champion.

TAXI

PAUL FREEMAN

Every choice has a consequence...

A moment in time, unforeseen, unavoidable, can change a life forever.

A Dublin taxi driver's life pivots on a moment of insanity when a teenage girl loses her life.

So begins a dark journey for Danny Coyne; he's not responsible for her death, yet he carries the guilt. He seeks solace in drinking and pushes away those closest to him as he steps into the life of the dead girl and forms a bond with her best friend. His self control will be tested to the limit as he seeks to mete out justice on those responsible and fight his own inner demons.

Every choice has a consequence.

AFTER THE FALL: CHILDREN OF THE NEPHILIM

No one knew where they came from or why they chose that moment to crawl out from the shadows. In a devastating orgy of terror and violence blood-drinking monsters rose from the dark to gorge themselves on the blood of humans. Facing this threat, mankind turned on itself in a devastating wave of self-destruction.

Twenty years after the Fall and what's left of mankind is eking out an existence in a post-apocalyptic world. With much of the Earth now a nuclear wasteland, civilization has been knocked back two hundred years. By day the remnants of humanity gather together in small groups drawing from the land what they can in their new technological wasteland. By night they hide behind walls and bank up fires in an attempt to ward off the evil stalking the land during the hours of darkness.

The world needs a savior. A hero unafraid to face his own fears and terror of the vampires. An ex-preacher disillusioned by the world and his god is not that man... or so he says.

MORE GREAT READS FROM LIR PRESS

LYKAIA

"We are the terrors that hunt the night. And we have never been human"

In Greek mythology there's a story of King Lykaonas of Arcadia and his fifty sons who were cursed by the father of the gods, Zeus, to become wolves. The very first Lycanthropes. Forensic pathologist, Sophia Katsaros, receives a cryptic phone call from Greece telling her that her brothers are missing and leaves to search for them. With the help of Illyanna, her brother's girlfriend, Sophia examines the evidence but cannot accept a bizarre possibility: Has one or both of her brothers been transformed during the Lykaia, the ceremony where Man is said to become Wolf? Who is Marcus, a dark stranger that both repels and excites her? And what is the real story behind the 5000 year old curse of King Lykaonas?